ALEX RYAN

is a pseudonym for authors Brian Andrews and Jeffrey Wilson. Both are US Navy veterans: Andrews served as an officer aboard a 688 class nuclear submarine and Wilson as a combat surgeon on multiple deployments in Iraq and Afghanistan supporting US Naval Special Warfare (SEALs). They have written 4 books individually and live in Kansas and Tampa, FL, respectively.

andrews-wilson.com

Recycling programs
for this product may
not exist in your area.

ISBN-13: 978-1-335-66138-8

Beijing Red

Copyright © 2016 by Brian Andrews and Jeff Wilson

A Worldwide Library Suspense/June 2018

First published by Crooked Lane Books, an imprint of The Quick Brown
Fox & Company LLC.

BEIJING RED

ALEX RYAN

TORONTO • NEW YORK • LONDON
AMSTERDAM • PARIS • SYDNEY • HAMBURG
STOCKHOLM • ATHENS • TOKYO • MILAN
MADRID • WARSAW • BUDAPEST • AUCKLAND

BEIJING RED

ONE

Rural irrigation project
Fifteen kilometers outside of Kizilsu
Kashgar Prefecture, Xinjiang
China
0730 hours local

WHEN HE WAS a boy, his father gave him a John Deere toy tractor set for his fifth birthday. Die-cast construction, green paint, rubber wheels—a toy that could actually dig up dirt, not the plastic crap they pawned off on kids today. His favorite piece had been the front-end loader, the one that came with an articulating shovel and a spreader in back. He'd played with that toy for hours in the backyard, scooping up dry, West Texas earth sand redistributing it. "Nick Foley Demolition and Construction," his father had declared with pride upon seeing his son's massive earthworks project, albeit executed at 1/32 scale. From that day on, his father had encouraged Nick to pursue a career in construction.

He'd become a Navy SEAL instead.

Now here he was, twenty-eight, out of the Navy, and back playing in the dirt. He surveyed the partially completed irrigation trench stretching off into the distance. Then he looked at the broken-down backhoe thirty meters away. *Not a John Deere*, he mused, reading the word "SUNCO" emblazoned on the side of the

bright-orange earthmover. He squatted and scooped up
a handful of dry, western China dirt and crumbled it
between his fingers. *'Bout the same as West Texas dirt*,
he thought. *Same kinda desert here, just on the other
side of the world.* He'd always liked the feel of soil in
his hands. It made him feel connected—a kinship to
the earth and every living thing that struggled to make
this planet a home. There was far more to life than living, he knew. Life was about stewardship, doing something good with the body and mind God had given. For
Nick, stewardship meant serving and protecting others without the caveat of personal gain. He hadn't spoken openly about his philosophy during his time in the
SEAL teams, but it was this simple ideology that had
led him to join the Navy in the first place.

And then later, it had led him away.

But today was today, and there was an irrigation
ditch that needed digging. He picked up a shovel—
one of many leaning against the defunct backhoe—
and headed toward the group of NGO volunteers and
paid laborers milling around the water station. This was
not a happy lot, and he didn't blame them. Digging by
hand was brutal work, but he knew from experience it
would be days before the backhoe got fixed. In Navy
speak, the machine was tango uniform—"tits up"—
for the foreseeable future. What this gang needed most
was motivation.

He stepped up onto a large, rusted toolbox.

"Good morning," he announced, smiling.

The paid Uyghur laborers—indigenous Muslims
from villages outside Kashi and Kizilsu—gave him
their attention. Everyone glanced over at him with a
perfunctory pause before resuming their grumbling.

"Must have been made in the USA, right?" he chuckled, gesturing with a thumb at the filthy orange machine behind him.

"Sounds about right, mate," said Ian, the Aussie, with an exaggerated grin.

Nick winked at his straight man. He could always count on Ian in a pinch. Since they'd shared their first pint of beer in China, their Aussie-versus-Yank banter had raged unabated, entertaining anyone and everyone who cared to listen.

"They tried to get a replacement," Nick went on, "but the company couldn't arrange the necessary vaccinations to bring in an Australian earthmover—two old mules and a plow, I believe."

There was a smattering of laughter from the other NGO volunteers, mostly Europeans and a couple of Brits, but only blank stares from the Uyghurs.

"Look, guys, I know this situation stinks, but if we wanted ordinary, we'd be working for multinational companies, making pointless widgets for myopic bosses who can't remember our names, right? If we wanted ordinary, we'd be sitting on our asses watching television, smartphones glued to our hands, tweeting about celebrity gossip." They laughed, and he knew he had their attention. He understood his audience—mostly young, motivated idealists—but sometimes even idealists need a kick in the ass. "Now, I realize that backbreaking manual labor in the desert is stretching our charter. And anyone who's not up for today's task can opt out. Nobody here is going to hold a grudge if you want to take the truck back into town. But me, I'm gonna dig, and anyone who's here with me at quitting time drinks beer on my tab tonight."

Nick stepped down, grabbed a shovel, slung it over his shoulder, and headed toward the irrigation ditch. The Uyghurs, who Nick knew did not comprehend a word of his little pep talk, mobilized en masse toward the trench, shovels in hand.

Nick glanced at Ian as he walked by the waffling group of NGO volunteers.

Ian winked at Nick. "I, for one, can't pass on free beer—especially when a Yank is paying."

Five minutes later, they were all down in the ditch, standing waist-deep and digging, with two dozen young, strong backs in the mix. As the dirt flew, Nick wondered if they weren't making better progress than yesterday, when the damn backhoe had actually been operational.

"Good working, Mister Nick," came a voice beside him.

Nick glanced right and saw Batur—a Uyghur he had befriended—standing in the ditch beside him. Batur's face and neck were dappled with sweat, despite the cool morning air. With a medic's discerning eye, Nick observed that his friend's deep-caramel-colored skin had taken on an uncharacteristic grayish tinge.

"You okay, Batur?" Nick asked.

Batur stared back with a blank expression that, from their many past conversations together, Nick understood meant incomprehension. Befriending Batur had been an interesting challenge. Nick didn't speak a word of Batur's native Karluk, and neither man had mastered Mandarin, so English had become the de facto language between them. As they got to know each other, Nick realized how desperately Batur wanted to learn English. In Batur's mind, speaking English was a prerequisite for a better life—a prerequisite for someday leaving

China. And so Nick made an effort to have conversations with the man whenever possible and subtly tutor his Uyghur friend on the basics of American English.

"Are you sick?" Nick asked, trying again. This time, he pointed to his stomach and made a sour face.

Batur nodded, getting it, and pointed at his own stomach.

"Batur eated some nasty bad shit, him thinking," the small, powerful-looking Uyghur said with a forced grin.

Nick couldn't help but laugh. "Been there, buddy," he said, shaking his head. "Don't work too hard today. Take a rest if you need to."

"Batur okay. Rest later," Batur said and went back to his digging.

Since his friend wasn't feeling well, Nick decided not to push an English lesson today. Both men worked in silence, and soon Nick had his own glisten of sweat going. He pulled his Texas A&M sweatshirt off over his head and tied the arms around his waist. He found a comfortable rhythm and moved load after load of dirt up and out of the trench. After a while, his shoulders and back began to ache, but it was a *good* ache. In fact, he relished the feeling. He was using his body, and he took guilty pleasure in letting his mind drift aimlessly. Eventually, his thoughts wandered to Afghanistan, and suddenly the dirt felt heavier.

A powerful moment of déjà vu washed over him. It wasn't just the barren landscape and craggy mountain peaks on the horizon. It wasn't how the Chinese security forces walking the streets of Kashgar reminded him of US Marines patrolling the villages in Helmand province in Afghanistan. No, this déjà vu was a product of the people—people like Batur, who worked and sweated beside him in this ditch. The Uyghurs, like the Pashtun in Northeastern Afghanistan, had endured thousands of years of relentless conflict. Wars, persecution, and would-be conquerors scarred their history. Through centuries of aggression and infiltration, the Pashtun had remained steadfast—pathologically undisturbed by the miserable lot in life they had been dealt by being born in the crossroads of Europe, Africa, and Asia. For the Afgahnis, the choice was simple—lose their culture or die fighting to preserve it. With the influx of Chinese and the modernization of Kashgar, the native Uyghurs now believed they were being forced to make the same choice.

Kashgar—called Kashi in Chinese—was twenty-five hundred miles from Beijing. The city's indigenous Muslim Uyghur population was culturally and ethnically divergent from the Han Chinese that governed them. In Nick's opinion, most Uyghurs, like their Pashtun Afghani counterparts, simply wanted to be left alone. They wanted to be free to work, have children, and provide for their families. The problem for the Uyghurs of western China was that they also wanted freedom to practice Islam. Although not forbidden, religion's place in Communist China had always been dubious. The party institutionally recognized religion but carefully controlled the amount of autonomy and political influence regional religious sects were permitted. In the case of Islam, imams were appointed by the Chinese government in an effort to exert influence and control.

For young, devout Uyghur Muslims in Xinjiang province, the suppression of Islam by the Chinese government had sparked an underground rebellion. Whispers of jihad were spreading, and the influence of radical

Islam from the Middle East was creeping in. Over the past decade, Kashi had become the epicenter for Uyghur terrorist activity against their perceived Chinese oppressors. In response, the Chinese government conducted regular counterterrorism operations to combat the growing radical Islamic threat. Tensions in the region were high. And even though Nick was not Chinese, Uyghur, or Muslim, he'd felt that tension from the moment he arrived.

Nick's shovel clanged as it hit a large stone just beneath the surface. The vibration rang up his arm, and a flash of white-hot pain flared in his left shoulder—an unpleasant reminder of the wound he received on his first tour with the SEALs. But the physical injury was the least of the damage he suffered at the base of the Hindu Kush. The invisible wound, the one he carried inside, had yet to heal. Strange that a single night, in a life of so many nights, had made him into the man he was today. He had left the Navy and gone home, only to leave and fly to a place so much like the one he was trying to forget. He shook his head at the irony. Kabul was roughly five hundred miles from Kashi. That was closer than Dallas was to El Paso. Strange that he had wandered back to the crossroads of humanity. Why had he come here?

For atonement?

For forgiveness?

"So what is that tattoo, Nick?" asked a female voice, shaking him out of his thoughts.

He turned to find Yvette, a blond Belgian co-ed who'd been chatting him up lately, staring at the patch of body art that decorated his right shoulder. He'd gotten the tattoo in Virginia Beach after returning from his first deployment to help conceal a nasty patch of scar tissue. While he rarely thought about the shield and frog on his deltoid, he was proud to wear a visible reminder of his association with his brother SEALs—the bravest men he'd ever know.

"Oh, this?" he said, craning his neck to look at the tattoo. "It's a reminder not to get drunk in a Navy town."

The blond laughed, but he wasn't sure she really got the joke. Nick watched a drop of sweat trickle down her neck and disappear in the cleavage between her modest but shapely breasts. Yvette was young and had the figure of an endurance athlete. She caught him looking, and it seemed to please her.

They worked together in silence for a while, grunting over their shovels and occasionally trading glances while reaching for their bottles of water. He felt her eyes on him and turned to catch her blatantly checking him out. Busted. She flashed him a coy smile and made a joke about a Belgian reality TV show where strangers are paired up and sent to a deserted island for thirty days to find romance. He chuckled and nodded, wondering if she had just solicited him for a reality TV show. He liked Yvette well enough, and maybe there could be a spark, but he suddenly found himself wishing he were alone.

Alone to work, and think, and brood.

As the morning wore on, chatter in the trench died away, replaced by weary grunts and the occasional expletive when someone's shovel hit an unexpected stone. Nick felt the enthusiasm of the group waning. With the exception of the paid Uyghur laborers, who were capable of working without pause until ordered to stop, the work detail was wearing down. Nick felt the mood darkening and progress slowing by the minute.

Time for another morale booster.

"I have a question for the group," he hollered. When he had everyone's attention, he scooped and flung a shovelful of dirt out of the trench with all his might. "I'm lookin' around at the progress in this ditch and wondering, who are the best diggers? Aussies, Brits, Germans, Belgians, Americans, or Uyghurs?"

"I hope you're joking," Ian hollered, ten meters down the trench. "You're five years younger than me and former military," the Aussie said, grunting loudly and flinging a load of dirt higher and farther than Nick's effort. "And I still can out-dig you."

"That was a good throw for a tourist, but I think the answer is obvious," came another voice, this one heavily accented in German. "The Uyghurs out-dig us all."

Everyone laughed and cheered at this, especially the Uyghurs, and dirt began to fly with renewed vigor all along the line.

Yvette sidled up beside Nick and bumped her hip playfully into his.

He did a double take at the blond and was about to make an equally playful retort when he noticed she was looking past him. He watched the color drain from her face and her hand come up to cover her mouth.

A shovel clattered in the dirt, and Nick heard a heavy thud behind him.

Yvette hollered, "God, oh God!" in her Belgian Dutch accent as Nick spun around. At his feet, Batur lay face down in the dirt. He knelt beside his friend just as Yvette regained her composure and dashed over, kneeling on Batur's other side.

"Help me," Nick said, and he grabbed beneath one armpit as Yvette did the same. Together they heaved the stout little man up onto the side of the ditch and rolled him onto his back.

Yvette screamed and bicycled her feet, propelling herself backward away from Batur like a crab. Nick choked back bile at the face no longer recognizable as his friend's. Batur's cheeks were hollow and sunken, like the gray skin of a corpse. In horrible contrast, the man's purple lips had swollen to the point where the bottom lip split in two places and impossibly dark blood leaked across his chin. Like his lips, Batur's eyelids were like two bulging balloons, hematomas swollen to enormous size and expanding away from the face. The skin seemed so thin that Nick imagined a single touch would cause the eyelids to explode in a gory puff. The slits between the upper and lower lids were barely visible, like lines painted on as an afterthought, and from the misshapen corners of the eyes came a trickle of dark blood.

"What's wrong with him?" Yvette sobbed from somewhere behind him.

For a moment, Nick thought he was looking at a corpse, but suddenly the body twitched. Batur's chest heaved as he tried to suck air through his impossibly swollen lips. An awful, wet, snoring sound came from his mouth but then abruptly stopped. Nick inched closer. He needed to clear Batur's airway—tilt the head back, tip the chin up. As he reached out to do just that, a hand grasped his shoulder from behind and held him back.

"No, Nick," a voice said in perfect, Chinese-accented English. "This man is very sick. You should not touch him."

Nick craned his neck around to find Hon Bai, the Han Chinese man who served as their NGO sponsor. "He can't breathe," Nick said.

Bai nodded nervously. "Yes, but what if he makes you sick? Or the others?"

Nick frantically tried to remember illnesses he had learned about during his year of training as a SEAL medic—an "Eighteen Delta," as they were known in the community. A whirlwind of symptoms and reactions raced through his mind. He remembered how Batur had looked when they first start digging and compared the memory to the grotesque, misshapen face before him. The transformation had happened so quickly. It couldn't possibly be an illness. It had to be a reaction, he thought. An allergic reaction to something—anaphylaxis, his training told him. Severe nut allergy? Bee sting? Or maybe this was a reaction to a toxin. Maybe Batur was bitten by a snake or a scorpion? Yes, that made the most sense.

"I can't just watch him suffocate," Nick said at last, looking up at Bai and trying to sound more confident than he felt. He couldn't stand by and watch the man suffocate under his own swollen face. He had chosen to become a combat medic in the SEALs because of the overpowering desire to help people in need. The war fighter in him had always served as a means to an end—stopping the misery, pain, and suffering inflicted by tyrants and terrorists on those unable to defend themselves. Today, the war fighter was gone, but not the medic. Not the steward. He refused to let Batur die on his watch without a fight.

"Until we know what is wrong, I would not touch him, Nick," Bai said, shaking his head nervously.

Nick noticed a pair of work gloves tucked inside the waistband of Bai's jeans. "Toss me your gloves, Bai."

Bai nodded and handed them over.

Nick donned the worn, leather gloves and tilted Batur's chin up and head back; a high-pitched whistle pierced the silence as the dying man sucked air through his swollen face. "He needs a doctor," Nick barked, his adrenaline ramping up. "We need to get him to Kashi."

Bai nodded. "The hospital in Kizilsu is closer. We can take him there."

"I'll pull a truck around," Ian said.

Nick heard the Australian dash off toward the pickup trucks parked beside the broken backhoe.

Ian swung a truck around in a spray of gravel and dirt. A crowd of horrified NGO volunteers and paid workers encircled them as Nick, Yvette, and Bai heaved Batur's oozing body into the bed of the pickup.

"I'll drive," said Bai, opening the driver's-side door and waiving for Ian to get out. "Ian, you're in charge here until I return."

Nick leapt up into the bed of the truck while Yvette scrambled in on the other side of Batur.

He shot her his best *What the hell do you think you're doing?* look.

"I'm coming with you," she said, her pale-blue eyes wide with misplaced worry. He realized then that she was coming for his sake—not Batur's—but there was no time to argue.

"All right," Nick said, fighting to keep Batur's airway open as the pickup truck wobbled and bounced along the dirt road. "Help me keep him steady."

"How far?" Yvette shouted over the wind and the engine noise.

"Forty kilometers."

"Do you think he'll make it?"

"If we can keep him breathing, yeah, I think so," Nick lied.

He didn't have the heart to tell her their friend would probably be dead in minutes.

TWO

TO NICK'S ASTONISHMENT, Batur survived the dusty, ago-nizing drive to Kizilsu.

Whatever was killing Batur was horrible—the stuff of nightmares. If it was infectious, Nick was screwed. They were all screwed. He'd had plenty of time during the drive, bouncing in the back of the filthy truck, try-ing to keep Batur's airway open, to think about that. Batur's symptoms—abdominal pain, fever, and bleed-ing from the eyes, nose, and mouth—made Nick think of Ebola. But from everything he'd heard about the deadly African filovirus, the timing was wrong. Ebola could kill quickly, but the illness progressed over the course of days, not hours. Batur had practically trans-formed right before their eyes. Nick's mind kept com-ing back to anaphylactic shock or acute toxicity as the culprit, but what the hell did he know? He was trained in battlefield trauma, not epidemiology. Sure, he knew how to stabilize gunshot wounds and manage broken bones, but that was a hell of a long way from medical school, residency, and a fellowship in infectious dis-eases. Expert or not, one thing was certain: he had been an idiot. He had gambled his life—and the lives of Bai and Yvette, for that matter—by treating Batur like an injured SEAL on the battlefield.

The truck swerved around a slower-moving car, knocking Nick against the bed rail and snapping him out of his moment of self-flagellation. He recognized the Artux mosque as Bai piloted the little pickup through the central square at a lunatic pace. He glanced over at Yvette, who was holding on with white knuckles. *She should have ridden in the cab*, he thought, looking at her now. She was terrified and beat to hell from the drive.

The truck skidded to a stop in front of a gray, industrial-looking hospital that was bigger than Nick had expected. China had very advanced medicine, rivaling or even exceeding the West in some fields, but this building was nothing like the sleek, modern hospitals he had trained in with the Navy. Still, any hospital was better than him trying to keep Batur alive at the side of an irrigation ditch waiting on Kizilsu EMTs that might never come.

He glanced down at Batur's barely human face.

Across from him, Yvette was already climbing out of the bed of the truck, taking care to avert her eyes from the grotesque, hemorrhaging thing that had once been Batur. She had stopped trying to help Nick only five minutes into the drive. He'd watched her vomit over the side, and after that, it was all she could do to keep her gaze focused in the middle distance. At first, he'd worried she was becoming sick—sick like Batur, that is—but her color was good and she showed no signs of fever.

"I'll get some help," she said, opening the tailgate and then setting off on unsteady legs.

She didn't make it far.

Help found them instead.

Twenty meters away, Nick saw three figures—clad in hospital scrubs, gloves, and surgical masks—running toward them with a metal gurney. The gurney was painted bright yellow and loaded with crash equipment.

When they got within five meters, the driver's-side door swung open, and Bai jumped out of the cab. He immediately stepped away from the truck and took a position several paces away.

"Are you okay, Nick Foley?" he asked, his jaw tight with worry.

"Yeah," Nick said, forcing a grin. "I'm good."

Bai nodded robotically. "Is the Uyghur dead?"

Nick gritted he teeth. He liked Bai, and he understood the cultural rift between the Uyghurs and the Han Chinese, but Batur was more than just "the Uyghur."

"No," he said with a hard glance at the NGO coordinator. "Not yet, anyway."

The welcome party arrived a few seconds later, and Nick realized from their expressions that Batur was not the first. This team had been prepped and waiting.

Not the first, he thought.

Shit.

A stern woman at the head of the stretcher barked something at him in Chinese. He shook his head and locked eyes with her. She barked at him again, louder and with more vitriol, and this time, he understood without translation: *Get the hell outta our way.*

He twisted his body and swung his right leg, and then his left, over the side of the bed of the pickup. When his feet hit the ground, he wobbled and almost collapsed—both of his legs were numb from the long ride crouched beside Batur. He shuffled his feet in place, working the circulation back into his muscles as pins and needles flared everywhere from his hips down. He watched as two male hospital workers loaded Batur onto the gurney and connected monitor cables to his chest. In concert, the woman retrieved a bag mask and used it to force oxygen into the Uyghur's swollen face—each squeeze reverberating like wet, rhythmic flatulence.

Just as feeling was returning to his legs, the doctor barked at Nick again.

This time, he shrugged incomprehension.

Still keeping his distance, Bai intervened, rattling off several sentences in Mandarin so quickly Nick couldn't make out a single word.

"You come," she replied, exasperated and wagging a finger at Nick, Yvette, and Bai. "All come."

Yvette squeezed Nick's arm. "We are not responsible for what happened to him," she said, her voice both defensive and worried. "They know that, right?"

"Yes," he said, trying not to sound condescending. "Believe me, they know."

They entered the hospital via what Nick deduced was the emergency room entrance. Double glass doors swished open and a blast of cool, conditioned air washed over him as he trailed the EMS team inside. Yvette walked beside him, her expression grave, while Bai trailed reluctantly behind. Halfway down the long, gray hallway, the lead doctor pointed to an open door and barked a command in Chinese. This time, she looked only at Bai when she rattled off her instructions before spinning on a heel and charging off after her team down the corridor.

Bai folded his arms across his chest. "They wish for us to wait here," he said, gesturing at the open door. "They will need some information."

Nick nodded and stepped into a waiting room not much bigger than a closet. Rows of round-backed plastic chairs, all a horrible orange color, were bolted to two walls. Nick imagined the space was used as a consultation room where hurried doctors gave families shitty prognoses about their loved ones. He sighed in surrender and collapsed into one of the molded-plastic chairs. Bai took a seat across from him but kept his eyes downcast on the floor. Nick felt a headache coming on. He leaned his head back against the wall and groaned his displeasure at the world. Yvette dropped into the chair beside him. After a silent pause, she clutched his arm, leaned her head against his shoulder, and began to sob. He pulled his left arm free and wrapped it around her, then closed his eyes and tenderly stroked her shoulder while she wept. Her tears were not for Batur, he knew.

These were tears of dread.

The door clicked.

His eyes popped open, and he saw the waiting-room door had been pulled shut by someone from the outside. He wondered if it was courtesy for the grieving or a signal of isolation.

Both, if they're clever.

And since coming to this country, he had found the Chinese to be nothing if not clever.

"I have never seen anything like that. Never," said Yvette, her Belgian Dutch accent thicker than normal with emotion.

Nick nodded. "I know."

"I hope we are not to get sick, Nick Foley," Bai said in a tone that almost sounded accusatory.

Nick shifted his gaze to Bai, but the Chinese man was staring out the window, his brow furrowed with

anxiety. Like his companions, Nick felt dread perco-
lating inside. In his haste to help Batur, he had made a
mistake—quite possibly a deadly mistake—by expos-
ing them all to this unknown scourge. Bai talked often
and fondly of his wife and two children. Nick didn't
know if he could bear the guilt if those kids lost their
father because of him.

Suddenly, Bai jumped to his feet, eyes riveted out the
window. He mumbled something in Chinese, his voice
harried. Nick was about to ask what he saw when the
door to the room burst open. In the doorway stood a man
dressed in a blue suit with an integrated hood, yellow
gloves that reached nearly to his elbows, and heavy rubber boots. He wore a gray mask, like a fighter pilot, only
this one had purple straps that bunched the blue hood
around his cheeks. He eyed each of them in turn from
behind bug-eyed protective goggles and then barked a
stern warning in Chinese. He repeated the command
for effect. Nick noticed an unmistakable quiver in the
man's voice, one borne more of fear than anger. Without
giving any of them a chance to ask questions, the suited
figure slammed the door and locked it from the outside.

"What the hell was that?" Nick demanded, turning
to Bai.

"He said we cannot leave this room."

"For how long?"

Bai shrugged.

"Why is he in MOPP gear?"

Bai looked at him, confused. "I don't know this
word."

"MOPP gear," Nick repeated, his frustration mounting. "You know, military protection equipment—a
hazmat suit with respirator, boots, gloves, and goggles."

"I don't know, Nick Foley," Bai said.

"They weren't dressed like that when we arrived and they came to get Batur with the rolling stretcher," Yvette said and hugged her chest.

She's right, Nick thought, wondering what had changed. He stood and walked over to the tall, narrow window. Peering out into the parking lot, he saw several military-style SUVs and a gray armored personnel carrier parked around Bai's pickup truck. Beyond them, at least two-dozen men in gray shirts, dark pants, and black tactical vests were setting up a makeshift perimeter. From what he could tell, all of them were armed—some had pistols in drop holsters, and others wore automatic weapons slung combat style across their chests. Two men were already in the busy street, directing traffic and turning away cars.

An image of Batur's grotesque visage, eyes weeping blood, flashed into Nick's head. He tasted bile in the back of his throat and felt a surge of panic wash over him. The alien emotion took him by surprise. He was a combat veteran, a blooded Navy SEAL with years of training, so why was he rattled? He forced himself to perform several rounds of slow, four-count tactical breathing to calm himself. As he scrubbed his friend's image from his mind's eye, he realized that even with all his training and combat tours, he had never been this terrified before.

He began to pace, and a bead of cold sweat trickled down from his armpit over his ribs.

We're dead, he thought, looking around the room at his friends.

We're all the walking dead.

THREE

Chinese Centers for Disease Control and Prevention
155 Changbai Road, Changping District
Beijing
1445 hours local

CHEN DAZHONG STARED expectantly at the phone on her desk. Any second now, it would ring and the director would be on the other end of the line. She knew exactly how the conversation would go. He would ask her how she liked her new office in the CDC's state-of-the-art main campus in the Changping District. She would reply, graciously, that the office was most satisfactory. Then there would be an awkward pause, after which he would ask her if she knew about the crisis brewing in Kizilsu forty kilometers outside of Kashgar. She would reply, "Yes, the initial reports are most troubling," to which he would solemnly agree and then tell her that he was sending her to lead the CDC's emergency response on the ground. She would accept the assignment, with all the professional enthusiasm she could muster, and thank him for yet another opportunity to serve her country and the CDC. She would not demand hazard pay, nor would she put stipulations on her acceptance. She would not remind him that today was technically her last day working for the Office of Disease Control and Emergency Response, *and* that it had been less than a week since she completed her twenty-one-day quarantine after Liberia, *and* that deploying to Kizilsu would likely strain her already troubled marriage to the breaking point. No, she would not say any of these things, because she was a good little soldier, and good little soldiers followed orders without condition or complaint.

She exhaled, trying to calm herself.

No, she told herself, *it was not simply about following orders*. It was not simply about duty. Going to Kizilsu was about pride and expectation, opportunity and advancement. Director Wong had selected her—a woman—to lead China's highly publicized Ebola aid mission in Liberia. Her success launching China's first Ebola relief hospital in Africa had reflected positively on the CDC and China in the eyes of the international community. Over the last five months, she had worked closely with the director, dialoguing with him on an almost daily basis. Her optimism, work ethic, and results-driven mentality had won his respect. Her new appointment at headquarters—project director for research, screening, and testing of emerging diseases—had been her reward. She was now officially on the fast track. On the day of the announcement, one of her colleagues had called her "a model for professional women in China everywhere" and then later whispered, "Careful, Dazhong. Don't fuck it up." Since that day, she'd felt the gaze of envy from her scores of male compeers—men who would not hesitate to derail her career at the slightest opportunity. She would not make it easy on them. No matter what pitfalls awaited her in Kizilsu, she had to say yes.

The phone rang.

Her stomach instantly went to knots. She glanced at

the LCD window above the keypad and saw the director's internal caller ID. She picked up the handset before the second ring and pressed it to her ear.

The conversation unfolded exactly as she had imagined, until the end.

"Dazhong, there is one last matter we need to discuss," the director said, his voice suddenly taking on a strange undertone.

The shift made her nervous and set her lower left eyelid to twitching, a tick that surfaced whenever she was both stressed and exhausted.

"Yes?" she said, pressing the knuckle of her index finger against it to make it stop.

"This assignment is not the same as your last mission. There are complicating factors you need to stay cognizant of at all times. Xinjiang province is not Liberia. There are political implications for every decision you make—political implications not only for this office with the State Council but also for China in the eyes of the world. The stakes are high. Do you understand?"

She swallowed, unsure how to respond. To presume she understood his unspoken agenda could be disastrous later, yet to ask for clarification now would signal her ignorance and inexperience in such matters. She decided to err on the side of caution and said, "I presume you are referring to the Muslim extremists in Xinjiang?"

"Yes," he said, his voice hard and low. "Tensions are high, especially in Kashgar. You must go into this situation with your eyes wide open. I would not be surprised if these initial reports of an Ebola outbreak prove to be erroneous."

"I was of a similar mind. Anything is possible, of course, but Kashi is so remote. A West African vector causing an outbreak in Hong Kong or Beijing, yes maybe, but Kashi? I would be curious to know if the Civil Aviation Administration of China has records—"

"I've already spoken to my counterpart at CAAC on the matter," he interrupted, "and requested passenger manifests for airline passengers traveling into or connecting through Kashgar who have been in West Africa anytime during the past month. As soon as this information is available, it will be analyzed and forwarded to you."

"Thank you, sir."

"Of course."

"And if it's not Ebola, then what?"

"Then you need to be prepared for something worse."

"Worse than Ebola?" she balked. "What could possibly be worse?"

"A chemical or biological weapon attack. Something weapons grade. Something new; something we haven't seen before."

A chill chased down her spine, and her office suddenly felt as cold and still as deep space.

"But I'm not trained for that," she heard herself say, and then she quickly added, "Forgive me, Director Wong, I misspoke. Whatever the crisis in Kashi, I can manage it with the tools and procedures of the DCER."

She heard him laugh into the receiver. "No, Dazhong, you have every right to be concerned. Which is why I am not sending you on this assignment alone. You and your CDC team will be part of a multidiscipline, multiministry Quick Reaction Task Force conceived precisely for situations like this. You will be traveling with the Snow Leopard Counterterrorism Commando Unit's Ninth Squadron—the Ninth SLCU—as well as Major

Li Shengkun and his staff from the PLA's NBC Regiment 54423 in Shenzhen."

She sat speechless, phone receiver pressed against her ear.

"Dazhong?" she heard him say.

"I've never heard of this task force before," she managed at last.

"That's because until now, it only existed on paper. I was on the committee that devised it—a tactical contingency for scenarios such as this."

"I see," she said. It made sense, perfect sense, but the prospect of teaming with both the army and China's most elite counterterrorism unit rattled her. She was a civilian. They were not. She was one woman. They were a regiment. For battle, she would be wearing scrubs and a carrying a noncontact thermometer. They would be wearing tactical gear and carrying automatic weapons. It did not take a genius to imagine how this scenario would play out. They would patronize her, marginalize her, undermine her authority at every turn—she knew this because she had played this game before.

She had played it for years...with her husband.

"Who is in charge?" she asked. "Of the operation, that is?"

"You are in charge of disease containment and all health- and welfare-related matters. Commander Zhang of the Ninth SLCU is in charge of security and threat prosecution. He has been instructed not to get in your way, just as I am telling you now not to get in his. The situation on the ground in Kizilsu will dictate whether this is a counterterrorism operation or an emergency response to an outbreak. By the time you land in Kashi, we should have a much better picture of the situation."

"And what about Major Li from Regiment 54423? Where does he fit into this equation?"

"Major Li's immediate priority is to determine if a chemical or biological agent has been deployed. Our single greatest concern is that some weaponized or biologically modified pathogen has been released as an act of terrorism."

"I should probably speak with Major Li before I depart," she said. "Make sure that we are properly equipped. Immunofluorescence assays will need to be performed. Serology tests run. We'll need the capability to perform PCR amplification and ELISA screening. All this will require special equipment. We'll also need experienced laboratory technicians, otherwise we'll be forced to shuttle biosafety level-four samples back and forth between Kashi and Wuhan."

"All this has already been taken care of. Remember, I was on the committee that developed this contingency plan. Also, I have given great consideration to the lessons you learned in Liberia. The Ebola response protocols you outlined in your final mission report have all been transmitted to the hospital director at the Artux People's Hospital in Kizilsu."

"Yes, sir."

"Is your 'go bag' packed and ready?"

"Yes."

"Good, because your plane leaves in one hour. There is a car and a Beijing police escort waiting at the front of the building to take you to the airport."

"Do I have time to stop by my apartment and say good-bye to my husband?"

"I'm sorry, Dazhong, but there is no time. You may call him, of course, and if he can make it to the airport before your departure, I will make sure that security lets him see you off."

Dazhong felt a wave of relief and then a twinge of guilt at her gladness that she would not be forced to see her husband and deal with the inevitable conflict that would follow. Perhaps she would wait awhile to call.

"I understand."

"Good luck, Dr. Chen."

"Thank you, Director Wong," she said, and then quickly added, "I won't let you down."

"I know," he said. "That's why I chose you."

Dazhong slumped in her chair, suddenly exhausted. Another separation from her husband was a needed respite, but she worried about the repercussions. Her unexpected departure would make him angry, and his anger would have days, if not weeks, to steep. She exhaled through pursed lips. She didn't have time to worry about *him* right now. She had much bigger problems to fret over. The situation in Kizilsu had the makings of something terrible. Something terrifying. Deep inside, she had always considered the possibility of an outbreak in China, but now that it was happening, she felt unprepared.

A tight-lipped, ironic smile spread across her face.

Maybe they would get lucky...

Maybe this was *just* Ebola.

FOUR

THE HOURS CREPT BY.

Nick didn't know if the room had become stuffy or if he was just becoming claustrophobic in the small space. The locked door and a window too narrow to accommodate escape amplified the feeling of captivity. He was a prisoner of the Artux People's Hospital until someone in hazmat gear said otherwise.

"There is no air in here," Yvette said with agitation.

Nick stopped pacing and turned to her. She had a light dapple of sweat on her face and neck. Might she also have a fever? He wiped his own forehead with the back of his hand and felt the dampness there. His throat was dry and sore, and his headache seemed to be getting worse by the minute.

"We're just feeling claustrophobic and probably a bit dehydrated," he said, trying to summon a reassuring smile. "Take a couple of deep breaths and the feeling will pass."

She looked down at her hands, unconvinced. Nick looked out the window and pressed his hands against the wall on either side.

A small army had gathered outside the hospital. The

local police, who had secured the entrance initially, were now outnumbered five to one by soldiers dressed in mottled cammie uniforms. Nick noticed that unlike the hospital EMS response team, the soldiers were all wearing CBR respirators designed to protect them from chemical, biological, and radioactive airborne contaminant. In addition to their cammies, kits, and respirators, they carried QBZ-95 automatic assault rifles—a modern, compact 5.8 mm weapon that clearly marked them as military. The weapons had a cool, sci-fi look, an obvious contrast to the Type 81 rifles carried by the policemen, which had more of an old, cold-war vibe to them. Of course, the older rifles used the larger, 7.62 mm rounds that Team guys loved, so it was a toss-up as to which weapon he'd prefer in a firefight. Nick laughed at himself for remembering the details of relatively obscure weapons while still not being able to come up with the name of the antibiotic used to treat anthrax. He guessed that knowledge pounded into you by a SEAL Senior Chief during SQT—the Seal Qualification Training that began immediately after BUD/S—stuck better than medical facts learned from a book.

"It's like a war zone out there," Yvette said from beside him. Nick startled at her presence. Apparently, he was losing his SEAL edge. After his first tour in Afghanistan, anyone creeping up behind him risked being on the receiving end of a reflexive elbow to the throat.

"They're setting up security to keep people out."

"And in," Bai pointed out from where he sat crosslegged on the floor.

Right, Nick thought. *And in.*

Nick remembered the American CDC's anemic, arm's-length response to the first Ebola case on US soil in Dallas, Texas, and contrasted it to what he was watching here. The Chinese response was so much more martial and robust, which begged the question—did that bode well or ill for their fate?

The door behind him clicked sharply, making Yvette jump, but then she set her jaw. Bai scrambled to his feet, and Nick turned with arms folded across his chest. The person at the door was protected head to toe by a yellow exposure suit. The tinted faceplate on the helmet made it difficult to discern the gender of the face inside. The self-contained respirator wheezed with each breath. Behind stood a security detail of two men. They wore the same exposure suits but brandished QBZ-95 rifles— combat slung and at the ready, hands on the grip and shooting fingers along the trigger guard.

The leader barked something in Chinese, the voice not settling the gender debate for Nick. Bai walked across the room and away from the door, positioning himself in the corner farthest from Nick and Yvette. The space-suited figure at the door placed a large canvas bag on the floor and slid it into the middle of the room. Instructions were given and the leader awkwardly backed out of the room, accidently bumping into one of the soldiers in the process and almost tumbling to the ground. The other guard shut the door, and Nick saw Yvette flinch at the ominous click of the lock. Nick looked at Bai and raised an eyebrow.

"What did they say?" Yvette asked.

"We are to change into the clothing in the bag." Bai explained. "We are to remove all our clothing and all personal items, including jewelry," he said with a nod at Yvette. "We then place our clothing along the wall underneath the window and someone will come back to take us."

Bai scurried to the center of the room and rummaged through the bag.

"Take us?" Yvette asked, the timbre of her voice indicating she was as angry as she was scared. "What do you mean 'take us'? Where are they taking us?"

"I don't know," Bai said, retreating back to his corner.

Nick grabbed the bag and retrieved the two remaining jumpsuits from inside. The suits opened in the back via a long slit that closed with Velcro patches. The suits reminded him of old-fashioned footy pajamas, except these had integrated gloves and hoods that drew at the face with elastic.

"Where am I supposed to change?" Yvette asked, looking around the small room.

Nick smiled. A few hours ago, she'd been shameless, and now she was modest. Go figure. "We'll turn our backs," he promised.

And they did.

A moment later, she was in her baggy suit, the hood pinched in on her cheeks and her clothes, jewelry, and underwear in a pile under the window. Nick pulled off his own clothes. Before even trying the Velcro, he recognized the fit was going to be a problem. The suits were made for Chinese adults, not six-foot-three American former SEALs. His suit pulled tight at his feet and, worse, in *other* places. He tossed his own clothes onto the pile, everything except for the five-fifty paracord bracelet he wore on his left wrist. The bracelet had been a gift from a teammate in Iraq, and he'd worn it everyday for the past three years. He wasn't giving it up without a fight.

He thought about sitting down but felt sure the suit would either rip at the seams or emasculate him, so he tried to fold his arms instead, the Velcro popping open in the back at the motion. He started to make a joke but then saw that Yvette had begun to cry and Bai was huddled defensively back in his corner, and he thought better of it.

There was a loud click and the door opened again.

A very small box was handed to Bai with another curt order. Bai pulled a surgical mask from the box and then slid the box over to them.

"Put on," the suited spaceman said from the door.

Nick pulled out a mask and handed it to Yvette and then fit one over his own mouth and nose.

"How is our friend?" Nick asked. "How is Batur?"

Bai translated Nick's question, and the spacesuit turned to face Nick.

"Uyghur dead," the hollow voice said, echoing inside the helmet.

Nick felt his throat tighten. Behind him, Yvette's sobbing grew louder.

"Come," the spacesuit ordered and gestured for them to follow.

The two sentries backed away from the door. Nick followed the small, suited figure down the deserted hallway, with Yvette and Bai in trail. Over his shoulder, Nick could see that a security checkpoint had been set up at the glass doors they had entered earlier; plastic sheeting stretched between the floor and ceiling a few feet from the doors, giving only a hazy, translucent view down the hall.

"Where are they taking us?" Yvette whispered.

"Isolation," Nick answered.

"I thought we were in isolation."

"No," he said quietly. "That was keeping us out of the way until they got organized. If I had to guess, they're taking us to a quarantine ward."

"Quarantine?" she gasped. "Where the infected people are?"

He nodded. "Probably."

"But Nick, this suit has gaps in the back," she said. "It will not protect us."

"The suit and mask are not for our protection," he said gravely. "It's for theirs."

FIVE

DAZHONG ENTERED THE hospital's north stairwell and began the trek up to level five. She had e-mailed a comprehensive list of biosafety protocols to the hospital director before leaving Beijing, and to her astonishment, he had implemented the instructions to the letter. His obedience and attention to detail had impressed her. Swift and comprehensive action was the key to containing an outbreak. If they were lucky, this outbreak—caused by whatever insidious scourge this was—would not spread beyond the walls of the hospital.

The north stairwell was designated a "hot zone," as was the emergency room and all of levels one, two, and three. Level four had a special designation as a quarantine zone for asymptomatic individuals who had been in close contact with infected patients. Levels five through nine were designated clean zones. She had restricted elevator use to emergency situations only, due to the risk of shuttling infected air between the lower and upper floors. The south stairwell was also designated a clean zone, reserved for access to and from the outside world without having to use the main entrance, which was now contaminated from patient admittance since the crisis began.

Her blue coveralls swished as she climbed. The baggy, lightweight material was lined with an impermeable membrane that served as a protective barrier for the wearer against deadly pathogens. Unlike the positive-pressure "space suits" worn by technicians in the BSL-4 labs—with their clean, cool, regulated air—field suits were basically fancy, expensive plastic bags. Within hours of their arrival, Major Li had confiscated all space suits in the building for use by his technicians in the lab. She had fought him on it, but soldiers with guns have a way of trumping civilians. So she had put her Liberia training to immediate use, breaking out the field suits and training everyone on the hospital team on how to dress out and decontaminate.

By design, exposure-suit material does not breathe. Within minutes of donning the suit, the air temperature inside "the blue bag" equalizes with the occupant's body temperature, making it unbearably hot. In Liberia, where the outside ambient temperature was often above thirty degrees Celsius, working a shift in a blue bag bordered on corporal punishment. On one occasion, she had become so overheated and dehydrated that she collapsed from heatstroke two hours into her shift. When she came to, she found herself lying on a cot in the admin tent, hooked up to an IV bag of electrolytes, surrounded by her staff. They each took turns scolding her for pushing herself too hard, and they did not leave her bedside until she ordered them away. She would always remember that day, not because of the heatstroke, but because that was the day she realized she had earned her coworkers loyalty and admiration.

Despite the air-conditioned environment inside the Artux People's Hospital, she was dripping with perspiration inside her suit. Sweat was beginning to pool inside her rubber gloves and boots; she could feel her hands and the soles of her feet beginning to prune. Her goggles were fogged, making it hard to see. The air inside her M5 antimicrobial mask had gone rank long ago. In fact, the smell of her captive breath was growing more and more nauseating with each passing minute. She was ready to decontaminate and strip off her PPE—her personal protective equipment.

So very, very ready.

By the time she reached the fifth-floor landing, she was panting. Yes, she was young, only thirty-one, but not a particularly robust thirty-one. Long, stressful working hours, perpetual sleep deprivation, and a diet composed primarily of noodles, bings, and caffeinated beverages were beginning to take a toll. Her aversion to exercise didn't help either. Her husband told her repeatedly that she was too thin, that she needed to eat more nourishing foods. "It's no mystery why we haven't conceived a child, Dazhong," he liked to say. "Look at how you treat your body." Hopefully, now that she had been promoted to department head for a research track, she would be able to keep more reasonable, regular hours. Also, transferring out of the Office of Disease Control and Emergency Response would mean less travel and more time at home—a double-edged sword as far as she was concerned. She tried hard to be both the professional scientist and the dutiful wife her culture demanded, but maintaining balance was becoming increasingly difficult.

When she finally reached the level-five landing, an orderly dressed in PPE identical to her own greeted her. In his left hand, he held a garden-variety, hand-pump, ten-liter plastic bug sprayer filled with an aqueous solution of chlorine dioxide. In his right hand, he held the sprayer wand. He gestured for her to step into a blue plastic tub filled to a depth of three centimeters with the same disinfectant. As a biocide, chlorine dioxide outperformed chlorinated water. It was extremely effective against a wide range of pathogenic microbes—killing viruses, bacteria, protozoa, and toxic molds within seconds—which was why she had stipulated its use here. The unspoken truth was that she had no idea what they were dealing with here, and she wasn't taking any chances.

She stepped into the plastic tub, positioned her feet shoulder-width apart, and held her arms out from her sides. Because level five was a clean zone, disinfection was mandatory prior to admittance. The carefully orchestrated decontamination ritual was critical to safeguarding not only her but everyone in the clean zone she was about to enter.

"Ready," she said, looking up at the orderly through her fogged goggles.

On that cue, the decontamination man methodically misted her from head to toe with biocide. When he stopped spraying, she rotated so that her back was to him. After finishing, he simply said, "Clear."

She rotated and stepped out of the plastic tub and onto an absorbent pad. Next to the pad sat a second blue sterilization tub, an oversized laundry hamper, and a trash receptacle marked with a biohazard sign. First, she removed her goggles and gently—so as not to make a splash—deposited them in the tub where a dozen other pairs of goggles and boots were soaking. Next, she held out her hands to the orderly for him to remove the tape sealing the cuffs of her rubber gloves to the sleeves of her suit. Once the tape was stripped off, he removed her gloves and placed them into the waste receptacle, leaving her inner pair of purple nitrile gloves untouched. After that, she stepped out of her rubber boots and waited while the orderly gently deposited them into the blue tub for soaking. Finally, she let him strip off her coveralls and dispose of them in a trash receptacle.

"Ready," she said.

"Clear," he replied and opened the heavy steel fire door with his gloved hand.

She stepped out of the stairwell and onto an oversized absorbent pad taped to the linoleum tile floor just inside the level-five corridor. She waited until the door closed behind her before removing her mask and tossing it into another prestaged biowaste receptacle. She then slipped on a pair of sterile foot covers and disposed of her nitrile gloves.

Decontamination ritual complete.

Absent her blue suit, the cool, dry, air-conditioned atmosphere of level five sent a chill careening across her sweat-soaked skin. Her damp, thin cotton scrubs offered no insulation, and gooseflesh stood up on her forearms and the nape of her neck. She shuddered involuntarily and headed toward a stack of fresh, dry hand towels, neatly folded, staged on a chair against the opposite wall. Towel in hand, she set off down the hall, wiping the sweat from her face and neck. When she reached the middle of the corridor, she stopped outside a pair of double doors labeled Gastrointestinal Department. Within an hour of her arrival, she and Commander Zhang had commandeered the space, and it had served as the Tactical Operations and Communications Center for their multidisciplinary task force ever since.

She tossed the towel into a laundry hamper and pulled open the door to the TOCC.

"Dr. Chen," Commander Zhang said, walking to greet her the instant the door opened.

"Commander Zhang," she said, nodding cordially.

"You're shivering," he said, noting how she was hugging her chest. "Sergeant Tan, get Dr. Chen a jacket."

"Sir," acknowledged the young, fit Snow Leopard soldier standing beside Zhang.

"Thank you, Commander, but that is not necessary."

"Of course it is," he said with a smile. "You are the last person on this task force I can afford catching a cold."

Before she could protest further, Sergeant Tan returned with a SLCU tactical jacket and draped it over her shoulders. The coarse, black material swallowed her tiny torso. Under its weight, she felt small and fragile. It was the same jacket that Commander Zhang wore, with the same embroidered patches on the left shoulder. The unit patch had a blue background and a golden border. In the center, a growling snow leopard was depicted over a map of China, framed by golden laurel, and resting above a pair of machine guns crossed at the barrel. Above the Snow Leopard patch, an embroidered Chinese flag was stitched—bright, bold, and red. Together, the two patches were dramatic and stark, contrasting both each other and the solid-black fabric onto which they were sewn.

"Thank you," she said at last, shifting her attention to the sergeant.

The junior soldier nodded at her and wordlessly returned to Zhang's side.

"How do you like it?" Zhang said, the crook of his mouth turning up at one corner.

"It is…" She hesitated. "A very handsome jacket." Then, with a smile, she added, "But maybe a little big for me."

"There are no female commandos in our unit," he said. "But when we come out of this crisis as heroes, I will mail you an insignia patch—so you will always remember your time with the Snow Leopards in Kizilsu."

"I would like that," she said, with as much earnestness as she could muster. "Very much."

This seemed to please the Snow Leopard Commander, because he smiled broadly at her. She knew Zhang found her attractive. It was obvious from the way he treated her. Boys and men had been pining for her affection since her fourteenth year. She had been blessed with a symmetrical and profoundly feminine face, with a petite nose, wide almond eyes, and shapely lips. In adolescence, she had come to understand that her beauty was a powerful asset when properly and demurely showcased. As she matured, she learned how to leverage her beauty to open doors and engender lasting but unrequited professional affections. The key was to entice, not tease. Allure, but not seduce. Men despised a cocktease but would wield sword and shield for a maiden. Commander Zhang was no exception. He was only doing what came naturally for men like him— subconsciously falling into the archetype that suited his ego. Should she ask, he would gladly become her champion.

Major Li, from Regiment 54423 of the People's Liberation Army, however, was another story altogether.

She leaned left to glance past Zhang into the TOCC behind him. "Is Major Li here?" she asked.

"No," Zhang said, his voice deepening. "Major Li has not returned from the laboratory."

"Hmm," she said. "I would have expected him to have the test results by now."

Zhang nodded pensively, then asked, "How are the patients doing?"

"Not good," she said, shaking her head. "Not good at all."

During her time in Liberia, she began to detach herself from the gruesome, heartbreaking patient interactions that she, and every other Ebola worker, had to face on a daily basis. Pain, suffering, and death were everywhere and unavoidable, so she learned to compartmentalize her feelings, her empathy, her fear. To function in the face of great adversity and risk, a doctor must become...clinical.

"How bad is it?" he asked.

"Seventy percent mortality, and we are losing more every hour. With the type of progression I'm seeing, I would not be surprised if the mortality rate reaches ninety percent or more."

"Is that normal for Ebola?"

"I don't believe we're dealing with Ebola."

Zhang took a step back. "If not Ebola, then what?"

"I don't know," she said, and then felt her pulse quicken as she added, "Something worse."

SIX

NICK STRETCHED HIS back and felt the overwhelming urge to start pacing again. He was not a jumpy guy by nature, but with the toxic, nervous energy coursing through his veins, he couldn't sit still. Lying in the short, uncomfortable Chinese hospital bed was unbearable. He simply could not relax.

So he paced like a caged animal.

Since the androgynous bubble-suit doctor and his or her two guards had locked the three of them in this room, they had been poked, prodded, and kept completely in the dark. Meals and water were being provided, but the hospital rations were not substantial enough to quell his rumbling belly. Taming hunger on a SEAL mission was an entirely different beast than in quarantine. On a mission, even in the desert, there was sensory nourishment for the mind to help offset bodily hunger. In here, in this horrible, gray-and-white, windowless room, with its linoleum tile floor and fiberboard drop ceiling, there was nothing to see, nothing to smell, nothing to hear. The room reminded him of a treatment bay. Rolling beds with metal side rails had been brought in for them to sleep on, but they did not have chairs. Their room was separated from a half-dozen similar rooms by folding glass partitions that had been pulled closed. He could count three other rooms with quarantine patients inside, one of them packed with at least ten people, including three small children. Nick guessed they were kept together in groups based on how and when they had been exposed. Whatever the hell this disease was, Nick was now certain that Batur was not the only victim.

He glanced up at the television suspended from the ceiling, where men in Western suits were yelling at each other behind an oversized desk. The volume was on mute, and he could not read the Chinese subtitles. He did not recognize the show, but it looked like some variant of the wildly popular CSI series.

Ironic, he thought.

"I don't feel sick," said Yvette, her voice small and sure.

He looked over at her. Sometime during the past six hours, she had drifted into an eerie and unsettling state of calm. This was the fourth time she had made this comment.

"You don't look sick," he said, realizing this was the fourth time he made the same reply. He did not like seeing her with this new, creepy Stepford Wife tranquility. In fact, he liked her better when she was teetering on panic. At least then he could satiate his instinct to comfort and protect her. Her hysteria had given him something to focus on besides questioning whether his lips and eyelids felt like they were beginning to swell.

"How long has it been?" she asked, smiling at him.

"Almost two days, I guess."

"If we were going to get it, don't you think we would be sick by now?"

He desperately wanted to point out that he had no friggin' idea. Without knowing the time from Batur's initial exposure to the point when his face exploded with edema and he began bleeding from the eyes, it was impossible to make predictions about the disease's incubation period. In Nick's mind, two days "symptom-free" was no guarantee they were out of the woods. But he heard soft hope in Yvette's voice and decided to keep these thoughts to himself.

"Definitely," he said. "I think we're good."

He looked past Yvette at the body lying motionless in the bed beside her. Bai was staring so intensely at the ceiling that, for a moment, Nick thought the man was sleeping with his eyes open. Yesterday, the hospital had allowed Bai to call his family. He had not been permitted to tell them where he was or any details of his detainment, but he had been allowed to say he was okay. Since making that call, Bai had not said a word.

"How long do you think until they let us leave?" Yvette asked.

"Soon," Nick said, and he winked. "You ready for that beer I promised?"

Yvette shook her head, her lips tight.

"When we are allowed to leave, I will go straight to the airport in Kashi to find a flight home." She looked up at him, and to Nick she suddenly seemed younger. "My mother will be worried," she said, and a tear rolled down her cheek.

He had no reply. The girl probably should go home to her parents. As far as his plans when he "got out," he had not given the matter any thought until now. Given the choice, his preference would be to finish the project. He felt the same about the mission now as he did before, if not stronger. But if Chinese government suspended or cancelled the project, then he would have no choice but to go home to Texas. His mother would certainly welcome him with open arms, but he wasn't ready to go home yet. His work here felt unfinished, and he didn't want to walk away from the NGO life. He didn't want to walk away from China.

The glass doors opened and a nurse walked in carrying meal trays stacked three high. The woman was dressed in blue coveralls, complete with mask, gloves, and goggles, but she was *not* wearing a space suit.

That has to be good, he thought. *Right?*

Bai sat up, and Nick wondered if he was thinking the same thing.

"She's not in a pressure suit anymore!" Yvette noted.

"Ask her if there is any news," he told Bai excitedly.

Bai chattered with the woman a moment. Then he nodded to her as she set down the trays and left.

"Well?" Yvette asked before Bai could even take a breath.

"I don't know," he said. "She says the soldiers took the pressure suits, and they were told by the CDC doctor to use these suits now. I asked her if she knows our test results, and she said she does not know."

Nick nodded, not sure if this was good news or not.

"Someone will come to talk to us soon, she says," Bai added after a beat.

Nick grabbed the three trays and handed them out to the others.

"Celebratory dinner, anyone?" he asked, setting his tray on his bed.

"I think it's lunch time," Yvette said.

"Close enough," Nick said as he sat down on the

corner of his bed, his Chinese-sized green scrubs lifting to his knees. He raised a cup of juice to Bai, who
tried to smile for the first time since they had arrived.
"To not being sick."

"To getting out of here," Yvette added.

Bai nodded but did not raise his own cup. "I just want
to see my family again."

SEVEN

TOCC, fifth floor
Artux People's Hospital

DAZHONG HATED SUPPOSITION, but during her career at the CDC, she'd learned that men like Commander Zhang hated being kept in the dark even more. Their working relationship would go smoother if she shared what she knew, as she came to know it, even if her working conclusions later turned out erroneous. Based on the patients she'd observed and treated so far, her medical instincts told her this was not an Ebola outbreak. Her reasoning for this had a textbook component and was also based on her intimate familiarity with the disease from her time in Liberia. Zhang was a counterterrorism operative, not an epidemiologist, and so much of what she wanted to tell him would fall well outside his area of expertise. Yet during the short time they'd worked together, she'd recognized that Zhang possessed a shrewd and logical mind. If she dumbed down the discussion, she might risk offending him. She decided to talk to him as a peer and put the burden of asking for clarification on his shoulders.

Zhang stared at her, his lips still parted in surprise at the bombshell news she'd dropped on him seconds ago.

"Initially, I thought this could be Ebola because the late-stage presentation of this infection is similar to

Ebola," she said, restarting the conversation. "Diarrhea, chest and abdominal pain, bleeding from the eyes, nose, and rectum, and pronounced edema are all present. But the disease progression is too fast, the tissue damage looks different, and the incubation period is not consistent with what we know about Ebola."

"What do you mean by that last point?" he asked.

"Ebola has a variable incubation period, anywhere from two to twenty-one days. We've admitted sixty-two infected patients who all presented symptoms within the past twenty-four hours. What is the likelihood that all of these people were exposed to Ebola in Kizilsu Prefecture and all fell ill at the same exact time?"

"Are you saying this may not be a naturally occurring outbreak?"

She nodded. "The consistency of disease progression across this initial wave of victims points to a bioterrorism event."

Zhang's expression darkened. "What bioweapon are we dealing with here?"

"Unfortunately, I can't tell you what it is, but I can tell you what it's not."

"Okay."

"It's not smallpox, anthrax, or plague, which are the three most probable agents that a terrorist would select. Smallpox victims present with a progressive skin rash that follows a predictable pattern: flat, red spots that become raised bumps, which turn into fluid-filled blisters, and then morph into pustules. The skin lesions we're seeing bear no resemblance."

"What about anthrax and plague?" Zhang asked.

"The only forms of anthrax and plague that kill this rapidly are the inhalation variants, and we are not seeing pulmonary pneumonia, hemoptysis, or shock induced by respiratory collapse. I've taken chest x-rays of multiple patients, and the images do not support respiratory infection as the cause of death."

"If it's not Ebola, not smallpox, not anthrax, and not plague, what else could it be?"

"This is really a conversation we should be having in conference with Major Li," Dazhong said, her irritation growing by the second. She shrugged off the oversized tactical jacket and handed it back to Sergeant Tan. "I think it's time we go see him."

"Agreed," said Zhang, and he headed for the door.

She trotted after him, down the corridor to the south stairwell. The door was guarded by one of Zhang's men, who stepped aside as his Commander approached.

"Any unauthorized entry attempts?" Zhang asked.

"No sir."

"Very well," he said, pushing open the door.

The south stairwell was designated as a clean zone, so PPE was not required for entry or egress. She followed Zhang up the stairs to the sixth floor, where Major Li and his team from the army's NBC Regiment 54423 had set up their laboratory equipment in the hospital's Radiology Department.

Dazhong had to jog to keep pace with the long-legged Zhang as he strode down the corridor. When they reached their destination, she was surprised to find two army sentries posted in front of the double doors leading into radiology. They were dressed in digital camo BDUs patterned in green and gray, and both men were armed with pistols worn in drop holsters. She glanced at Zhang and saw him smirk at the scene. He took a position no more than thirty centimeters in front of one of the sentries, blatantly invading the soldier's personal space. Next to the tall and powerfully built Snow Leopard Commander, the army sentry looked like a child. Nonetheless, the soldier did not flinch.

"Step aside, soldier," Zhang ordered, his voice baritone and ripe with authority.

"Laboratory access is not permitted at this time," the young solider replied, eyes fixed straight ahead.

Zhang glanced at the soldier's rank insignia. "I said, step aside, Corporal," he barked. "That's an order."

"I'm sorry, sir, but you are not in my chain of command. My orders come directly from Major Li. No unauthorized personnel are permitted to enter the lab."

Zhang clenched his jaw, and Dazhong saw the veins on his forehead stand up.

"I am Commander Zhang of the SLCU—the senior ranking officer of this joint task force. Every member of this operation, including Major Li, reports to me," he said. Then, gesturing to Dazhong, he added, "This is Dr. Chen from the CDC, and she is the senior ranking civilian administrator on the premises. The Artux People's Hospital is under her control, as is this laboratory. Now, if you do not step aside in the next five seconds, you are going to find out what happens to soldiers who disobey direct orders."

The soldier glanced at the sentry to his right. The second soldier nodded and shifted his right hand to the butt of his weapon.

What happened next, she did not fully comprehend until it was over. A black shadow whirled and danced in a blur of movement, bodies twisted and fell, and when she blinked, Commander Zhang was holding a pistol in each hand. The two army sentries were on the ground—one sitting, holding his knee, and the other lying flat on his back groaning.

Mouth agape, she stared at Zhang; he did not notice. His attention was still focused on the two sentries he had just disarmed. He opened his mouth to speak but was interrupted as the right-hand door to the laboratory swung open. Major Li stepped into the doorway. He glanced at each of the sentries and then fixed a steely glower on the Snow Leopard Commander. She watched Li purse his lips at Zhang.

"Your men attempted to draw their side arms," Zhang said, looking down at Li, who stood nearly a head shorter. "That was a mistake."

Major Li shot Dazhong an accusing stare—part disdain, part rebuke—as if *she* were to blame for this absurd display of hypermasculine turf fighting.

She met his stare but said nothing. She knew better than to step in between two raging bears.

Finally, Li shifted his gaze back to Zhang. "The sentries were following orders, Commander. Your decision to assault my men, however, is something you will come to regret." Major Li extended both palms to Zhang. "Hand over their weapons. Now!"

Zhang screwed up his face at the other man and brazenly stuffed the two semiautomatic handguns into the oversized cargo pockets on the outside of his pant legs. "I think it's time we made something clear, Major Li. I am the ranking officer of this joint task force. You do not threaten me. You do not give me orders."

Li sniffed and retrieved a folded piece of paper from his left breast pocket. He handed it to Zhang and said, "You *were* the ranking officer of this task force. Not anymore."

Zhang cocked an eyebrow at Dazhong and snatched the document from Li's outstretched hand. He unfolded the paper and read. When he was finished, he handed the paper to her. It was a letter issued from the office of the Central National Security Commission—the CNSC—and signed by Deputy Chairman Hu Zedong. The message was succinct and clear. The joint task force had been officially reclassified as a military operation, with all personnel now serving under the command and authority of Major Li Shengkun. She looked back at Zhang, who shook his head in disbelief.

She handed the letter back to Major Li, who took it and returned it to his breast pocket, looking smug. The two army sentries whom Zhang had humiliated were now back on their feet, flanking the major.

"Commander Zhang," Li said, his voice cold and harsh. "The weapons."

Zhang retrieved the handguns he'd confiscated and returned them to the soldiers.

An awkward silence persisted in the corridor of level six of the Artux People's Hospital in Kizilsu Prefecture until at last the lone woman in the group finally spoke.

"Well, gentlemen," Dazhong said, "hopefully we can all put this misunderstanding behind us and focus on the crisis at hand. Major Li, the Commander and I wish to conference with you. I was hoping to review the test results for the blood samples I sent to the lab four hours ago. If we could step into the lab and—"

"I'm sorry, Dr. Chen," Major Li interrupted, "but the samples are still in process. I don't have any results to share at this time."

"But surely you must have something to report. Four hours is more than sufficient—"

He raised a hand, cutting her off. "The samples are still being analyzed. When I have results to share with you and the rest of the team, I will do so."

She looked expectantly at Zhang.

The Snow Leopard Commander read her mind. "Major Li, it is imperative that we conference now. Dr. Chen has spent the last several hours observing infected patients, and based on her observations, she is convinced this outbreak is *not* Ebola."

"I concur," Li said simply.

"In that case, you should know that both Dr. Chen and I are concerned this outbreak was caused by an act of bioterrorism," Zhang continued.

"In that case, shouldn't you be out there?" Li said, gesturing with his right hand to indicate the world outside the hospital. "Shouldn't you be hunting down the terrorists responsible for this tragedy? After all, Commander Zhang, you are the head of China's elite Snow Leopard counterterrorism unit. Maybe it's time you leave the science to the scientists and concentrate on doing the job you were sent here to do."

Dazhong watched Zhang bristle, but the Commander kept his temper in check.

Li straightened his uniform. "When it's time to conference, I'll have someone contact you." Then, without another word, he turned and disappeared back into the lab.

Dazhong and Zhang exchanged glances and then departed in silence for the south stairwell. As they walked the length of the corridor, the only sound was the echo of Zhang's combat boots on the tile floor. When they reached the stairwell, Zhang pushed the heavy metal door open for her, and they both stepped across the threshold. The instant it slammed shut behind them, they both started jabbering at the same time.

They paused simultaneously.

"You first," Dazhong said.

Zhang smiled. "No, you go."

She took a deep breath and said, "What was that all about back there?"

He shook his head. "I apologize, Dr. Chen. I lost my temper and my conduct was unprofessional."

"No, no, that's not what I meant. What happened with Major Li taking over the operation and cutting us out of the information loop?"

"I'm as surprised as you," he said. "I've conducted many joint operations with the army, and I've never experienced anything like this."

"Do you believe him?"

"The letter was issued by the CNSC. It looked legitimate."

"I'm not talking about the letter," she said, frustrated that they'd somehow now fallen out of synch. "I mean, do you believe that the samples are still in process?"

"From a scientist's perspective, you'd know the answer to the question better than I would. But from a trained interrogator's perspective, I'm convinced Li is hiding something."

When they reached the landing outside the door to level five, she stopped and turned to face him. "Without those test results, we're stuck running in place. I can't develop a treatment and containment protocol if he won't tell me what disease we're fighting."

Zhang nodded. "I understand. I plan to call my superiors in Beijing. I suggest you consider doing the same.

Perhaps your CDC director has access to the information Li is withholding."

"Perhaps," she said.

"In the meantime, if you have a few minutes to spare, I could use your help with something," Zhang said.

"Of course. What do you need?"

"On the flight from Beijing, I was reviewing your CV, and I noticed that you lived and studied in America for several years."

"Yes. I did two years of postgraduate work at Johns Hopkins in Baltimore. Why?"

"Excellent," he said with a hint of embarrassment. "My English is not so good, and I could use translation help with someone."

"Who?"

"An American named Nick Foley," Zhang said. "He's being held in observational quarantine, down on level four."

"Certainly. What's the purpose of the interview?"

"Oh, it's not an interview," China's preeminent counterterrorism Commander said with a smirk. "It's an interrogation."

EIGHT

Isolation Ward, fourth floor
Artux People's Hospital

NICK DID NOT like this change of venue. The relief of no longer seeing the hospital staff in pressure suits was ebbing in the face of this new twist. Two armed guards had taken him from the quarantine quarters to this closet of a room. Unlike the soldiers he had encountered before, these men carried themselves with a different military bearing. They were elite—undoubtedly Special Forces.

Takes one to know one.

The windowless room was small and barren. Judging by the countertop along the rear wall with a built-in sink, he guessed this had been a break room before being commandeered and stripped bare by the military. He imagined a coffee machine and snacks… God, what he would give for a cup of coffee. He sat at a white Formica table, drumming his fingertips impatiently on the surface with nothing to do but stare at the two empty chairs across from him. The overhead fluorescent light buzzed incessantly, needling his nerves. He had been waiting for thirty minutes by his count, a number he estimated, since there was no clock in the room. They had yet to return his clothes, his watch, and his wallet since he had stripped naked the day of his arrival, and it was finally beginning to piss him off. He was tired of being locked in quarantine. He was tired of being bossed around and manhandled without explanation.

The door opened.

A nurse entered and took his temperature with a noncontact thermometer; she conducted her business in silence and was careful not to show him the LCD window on the device. He thought about asking her about his blood-test results, but what was the point? Even if she knew, she wouldn't tell him. Besides, she probably didn't speak English anyway. The nurse left and the waiting began anew. With each passing minute, he felt less like a hospital patient and more like a prison inmate waiting to be grilled by a prosecutor. Seeing the shoulder of the armed guard standing outside the door cemented the feeling. He shuddered, perhaps from the chill of wearing only the ridiculous, paper-thin cotton scrubs they'd given him, or more likely from the realization that he might soon have to put his SERE interrogation training to use.

No problem—like riding a bike. I just need to work within the system and get the hell out of here. Then I'll figure out what to do next.

The door opened.

A different woman stepped in and took the seat directly across from him. She nodded politely and opened a leather notebook. When she looked up at him, he knew this woman did not work for an intelligence agency, nor was she a military interrogator. Her demeanor was pleasant, yet slightly nervous. She had bright, almond-colored eyes and creamy, unblemished skin, which gave her an aura of royalty. Her unlined forehead and high cheekbones were framed by thick, onyx hair she wore tucked behind one ear. She wore a thin surgical mask hiding the bottom half of her face, but Nick imagined a perfect nose and full, ruby lips underneath. Unlike the other hospital workers he'd encountered thus far, she wore regular scrubs and thin surgical gloves. No space suit. No hood. No blue coveralls with boots and goggles.

He exhaled, breathing easy for the first time in days.

He waited patiently while she jotted down some notes. Perhaps she was waiting for an interpreter. Then she raised her eyes and held his gaze in a way uncharacteristic of a woman in the misogynistic Chinese culture. Her confidence made her even more attractive, and Nick realized that he had been "out of the game" much too long.

"Good day, Mr. Nick Foley," she said in clipped but perfect English.

Nick raised his eyebrows in surprise. "Good day," he said, and then he chuckled at the ridiculousness of these pleasantries under the circumstances.

"My name is Dr. Dazhong Chen," the woman said, smiling politely with her eyes. "How are you feeling today?"

Nick settled back in his chair.

"I feel very well, thank you," he said. Apparently, he had misread the situation entirely. This woman was a doctor, which meant this was a medical evaluation, not an interrogation. "Obviously, I'm concerned and frightened about what's going on here," he continued. "My friends and I have been locked in quarantine with no information, waiting on our test results to learn if we are sick with, uh, whatever this thing is."

"I am sorry you have been frightened," the woman said. "We are doing everything we can to ensure you and the others are kept safe after your exposure. I must ask you some questions, if you please."

"Shoot," Nick said. The woman raised an eyebrow, apparently confused. "Go ahead," he said, clarifying.

"Thank you, Mr. Foley. Have you had any nausea or vomiting since your arrival or immediately before coming to Artux hospital?"

"No," Nick answered. Surely they would know that already. If he had vomited, he imagined alarms would have gone off in his little cage with Yvette and Bai.

"And before you came to this hospital, did you have any sore throat or fever? Any muscle aches or strange weakness?"

"No."

"And since you came to this hospital?"

"No," Nick said, choosing to dismiss the effects of dehydration and nerves he had certainly been experiencing. He felt himself begin to relax. The conversation was beginning to sound like a final exit evaluation before being cleared and released. He swallowed his excitement at the thought that this nightmare might finally be over.

"Any shortness of breath or dizziness—either after you came here or in the days before?"

"No."

"No rash or headaches?"

"No."

"Any stomachaches or muscle cramps? Any sweating?"

"No," Nick said, and the image of Batur popped into his head.

Any bloating of your eyelids and lips, and blood

from your eyes, ears, nose, mouth, and ass? Any turning gray, puffing up like a blowfish, and dying?

He shook the image away.

"Any diarrhea or blood in your urine or stools?"

"No," he said, and then quickly interjected, "Are you the doctor in charge of the medical staff here?" He leaned forward and made eye contact with her.

"I am one of the medical team members."

He noted that she did not break eye contact or lean back away from him. *Impressive, under the circumstances.* He leaned in closer and lowered his voice. "So what is this thing? And do I have it?"

She glanced over her shoulder—unconsciously, he guessed—and in that instant, he realized she did not have full authority here.

"Your tests are negative."

"Negative for what?"

The woman sighed and folded her hands. "I am not able to discuss the particular details with you, Mr. Foley. I must apologize and ask for your understanding on this matter."

Nick nodded, the uneasiness beginning to creep back in. "And my friends?"

"Negative for your friends as well."

The door burst open before he could ask his next question.

The man who entered was tall for a Han Chinese—around six feet tall, Nick estimated. He wore scrubs, but his level of fitness and catlike movements gave him away as Special Forces. From his demeanor and confidence, Nick pegged him as the likely Commander of the two who had escorted him here.

The man spoke softly but with authority to the

woman and sat down beside her. The doctor nodded and looked down at her hands.

The military man folded his hands on the table and fixed Nick with a cold stare. Then he began speaking in Chinese. As he spoke, the doctor began to interpret in English, both speaker and interpreter maintaining their respective and unbroken cadence. As the man spoke, his gaze did not waiver, and Nick shifted uneasily under the weight of the other man's soul-searching stare.

"My name is Commander Zhang. I am the Commander of the Snow Leopard counterterrorism unit sent with the disease control specialists to investigate this horrible event," he said through the woman. After a few disorienting seconds, Nick's brain made the shift, and it was as if the Commander was speaking to him with the doctor's soft voice. "What is your name, please?"

"I am Nick Foley, an American NGO volunteer working on a water project nearby."

Zhang huffed with irritation, leaned over to his interpreter, and whispered something in her ear.

"I am sorry," the woman said softly. "The Commander asks that you please answer simply and only the questions you are being asked."

"What is going on here?" Nick asked, looking at the beautiful Chinese doctor for the first time since the Commander had entered the room. "Have I done something wrong?"

There was another exchange between the two, and then the woman said, "Commander Zhang says that is what we are here to determine. He again asks that you please answer only the questions he asks."

Nick sighed and again turned to the Commander. "Okay," he said. "Shoot."

"Why are you in Kashi?"

"As I already said, I am an NGO volunteer working on a clean water project." He started to explain more but stopped himself. He thought he saw some satisfaction in the eyes of the military Commander, who controlled the conversation on multiple levels.

"How do you know the Uyghur named Batur?"

"He is a paid worker on my project."

"He is your friend?"

"Yes," Nick said, then his throat tightened. "He was."

The Commander continued through the doctor.

"Have you prayed with him at the Id Kah Mosque or attended prayers there before?"

"The mosque?" Nick asked, confused by the direction of the conversation. "No, never."

"Are you Muslim?"

Nick was startled by the question. What the hell did that have to do with anything? He knew, of course, of the rising tensions between the Han Chinese and the Muslim Uyghur minority in the region. Those tensions had come to a violent head after the murder of the state-appointed imam of the Id Kah Mosque, Juma Tahir. He did not like where this conversation was heading, and he understood the reason even less.

"No," he answered finally. "I am not Muslim. I was raised Presbyterian, if that is relevant to this outbreak somehow."

The Commander again leaned to the woman doctor and said something with what Nick felt was exaggerated irritation. The woman said something back, and the Commander shook his head and sighed. Then he straightened up and drilled his laser-beam eyes into Nick's forehead.

"What do you know of Batur and his ties to terrorism?" the Commander asked, in Dr. Chen's demure voice.

"Ties to terrorism?" This time there was real surprise in Nick's voice. "Nothing," he said, sounding more defensive than he meant. "I very much doubt that Batur was a terrorist."

There was no way in hell that Batur was tied to terrorism. If anything, it seemed to Nick the Uyghurs were victims of paranoia, sparked by the actions of a crazy few. He sure as hell didn't like the way this was going. He tried to read something—anything—in the cold, dark eyes of the Snow Leopard Commander, but he saw nothing. A terrible dread washed over Nick. If Zhang knew about his special operations background, the session would not end well.

"Do you understand the question, Mr. Foley?"

"What?" Nick asked.

The interrogator, speaking with the beautiful doctor's voice, had apparently asked another question.

"Do you work for the United States government?"

Shit, he knows. He knows I was a SEAL.

Nick felt a shift inside, and suddenly the conditioning from the grueling training he endured in the cold, Pacific Northwest woods kicked in. He'd been conditioned to resist this kind of questioning during SERE school. He slipped the mask on, and the mask felt good. The mask gave him strength, and confidence, and certitude.

"I do not," Nick said. "I work for an international NGO providing clean water to poor people around the globe."

"Do you collect information during your travels on

the countries you work in and provide this information
to the US government?"

"You mean am I a spy?"

The Commander leaned over and spoke softly again
to the doctor.

"Do you hate Muslims?" the counterterrorism soldier asked through the woman.

"What? No, of course not."

"Are you a terrorist, Mr. Foley?"

Zhang was trying to shake him; he would not crum-
ble.

"No," he said, evenly holding the interrogator's gaze.
"I am not a terrorist. And I do not hate Muslims."

The Snow Leopard Commander leaned back and
crossed his arms across his chest.

"Yet you killed many Muslims in Afghanistan, did
you not, Mr. Foley? And in Iraq as well, I believe."

Both Nick and the doctor stared wide-eyed at the
Commander after his sudden display of perfect English.
Zhang turned to the doctor. "You may leave now, Dr.
Chen," he said.

The woman's face flushed, but she quickly collected
herself.

"I prefer to stay," she said in English.

The Commander shrugged and rose from his chair.

"As you wish," he said. He paced behind the doctor's
chair. He smiled again at Nick. "You were saying, Mr.
Foley? About the Muslims you killed?"

Nick said nothing. *Time to keep silent*, he decided.

"You *did* serve in the United States Navy, did you
not?"

"Yes," Nick answered.

"As a SEAL, yes?" the Commander asked, leaning now on the back of the doctor's chair.

Nick said nothing and then leaned forward.

"I would like to speak to someone from the US embassy now."

The Commander waved his hand, as if shooing away a fly, and chuckled.

"There is no reason for that, I assure you, Special Operator Second Class Foley," the Commander said, using Nick's final rank when he had left the Teams. "We are both soldiers—both men of action, yes? And the lies and maneuvers of bureaucrats do not suit us. Let us talk as soldiers."

Zhang took his seat. He leaned in, making a little temple with his long, thick fingers. "As a SEAL, you are well trained in terrorism operations, correct?"

"I am well-versed in *counter*terrorism operations."

"Of course. Counterterrorism," the Commander said, the thin smile still on his face. "So you learned to kill Muslims and to use the tools of terror, and now you are here—a former Navy SEAL in China making clean water. And after only a few weeks, we have dozens of dead Muslims in what appears to me to be a terror attack." Zhang leaned in, his smile gone and his eyes burning a hole in Nick's forehead. "What am I supposed to think, Mr. Foley?"

Nick's mind went into overdrive as he recognized Zhang springing the trap.

Time to go on the offensive.

"You are a Snow Leopard Commando—one of China's most revered counterterrorism experts—so you know full well what you are saying is bullshit," Nick said, his voice rising as he resisted the urge to rise from his seat as well. "I was a soldier—not a terrorist. I fought terrorists—not Muslims. And," he added, lowering his voice, "Batur was my friend."

The Commander leaned back and again crossed his arms across his chest.

"Yes," he said. "Yes, so you have said. But still, what would you think—one soldier to another, one *coun-ter*terrorist expert to another—were you sitting in my chair, hmm?"

"If I were sitting in your chair, I would ask myself the following questions: Why would a man secretly working for the US government attack the most despised minority in China, in the middle of the desert, where no one is likely to notice, let alone care? Conversely, if I were a terrorist, why would I target Muslims over Han Chinese? And why would I select Kizilsu over Beijing, or Shanghai, or Hong Kong if my goal was to create mass hysteria and panic? Because that is exactly what terrorists do, Commander Zhang—they go for the throat."

His anger properly ventilated, Nick took a long, deep breath.

"What else would you ask yourself, Mr. Foley?"

It was the beautiful Chinese doctor who spoke this time, and immediately the Snow Leopard Commander shot her a critical look.

"I would ask myself," Nick said, gaining control for the first time in the conversation, "if this is a terrorist attack—not an epidemic, or a toxic chemical release, or whatever the hell *this* is—then who has the most to gain from it?"

She fixed her bright, almond eyes on him, and Nick felt a moment of communion.

Then, Commander Zhang leaned in to conference

with her, and the moment was gone. They traded harsh whispers back and forth in Chinese. The argument ended abruptly with Zhang standing. He glared at her, and she popped to her feet a heartbeat later, looking diminutive beside the powerfully built Snow Leopard.

"You will be discharged soon," Commander Zhang said. "We may wish to speak with you again, but until then," he said, waving a familiar-looking, worn, blue rectangle in his right hand, "I will be holding on to this." He flashed Nick's passport between them and then slipped it into his pocket.

"Of course," Nick said, forcing calm into his voice. "And I would be happy to help in any way I can."

"I'm sure," the Commander said.

"As I said, Batur was my friend."

"Of course."

Then the Commander spun on a heel and led the doctor out of the room gently by the arm. At the threshold, she glanced over her shoulder at Nick with curious eyes. He met her gaze with a blank stare. In situations like this, he followed one simple rule: Trust no one, and beautiful women least of all.

After all, wars had been started by such women.

NINE

TWO HOURS LATER, Nick was ushered out of quarantine and into the light of day.

He paused on the front steps and let the sun beat on his face and fresh air fill his lungs. Freedom was an even sweeter elixir than Nick had imagined. The last three days, especially the last twenty-four hours, had been both physically and mentally exhausting. Finally, the nightmare was over.

He was free.

"Nick!"

He turned and Yvette was there. She flung her arms around his neck in a tight hug; any sexual tension he had once sensed in their relationship was now gone. She hugged him like a sister, and he hugged her back accordingly. After they had been separated for his interrogation, he had not expected to see her again. He'd figured by now she would be cruising in an Airbus at forty thousand feet on a one-way flight to Brussels. Her presence indicated that perhaps she and Bai were also suspects. Maybe you didn't have to be a Navy SEAL to be interrogated and accused of colluding with terrorists.

"How are you?" he asked, pulling back from her embrace.

"I feel fine... You?"

"Fine," he said. He wondered how long until the poor girl could go home to her family. "Are you out of here soon?"

She nodded.

"They tell me I will be allowed to leave the country in one or two days. I have no idea what to do until then. I'm done digging trenches, I can tell you that. I have no desire to go back where Batur got sick."

Nick nodded. That was for damn sure.

"There's no need," said a voice behind them.

Nick looked past Yvette to see Bai walking toward them from the glass doors of the hospital. The NGO coordinator was wearing a smile on his face—an embarrassed smile, but a real one nonetheless. Nick could not remember the last time he'd seen Bai smile like that.

"I have arranged rooms at the Qidong Grand Hotel for each of us," Bai said as he extended a hand toward Nick.

Nick shook it firmly and placed his other hand affectionately on the smaller man's shoulder. There was something about a shared trauma like this that bonded people, he knew. "That's very generous, Bai," he said, wondering if this was the man's way of apologizing for his aloofness and suspicion the last few days. "And unnecessary."

"I disagree," Bai said with a slight bow. "Our staff already collected your belongings from the work site. Your bags are waiting for you in your rooms."

"You will get no arguments from me," Yvette said. "Where is your truck?" she asked looking around.

"Taken by the government officials, I'm afraid," Bai said. "The good news is the hotel is only a short walk from here."

"I'm more than happy to walk," Nick said, stretching out his back. He had not walked farther than a few paces to the shared bathroom until yesterday when they led him down the hall to his interrogation. Since then, he had sat alone in a small hospital room, under guard.

Bai gestured left, and they followed him northeast along Pami'er Road. They arrived at the hotel in less than fifteen minutes.

By American standards, the hotel was equivalent to a Motel 6, but after living for weeks in the NGO tents and then spending three days in quarantine, the place might as well have been the Four Seasons. They walked beneath the movie theater–like marquis and into the small lobby, where Bai handed each of them a key.

"Your rooms are on the second floor, just up the stairs," he said. "Would you let me take you to dinner?"

"Of course," Yvette said.

"Sounds great," Nick said.

Nick and Yvette followed Bai up the gently sweeping stairs, looking at the gaudy, yellow-and-brown sunburst chandelier that reminded Nick of Orlando for some reason. At the top of the stairs, they split up and headed to their respective rooms.

"Out front in an hour?" Nick asked, and his companions nodded in agreement.

The room was a far cry from big-city US luxury, but Nick had no doubt that booking three rooms at the Qidong Grand was a blow to Bai's meager NGO budget, and so he appreciated the gesture. He tossed his oversized backpack on the bed and stripped off his clothes. Moments later, he was standing in a steaming-hot shower. He put his palms against the wall and let the heat unkink his aching back and shoulders.

While the water did its work, he let his mind wander. *What the hell am I doing here?* *What the hell am I doing with my life?*

This was not the first time he had asked these questions. A part of him wanted to go back to Texas, put his education to work in the construction business, find a girl, and live the American dream. Another part of him wished he had never left the Navy. He supposed he could always try to get back in the game—use his SEAL pedigree to work as a security specialist like so many former operators did. That had to be better than toiling for free in this barren outland of western China, a stone's throw from the rugged Afghan country that was the crucible of his guilt.

The guilt was always there, just below the surface. Gnawing and burning...gnawing and burning.

Now he could add the bloated death mask of his Uyghur friend to the gruesome mental catalog he kept of the charred, dismembered corpses of women and children who had been killed in the hellfires of Afghanistan. *Batur was collateral damage in someone else's war*, he told himself, but this did not make him feel better. He envied his SEAL brothers who could operate in the black-and-white world of combat. For Nick, everything was shades of gray.

He shuddered.

He felt the water temperature drifting lukewarm, and he immediately spun the handle to stop the spray before it turned cold. Most people thought that SEALs enjoyed the cold, became conditioned to it after shivering for

hours in the freezing surf in BUD/S—the first stage of
Navy SEAL training where 80 percent or more of candidates washed out. The truth was, for Nick anyway, he
had once enjoyed the cold, but BUD/S had stolen that
joy forever. He frigging hated the cold now. He shiv-
ered and smirked at the notion that he and Yvette had
single-handedly exhausted the hotel's entire hot water
supply with their postquarantine showers. He toweled
off and looked longingly at the bed, suddenly desperate to slip between real cotton sheets and drift away.
But if he napped, he would not be able to drag himself
out of bed to meet Yvette and Bai for dinner. So he immediately dressed—pulling on clean underwear, cargo
pants, a black T-shirt, and a gray flannel shirt. He sat
on the edge of the bed and slipped on his "camp" shoes
instead of the work boots he usually wore. The pair of
KEENs felt amazing on his abused and blistered feet.

An audible growl from his stomach reminded him
just how hungry he was. With his mind on roasted
chicken and rice, he slipped on a jacket, dropped his
wallet and key into his left cargo pocket, and headed
downstairs to meet Bai and Yvette. He glanced at his
watch and realized he was a few minutes early. He
thought about grabbing a beer. A cold beer would be
amazing, but one beer would lead to two, and two to
three… In his state, that would be a disaster.

Instead, he paced the lobby.

"Excuse me, please," said a woman's voice behind
him.

"Oops, sorry," he said, sidestepping clear of the lobby
doors to clear the path. Even under the caustic yellow
lights of the oversized marquis, he recognized the
woman immediately— the interrogator's accomplice.

She dismissed him with a wave and looked down at her phone.

What the hell was the name she had used? He was terrible with Chinese names and decided to simply go with "Doctor."

"Excuse me, Doctor?" he said.

She looked up and he met her eyes. She did a double take, and for a moment looked panicked.

"Nick Foley—the American from the hospital," he said, but she knew exactly who he was. "Are you staying here at the hotel?"

"I am late for a meeting," she said, composing herself. "Please excuse me."

She turned abruptly to leave, and he resisted the urge to grab her by the arm. He needed to be careful—she was one of them, a part of the Chinese government machine with the power to kick him out of the country or, worse, toss him in a Chinese prison to rot. He fell in step beside her as she headed out of the lobby.

"I have a few questions," he said as they pushed through the doors together. "Can I walk with you?"

She turned to him, her eyes hot with emotion. Anger, irritation, exasperation? He could not tell.

"No," she said sharply. "I am sorry, but I have no information for you. You will need to speak to Major Li."

She picked up her pace.

"Who is Major Li?" he asked.

"We should not be talking," she said.

With a quick glance right and then left, she abruptly dashed across the street, leaving him standing alone on the sidewalk.

"Who the hell is Major Li?" he hollered after her.

She ignored him and did not look back.

For a moment, he contemplated chasing after her—
he had plenty of questions for the beautiful CDC doctor—but he knew that would be a mistake. He needed
to lay low, get his passport back, and then…and then
what? How could he walk away from something like
this? His instincts told him there was more to this outbreak than met the eye.

A hand on his shoulder triggered an automatic combat response. He spun to face the aggressor, his left hand
shooting up to block at the wrist and his right hand re-
coiling for a hammer fist blow.

Yvette jerked her hand away, eyes wide with fear
and confusion.

"Sorry," he grumbled and dropped his hands to his
side. "You startled me."

"Are you okay, Nick?" asked a worried-looking Bai,
who was standing at the Belgian girl's side.

Nick found a smile and flashed it at his friends. "Exhausted," he said. "And hungry."

"Me too," Yvette said. "I'm so hungry, I could eat
a goat."

"At the place where we're going, that can be arranged," Bai said, grinning.

They all laughed out loud as Bai led the way, crossing the street and walking them in the same direction
as the CDC doctor had gone. Nick scanned the street
ahead for her, but she was long gone—disappeared into
the night.

TEN

DAZHONG CLENCHED HER fists and seethed as she made the trek to the hospital from the hotel. She was furious and exhausted, which is always a terrible combination, because the two emotional states, while incongruous, amplify each other to ill effect. Thirty-six hours straight, she had been in that hospital, working without sleep and waiting for Major Li to share his findings to no avail. An hour ago, a concerned and equally exhausted Commander Zhang had ordered her back to the hotel to get a few hours of sleep. She had objected at first, but he promised to call her the instant Major Li spontaneously transformed into a leader who valued transparency and cooperation with his task force members. They had both laughed punch-drunk at this absurdity, the way one only can at the breaking point of fatigue.

"Are you sure?" she had said, debating. "I don't think it's a good idea for me to leave."

"The hospital and this debacle will still be here in three hours when you wake up, I can promise you that," he'd said. "Now go, take a nap and clear your head."

At that, she'd acquiesced. Secretly, she'd been grateful for his offer and respected him all the more for covering for her. She'd fallen asleep instantly, fully dressed on the hotel bed. But she had not been asleep ten minutes before her mobile phone rang, waking her up. A sheepish Commander Zhang was on other end, reporting that Li had summoned them both to discuss the laboratory findings.

Typical.

She reached the south entrance and found Zhang waiting for her.

"I'm sorry," he said, his voice ripe with ironic apology. "I should have known."

"It's not your fault," she said. "I appreciated the gesture."

Zhang motioned for her to lead the way up the south stairwell, which was still designated as a "clean zone" and thus did not require PPE.

"Where does Li want to meet?" she asked over her shoulder.

"The laboratory."

"Why not the TOCC?"

"I assume because he wants to exclude as many people as possible from learning the truth," he said. "I imagine he'll only grant access to the two of us."

She grunted understanding and looked up the foreboding stairwell. Anger and curiosity were poor substitutes for rest and nourishment, and she wondered how long she would last before collapsing from exhaustion. By the third floor, her legs were jelly, and she questioned whether she could make it to the sixth floor. Maybe she could ask Commander Zhang for a piggyback ride the rest of the way. The thought made her giggle.

"What's so funny?" he asked.

"It's nothing."

"Tell me. I could use a good laugh right about now."

"Oh, just that my legs are so tired I was contemplating asking you to carry me the rest of the way up," she said, grinning and glancing over her shoulder to catch his reaction.

"Rescue carries are part of our unit's training program. Compared to some of the brutes I've carried, I could sling you over my shoulder and not even notice." He smiled and slapped his right shoulder. "Hop on."

"As tempting as it is, I don't think my husband would approve," she said with a deflecting chuckle.

After an awkward beat, he said, "I didn't realize you were married."

The disappointment in his voice was unmistakable, confirming her earlier suspicions. The commander of China's most elite counterterrorism unit had a crush on her. She couldn't help but warm at the thought. Zhang was bright, held a powerful position, and was ruggedly handsome. If circumstances were different…

"In my line of work," she said, "wearing any kind of jewelry, especially diamond wedding rings, is a liability. Rip a suit or a glove inside a hot zone, and it could cost you your life."

"Understood," he said. "Wearing jewelry is prohibited in uniform for similar reasons."

"So…are you married as well?" she asked, making her tone upbeat and curious.

"No."

"Really? I would have thought women would line up around the block at the opportunity to be Mrs. Snow Leopard Commander."

"You'd be surprised," he said, his voice flat. "It's tough to have a healthy relationship in my line of work."

"Mine too," she said, matching his intonation.

Mine too.

Panting, she finally stepped onto the sixth-floor landing. She glanced at Zhang and was annoyed to see him utterly unaffected by the climb. She couldn't imagine the level of physical conditioning the Snow Leopards must endure for their profession. The heavy steel door leading to the level-six corridor loomed in front of her; she did not even feign an attempt to open it.

With a smirk, Zhang reached out and pulled the handle with ease.

They walked shoulder to shoulder down the corridor to Li's laboratory. She was relieved to see that the two guards stationed outside the entrance were *not* the same two guards that Zhang had humiliated the day before. Flaring tempers were the last thing she needed right now.

"Commander Zhang and Dr. Chen to see Major Li," Zhang announced, stopping in front of the guards, his voice all business.

"Yes, sir," the guard on the right said and then disappeared inside.

Thirty seconds later, the door opened and the guard reappeared. He waved them inside and they found Major Li waiting, a brown folder tucked under his right arm.

"Commander Zhang... Dr. Chen," he said as they approached.

"Major," they responded in unison, formal and frosty.

Li led them to a doctor's office he had commandeered and shut the door behind them. He took a seat behind a metal desk, and they seated themselves across from him. He slid the brown folder across the desktop. Dazhong scooped up the folder and opened it on the desk so that Zhang could read it at the same time. She hadn't turned past the first page of the report and already her temper was on fire. This document was *not* the laboratory patient test results; rather, it was the Joint Task Force Kizilsu incident report ready for submittal to the Central National Security Commission. Li had written the entire report without input or feedback from her or Zhang. The audacity of this man apparently had no bounds. She glanced at Zhang and deduced from his clenched-jawed expression that he too was boiling mad inside. Zhang, however, had his gaze fixed squarely on Major Li; the Snow Leopard Commander did not seem to care about the report any longer. Turning her attention back to the folder, she flipped immediately to the section titled "Disease Pathology and Diagnosis." She did not even finish reading the third sentence before erupting at the army officer seated across the table.

"Is this some kind of a joke?" she said with such venom that she surprised herself.

"There is nothing humorous about poison gas, Dr. Chen," Li said without affectation, knitting his fingers together on the desk.

"These people did not die from—" She paused and looked down at the file to quote verbatim from the report. "From an 'exposure to a toxic chemical plume discharged during an industrial accident.'"

Li shook his head dismissively. "I'm sorry, Dr. Chen, but data do not lie. Read the laboratory reports. All the proof you need is right there in front of you. Case closed."

"Not as far as I'm concerned. I want independent laboratory confirmation of these findings."

"I'm afraid that's not possible."

"Oh yes it is," she said, getting to her feet. "If I have

to draw the blood samples and perform the analyses myself, then that is what I'm going to do."

"You cannot take samples because the last two victims expired twenty minutes ago," Li said. "All the corpses are under my control and are being processed for transport and cremation in accordance with appropriate biohazard protocols."

She felt her face flush hot as anger welled up inside her. "This is…is…completely unacceptable. I'm calling the CDC director. We'll see what he has to say about this."

Li flashed her a wolf's smile. "Director Wong has already been briefed, and he is in full agreement. I took the liberty of forwarding him an advance copy of the report. All that is needed now is your signature."

She took Li's circumvention like a punch to the gut and felt like she could start hyperventilating at any moment.

Li ignored her distress and shifted his gaze to Zhang. "Commander Zhang, these findings are relevant to you as well. Because this incident has been deemed an industrial accident, your counterterrorism investigation is now officially closed. I have spoken to Commissar Sun at the People's Armed Police headquarters in Beijing, and he understands that SLCU involvement in this operation is no longer required." Li extended an ink pen across the table. "As of this moment, the joint Quick Reaction Task Force is officially dissolved, it's mission complete. If you could both sign and date the last page of the report…"

Without a word, Zhang snatched the pen from Li's outstretched hand, flipped to the back of the report, and scribbled an illegible signature and date. He passed the pen to Dazhong. Feeling dazed, she took the pen and signed.

Zhang stood and faced her. "Dr. Chen," he said, his voice low and tight, "it appears our work is done here."

"Yes," she said, turning toward the door. "Apparently, Major Li has everything under control."

ELEVEN

Four Seasons Hotel
Beijing
2015 hours local

MAXIM VLADIMIR POLAKOV pulled back the French cuff of his dress shirt and checked the time on his Omega Constellation watch. He gritted his teeth; he was going to be late. His asset was easily spooked, interpreting any deviation from the plan as an abort signal. "Spooked" was perhaps too kind a word—unpredictable and recalcitrant were more accurate. Polakov had threatened that the next no-show would warrant a stiff consequence, but they both knew this was a hollow threat. Moscow very much wanted what "Prizrak"—the Russian codename for his asset, *Ghost*—had to offer. Those closest to the Russian president whispered that his interest in the weapon bordered on obsession, and Polakov was one of only a handful of people on earth who understood why. Now that the weapon had transitioned from "theoretical" to "operational," the Russian president was growing more impatient by the hour. As far as the center was concerned, Kizilsu was an unsanctioned test. The scale of the event had already drawn unwanted attention from the Chinese government, and if the Americans started snooping around…*govno*, he didn't want to go there. An intervention by either power would be detrimental not only to Polakov's career but also quite possibly to his tenure on this earth. Prizrak's antics were jeopardizing everything. He needed to close the deal—and soon.

The problem was Prizrak. Like so many assets, as the end game drew near, the Chinese scientist decided to change the rules. But the game doesn't work that way. It never has.

It never will.

During their first meeting six years ago, Polakov had instantly recognized the Chinese researcher's brilliance, but he had also recognized something else. Unlike most scientists, Prizrak oozed ambition and charisma. In his first report to Moscow, Polakov had described the Chinese scientist as a modern-day, Chinese Robert Oppenheimer—a man capable of leading a "Manhattan Project in biotechnology." It was Polakov who first recognized the potential to weaponize Prizrak's cancer treatment research. That realization required a paradigm shift, one that the Russian military mind seemed automatically programmed to perform. He had not shared his insight with Prizrak in the beginning; that would have been a mistake. First, he'd needed to understand the man. Second, he'd had to establish trust.

Polakov spent the first six months of the recruitment developing a psychological profile of the military scientist. Prizrak was a charismatic egoist with eclectic tastes. Like many egoists, the man was acutely socially aware, but sometimes to a fault—his perceptions often bordering on paranoia. He was quick-witted and outgoing but emotionally shallow and insecure. He demonstrated great professional focus but was prone to interpersonal distractions and infatuations. By understanding the man's contradictory traits—exploiting some and mollifying others—Polakov had been able to mold Prizrak into the rising star he was today. But now, with Prizrak's increasingly unpredictable behavior, Polakov felt his grip over his asset slipping. He suspected that once this mission was complete and the weapon was safely in the hands of the Russian military, he would be forced to eliminate his prized asset. He would hate to do it. Prizrak's contribution would be legendary—a gift that would shift the global balance of military power and return Russia to its rightful place as the world's dominant superpower. Also, he would miss his trips to Beijing, a city full of pleasures and excesses he had very much come to enjoy on the Center's tab.

As his heels clicked against the polished marble floor of the Beijing Four Seasons' hotel lobby, an ironic smile spread across his face. The city had changed so much over the years, becoming a decadent caricature of the very Western excesses that the Chinese Communist government claimed to detest. Communism was intended for the common people, not the ruling class. Nowhere was this more evident than in the capital.

He strolled up to the sleek, modern reception desk. Behind it hung an immense modern painting, which to him looked like nothing but ink splashed across canvas. Two very attractive Chinese women stood straight-backed and smiling. He placed his hands on the counter and smiled back.

"How may I help you, sir?" the taller of the two girls asked in English.

"Any messages left for me?" he asked in fluent Chinese. "My name is Andrej Sablic."

No messages were waiting for him; no messages ever were. He used the time while the receptionist flipped through the message box to casually scan the lobby for any ticks that may have followed him inside. He did not recognize a soul. His countersurveillance efforts had taken nearly two hours, with five cover stops and multiple car changes to be certain he had lost his MSS—Ministry of State Security—surveillance team. Their presence was more of a nuisance than a concern. He was good at his job. All the years he'd been operating in China, he had never been observed together with Prizrak. He knew this because even now, he did not rate anything more than a junior, two-man surveillance team. Some nights, he wasn't followed at all. Ministry surveillance was standard fare for foreign businessmen of his supposed stature as well as for diplomats; careful countersurveillance was the price of being a spy. If he grew complacent and sloppy and happened to be spotted with Prizrak, he would be flagged by the MSS and everything would change. He could not afford to make that mistake.

Ever.

"I'm sorry, sir," the girl said finally. "I have no message for you." She looked distressed to have failed him.

"No matter, my dear," he said with a smile. "All is well."

Polakov turned and walked away. He was tempted to skip his last counter-surveillance move, but caution trumped laziness. So he rode the Four Seasons lobby elevator, with its opulent bronze doors and a marble floor, to the fifth floor and disembarked. He turned left, strode quickly to the end of the hall, and then took the stairs back down to the ground floor. The stairwell emptied around the corner from the hostess stand into the Italian fine-dining restaurant Mio, conveniently out of sight from the elevator and the main entrance.

"Good evening, Mr. Sablic," a tuxedoed man said from behind a young woman in an impossibly tight black dress. "You are dining with us tonight?"

"Of course," he answered. In Beijing, he was always Andrej Sablic, a business tycoon from Croatia's emerging economy.

"I'm so sorry," the woman said from her computer. "I don't see a reservation under Sablic."

"Nonsense," the maître d' said with a harsh glance that made the girl blush. "I will take you to your usual table, Mr. Sablic."

Polakov smiled at the girl and then followed the man through neatly arranged rows of four-top tables surrounded by low-back, circular cherrywood chairs. Everything about the restaurant screamed of wealth. From the wood-paneled walls and glimmering tapestries to the spherical architectural lighting between ornate dining tables—the balance and beauty of the space rivaled any restaurant he'd visited in all his years of travel. The sharp click of the maître d's heels on the white-and-black checkered marble floor caught his attention and he imperceptibly matched stride with the man. They walked to the very last table on the right, just off the corner of the bar. Adjacent to the table was a pair of leather club chairs separated by a cocktail table. In the rightmost chair sat a middle-aged Chinese man with graying temples and a finely tailored suit, talking on his mobile phone.

Polakov smiled tightly.

"Here you are, Mr. Sablic."

"Thank you," Polakov said. He sat in the chair with a view of the dining room, placing him back to back with Prizrak, seated in the club chair behind him. Three meters away, two Western businessmen sat on barstools, sipping cocktails and engaging in separate conversations on their cell phones.

"Shall I bring you your usual cocktail, sir?" The maître d' asked, bowing and smiling.

"Please," Polakov said.

The maître d' snapped his fingers, and a waiter who had been standing beside the bar handed Polakov a black, leather-bound dinner menu. Then both men disappeared. A moment later, the waiter returned and Polakov ordered the tonno tonnato appetizer and fassone veal crepinette without looking at the menu.

Polakov surveyed the room while he waited for his cocktail. *Still clean*, he reassured himself. When the waiter returned with his drink, he made a show of pulling his supposedly vibrating phone from his coat pocket, looking at the screen, and then rolling his eyes as he answered.

"Hello? Yes, thanks for calling. How is work progressing?" he said in German into the phone, which was actually powered off. It wouldn't do for a real call to come in during this facade.

Beside him, Prizrak made a similar show of dialing a number on his phone and then placing the phone to his ear. This was a modified version of an old-school Cold-War technique where two teams shared information by engaging in separate conversations at adjoining tables. Two distinct dialogues, carried out in different languages, but languages spoken with mutual fluency by the actors. The advent of the cell phone made the game so much easier.

"You're late," Prizrak said in Russian from beside him.

The Russian agent glanced around the room. He doubted anyone else in earshot spoke Russian or German.

"I know, but it couldn't be helped," Polakov said, still feigning a conversation in German on his phone. Behind him, the Chinese man gave an irritated huff. "Relax, old friend. I had a team on me when I left the office. You know the game; these procedures are more for your protection than mine."

"You kept me waiting too long. I was just about to leave."

"I am getting heat about the test. Moscow is not pleased," Polakov said, getting down to business. "We authorized a limited, small-scale test, but our sources tell us that you have infected dozens in Kizilsu. This is not what we agreed to."

"I know, but it couldn't be helped," Prizrak said, mimicking Polakov's own excuse. "A robust field test was necessary."

"Necessary? Why?"

"Laboratory testing provides proof of concept, but proof of concept means nothing in the real world. You have tasked me with developing a weapon that will change the nature of warfare, and that is what I have done. The Kizilsu test was the only way to demonstrate to Moscow that I have fulfilled my obligation."

"Yes, but—"

"The mortality rate was one hundred percent with zero cross-infection," Prizrak interrupted. "Zero, Andrej!"

"Control yourself," Polakov snapped and resisted the urge to look behind him at the man whose voice was rising enough to draw attention.

"The weapon is perfect," Prizrak said, lowering his voice.

"Perhaps," the Russian agent conceded. "But you have made it more dangerous for all of us. The Snow Leopards are in Kizilsu as we speak, investigating."

"They will find nothing, because there is nothing to find," Prizrak said proudly.

There was a mania in the man's voice Polakov found disturbing. He needed to complete the technology transfer before he lost control of his asset. "How can you be so sure?"

"Because that is the beauty of the weapon. It leaves no trace. They are glorified policemen, not technologists. Once they run out of people to interrogate, they will lose interest. Besides, Kizilsu is the middle of nowhere, far from real China. And no one gives a shit about the Uyghurs."

Polakov hoped his asset was right about that. He supposed having the elite counterterror unit isolated thousands of miles from Beijing was better than having them here snooping around.

"When will you be prepared for the technology transfer, Prizrak?"

"When my new demands have been met," the scientist said.

"What new demands?" Polakov said, his stomach suddenly going sour.

"I e-mailed them to your secure address ten minutes ago." And with that, the man called Prizrak pocketed his phone, swallowed the final sip of his cocktail, and walked away without a backward glance.

Polakov felt his face flush with rage. He wanted to chase the arrogant bastard down and strangle him, but he forced himself to remain seated. He made a show of continuing his "conversation" on his cell phone and surveyed the restaurant for eyes fixed in his direction. No one was looking. After a moment, he feigned a laugh, uttered an overtly good-natured good-bye, and set his phone on the table beside his plate.

New demands? New demands!

What else could it be? They had already offered him everything—a new identity, plastic surgery, twenty million dollars in a Swiss bank account, and a seaside villa in Mali Losinj. This was insanity, and Moscow would not tolerate it.

He took a deep breath and contemplated his next move. Whatever Prizrak's new demands, he would advise Moscow to acquiesce. Then, once the weapon was safely in Russia's hands, he would personally make Prizrak disappear. As Stalin said, "Death solves all problems. No man, no problem."

He raised his soon-to-be-empty cocktail glass to the waiter, who smiled, nodded, and hustled over to the bar to prepare a refill.

He would miss the Mio restaurant and the Beijing Four Seasons when this was over. He should be the one retiring in Mali Losinj, not Prizrak. The muscles in his shoulders and neck were tight and knotted. He did not need the stress of this life anymore. Perhaps he would get a massage when he finished his meal. He had much thinking to do, and he needed to purge himself of all this tension. He thought of the petite, pretty Asian masseuse he visited regularly and of her strong, capable hands.

Forget the massage, perhaps he would go straight to his room and treat himself to something more. Tomorrow, he would deal with *Prizrak*.

TWELVE

FOR HER EIGHTH BIRTHDAY, Dazhong's father gave her an ornate, wooden puzzle box. It was small, about the size of an apple, and intricately hand painted, with five sides depicting the five elements of the Chinese zodiac: earth, wood, metal, fire, and water. The sixth was painted with the universal binding forces of duality—yin and yang. She had never seen a puzzle box before, and so after a cursory examination, she thanked her father for the beautifully painted thing and added it to her modest collection of childhood treasures.

One week later, her father asked her if she liked her birthday present, to which she replied with as much sincerity as she could muster, "Yes father, it is beautiful box. Thank you." His laughter took her by surprise, and she felt her cheeks flash crimson with girlish anger and embarrassment over his callous dismissal of her gratitude.

"Dazhong, my flower, the box is not meant to be your present; it is only a box," he said, bending to kiss her forehead. "Your actual present is *inside* the box."

Dubious and excited, she ran and fetched the box. With her father looking on, she turned the box over and around, and around and over, in her hands looking for access. With each revolution, she heard something shift inside.

"I can hear it moving," she said, grinning at him.

"Yes, but be careful. The treasure within is delicate."

"But how do I open this box?" she asked, scanning every surface for the umpteenth time. "There is no lid."

"It is a puzzle box," he said, grinning. "To open it, you must solve the puzzle." Then, suddenly turning serious, he added, "But be careful not to break the box, because if you do, you will destroy the gift inside."

"I do not understand, father," she complained. "There are no hinges, no keyholes, no little doors to open. It is just a painted box."

"Looks can be deceiving," he said. "To open this box requires twelve manipulations, one for each of the twelve animals of the zodiac calendar. The man who sold it to me taught me the secret, so I know it can be opened."

"Are you sure?" she said, cocking her head skeptically.

"Of course, how else do you think I was able to put your present inside?"

She studied the box, and after a moment, fine lines in the wood revealed themselves to her, each seam skillfully camouflaged by painted streaks of artistry. With her thumbs, she pressed and swiped here and there until at last a section of the box shifted. She giggled with excitement at the tiny victory and looked up at her father for recognition.

"Like so," he said, nodding with approval.

"Only eleven moves to go," she said, proudly.

"Not necessarily," he tsked. "That may or may not be the first manipulation. If you perform the moves out of sequence, the box will not open."

A week later, he returned to her.

"Have you retrieved your treasure yet?" he asked.

"No," she sulked. "It is impossible. I will never open this box."

"Perhaps I made a mistake," he said, frowning. "I should not have given you this box until you were older. Eleven or twelve, I think. I am sorry, Dazhong. I did not mean to torment you."

"Then will you open the box for me?" she said, fighting back tears of desperate aggravation. "Please, father."

"I would gladly open it for you, except then I would ruin the magic," he said. "And that will not do."

"The magic?" she asked, her curiosity recharging.

"Yes, the magic. Whenever a puzzle box is given as a gift, it is magically bound to the recipient. If I open the box, then the magic will be ruined. This is your box now, and so only you must open it."

She thought about this and said, "Well, I don't want the magic to be ruined, that's for sure. Maybe you can give me a little hint, just to get me started."

"A hint?" he echoed playfully.

"Yes," she said.

"Hmm," he muttered, rubbing his chin. "I suppose I can tell you this—to open the box, you must understand the five elements of the zodiac and the binding force of the universe. If you study hard and come to truly understand the nature of these things, the box will reveal it's secret to you."

Over the next month, she studied the elements—earth, wood, metal, fire, and water—asking her father endless questions about the nature of things. When she had learned all she could, she asked him about yin and yang and the duality of the world. During her quest for knowledge, she spent more one-on-one time with her father than ever before, and his enthusiasm, patience, and attention brought them closer together. Instead of resenting the puzzle box for its impenetrability, she came to love it for its elegant beauty and curious magic. Then one night, she had a dream about a great and terrible storm, in which the elements of the earth went to war with each other. As the war raged, she soon recognized that there could be no single victor, because when the fire burned the wood, water extinguished the blaze. And when the water flooded the earth, metal dug culverts to channel the water away, and so on and so on. For every move, a countermove. Yin and yang swirling in opposition, yet in harmony. And when she woke, she smiled, because she finally understood. She reached for the puzzle box and her fingers went to work. Press a block of water, and a block of fire shifts out on the other side. Slide a piece of earth to the left to shift a piece of metal to the right. Ying and yang. Action and reaction. The twelve manipulations came to her as easy as a breath, and the box was suddenly open in her hands.

"Dr. Chen," the voice said, shaking her from the memory. "Dr. Chen, we've arrived."

She turned, disoriented, to look at the driver holding the rear passenger door open for her. "Thank you," she said, gaining her bearings. "If you wouldn't mind grabbing my bags from the trunk."

"Yes, of course, Dr. Chen." The man disappeared behind the hired car while she stepped out onto the curb.

When he returned with her luggage, she said, "Thank you. How much do I owe you for the ride from the airport?"

"The fare is already settled," he said. "On your husband's account. Have a pleasant evening, Dr. Chen."

"Thank you," she said, turning toward the apartment lobby, and suddenly her legs turned to stone. Behind her, she heard the engine rev and the sound of tires on wet pavement as the car drove away, and still she could not bring herself to take a step. Inside, lurking on the thirteenth floor, her husband, Dr. Chen Qing, waited for her. They had not spoken the entire time she was in Kizilsu. She had called him from the airport in Kashi, hoping to gauge his mood, but her call went straight to voicemail. She'd left him a message with news of her imminent return and her travel itinerary. She assumed the driver who had met her at the airport had been provided by the CDC, certainly not her husband.

She willed her right foot to move.

And then her left.

It will be okay, she told herself. *Be brave and strong and everything will be okay.*

It was past eight o'clock, so hopefully he would already have several drinks in him. She liked him better when he was drunk. Sometimes, in inebriation she could steal moments with the old Qing—the man he was before they married. The man who made her laugh, dreamed about the future, and made love to her as a woman. Not the cold, cruel, calculating creature who paraded as her husband now.

The grand marble lobby was empty.

She rode the elevator up, alone.

A moment later, she found herself standing outside apartment 13B.

She steeled herself and then reached for the doorknob, but the door swung open before her fingertips touched brass. And then he was standing there, smiling.

"Welcome home, Dr. Chen," he said playfully, teleporting her back in time—back to the early days of their courtship, when she had just earned her PhD and he insisted on calling her Dr. Chen at every opportunity.

"It's good to be home, Dr. Chen," she fired back, along with a tentative smile.

He reached out and took her luggage from her. She followed him inside. The smell of her favorite meal—Hong Kong–style pan-fried noodles with crispy duck—enveloped her. She inhaled deeply and her stomach promptly growled.

"I hope you're hungry," he said. "I ordered in."

"I'm starving," she said, shrugging off her travel coat.

"Undoubtedly," he said, taking her coat. "I hear the food in Kashgar is terrible. They say it tastes like dirt, no doubt from the Uyghurs working in the kitchen."

She lowered her eyebrows at him.

"I'm joking, Dazhong," he said. "Relax."

She walked over to their dining table and was surprised to see that two place settings had been thoughtfully arranged, and atop one of the plates was a small box tied with a bow. She could feel his eyes on her as she approached her seat. "For me?" she asked, picking up the box and turning to look at him.

He nodded.

She tugged at the ribbon, and the cardboard top flaps popped open. She peeked inside and smiled at the honey- rose-flavored pastry within. "From Daoxiangcun bakery?"

"Your favorite—a xianhua meigui bing," he said, evidently quite pleased with himself.

Why is he being so nice?

The thought was so loud in her mind, her heart skipped a beat, worried she might have slipped and actually spoken the words aloud.

"You don't look pleased," he said, his brow furrowing.

She smiled. "No, I am pleased, just…confused."

"Confused about what?"

Flustered, she fumbled for words. "I seem to remember a recent conversation when you told me I should stop eating pastries because too much sugar is not good for my health."

"Yes, but you are too thin, Dazhong. When you work hard, you forget to eat, and you have been working too hard," he said, looking her up and down. "Maintaining the optimal amount of body fat is critical for fertility."

Uncertain how to respond, she smiled politely and simply said, "Thank you for the pastry. It was very thoughtful."

"You're welcome," he said. "Let's have dinner."

She carried both their plates to the kitchen while he took a seat at the table. She served a generous portion of noodles and duck onto his plate first and then served herself a lesser portion. She returned to the table and placed his food in front of him before taking her seat on the opposite side of the glass table.

"At least this time you can self-monitor in quarantine at home," he mumbled through a mouthful of noodles. "Last time was dreadful, you staying in Liberia twenty-one extra days."

"I am not under quarantine."

He cocked an eyebrow at her. "But it was an Ebola outbreak, was it not?"

"No," she said. "The official position of the CDC

is that the deaths in Kizilsu can be attributed to an industrial accident resulting in a toxic chemical release."

"What?" he said, setting down his chopsticks. "I heard rumors of patients with symptoms consistent with hemorrhagic fever."

"Where did you hear that?"

"There have been many rumors swirling around the past few days. Some people say it was a terrorist attack. Other reports describe victims with Ebola symptoms. Since the CDC sent you, I assumed it must have been the latter. After all, you are the CDC's department head in disease control and emergency response for Ebola."

"As of tomorrow, I start my new job, and I will be washing my hands of all this. If someone has a question about it, I will direct them to the CDC press secretary."

"You don't sound pleased by the outcome."

"I support the official position of the CDC," she said, staring at her plate.

Qing thumped his knuckles on the table hard enough to give her a start. "What really happened out there, Dazhong?"

"I've said too much already," she said, meeting his gaze.

"Nonsense. You've given me the party line, the same party line that is going to be spoon fed to the media cows when they finally wake up."

"I'm sorry, Qing, but I am bound to confidentiality agreements under the joint task force. Each of the team leaders, Zhang, Li, and myself, are all equally and directly accountable to the Central National Security Commission. Violating the agreement could land me in jail."

"Captain Li Shengkun?" he asked abruptly, his eyes laser beams burning into her skull.

"He is a Major now, but yes."

"From the PLA's NBC Regiment?"

"Yes, do you know him?"

Qing smiled broadly, his demeanor shifting. "Of course! Our community is such a small one when you really think about it. Li and I were contemporaries at Beijing University. We took many of the same grad-uate courses together... I'm sure he must have men-tioned that."

"No," she said, her curiosity piqued. "He did not."

"Well, I'm not surprised. He was never one for small talk. I'm not surprised he stayed in the army. A very serious guy, that Li."

"A little too serious if you ask me," she mumbled, nodding.

"Would you like more duck?" he asked, scooting his chair back from the table.

"No, thank you, but I'll do that," she said, jumping to her feet.

"Sit, Dr. Chen. Relax. You've had a harrowing week," he said, smiling. "It's fine."

She folded her arms across her chest. *Who are you, and what have you done with my husband?*

"Who is Zhang?" he called from the kitchen.

"What's that?" she called back.

"Zhang," he said, returning to the table, his plate full again. "You mentioned Li and also someone called Zhang on the task force?"

"Oh, I would be surprised if you knew Zhang," she chuckled.

"What's so funny? Is he military as well?"

"Not exactly," she said, wiping her mouth with her napkin. "Commander Zhang is the head of the Snow Leopard commandos—Beijing's elite counterterrorism police unit."

"Yes, I've heard of them," he said, snatching a piece of duck with his chopsticks with more malice than any piece of duck deserved. "I suppose Commander Zhang is going to be a busy man for the foreseeable future—chasing Muslim terrorists around the Kashgar Prefecture."

She shrugged. "I'm not so sure. He told me he planned to return to Beijing within the week, if not directly, to follow a lead."

Qing finished chewing and then smiled at her. "You look beautiful tonight, Dazhong. Thin, but beautiful."

That's my cue.

"Thank you," she said. Then she looked at his plate, which was still full of food. "Aren't you going to finish?"

"It seems I've lost my appetite."

She had come to hate that look on his face—the smug satisfaction of his dominance. She buried the thought and smiled demurely. She hoped the smile looked genuine enough. He scooted his chair back from the table, and she did the same. He was in such an uncharacteristically good mood tonight, hopefully that meant he would be gentle with her. She followed him into the bedroom, not another word spoken between them.

While he disappeared into the bathroom, she performed her precoital ritual. Robotically, she stripped off all her clothes and laid them neatly on a chair in the corner. Then she gathered her hair into a ponytail and applied a dab of perfume behind each ear, along the nape of her neck, and between her breasts. As soon as he finished in the bathroom, it was her turn. She closed the door and relieved herself. With the water running, she quickly fetched a tube of lubricant she kept hidden under the sink and prepared herself. She was not attracted to the man. Not anymore. Her body no longer responded to his touch. It took an effort to suppress her physical revulsion for him, so it was better for her this way. Much better. And he was too self-absorbed to notice. She had other secrets, too—secrets Qing would not be pleased to discover.

She looked at herself in the vanity mirror.

Ornately painted on the outside...with hidden treasures locked safely inside.

Just like her puzzle box.

She washed and dried her hands and then returned to the bedroom, where she found him pacing—vulpine and anxious.

He stopped midstride to study her naked body. More judgment than lust, she thought.

Then he took her.

She let him settle into a rhythm, rocking and thrusting her from behind, before detaching her mind completely.

Tomorrow will be a very busy day. I'm nervous about my meeting with Director Wong. Our last conversation over the telephone from Kizilsu had been awkward and forced. And brief. Much too brief. I tried to protest Major Li's findings. I was prepared to tell the director I would not sign the final report, but he silenced me before I could get the words out. It was almost as if he anticipated my protest.

This entire situation reeks of foul play. And it doesn't

make any sense. Why would Major Li falsify lab reports and tell the National Security Commission that the deaths in Kizilsu were caused by a toxic chemical release from an industrial accident? Why would he sell such a ludicrous story up the chain of command? Unless...

Maybe I have it backward. Maybe the order came down from above, and Major Li was given the impossible task of trying to fit a square peg in a round hole. I should ask Director Wong about this tomorrow when we debrief. Certainly he will have an opinion on the matter. But what if he was complicit? Can I even trust him? Who can I trust?

Commander Zhang?

Too dangerous to trust anyone.

The heavy pounding she was taking from Qing jerked her out of her mental refuge. She glanced back over her shoulder and saw his faced contorted with an anguished pleasure as he climaxed.

She looked away at the puzzle box on her nightstand. A wry smile spread across her face.

No sons for you, Chen Qing.

Not tonight.

Not ever.

THIRTEEN

Four Seasons Hotel
Chaoyang District, Beijing
1630 hours local

NICK ADJUSTED THE incline angle on the treadmill—up
10 percent. He pressed the green pace button with his
thumb—up 10 percent. Three miles down, four to go.
He hated treadmills, but like all tools, they filled a need
in those places where running outdoors was impossible.
Like on a submarine, in a war zone, or in a city where
the air pollution index was over 150. He had actually
stepped outside, ready to tear up the streets of Beijing
for his typical seven-mile jaunt, but when he couldn't
see the buildings two blocks away through the gray-
yellow haze, he executed an about-face and headed for
the hotel gym. The air conditioner was cranked to frigid
in the undersized gym, but at least he could breathe.

Bai had not come to see him since he'd checked in
nearly thirty-six hours ago. That surprised him. During the flight from Kashi to Beijing, Bai had made Nick
an offer for full-time employment as Director of Field
Operations, but Nick had balked, asking for time to
think about it. Five days ago, he would have jumped at
the chance; the NGO had operations all over the world
and an ambitious plan to double the number of projects
over the next two years. This was the opportunity he'd

been waiting for. But the events in Kizilsu had left him unsettled and uncertain. He couldn't shake the feeling that what had happened to Batur was no accident. Tragedy he could accept, but this was more than a random outbreak. The rumors were swirling. According to Bai, every person who died in that hospital was a Muslim Uyghur. Couple that with the knowledge that the Red Army had taken control of the entire operation, and it was obvious that something disturbing was going on. The Chinese military was engaged in cover-up operations, and someone needed to find out why.

He knew that someone should not be him, but when had that ever stopped him before?

Mile four clicked by.

Incline up 10 percent.

Speed up 10 percent.

Maybe Bai's reticence to contact him was the Snow Leopard Commander's doing. Zhang still held Nick's passport, and God only knew what sort of case that asshole was trying to build against him. The image of a dank, windowless prison cell with a metal shit pail in the corner popped into Nick's mind. He shook it off. He hated confinement. He hated feeling trapped, even in a fancy-ass hotel like this. He would much prefer the open, outdoor, barracks-style accommodations back in Kashi. At first, he had wondered why Zhang would pamper a criminal suspect in a luxury hotel in the business district of Beijing. Then it hit him. The Chinese intelligence community undoubtedly had sections of this property—a popular choice for international businessmen and diplomatic visitors—properly "equipped." The fact that he'd been placed in a premier room on the eighteenth floor simply meant those rooms were wired for video and audio surveillance. One of Zhang's minions was probably watching him grunt and sweat his ass off even now.

The irony of the entire situation made Nick laugh. They could monitor him for a year and it wouldn't matter. He had nothing to hide. He wasn't a spy or a terrorist. He was just a guy who was good with his hands, wandering the world with a guilty conscience, looking for something to fix. Be it a broken leg or a broken water main, he didn't care—so long as someone gave him a problem to solve.

Anything but isolation, boredom, and purposelessness.

He had to get out of here.

Five miles down.

Incline up 10 percent.

Speed up 10 percent.

He could go to the US embassy, but that would probably change nothing. In fact, it might even make things worse by pissing off Zhang. Best to just wait it out. The last thing he needed was to be a political headline on CNN. Speaking of headlines, it was odd there hadn't been a single story on the Beijing news about Kizilsu. The entire event had been sanitized. That spoke volumes. Not to mention the presence of the elite Chinese counterterrorism unit working hand in hand with the Chinese CDC. Still, none of it made sense. Who, other than the Chinese, would attack a Muslim minority in the western high desert? And if it was the Chinese, then why use a bioweapon? And what the hell kind of a bioweapon was it? Nothing like anything he'd heard of before. Anthrax and the other bioweapon agents have longer incubation periods and are difficult to contain.

A viral or bacterial pathogen should have kicked off an epidemic. Right? He had been exposed. Yvette and Bai had been exposed. But they had not gotten sick. Somehow this attack—if it was an attack—had been surgical. More like a controlled toxin release. A chemical weapon of some sort? But who in China possessed chemical weapons other than the Chinese military? And if the Chinese military was behind it, why investigate a state-authorized military strike with a state-run counterterrorism unit?

Plenty of questions, but not one damn answer.

Six miles down.

He raised the incline to maximum.

He increased the speed to maximum.

The treadmill shuddered and growled under the rapid-fire, pounding blows from his strides. Sweat rained down everywhere and on everything. His heart pounded. His lungs churned. His muscles burned, and it felt good. He felt strong, and powerful, and alive. As he sprinted, he imagined that he was running in the desert, beneath a bright-yellow sun shining in a bright-blue sky. For a fleeting moment, he felt free...

Seven miles.

With his thumb, he backed the speed down from 10.0 to 1.5, slowing rapidly from a sprint to a walk. Next, he lowered the incline, from 10.0 to 0.0.

"Not bad," he murmured, checking his time, "for an ex-SEAL as outta shape as me."

Nick felt someone's eyes on him. He turned his head left and saw a young Chinese girl—no older than six—standing five feet away, mouth agape and staring at him. Her harried mother, blushing and apologetic, came to gather her.

"He Superman?" the girl said, pointing and grinning at Nick. "Superman!"

The mother hushed her daughter with Chinese words Nick did not understand and ushered the little girl away. As they left, the little girl looked over her shoulder at Nick one last time. They made eye contact and Nick felt a surge of déjà vu.

The girl's bright, almond eyes reminded him of the hauntingly beautiful eyes of the CDC doctor who had interviewed him in Kizilsu. Maybe now that things had calmed down, she would be ready to answer a few questions. She worked for the Chinese government, and she had assisted Zhang with his interrogation, but she wasn't army. Their last encounter—albeit brief—had been telling. It was obvious she had been sidelined. Major Li, whoever the hell that was, had taken control of the operation in Kizilsu and sent her and Commander Zhang back to Beijing. If the good doctor was pissed off enough about how she had been treated, maybe he could prod her into giving him some idea as to what was going on. It was a moonshot, but where else could he start?

Unfortunately, he had no idea how to contact her. He couldn't even remember her name. He tried picturing the nametag on her lab coat—Chen Dashing? Chen Dashon? He couldn't remember. Chinese protocol was to place the surname before the given name. In America, Hon Bai would be called Bai Han. So that meant her last name was Chen and her first name was "Dash" something or other.

"Dr. Dash," he said aloud with a grin. "I wonder if Chinese people use nicknames."

Nick sighed and grabbed a towel to wipe the sweat

from his face and brow. Then he tossed it around his neck and headed back to his room to shower and change.

He should let it go.

Instead, he picked up his mobile phone and dialed Bai.

"Hello, Nick Foley," Bai said on the line, his voice cheerful and maybe hopeful.

"Hello, Bai," Nick said. "How is your family? All is well, I hope."

"Very well, Nick. And you? You are ready to accept the new position?"

Nick paused.

"About that," he said. "I would love to finish the Kizilsu project before moving on to something else."

There was a pause.

"That project is closed, Nick," Bai said quietly. "For a long time, anyway. Maybe forever."

"What about Yvette, and Ian, and the others?"

Another pause made Nick wonder what Bai might be keeping from him.

"Yvette went home, Nick," Bai said. "I offered her another project, but she said no. I am sure she will not be coming back. Ian moved on to a new project in Cambodia. He will be the project manager there."

"He'll be perfect," Nick said. He would miss them both.

"As far as the others on the Kizilsu team, most went home," Bai said. "It was quite a scary thing, this outbreak."

"Yes," Nick said. Bai's segue was perfect. Right where he wanted to go. "Speaking of the outbreak, what else have you heard, my friend? Any rumors or details emerging? Has the government released an official statement yet?"

"A statement has been released, Nick. The cause of the deaths was an industrial accident at a chemical factory in Kizilsu."

Nick's cheeks flashed hot. "Oh, that's bullshit, Bai. We both know that."

"Be careful, Nick," Bai said and then paused as if choosing his next words. "It is different in China than America. People here do not feel so much a need—or perhaps a right—to know everything. I trust that it will be resolved by the people best qualified to take care of such things."

"Of course," Nick said through clenched teeth. "I was just curious…"

"Yes, I understand," Bai answered.

Nick felt the awkwardness through the ether. The momentum of the dialogue was fading. It was now or never: "Did you happen to have any other conversations with the woman doctor we met at the hospital? I can't remember her name."

"The one from the CDC? Her name is Dr. Chen, and no, I have not spoken with her."

"Do you know a way I could contact her? A phone number perhaps? Maybe she could answer some of my questions about what happened."

This time the pause was longer—uncomfortably long, in fact—and for a moment, Nick wondered if the call had dropped. He pulled the phone away from his ear and glanced at the screen just to make sure.

"I do not," Bai said finally. "As I said, Nick, it is best not to investigate such things. It will be very bad for you to be asking these questions—especially if you wish to obtain a work visa to take over operations for us. I suggest you forget about what happened in Kizilsu. The CDC and the military will get to the bottom of this. It is not for us—especially not for you—to be investigating. Do you understand?"

"Of course," Nick said, trying to sound as casual as possible. "I was just curious."

"It's time to move on, Nick. We are ready for you to take a larger role in operations. Have you made a decision about my offer?" Bai asked, trying to sound cheerful but failing.

"I'll call you tomorrow," Nick said and looked at his watch. "I really want the job, Bai. I'm flattered and excited by the opportunity, but I haven't been able to reach my family in Texas. Before I accept a permanent position, I need to contact them first."

"Of course," Bai said. "Take a few days if you need. Perhaps you can let me know before the weekend?"

"Absolutely," Nick promised. "Thank you for this opportunity, Bai."

"We will be very pleased to have you, Nick," Bai said.

Nick ended the call and tossed his phone on the bed.

Time to face the facts. He'd be lucky to get out of this mess with his passport and dignity intact. He was never going to find out what really happened in Kizilsu, and he was certainly never going to see the beautiful Dr. Dash again.

He sat on the edge of his bed and sighed. Was this really a rabbit hole he wanted to plunge down? He felt himself tumbling already—back to a life he had left. There were many things he missed about being a SEAL, but most of all he missed the sense of purpose and brotherhood. He had hoped that by working for an

NGO, he would be able to rekindle that same sense of purpose and feeling of fraternity, only without the violence and bloodshed. And he thought he had, until Batur collapsed unconscious in a ditch next to him and died mysteriously a few hours later. Dozens of innocent civilians were dead in Kizilsu, and now cover-up operations were clearly under way. A floodgate opened in his mind, and a torrent of painful memories consumed him—memories of a similar event that happened not all that far from Kizilsu, in fact.

Nick stretched out on the bed and closed his eyes, and for the first time in a long time, he let his mind drift back to the rugged foothills of Jalalabad in Afghanistan.

FOURTEEN

Six years earlier
SEAL team platoon, call sign Mustang
Southeast of Jalalabad, Afghanistan
0230 hours local, October 2010

NICK BOUNCED THE heel of his left boot up and down against the armored floor of the modified Humvee. Not because he was anxious. Not because he was afraid. This was pent-up energy leaking out at the seams. He was like a bottle of soda all shaken up—if he didn't unscrew the cap and bleed off some pressure before the party, he just might pop.

His unit had been operating in the shadows of the Hindu Kush in northeastern Afghanistan for several weeks now, and this was the first time they had real, actionable intelligence they had to move against. According to the CIA spooks, some notorious Taliban badasses were hiding out at an isolated compound in the mountains. Tonight's mission was a capture/kill raid: take whoever or whatever they could off the target list and neutralize whoever or whatever they couldn't. All their previous ops had turned into relationship-building endeavors—winning the hearts and minds of the locals. Basic intelligence gathering begins with grassroots relationships, or so he'd been told by the career guys. With the enthusiasm of a rookie who was trying to prove his worth, Nick had immersed himself in the task. Tonight, however, he was beginning to wonder if he was becoming *too* invested in the lives of the locals he'd met.

Unlike some of his SEAL teammates who preferred to live in the black-and-white world of "us versus them," Nick often found himself wandering in the gray divide. He had never planned to be a SEAL. In fact, his plan had been to join the Peace Corps and travel the world to help the less fortunate. But during his junior year of college, he had taken a twentieth-century military history class on a whim. He had always been a fan of history, and with all that was going on around the world since 9/11, the course sounded fascinating. The professor, a retired Navy admiral, had been a SEAL and had argued that unless the forces of evil spreading oppression were unseated, the oppressed peoples of the world would never live in peace and prosperity—no matter how many bridges, or irrigation systems, or primary schools the NGOs of the world built. There *is* evil in the world, and evil must be stopped, no matter the risk. No matter the personal sacrifice. Three days after the semester ended, Nick had dropped out of college—to the shock and dismay of his mother—and had enlisted in the Navy, intent on becoming a Navy SEAL.

During his time in Afghanistan, Nick had come to understand how war—unlike combat—lingers after the bullets stop flying. Long after his unit finished its tour and headed home, the Pashtun would still be here, struggling to safeguard their families from the al-Qaeda and Taliban crazies that infested their homeland. No matter how long coalition forces remained in the country, no matter how many covert operations the SEALs completed, Nick knew they would never eliminate violent

Islamic extremism from Afghanistan. In war, ideology is bulletproof. He thought about the village children—showing off their street soccer skills and then dancing for joy when he surprised them with chocolate bars afterward. How many of those kids would reach adulthood? How many of those kids would live long enough to play soccer with children of their own?

Not enough, he told himself.

Not nearly enough.

"About ten minutes to our IP," the Senior Chief, Nick's SEAL platoon leader, said into his headset.

Nick pushed the thoughts from his mind and concentrated on the mission at hand. He checked his kit by feel, counting extra magazines for his rifle and the pistol in the drop holster on his right thigh. He tapped the fragmentation grenades on the left side of his kit and shifted in his seat to retrieve the trauma bag from his back. After a quick inventory of his medical gear, he said a silent prayer that he would not need any of it tonight. He was ready.

A few minutes later, the three Humvees formed a tight circle and the SEALs jumped out. They formed up into two groups of six, each warrior scanning the perimeter through their night vision goggles while the Senior Chief radioed the Head Shed. After getting confirmation that the mission was a go, Senior made two quick hand gestures and they headed west. The assault teams diverged as they moved down a shallow, sloping embankment toward the compound. They would make their assault from different vectors, offset by one hundred twenty degrees. They moved quickly and quietly over the shale and gravel toward the target, which was now only about a kilometer away. Nick pictured the details of the compound from the aerial surveillance pictures in their briefing. The compound comprised four single-story buildings with a crumbling stone wall encircling the perimeter. In his mind's eye, he surveyed every nook and cranny in advance—noting hideouts for the bad guys and cover for the good guys. Senior had briefed that "one way or the other," they would be in and out of the compound in under five minutes. The aggressive timetable was designed for team security, since the sounds of the firefight would echo for miles in the mountain passes and valleys.

According to the CIA liaison providing intelligence for the op, the closest Taliban reinforcements were miles away from the compound. Equally important, there were no civilians in the area, which meant that everyone on the "X" was a bad guy. For Nick, this changed the entire dynamic of the mission and took a ton of pressure off. In this scenario, capture or kill decisions were dictated by team safety and nothing more. The CIA spook finished his brief with a promise that "the high-value targets will be there." Nick noticed that the more senior SEALs had traded cynical glances at this comment. During the Humvee ride over, Nick had asked one of the NCOs why he didn't trust spooks. As far as Nick was concerned, all intelligence provided to date had been spot on, and the grassroots work their unit had been doing supported the claim that the Taliban was operating out of this particular compound. The senior SEAL had smiled and simply said, "It's the shit they *don't* tell you that gets guys killed."

Now, as he scanned over his rifle for movement in the eerie green-gray world of night vision, he tried not to think about that.

"Hold."

Nick took a knee on the Senior Chief's command in his headset. He felt the muscles in his neck tighten, and he immediately began the tactical breathing he had been taught to slow his pulse. He scanned his sector and saw nothing but small rocks and scrub bushes sparsely scattered throughout the last twenty yards to the compound—absolutely no cover should they need it. This was no-man's land, the most dangerous part of the approach before the perimeter breach.

His headset crackled.

"Alpha set," he heard the Senior Chief say softly in his ears. Nick tapped the focus adjust on his night vision goggles and the crumbling rock wall ten meters ahead sharpened with perfect clarity. He tightened the grip on his M4 rifle and scanned along the top.

"Bravo is ready," came the voice of "Bronco," a former rodeo star who led the other half of the team.

"The spooks didn't get us that Predator overflight I wanted," Senior grumbled under his breath next to Nick. "Hopefully everything's the same as a few hours ago." He sounded irritated but not worried, so Nick decided not to worry either. Twelve SEALs on eight to ten bad guys was an easy day—like target practice on the range.

Senior keyed his mic. "Set."

Nick rose into a combat crouch. His fellow SEALs did the same, and the team spread out into assault formation.

"Go."

They closed on the perimeter in unison, rifles up, legs churning beneath controlled torsos. Nick was on the left, with the other five SEALs spread out and offset just enough to cover the target without putting each other at risk from overlapping fire. Upon reaching the wall, he steadied his rifle atop the stone ledge and scanned ahead. A single light shone through the windows from the closest of the four structures, but he saw no movement inside. Senior signaled and the SEALs slipped over the rock wall into the compound.

A heartbeat later, the night erupted—with light, and tumult, and pain.

Chunks of the wall exploded beside Nick's head, and he felt a searing burn in his right shoulder. He jerked reflexively away from the line of fire. His elbow went white hot with pain, and the two fingers on the outside of his right hand went numb. He ignored all this and took aim at the muzzle flares on the rooftop of the building directly in front of him. He squeezed the trigger, sending bullets flying at a roof sniper. Gunfire flashed all around them—from the rooftops, the windows, and the covered corners.

"Heavy contact—heavy contact!" barked Senior's voice in his ear. "Pull back over the wall."

They backpedaled to the rock wall, returning fire as a storm of enemy bullets whirled around them.

Nick vaulted over the perimeter wall and landed in the dirt. He crabbed low over the ground until his back was pressed against the wall. "Eight to ten guys my ass," he heard someone say. Nick closed his eyes and collected himself with two deep breaths. Then he rose and sighted. He spied a Taliban sniper on the rooftop, squeezed the trigger, and noted the impact location of his missed shot. He adjusted, squeezed again, and watched the figure crumple. He dropped down below the wall and slowed his breathing.

Fire and move, fire and move, he told himself. *Find a controlled rhythm.*

He popped up again, but this time a flash of bright light washed out his night vision. "RPG!" He yelled, dropping to the ground. The world vibrated with a deafening explosion. When the dust cleared, he saw that a huge section of wall had been vaporized five feet beside him.

"To the east corner," Senior announced. "On me."

They moved together, hunched and taking turns rising and engaging targets inside the compound as they covered fifty yards along the perimeter in a blur. Nick could hear converging fire as the other team of six SEALs approached the rally point from other side. He recalled an aerial view of the compound in his mind, based on the satellite imagery from the premission CIA brief. From the east corner, they could retreat into a snaking ravine that stretched out for miles. There, they would find cover—scattered boulders, scrub trees, and access to rising terrain. Given the overwhelming enemy force of fire, retreat to the Humvees back across no-man's land was impossible.

The burning in his right hand reminded Nick that he had not made it through "round one" unscathed. Immediately, he wondered if anyone else on the team had been hit. He counted five crouching silhouettes beside him and exhaled a sigh of relief. His half of the assault team was intact, with no mortal injuries. He could assess the other half of the unit when they regrouped.

Step one in treating the injured in combat is to defeat the enemy or move to safety, he reminded himself. *Rendering care is impossible when you're being cut to shreds.*

"Shit, Senior," someone whispered from the dark, "that's gotta be twenty to thirty fighters. What the fuck is wrong with those intel assholes?"

"Save it," Senior barked back. "We're gonna pull back to the ravine, regroup, and then reengage." The seasoned veteran operator keyed his mic. "Bravo, sitrep?"

"Moving east for cover in the ravine," came the reply.

They fanned out in a reverse *V*, crouching and firing at the compound as they retreated. They hadn't made fifteen yards when muzzle flashes lit up the darkness on their right. Nick counted at least six muzzle flashes, coming from the hill they had descended on their approach.

"Contact right," he hollered, returning fire as bullets smacked the ground around him.

"Where the hell did they come from?" someone yelled as the twelve SEALs spread out to find cover among the boulders on the sloping wall of the ravine. For an instant, a terrifying image popped into Nick's mind—a dozen SEALs, hands bound and kneeling before a black-robed jihadist with a camcorder, waiting to have their heads sawed off. "Screw that," he mumbled. He sighted a fighter moving down the loose shale hill, put the red dot of his infrared sight just ahead, and squeezed the trigger. The terrorist crumpled in a heap to the ground as Nick's magazine clicked to empty.

Muzzle flashes lit up the countryside as the Taliban fighters engaged en masse.

There was no "fire and move" now—there was barely enough cover for the team where they were. Nick pulled his head down and tried to sink closer to the ground while the rounds ricocheted around him.

He swapped magazines in his rifle and waited for a lull to return fire.

"Mustang Main, this is Mustang Actual," he heard Senior on the encrypted radio behind him. "Heavy contact. We need air support right now. We are pinned down and in deep shit."

The NCO was on a different frequency, so Nick didn't hear the reply, but a moment later he heard Senior on the radio again, now on the frequency for the air support.

"Chevy two-five, Chevy two-five, this is Mustang Actual. We are in the ravine just east of the compound. Twelve souls—all to the east. The compound is enemy fighters only. Cleared in hot. Danger close—I say again—danger close."

Danger close, Nick thought. *A request reserved for situations where the requestor believed the alternative was certain death at the hands of the enemy.* The Senior Chief had just authorized the pilots to break the rules and drop ordinance perilously close to their position. As the team's leader, Senior was taking full responsibility for their lives. In the unfortunate event the ordinance delivery was off target by the slightest margin, and one or more SEALs died from friendly fire, the pilots were not to blame. Ironically, the thought of being vaporized by an Apache gunship was much more appealing to Nick than having his head chopped off and streamed on the Internet for his mom and dad to see.

"Two minutes," the Senior Chief called out.

Taliban rounds ricocheted off the rocks all around, kicking up dust and spraying them with stone fragments.

"Oh, shit," said a voice to Nick's right.

Nick glanced right and saw Simmons burrowed between a shallow groove in the ground and a pitiful excuse for a rock, barely big enough to shield a child.

"You all right?" Nick called.

"I'm hit," Simmons said. "It's bad."

"I'm coming," Nick said and mentally ran through his trauma procedures as he popped his head up and fired several shots at the hillside. Despite having a heavy pack full of advanced trauma equipment on his back, for expediency Nick decided he would use the blow-out kit in Simmons's own left cargo pocket. The cover by Simmons was shit, and he didn't dare try to unpack.

"Hold where you are, Foley," Senior barked. "There's too much fire, and we have danger close incoming less than a minute out."

Nick jerked his head back behind his own rock, closed his eyes, and made a decision. If they made it out, he'd tell Senior he didn't hear the order. He was the team medic; if he didn't take the initiative to help his wounded teammates, he didn't deserve the position. He rolled to his right and then slithered forward. He came first to Simmons's Oakley boot and inched along his teammate's right side. He leaned against the rock and raised partway up on a knee. Muzzle flares lit up the hillside again, and twice as many flashed from the rooftops in the compound. The tracers looked like a laser blasts in a Star Wars movie, crisscrossing the night sky in both directions as the SEALs returned fire.

"It's me, Tom. It's Nick. Where are you hit?"

The voice beneath him was no longer that of a tough Navy SEAL.

"Right shoulder, at the base of my neck." The voice was muffled and wet, like someone had shoved soaked cotton in Simmons's mouth. "I can feel the blood spraying out of me."

Nick saw a shadow on the hillside moving in his direction, maybe twenty yards away and lit from behind by orange tracers. He lifted his rifle, aimed, and fired. The figure arced backward and fell.

"Pull out your blow-out kit and hand me the packing," Nick yelled, as enemy gunfire erupted ahead. Bullets ricocheted off the rock beside him, blasting his cheek with rock shards.

"Here," Simmons said, shoving a thick trauma dressing up at him.

Nick knew it would be a mistake to sling his rifle. "The best care under fire is to return fire," went the mantra. He grabbed the dressing in his left hand and steadied his M4 in his right, firing at movement on the rooftop closest to him. He looked down through his night vision goggles at the black puddle pooling beneath Simmons's head. He shoved the dressing into an impossibly large, gaping hole in the base of his Simmons's neck and felt hot, wet blood soak through his left glove.

Fuck, that's a lot of blood.

"Everyone down," Senior Chief shouted just as the roar of the two Apaches engulfed the ravine. "Incoming!"

Nick pressed the already soaked dressing hard into Simmons's neck and then used his body to shield his teammate from the coming firestorm. Four streaks of orange fire stretched out from the attack helicopters like the fiery fingers of an angry god. Nick hugged Simmons, closed his eyes, and tried to make himself small.

For a moment, it seemed his worst fear had been realized...he was being vaporized by a Hellfire missile.

It was as if the sun had swallowed the earth—light so bright, it penetrated him; heat so hot, it weighed like a blanket; and noise so loud, it shook his bones to dust. Then, a microsecond later, it was dark, cool, and quiet.

Nick raised his head and saw the entire compound engulfed in flames. On the far rooftop, fire moved across the roof and then fell into the compound. It took Nick a moment to realize it was a terrorist engulfed in flames, running until he fell off the roof. Sporadic gunfire continued from the hillside, but what was left of the enemy force was retreating. He thought about returning fire, but he was shaking too much to steady his rifle. In his peripheral vision, he saw his fellow SEALs rising into tactical crouches, rifles up and engaging the fleeing terrorists on the hill.

"Secure the compound," Senior's voice rasped in his earpiece. "Exfil in fifteen mikes."

Fifteen minutes until the Blackhawks arrived to pull them out. During that time, they would scour the compound for any potential intelligence that survived the missile strike. They would be vulnerable to another attack if the surviving members of the enemy force regrouped, but this time, the SEALs would have the defensible position. Nick looked at the wounded SEAL lying beneath him. Despite the monochrome gray of his night vision, he could see that Simmons's eyes were bright—not that glazed and absent look he had seen in trauma patients who were slipping away.

"You okay?" he asked Simmons.

"Better if you get the fuck off me," came the haggard reply.

"I have an urgent medical," Nick said into his mic

for the Senior Chief and the rest of the team. "Urgent CASEVAC with a gunshot wound to the neck."

Simmons was a tough bastard, but the wound was dangerously close to being fatal. He needed to be stabilized before the Blackhawks arrived. As if reading his mind, seconds later, two SEALs were beside him.

"Whatcha need, Doc?" the SEAL on his right asked.

Now that someone was hurt, he was Doc.

"We need to get him to cover inside the compound."

It was impossible to imagine that anyone was still alive inside the enemy compound in the wake of destruction unleashed by the appropriately named Hellfire missiles. Nick heard the Apaches circling back for a mop-up pass and felt confident the gunships would drive the remaining Taliban fighters into the hills, forestalling a second assault. A loud, long burp echoed through the ravine as one of the warbirds let loose a stream of cannon fire on the hillside.

Nick looked back at Simmons. "Can you hold pressure here while we carry you?"

"Yeah, man, I got ya," the SEAL said, with steely warrior eyes. "Help me get my rifle up."

Nick smiled. That was a SEAL to the core.

He slid Simmons's M4 into the SEAL's right hand and then counted to three while the other two lifted their wounded teammate by his legs and shoulders. The lead SEAL slung both legs over his own shoulders at the knees, securing them with his left forearm while he steadied his rifle with his right. The other teammate wrapped Simmons's arm around his own neck and held the forearm in his free hand, leaving his own rifle in play.

"Dude," the SEAL told Simmons. "Let go of your rifle, bro, you're choking the shit out of me."

Simmons reluctantly took his hand off the grip of his M4 and held onto the wrist of his teammate instead. Nick helped hold pressure on Simmons's neck and scanned around with his own rifle, but the enemy was in full retreat mode now, being driven back by the Apaches. Moments later, they were over the perimeter wall.

"This way," the Senior Chief said, moving up alongside the group. "Get him inside until the CASEVAC is here in eight mikes. We'll land the bird inside the wall."

As they moved through what remained of the compound, Nick choked on the acrid smell of smoke and burning wood. But it was not just smoke; there was an undercurrent of something else that smelled like… burnt meat.

The Senior Chief led them into the charred remnants of the first house, where Nick had watched the flaming shooter fall off the roof. The roof was gone now, as was the back wall. Nick's boot squished into something soft, and he recoiled in horror at the human carnage underfoot. He pulled his eyes away from the charred remains and focused on his job. They laid Simmons against the wall, and Nick slid his pack off to get to his meds and set an IV with a bag of Hespan—a fluid to expand Simmons's blood volume until he could get a transfusion at the Cache, the advanced trauma hospital a short flight away.

"How is he?" Senior whispered.

"I'm gonna get an IV going to keep his BP up. I think he has a vascular injury. He lost a lot of blood and needs surgery, but as long as we keep pressure on that wound, he'll be stable."

As he fumbled with the IV tubing, Nick's eyes were drawn again to the carnage around him. Along the back wall, a body was still smoking, brightly colored cloth still visible around the upper torso. Beneath was nothing but half of one leg. But something was off—the body was too small. Nick felt bile in his throat, and his breath caught in his chest.

"Are those children?" he barely whispered, turning to look at Senior.

"Don't look," Senior said softly. "Focus on Simmons, Nick."

"But the CIA said no civilians were present," Nick said, his voice cracking.

"And they also said there would only be eight to ten bad guys with no reinforcements in the area. I guess they fucked everything up."

Nick fought nausea at the smell of the smoldering bodies. His hands trembled as he worked to set up the IV. He tried to immerse himself in the task at hand, wiping Simmons's forearm with an alcohol wipe and readying the sixteen-gauge needle, but the emotion was a tidal wave he couldn't beat back. He squeezed his eyes shut and blinked repeatedly, clearing the tears so he could slip the needle into Simmons's vein.

He had joined the teams to make a difference—to help people and protect his country. He knew *this* was not his fault. It was not even the Senior Chief's fault for calling in the Apaches. They were under heavy fire, and Senior made the call to save the team. Of course they had to return fire. Of course they needed air support…

What kind of enemy surrounds himself with women and children?

Nick clenched his teeth together, because if he didn't, he knew the rage and anxiety building inside would find a voice.

The distant thump, thump of an approaching Black-hawk brought him back to the moment.

"One minute, Nick," said Senior. "Is he ready to go?"

Nick connected the IV tubing from the back of the Hespan to the needle in Simmons's arm and then pulled off a piece of tape.

"Yeah, he's set," he said.

"Go with him, Nick. Our exfil is right behind them. We'll see you at the Cache."

"Check," Nick said, hoping the relief was not evident in his voice.

He was proud to be a SEAL. He believed in the mission of fighting terrorism. He believed in his team-mates, men whom he had come to love like brothers. But a switch had flipped in his mind. The job was not the same now. He was not the same now, and no matter how much he wanted to flip that switch back, he knew he couldn't.

Not ever.

FIFTEEN

Chinese Centers for Disease Control and Prevention
1752 hours local

DAZHONG FOLDED HER arms across her chest. She was angry and frustrated. She had expected more from Director Wong. And less. To hear him talk, the CDC director supported Major Li's fantastical claim about a toxic chemical release as the root cause for sixty-seven civilian deaths in Kizilsu. Wong's body language, however, told a different story. He was anxious and taking great care to toe the party line in front of her. This aggravated her. They were scientists, not bureaucrats, and they both knew it.

She pressed, and of course her emotions got the better of her. Her true feelings about Major Li's bogus report came spilling out like a vomitus purge. She regretted this misstep as the words were still burbling from her lips, but it was too late. Backpedaling was not an option, so she didn't even try. Now a dense silence hung in the air between them like a foul odor. She waited, putting the burden of rebuttal on him.

At last, he spoke.

"I want you to hear me, Dr. Chen," he said, closing the gap between them and putting a hand on her shoulder. "It is important that you understand what I'm about to tell you and you take it to heart."

She nodded coolly but could not bring herself to make eye contact with him.

"This is the last time you will speak of this matter, to anyone. I want you to promise me you will not contact Major Li, you will not discuss these feelings and misgivings with any of your colleagues, and most importantly, you will not submit any unsolicited written statements or contradictory findings to the commission ex post facto. Do I make myself clear?"

"Yes, Director Wong."

"Good. Now go home, Dazhong. Enjoy the rest of your evening, and when you come into work tomorrow, be ready to put all this business behind you and get started on your next project."

She looked up and met his gaze. Instead of finding irritation or accusation in his eyes, she saw the stately calm of an elder. The interaction reminded her of how her father had often managed her as an emotional, irrational teenager of fourteen. Yet in this case, she was not irrational, nor was she a teenager. She was emotional, however, and Director Wong had listened to her protest with patience and without reprisal. For this, she was grateful.

"I understand," she said at last. "Thank you, Director Wong."

She left his office and walked directly to her own. She shut the door and immediately began to pace. *Director Wong is right*, she told herself. *Just let it go and move on*. Simple enough advice. Unfortunately, she couldn't let it go. Major Li was hiding something, and she needed to find out what.

They've boxed me out, she thought. *My only hope is to find someone on the inside whom I can trust. But who?*

If word circulated that she was snooping around, she risked terrible consequences—getting fired from the CDC, prosecution, jail time, or worse. The only person besides Director Wong she trusted enough to even broach the subject with was Commander Zhang of the Snow Leopards. But talking to Zhang was a risk, too. As a senior officer in Beijing's elite counterterrorism unit, he was tightly integrated into the political-military complex. Her entire opinion of Zhang was based on only a few days of interaction. While she found him to be bright, pragmatic, and reasonable, she could only speculate on the nature of his patriotism. Would he view her unsanctioned investigation of a military conspiracy as an act of heroism or an act of treason? Unfortunately, the only way to know for sure was to ask for his help, and in doing so, she would show her colors and seal her fate.

No, I cannot go running to Zhang, no matter how tempting the idea is, she decided.

She walked over to the plate-glass window and stared out across the neatly kept entrance to the CDC. In the center courtyard, she watched three flags billowing in the wind. In the middle, the Chinese national flag waved crimson. To its left hung the flag of the Chinese CDC, a majestic blue background inscribed with a white logo. And to the right flew an iconic star-spangled banner—the flag of the United States of America. This was the only place in China she had ever seen the American flag prominently on display. Here it was a symbol of solidarity with the American CDC in Atlanta, the organization upon which the Chinese CDC had been modeled. Every day, every CDC employee saw the Chinese and American flags waving side by side. It was by design—an omnipresent reminder: disease does not pick sides. Disease has no geopolitical agenda. It is ignorant of wealth, and power, and national borders. It transcends politics, race, and religion. Without scientific cooperation, without intellectual solidarity, the odds of surviving the next great epidemic could dwindle to single digits. Cooperation with America was essential...

The American Navy SEAL's face suddenly popped into her mind. Nick Foley was the one who had put the bold conspiratorial ideas into her head in the first place. During the interrogation in Kizilsu, Foley had asked the question that had set her down this path: *Who has the most to gain from this attack? Who has the most to gain from covering it up?*

That was the next logical question, was it not? What would Nick Foley say? Maybe I should ask him.

She shook her head.

Ridiculous.

But she found herself going to her computer anyway to print the list she and Commander Zhang had compiled of all the quarantined patients in Kizilsu. She had input the patients' serological and physical exam results, and Zhang had entered their personal data from background checks. Together, they had been able to generate an excellent profile of each detainee's social, fiscal, and physical status. She had been looking for vectors, Zhang for terrorists, and in the middle of it all, they had found Nick Foley. The only question now was, where in China was he?

Please, please, please have his mobile number.

She scrolled down the list until she found Foley's entry. Holding her breath, she scanned the column labeled "mobile phone." She exhaled with relief and entered Foley's number into her phone under the new contact "NF." Then she exited the program and shut down her computer. Before leaving for home, she gave one last look out the window at the American flag.

The entire drive back to her apartment, she tried to convince herself that contacting Nick Foley was the stupidest idea she'd ever had. It didn't work. Foley was the perfect sounding board. He was American, not Chinese, so the risk of him condemning her as traitor was virtually nil. He was a former Navy SEAL, which meant that he was familiar with this world of military cover-ups and how soldiers think—two things she most definitely was not. And best of all, he was completely divorced from those in power who could judge her. Nick Foley had nothing to lose or to gain by talking to her, which meant he was not a threat and his counsel would be objective.

She smiled at the idea, feeling empowered, even a little dangerous.

She entered the code to unlock her door and stepped inside to find her apartment empty. A note from Qing sat on the dining table, informing her that an urgent business matter had cropped up demanding his immediate attention in Shanghai. He offered no explanation and no mention of when he would be returning. Typical Qing. For some reason, he refused to communicate anything about his whereabouts or schedule with her via SMS. When it came to his travel plans, he insisted on leaving her notes.

All the better, she smirked, because his absence meant that tonight she was free.

She retrieved her mobile phone from her purse and sent a text to her girlfriend Jamie Lin.

DC: Guess what?

The reply came almost instantly.

JL: Q is out of town?!

DC: Yes JL: Delicious. Get dressed and meet me at Babyface.

DC: I'd prefer Vics tonight JL: Ok. what time?

DC: 930?

JL: see you then

Dazhong felt electric. She wanted to dance and drink and be fearless with her fearless best friend, Jamie Lin. Smiling, she returned her mobile phone to her purse and headed to the kitchen, where she fixed herself a small dinner of leftover noodles and duck. After that, she walked into the bedroom to shed her work clothes and dress for the night's adventure.

The instant she stepped into the bedroom, she noticed a white cardboard box tied with a silver string propped up against her pillow. She rolled her eyes, predicting *the gift* inside. With nimble fingers, she unfastened the bow and opened the box. Inside, she found expensive silk lingerie. With a sigh, she left it where it lay, untouched, and turned her attention to the puzzle box on her nightstand. She picked up the puzzle box and rotated it to the face painted with twisting tongues of elemental fire. Her fingers danced the intricate waltz in a blur—a series of manipulations now effortless from twenty years of repetition and practice. Shift, slide, push, pull, and the secret box lay open. Inside were three objects, each of which she kept hidden from Qing and each for a different reason: endearment, empowerment, and deception.

With a delicate touch, she retrieved the first item— a silver pendant necklace given to her by her father on her eighth birthday. She held it up for inspection. An intricately carved silver rat dangled in midair, suspended from a thin and finely fashioned chain.

"Hello, little friend," she said, kissing the miniature on the nose. "Have you missed me?"

The little totem bobbed to and fro in the air, as if to answer her.

"Good, because I've missed you, too."

She lowered it back into the puzzle box but stopped before releasing the chain. After a moment of hesitation, she changed her mind. The last time she'd worn the charm was on her birthday—a tradition she kept to celebrate her father's gift to honor her birth during the year of the rat. As a young girl, she had resented being associated with such a vile creature, until her father explained that the rat—along with the dragon and the monkey—occupied the powerful first trine of the zodiac. Of all the zodiac totems, the rat was understood to be the most ambitious, clever, and industrious.

"You should embrace the power of the zodiac, Dazhong," he had told her. "Leverage your strengths and know your weaknesses. If you are not careful, ambition can sour into greed, intelligence can mutate into ruthlessness, and industriousness can become exploitation. Whenever you feel weak, wear this charm around your neck. When you are feeling powerful, that is the time to take it off."

She'd been feeling weak lately; she fixed the pendant around her neck.

Despite having no monetary worth, her father's gift was more precious to her than all the gold, diamond, and pearl necklaces Qing had given her over the years. If he were ever to catch her wearing the silver rat charm instead of one of his expensive pendants, she knew he would rip it from her neck. And so, she never let him see it, wearing it only when he was traveling or when she was alone.

Next she retrieved the second item from the puzzle box—a stainless-steel key that opened a shallow footlocker that she kept under the bed. The footlocker agitated Qing to no end, and during the early years of their marriage, he had badgered her incessantly about opening it so he could inspect its contents. Despite his persistent requests for access and threats to break it open, she refused to give him access, claiming it contained nothing more than keepsakes and childhood treasures—emotionally personal items she would only share when and if she felt inclined to do so.

She had never felt inclined with Qing. She didn't think she ever would.

There were indeed a few childhood mementos inside, but of late, she had taken to storing *select* wardrobe additions, all of which had been purchased on shopping sprees with Jamie Lin. Undoubtedly, the collection of high heels, miniskirts, and revealing clubbing tops she had accumulated over the past year would send Qing into a furious tirade. As long as he never carried out

his threat to break open the trunk, her scandalous secret would be safe.

Smirking at the thought, she picked out a black skirt
and a low-cut silk tank top printed with a purple snake-
skin pattern. For undergarments, she selected a black
thong and push-up bra with extra padding. For shoes,
she went straight for the most expensive thing she
owned—a pair of Christian Louboutin Luciana black
leather pumps. Her hair and makeup took her thirty
minutes—fifteen of those minutes she spent on the eyes.
She always went dark and bold with the eyes.

Her eyes were her secret weapon.

Dressed and made up, she barely recognized herself
in the mirror. Were she to walk by Qing on the street
tonight, he would not know her as his wife. He would
stare, and he would gawk, but he would not recognize
her. She suddenly thought of Commander Zhang. Would
Zhang, with his elite training, be able to recognize her?
If he could, what would he think of her as she was now?

She forced Zhang's image from her mind, locked the
footlocker, and shoved it back under the bed. She placed
the key back into the puzzle box and retrieved the third
and final item inside—a white plastic clamshell container holding twenty-eight colored pills. Using her
thumb, she pressed today's birth control tablet through
the foil backing and into the palm of her hand. She
popped the little pink pill into her mouth and swallowed. *Betrayal*, she mused with a wry smile, *one dose
at a time*. It was a remarkable feat, if she really thought
about. For seven years, she had managed to keep this
dark secret from her husband. For seven years, she had
kept herself barren because of him.

Thirty minutes later, she was standing outside Club

Vic's waiting for Jamie Lin. Just as she was beginning to wonder if her friend was not going to show, she felt a tap on her shoulder. Dazhong turned to find Jamie Lin, dressed to kill and grinning ear to ear.

"You look hot, Chen," Jamie Lin said, looking her up and down. "Love that top."

"Thanks. You look, um, *strong*," she said, noting the lean cords of muscle showcased by her best friend's bare arms and midriff.

"Eye of the tiger, baby," Jamie Lin purred playfully.

Jamie Lin was not your typical Chinese girl. She was outspoken, wild, and obsessed with fitness. On the surface, the two women were total opposites—Jamie Lin seemed superficial, obsessed with clubbing, money, and curating her "Beijing Babydoll" Weibo feed. But over the last few months, Dazhong had begun to catch glimpses of a different side of her friend. In fact, she was beginning to suspect that there was a passionate and deeply cerebral soul caged behind the makeup and the muscles. This person was the woman Dazhong wanted to know, and the more Jamie Lin resisted her attempts at platonic intimacy, the more insatiable Dazhong's curiosity to truly know her friend had become.

Both women had been born in Beijing, but Jamie Lin's family had moved to the United States when she was seven. Jamie Lin had only moved back to China three years ago, and Dazhong could still pick out Western-accented undertones in Jamie Lin's Mandarin. True to form, Jamie Lin worked in corporate finance—her boss was some big shot in international tech. Whenever Dazhong asked Jamie Lin about her job, Jamie Lin played dumb, pretending her boss did all the work and she had been hired as corporate eye candy. Dazhong

knew better; she'd overheard Jamie Lin on the phone
with work colleagues enough times to know the girl
had a formidable grasp of the complex world of international business, finance, and technology. Sometimes,
Dazhong wondered if Jamie Lin was in fact the "the
boss," because she always sounded like the one giving
instructions.

"Are we gonna stand here all night, or are we gonna
dance?" Jamie Lin said coyly, one hand propped on a
hip.

Dazhong smiled. "Big Mac has a crush on you, not
me, remember? Go do your thing."

Jamie Lin grabbed her by the hand and tugged
Dazhong toward the front of the line. "Big Mac," the
club's lead bouncer, smirked as they approached. Jamie
Lin walked straight up to the thick, heavily tattooed
Asian and kissed him on the cheek, flattening her
breasts against his chest while slipping cash into his
front pants pocket. Big Mac nodded a stoic, wordless
approval and waved them inside.

Jamie Lin dragged Dazhong through the crowd to
the bar and ordered them a pair of cosmos. While they
waited, they watched one of Vic's famous bartenders
put on an aerial mixing show—juggling and flipping
bottles of hard liquor in the air as a circle of inebriated
spectators looked on, hooting and hollering. Jamie Lin
paid for the first round, and the two women quickly
drained their glasses so they could head to the dance
floor. Jamie Lin pushed her way into the middle of the
gyrating crowd and carved out a little cylinder of space
to groove as DJ QQ mixed Aphex Twin's album *Syro*
from the stage.

Dazhong lost herself in the music and rhythm for the

next hour, letting her mind go carnal, but eventually, thoughts of Kizilsu, Qing, Major Li, and the mysterious killer-disease conspiracy crept back in.

"What's wrong?" Jamie Lin shouted over the booming techno beat, zeroing in on the shift in mood.

"Nothing," Dazhong shouted back, forcing a smile.

"You look upset."

"I'm fine."

"Wanna talk about it?"

Dazhong considered her friend's offer but shook her head. "No, really, I'm fine. Cosmo is wearing off, that's all."

Jamie Lin flashed her a Cheshire grin. "In that case, I'll be right back."

While Dazhong waited for her second cosmo, she danced alone, letting the world blur around her. Boys and men tried to talk and dance with her, but she looked through them like rain and let them dribble away. She was inside herself, alone with her thoughts and her worries. Jamie Lin was right, she did need to talk to someone, and that person was Nick Foley. Maybe with a little liquid courage, she could make it happen.

The second cosmo tasted even better than the first, and by the time her cocktail glass was empty, Dazhong was buzzing pretty hard. She looked at her friend and smiled.

"What?" Jamie Lin said, grinning back.

"You're a good friend, you know that?"

"Why, because I make you dress like a slut and get you drunk?"

"No," Dazhong said with an inebriated giggle. "Because you remind me the secret to life is to take chances and have fun."

Jamie Lin shrugged. "It's not a secret, Chen. It's my dogma."

"Did you learn that in America?"

"Sort of. I learned it from an American boy I knew."

An image of the American Navy SEAL sitting across the interrogation table from her in the Artux People's Hospital popped into her mind, reminding her of what she needed to do.

"I've gotta go," she said, suddenly stepping forward and hugging Jamie Lin.

"Wait, what?" Jamie Lin said, halfheartedly hugging her back. "We just got here."

"I know. I'm sorry," she said. "There's just something I've got to do."

"Right now?"

Maybe it was the alcohol, or maybe it was something else inside her, but whatever it was, Dazhong knew she needed to act before the opportunity was gone.

"Yes, right now."

"Text me later," Jamie Lin said. "Let me know when you get home."

"I will," Dazhong said, turning away. "Bye bye, Babydoll."

Jamie Lin smiled, held up two fingers in a *V*, and blew her a kiss.

Dazhong pressed her way through the crowd, a little unsteady on her Lucianas, and left the club. Outside, on the sidewalk, the cool night air licked at the perspiration on her skin and sent a chill running down her arms and back. She retrieved her mobile phone from her handbag and looked up the "NF" contact entry she had made earlier that day. She stared at Nick Foley's phone number and felt her nerve waning.

Where should I meet him?

She scanned the buildings around her, looking for someplace close and suitable. Across the street, the neon sign for the popular Club Mix beckoned. Loud, crowded, and warm—perfect. She looked back at the glowing LCD screen in her hand, took a deep breath, and pressed the dial icon next to Nick Foley's mobile phone number.

SIXTEEN

NICK WOKE WITH a start, confused and in the dark.

A loud, rhythmic buzzing punctuated the silence.

"Where am I?" he mumbled as he jumped out of bed. He scanned the space around him. No enemy gunfire, no Hellfire missiles, no burning bodies—just city lights winking at him through the oversized plate-glass windows of his hotel room.

I'm in the Four Seasons, he reassured himself. *In Beijing.*

The buzzing was coming from his mobile phone on the wooden nightstand beside the bed. He picked up the offending device and checked the caller ID. He didn't recognize the number. He answered the call anyway.

"Nick Foley."

"Yes, hello…maybe you don't remember me," a nervous woman's voice said on the line. "We ran into each other in the hotel lobby the other night in Kizilsu."

Nick's pulse rate jumped.

"Yes, I remember. Hello."

"I am sorry to call you so late at night. Am I disturbing you?"

"No, no, of course not."

"Okay, good," she said. Then, awkwardly, she asked, "Can you meet me? I would like to ask you a few questions."

Nick's mind started racing. *Was it really her, Dr.*

*Chen, on the line? Or was it a confederate? Was this
a trap? Was this conversation being recorded? Is that
why she didn't say her name?*

"Hello? Are you still there?" she said, tension rising
in her voice.

"Yes, I'm here," he said. "When and where?"

"Club Mix," she said. "I will be waiting for you."

"Okay, I can leave immediately."

"Very good…oh, and please come alone."

"Understood."

She ended the call without a good-bye.

"Well, I'll be damned," he said, shaking his head. "I
did not expect that…"

Thirty minutes later, Nick was standing inside Club
Mix looking for the beautiful doctor whose name he
could not pronounce. The pounding music and flashing lights were already giving him a headache, reminding him why it had been so long since he'd been in a
club like this. And yeah, the last time gave him a headache, too.

He scanned the crowd, looking for a captivating pair
of almond eyes, but after an exhaustive sweep, he admitted defeat. "This is pointless," he grumbled. "Every
girl in the joint has almond eyes."

If she actually did show up, the burden was on her
to find him.

He headed to the bar, took a seat at the counter, and
ordered a beer. All around him, girls gyrated across the
lighted floor in tight, impossibly short skirts. After a
few minutes, he stopped watching. In stark contrast to
the party girls and club-hopping hipsters—laughing,
flirting, downing fancy cocktails and neon shooters—
Nick sipped stoically at his beer, waiting to be found.

As the minutes ticked by and his beer glass got empty, that hope began to fade. He checked his phone to see if he had missed a call or text. Perhaps he should dial the number she had called him from. Would she answer? On the phone, she had sounded nervous. His mood darkened.

This is a setup, he told himself. *Don't be an idiot. This is how the game is played. She's Zhang's honey trap, and I'm the mark.*

Across the bar, an inebriated teenage girl pointed at him and whispered into the ear of her blue-haired friend. Then they both blew him a kiss, and the blue-haired girl motioned for him to join them on the dance floor. Nick smiled politely, shook his head no, and looked down at the multicolored, lighted tiles shining up through his beer.

He took a long pull on his drink.

"Hello," said a woman's voice just behind him.

He swiveled to the right and came face to face with a girl who looked to be in her midtwenties. She wore the same heavy makeup as the other girls giggling in the booths and bouncing on the dance floor, but this girl had presence about her. He stared at her, hypnotized by the perfect jawline, delicate nose, and sensuous smile.

"No thank you," he said before she could ask him for a dance or a drink. "I'm meeting someone." With great effort, he redirected his gaze into the depths of his beer mug.

Undeterred, she placed her hand gently on his arm—igniting carnal urges in the primitive part of his brain. He'd never been with a girl this beautiful before. His imagination went to work, and he felt a stirring.

"Nick Foley?" she said.

His chest tightened.

How did this girl know his name? Was she the one who had called him?

He turned and locked eyes with the girl. If he ignored the heavy eye shadow and mascara…

The features were eerily familiar. Could it really be her?

"Dr. Dash?" he said, then blushing, he added, "I mean, Dr. Chen?"

"Yes, it's me," the woman said, rescuing him.

"I… I didn't recognize you," he stammered.

The corners of her lips curled into a knowing smile. "Perhaps you can accompany me to a quiet booth? Somewhere we might have a conversation in private?"

Her voice wasn't slurred, but he could tell she'd had a few drinks.

"Of course," he said and grabbed his beer from the bar, wondering where in a club with music this loud they could possibly find a *quiet* booth. He followed her—his gaze trained on the backside of her tight, black skirt. She led him through the crowd, descended a short set of stairs, and weaved through the modern, white-top tables until they reached an area populated with intimate, high-back booths. He noted that most of the booths were already occupied by other couples engaged in their own private conversations—the type of conversation just shy of intercourse.

They slid into one of the neon-green leather booths and the noise level dropped significantly. She sat opposite the cozy bistro table from him and crossed her legs at the knee and her hands at the wrists.

"You did not recognize me at the bar?" she said, toying with him straight out of the gate.

"No, I didn't," he said. "You look *different* than I remember."

"I should hope so. Last time we met, I was wearing a mask."

"And there's that," he said, flashing her his best self-deprecating smile.

"But you thought I was someone else? Some other girl?"

"Well, yes…er, I mean no… I wasn't sure."

"You called me a different name?"

"Oh, that was nothing. Just me badly mispronouncing your name."

"Dr. Chen is easy to say," she teased.

"Actually, I was trying to say your given name: *Dash-ing*," he said, his cheeks flaring hot. "Or is it *Dash-ong*? I'm sorry, my Chinese is horrendous."

She smiled broadly at this. "It's a good try, but that's not how to say it. My name is pronounced *Da-Chung.*"

He tried to mimic her intonation, but from the way she wrinkled her nose at him, clearly he'd failed miserably.

"It's okay. Most Americans have a hard time saying Chinese names. If you like, you can call me Dash," she said, smiling at him with her eyes. "I think it's nice."

"Yeah, me too."

"Then it is decided. Dash will be my American nickname with you."

"Just between us?"

"Just between us."

Nick reminded himself that she was probably still working with Commander Zhang, who may well still suspect Nick was involved in the events in Kizilsu. She'd probably played him from the beginning. *CDC doctor my ass*, he thought. He waited a beat for her to redirect the conversation. When she didn't, he decided to extend the small talk and see where things went.

Keep it casual. Let her think her flirting and smiling is working, then you can turn the tables on her.

"Cool club," he said, gesturing around them. "Do you party here often?"

"Not really," she replied without a hint of judgment or embarrassment. "I have a Western friend—an American in fact—who is a very bad influence on me." She looked out at the crowded dance floor and her lips curled into that same knowing smile. "My husband would kill me if he found me here with you. He would say I have been corrupted by the West, like so much of China." She looked back at him with eyes that seemed more focused now. "Perhaps he is right," she said, leaving him to wonder if she thought that was a good thing or a bad thing. "But," she added quickly, "I would never betray him, or break my marriage vows."

"Of course," Nick said, unsure what else to say.

Message received. And I don't pursue married women—especially those working for the Chinese government—so let's get down to business.

A waitress approached the table, wearing a skintight silver dress and carrying a lighted tray that seemed to change colors in rhythm to the music. She said something in Chinese, then looked at Nick and tried again in English. "Something to drink?"

"No thanks," Nick said, holding up his half-empty beer.

"A cosmopolitan," Dash said. She waited until the waitress had gone before leaning in to say, "I would like to ask you some questions."

"Of course," Nick said. A preemptive strike was needed. "But first I should probably ask, is Commander Zhang okay with us meeting like this?"

She blushed and shook her head, unable to hide the embarrassed, conspiratorial look on her face.

She's conflicted, he thought. *Either this girl is one hell of an actress, or she's flying solo.*

"Commander Zhang does not know I am here," she said, as if reading his mind. "I could get in much trouble for meeting you like this."

"I understand," he said. "It's a risk for me, too. Commander Zhang is still holding my passport. If he finds out that we met…well, let's just say the remainder of my stay in your country might become most unpleasant."

She nodded pensively at this. "That is not my wish, Nick Foley. Maybe this is not a good idea."

"No," he said, a beat too quickly. "You said on the phone you have questions for me. Well, I have questions for you, too."

She leaned in, about to talk, but snapped back upright when the waitress arrived with her cosmo. For a moment, he caught her scent—floral and profoundly feminine—and he had to beat back the carnal thoughts.

She waited for the waitress to leave and then leaned in again.

This time, he made a conscious effort to breathe through his mouth.

"I would like to continue our conversation from the interview we had in the hospital," she said.

"By interview, don't you mean my interrogation under duress as a suspected terrorist?" he said, surprised at the adversarial undertone his voice had taken on.

She rolled her eyes at this. "We both know you are

not a terrorist, Nick Foley. And so does Commander Zhang. He is simply not ready to admit it."

"Thank you," he said, feeling the knot in his chest loosen a bit. "It's good to hear you say that."

"Can we continue the interview?"

"Yes," he said, "provided that when I'm done answering your questions, you'll agree to answer mine."

She fidgeted in her seat. "I will agree to answer your questions as best I can. Is that acceptable?"

He nodded.

"Why did you say that what happened in Kizilsu could not be a terror attack?" she asked, her eyes darting about the room as if the Snow Leopards might fast-rope into the club at any moment.

"I didn't say that," he countered. "I said if it was a terror attack, it would make no sense for a hostile organization to hit China in the middle of nowhere and target a cultural minority that subsists at the fringes of Chinese society. If al-Qaeda, or ISIS, or even, God forbid, a world power like Japan wanted to attack China, they would not target a place as remote and inconsequential as Kizilsu. They would attack the financial district in Hong Kong, or government buildings in Beijing, or a target with cultural significance. Why would anyone interested in making an international statement target a Muslim minority in a village so remote that the world will never hear about it?"

"Yes, I have thought about this much since you said it." She took an absent-minded sip of her drink, lost in thought. "Commander Zhang says you hate Muslims," she said simply, her face a mask to her true opinion on the subject.

A hot flash of anger roiled him at the absurd accusation. "Commander Zhang is wrong. During my time in the Middle East, I fought shoulder to shoulder with many Muslims. Many of these men hold my profound respect, and some I even consider brothers." He took a deep breath to quell his rising emotion. "What *both* you and Zhang need to understand is that I don't hate Muslims. I hate *terrorists*. I hate them because they try to control people through fear by targeting innocents—even children—to further their agenda. I hate them because they are cowards."

His voice cracked with anger, but she did not recoil at his rage. Instead, she held his gaze, measuring him.

He took a defensive swig of beer.

"I do not agree with Commander Zhang," she said, reaching out to touch his hand but stopping short. "I have no experience with terrorists. I have never been in war. It must be...difficult."

He took another swallow from his glass. "Yes, it changes you. I apologize for losing my temper."

"Apology accepted."

"Next question," he said, forcing a smile.

"You said something else I've been thinking about. You said that you thought the only people who hated the Uyghurs enough to attack them were Han Chinese."

"I didn't mean you," Nick said.

"Yes, yes," she said, waving the comment away. "Of course not, but this idea has been bothering me very much. It makes no sense. If the attack was by Chinese, and the attackers had access to a biological weapon, then it must be connected to the government." She was whispering now, and Nick could barely make out the words over the din of the club. "But that makes no sense either. The government would have no need to use such a dangerous weapon. Counterterrorism police are already in Kashi. Commander Zhang could arrest every Uyghur troublemaker and no one would complain. This is not America—the lawyers and the media are not in charge here."

"My point exactly," he said.

"However, the threat of terrorism *is* growing in China. There are radical Muslims in Xinjiang province causing trouble. An imam was murdered in Kashi, but this murder was done by radical Uyghurs who believed the imam was a servant of Beijing rather than Allah. There have been some attacks against innocent Han Chinese. But all of this fighting is done by people who are—how do you say it in American?" She thought for a moment, searching her memory. "By people who are thunks, yes?"

Nick chuckled.

"You mean *thugs*?"

"Yes, thugs. That is correct, Nick Foley. They are thugs, not people who have access to a bioweapon of this type. It is very sophisticated."

Now she had his attention. He leaned in to talk but did a double take as a young man walked by staring at them. For a moment, he felt certain he had seen this kid hovering at the bar when Dash arrived. Nick shook off the paranoia—there were hundreds of twentysomething Chinese boys in here looking to get lucky, and they all had the same West-envy, hip-hop look. He looked again at Dash, who sipped absently on her drink, deep in thought again.

"Anthrax and sarin gas can be purchased on the black market. There have even been talks of suicide attackers intentionally infecting themselves with Ebola and then attacking a population by integrating during the incubation period or whatever. But that's not what happened in Kizilsu, is it?"

Dash held his gaze and nodded subtly. Before answering, she checked for any would-be eavesdroppers hanging around their booth. "What happened in Kizilsu is a mystery. What killed the people was not anthrax, Ebola, poison gas, or an industrial accident. In my opinion, what killed the people was an engineered weapon, not a biological agent," she whispered. "But I have no evidence. This is just my theory."

Nick had watched helplessly as Batur had bloated and then dissolved before his eyes. The speed of the transformation screamed chemical agent, but the symptoms presented like an infection. Was she suggesting there could be a weapon that was both? Some sort of hybrid biochemical weapon in the Chinese military's arsenal? If so, the superpower strategic landscape had just shifted beneath their feet. His heart was racing now as they danced around the truth. "I want to hear your theory. Tell me more."

"What is the biggest problem with a biological weapon?" She was leading him to the answer, just like the teaching doctors at the Navy base trauma center who constantly "pimped" him during rounds until things began to click.

"Well," he said. "I guess the biggest problem is how to avoid infecting yourself when you're trying to use it on someone else."

"Containment," she said, nodding. "Infecting yourself is a problem, of course, but the real problem is containing the agent to the intended target population. Once infected, the victims act as vectors, spreading the agent to others. This is how epidemics are born. It is very difficult to contain a contagious pathogen within a target population unless you can manage to completely isolate the infected. The longer the incubation period, the more difficult the task becomes. Biologics do not make a good terror weapon. A terrorist who attacks a country on the other side of the world is a fool if he thinks his homeland is safe from harm. A pandemic, no matter where it starts, will spread. The world is a small place. Biological weapons are not like bombs. They are not tactical."

"But you think this weapon was tactical? You think it acted like a bomb?"

"Yes." She pushed her cosmopolitan aside and leaned on her elbows, her hands now folded in front of her. "This agent appears to have infected a very specific group of people in a small area. Commander Zhang determined that every victim of the attack had attended morning prayers at the local mosque, but not a single victim acted as a vector. They were not contagious. Even close contacts of the victims showed no trace of infection."

"Containment," Nick said softly.

"Yes, total containment. Not one case in the community, in the hospital staff, or with people like you—people who had close contact with a victim."

"But it was lethal."

She nodded. "One hundred percent mortality."

Nick took a moment and let the gravity of what she was telling him sink in. This agent—this *weapon*—infected everyone exposed, killed quickly and completely, and did so without being contagious. That seemed impossible.

"What is it?" he asked.

"I don't know," she sighed, and suddenly, despite the movie-star makeup and plunging neckline of her silk top, he saw her in a new light. Like a scientist dressed as a party girl on Halloween. "The data make no sense."

"How so?"

"Well, first of all, the victims had moderately elevated immunoglobulin counts, but when we began using ELISA to dig deeper, we could not find a common viral antigen across the group of patients."

"What about bacteria?"

"All attempts to culture suspected bacterial or fungal species from the sputum, blood, or urine samples failed."

"Okay, if it's not a virus and it's not a bug…then it must be a chemical toxin of some sort."

"No," she said, shaking her head in frustration. "I thought this, too, but all of the victims had a very specific immunologic response. The innate immune system response was robust, but an adaptive immune response never occurred."

"I don't understand," Nick said.

"Sorry, sometimes I talk too technical," she said, flashing him a little grin. "What I mean is the immune system recognized an invasion was occurring, but it could not identify the invader. You see, the immune system has two parts. The first response is general. The second response—the adaptive response—is highly antigen specific. The immune system looks for markers on the subcellular level to identify each new invader. Then it catalogs the specific proteins for each new virus and bacteria and keeps a record so that on the next exposure, it can mount a strong defense."

"You were looking for these specific proteins to identify the bug, just like the police use a fingerprint to identify a criminal," he said.

"Yes, exactly," she said, excited that her dull student was able to understand this simple concept.

"And you didn't find any fingerprints?"

"Not yet," she said.

"Well, can't you keep looking?"

She slammed a hand on the table, surprising him. "The bodies are no longer available, and neither are the tissue samples."

"Why?"

She looked at him, fury in her eyes for the first time since they'd sat down.

"Because they were all taken!"

"By Commander Zhang?" he said, shaking his head disparagingly.

She cocked her head and looked confused. "No, not Commander Zhang. By the military."

"I thought Zhang was military?" he said. Now he was thoroughly confused.

"Not exactly. The Snow Leopards are a division of the People's Armed Police Force. I do not think you have this structure in America. They are in-between the regular police and the army. Very elite, but separate."

He nodded understanding—similar to the elite SWAT units operated by the DEA and the FBI. Now the pieces were clicking into place. "I see. It was the PLA that commandeered the bodies in the middle of your investigation and put Major Li in charge?"

"Yes. Commander Zhang and I were both surprised by this," she said, but then she hesitated and screwed up her face at him. "Wait, how do you know about Major Li?"

"From you, remember? The last time we spoke in the hotel lobby, you said if I had any questions, I should go ask Major Li."

She frowned. "I was upset. I should not have told you that."

"Too late now," he said with a reticent grin. "For what it's worth, I would have been pissed off too if I were in your shoes."

"It was terrible. Li confiscated all the reports and tissue samples for Regiment 54423 and then destroyed the bodies…at least that's what I've heard."

Nick resisted the urge to rub his chin. *So I was right*, he thought. *There is a conspiracy going on, and the Red Army is at the center of it.*

"What is Regiment 54423? I've not heard of this unit," he said.

"The army's nuclear, biological, and chemical weapons unit—a division of soldier-scientists."

"Well, there you go," he said. "It *is* a cover-up. The army must have tested a new weapon system on the Uyghurs, and now they are hiding the evidence."

"No," she said simply. "This is the story I would have believed, if I had not met you in Kizilsu."

Nick raised his eyebrows. *What the hell was that supposed to mean?*

"You told me during your interrogation that if we wanted to figure out who would do such a terrible thing, then we should ask ourselves who would benefit the most," she said, tapping her index finger against the side of her martini glass. "The army does not benefit from this attack."

"But the party leadership does. From what I understand, Beijing has been steadily stepping up the pressure against Muslim dissidents out west, right?"

"You were a soldier, so let me ask you this question: If the United States had an advanced, secret biological weapon, a weapon superior to all other biological weapons because it can be deployed with the accuracy of a bomb, would your government use it on a foe as unworthy as the Uyghurs in Kizilsu?"

He thought about the breadth of the firepower in the US arsenal. Then he thought about the percentage of that arsenal that *could* be used in the War on Terror but wasn't. He shook his head.

"Never in a million years."

"Exactly. In China, the government can deal with Muslim troublemakers harshly enough using the state police. They have no need to use such a weapon. Despite what you may believe about China in America, my government would never target women and children when dealing with such a problem."

"Women and children?" Nick felt a band tighten around his chest. Images of charred bodies—one smoking black body without legs and the remnants of a red scarf—crowded into his mind's eye. For a moment, he thought he might be sick. He exhaled slowly and looked at her.

"Yes," she said. Her voice had lost its rising passion and once again become cool and clinical. "Among the victims were two women and one child—an infant."

Nick rubbed a hand across his face and let the air hiss out through pursed lips. "Well, then it must have been a terrorist attack." He wasn't sure she was listening to him, and her headshake may have been to an internal thought rather than what he was saying. "Then we're back to the original question: who would benefit from launching such an attack?"

Dash looked up and her almond eyes were rimmed with tears. Nick wondered whether it was grief or frustration—maybe both.

"I don't know," she said. "This is why I contacted you. I was hoping you could help me answer this question."

He opened his mouth to say something but then realized he had no idea what to say. How could he help? He was an outsider—an outsider being investigated by the Snow Leopard Commando Counterterrorism Unit. He didn't have any allies in China. He didn't have access to privileged information. He was about to verbalize these things when she abruptly stood.

"I am sorry to have bothered you, Nick Foley," she said and gathered her small clutch. "It was a mistake to involve you. I do not wish to put you at any further risk. I simply thought—because you have fought terrorists—that maybe you could help me look at this problem differently. There is no one else I can approach. Major Li controls all the information. Commander Zhang has been ordered to end his investigation. My office has assigned me to other duties. I have no access to the bodies, or the tissue samples, or any of the lab data. I just…" She shook her head and turned to leave.

"Wait," he said, grabbing her by the arm. She recoiled at the touch like a whipped puppy. He released her instantly. "One of the victims was my friend. He was a husband and father and now…" He paused, struggling to find the right words. "What I'm trying to say is that I want to help you. I *will* help you."

She looked around, suddenly paranoid.

"I'm sorry, Nick Foley," she said, then leaned in closer. "Perhaps we can speak again. I don't know. I need time to think."

"At least let me call you a cab," he said, stepping out of the booth to accompany her. "It's late to be wandering the streets alone."

She shook her head.

"Thank you, but that is not necessary," she said. "I will take the subway, as I always do."

"Then let me walk you to the closest metro station," he insisted.

Dash shook her head again.

"It is best for us both not to be seen together. Thank you, Nick Foley. We may yet speak again."

He watched her as she weaved hastily through the crowd. What the hell had just happened? If he was being played by this woman, then he had no idea what her endgame was.

When she reached the steps leading up to the main club, he saw two men slide out of a booth and begin moving in her direction. This time he was certain he had seen both these men at the bar. It wasn't a coincidence.

He threw a handful of bills on the table and set off after her while keeping a discreet distance from the two men following her. By the time they had all navigated through the densely packed dance floor, his Navy SEAL instincts were ringing like alarm bells. At the door, the two men were joined by a third. They spoke briefly, pointed to the door, and then followed Dr. Chen out.

Nick moved swiftly after them, his body amped with adrenaline. He forced himself to pause and count to five before pushing his way out the door. He did not want her, or the three men, to spot him leaving the club.

He stepped outside and immediately felt a stab of panic. The street was teaming with cars, and the sidewalk was crowded with more people than he would have imagined given the late hour. He scanned left and right but couldn't find either Dash or the three men. He jogged five paces toward the curb, changing his vantage point, and caught a glimpse of one the men turning the corner at the end of the block to the right. With clenched fists, he set off after them, praying he could catch up before it was too late.

A crowd of people waiting for the traffic light to change blocked Nick's path at the intersection. He pushed through them with harried dread, knocking shoulders and stepping on toes. He ignored the dirty looks and clipped rebukes; rude was rude in any language. He pressed up on his toes to see over the crowd. At six foot three, he was taller than most Chinese, but it didn't matter. He'd lost sight of his marks. Emerging from the crowd, he paused at the curb and scanned down the street. A block and a half away, he spied what looked like a blue-and-white Beijing subway sign.

Had she already gone underground?

Had they followed her?

He didn't have time to wait for the damn light any longer.

Fuck it.

With his arms raised—palms facing out like a traffic cop with a death wish—he stepped into the street. Horns blared and brakes squealed while Nick tried to dodge and juke his way across four lanes of heavy traffic. A motorcycle, shooting the gap between the lanes, clipped his hip and sent him spinning onto the hood of a compact white sedan. He felt the thin sheet metal buckle beneath his weight as he rolled over the top and off the other side. He landed on his feet and felt the wind from a delivery truck passing by six inches from his face. He glanced back at the driver of the white car, who was making obscene gestures and screaming incomprehensible profanities out the window. Nick waved an apology and sprinted through a gap in traffic to safely reach the other side of the street.

With most of the pedestrians trapped behind him still waiting to cross at the intersection, the west sidewalk along Sanktun was relatively empty. He scanned straight ahead.

Nothing.

He looked down the sidewalk on the other side of the street and spied a woman walking between two men. A third man was walking in front, leading. The woman's posture was rigid, her gait a nervous shuffle.

That's her.

The man to Dash's left had a hand on her waist in an attempt to look familiar, but her body language screamed fear. He watched the lead man look up and down the street and then bark an order over his shoulder. The two others dragged Dash behind them into an alley halfway down the block. The leader looked left and right and, seemingly satisfied, disappeared into the alley.

By now, the light had changed, and the oncoming traffic was beginning to move.

Damn it. Not again.

Heart pounding, adrenaline surging, he bolted into traffic a second time.

He dodged a silver sports car but was not fast enough to clear the speeding red Chery Tiggo. The compact SUV swerved left just in time to avoid completely clobbering him, but he still slammed into the rear passenger door. The impact spun him right, and he slid down the rear fender, hitting the street hard on his left elbow. He rolled out of the fall—his training taking over—and vaulted upright with his right hand and leg. The Tiggo crashed into a taxi and mayhem erupted. Horns blared and all the traffic around him squealed to a stop.

Without missing a beat, he was through the gaps and sprinting down the sidewalk toward the alley. Something terrible was about to happen to Dash. He could feel it in his bones. He visualized the worst possible scenario and readied himself. He reached the corner of the white stone building that formed the corner of the alley and skidded to a stop, forcing himself to assess.

Assess...aim...fire...move.

Nick pressed himself against the wall and listened a moment. He heard angry but controlled Chinese, he assumed from the leader, and then heard a terrified, choking reply from Dash. He glanced around the corner for a microsecond and then jerked his head back against the wall. He closed his eyes and processed the mental snapshot: One man, his back to my approach, his right forearm wrapped around Dash from behind. A second man to the right, standing at a forty-five-degree angle. The third, facing Dash and the alley entrance, perhaps two paces separation from Dash.

He took a deep breath, opened his eyes, and turned the corner into the alley.

He wobbled like a drunken sailor and then chortled in a loud and obnoxious voice. Three more wobbly paces and he stumbled to his knees. One of the men barked an order at him in Chinese, no doubt an order to "go away."

"I'm looking for Gina." Nick hollered back in a thick slur. "Hey, is that Tony? What the hell are you doing here, man?"

The leader barked an order and the other two thugs turned to look at Nick. The jackass on the left spat onto the ground and pushed Dash into the leader's clutches. The other one reached into his pocket. They looked at each other, nodded, and began their approach. Nick looked at Dash and saw her eyes go wide with surprise and hope.

He winked at her.

He got to his feet and stumbled onward, closing the gap. The two meatheads began to diverge, preparing to hit him from both sides. He squinted his eyes as if trying to sharpen his vision and stumbled right, trying to center himself between the two men. They closed to within a yard of him and then the man on his left snapped out a short, metal baton that made a metallic click as it locked into place.

"Hey," Nick said with a burp and a laugh. "You're not Tony."

The two men exchanged grins, and the man on the left said something that made them both chuckle. The jackass with the baton raised his right arm, ready to turn Nick's brains into scrambled eggs, but the opportunity never came.

Nick shifted his weight onto the ball of his left foot and exploded forward. He blocked upward with his left arm as he spun. The outside of his wrist hit the assailant's wrist, stopping the baton midswing and deadening

the attacker's right forearm. Still rotating, Nick clasped
his foe's right arm and took control of the limb, pulling
the thug toward him and off balance. Simultaneously,
he drove his right elbow up into the man's left temple
with an audible crack. Still rotating counterclockwise,
Nick stepped across with his right foot so that his back
was now facing his dazed attacker, brought his strik-
ing arm up, relocked his elbow, and then dropped his
full weight onto the assailant's captured arm. The blow
landed between the thug's shoulder and elbow, and Nick
heard a crunch as the other man's humerus shattered.
The scream that followed reminded Nick of a wild animal. Nick released the arm, raised his right knee, and
then kicked sharply behind him, snapping the man's left
knee backward, parting the ligaments meant to prevent
the movement from their bony connections. A second
primal howl came from the man as he crumbled to the
ground behind Nick.

Nick turned to jackass number two, who stood,
mouth open and eyes wide, hands at his side. Without
a second's hesitation, Nick drove his right palm into the
thug's nose, rupturing bone and cartilage in an explosion of gore. With his left foot, Nick kicked the soft organs between the other man's legs, and then he stepped
through the gap, locked his left leg behind the man's
right ankle, and delivered a right hammer fist across
the man's throat, which sent the smaller man toppling
backward over Nick's leg. Jackass number two hit the
ground hard, his head whiplashing against the unfor-
giving pavement with an audible thud. The body went
limp and urine began to pool beneath.

The fight was over in less than three seconds.

Nick glanced down at his first adversary to make

sure the man with two broken limbs hadn't pulled a handgun while he was vanquishing the partner. Satisfied, he raised his hands in a combat spread and turned his attention to the crew leader.

The remaining thug stood behind Dash, one arm wrapped around her neck in a headlock-style choke hold. The leader met Nick's gaze while he whispered something in Dash's ear.

"Let her go," Nick said, his voice hard and clinical.

The leader released his grip on Dash's neck and shoved her roughly toward Nick, who caught her just as her left knee struck the pavement. She groaned in pain as the nameless thug disappeared into the night, abandoning his fallen accomplices. Nick lifted Dash to her feet and tilted her face up by her chin.

Her eyes swam in tears, which spilled down her exquisite cheekbones, leaving behind trails of mascara.

"Are you okay?" he asked.

She started to say something, couldn't, and then just nodded instead.

Nick knelt beside the unconscious man to his left, making sure to stay out of reach of the other moaning figure writhing in pain farther away. He began to rifle through the man's pockets.

"What are you doing?" Dash asked. There were tears on her cheeks, and she looked anxiously up and down the alley. "What if he comes back?"

"I'm looking for some identification—something to tell me who these assholes are. If they work for Zhang or Li, they'll be carrying military identification."

"That is insane. Commander Zhang would never try to hurt me, and Major Li already has control. I told you, this is not my government doing this."

Nick flipped the unconscious man unceremoniously over onto his face and pulled a wallet from his back pocket—no military ID, just cash and a civilian work ID.

"Besides, if they were military, how would you defeat them so easily?" Dash demanded. "No—these men are thunks."

Nick smiled and shook his head.

"You know, I am a Navy SEAL," he said as a way of explanation.

"I thought you were out of the military now?" She started dancing up and down, a bundle of nerves, her voice cracking as she spoke.

"It's not the type of training you forget." He stood up. "But you're right. They don't seem to be military."

"Of course not," she snorted. "Please," she said, looking at him and squeezing her eyes shut. "Get me out of here."

Nick put an arm around her waist and pulled her beside him. "C'mon, let's go," he whispered, and he felt her soft hand grip his forearm. They stepped around the two remaining assaulters, one motionless and the other gurgling in agony over his shattered arm and ruined knee, which was still bent backward at an unnatural angle.

Dash walked on her toes as they passed them as if she might somehow get contaminated by the carnage.

"How did you do that?" she whispered.

"An old friend taught me," he said.

An image of the Senior Chief—his big, powerful hands on his hips, standing victorious over Nick after taking him to the mat during close quarters combat training in SQT—flashed into Nick's mind. The SEAL instructor's words echoed in his head: *"Hand-to-hand combat is life or death. There is no time to think. You will practice these katas until they are automatic—until muscle memory makes the movements rote. Trust me, Foley, when you need the hammer, it will be there."*

Dash looked up at him, confused.

He smiled down at her. She pressed her face against his shoulder and squeezed his arm. When they reached the corner and stepped onto the sidewalk, she instantly collected herself and let go of his arm. She straightened her silk top, adjusted her skirt, and wiped her cheeks dry.

"Thank you, Nick Foley," she said, forcing a smile.

"You're welcome," he said, scanning up and down the street for the escaped thug and any other "reserve" threats.

"I really must go," she said, taking a step away from him toward the metro sign on the other side of the street.

"Not that way," Nick said, draping an arm around her shoulders and redirecting her toward the busy intersection a block away. "You're taking a cab. I insist."

When she again started to object, he silenced her with a look: *Trust me on this, will ya?*

She nodded in surrender and folded her arms across her chest.

They walked north back toward Workers Stadium North Road. A million questions raced through his head, but he didn't know where to start or how. He looked at her. Just minutes after being assaulted in an alley by three men, she had already found her composure. Most people would be catatonic. Or hysterical. Not Dash. There was mettle in this woman, despite the fact she couldn't weigh more than a buck ten.

"Did you know those men?" he asked. He was still a long way from trusting her, but there was something much bigger than both of them going on here.

She shook her head.

"What did the leader say to you? What did they want?"

He waited while she thought a moment, probably deciding what she should share.

"He told me to stop asking questions that were not my business. He said if I didn't stop meddling, they would come back and hurt me. That is when you came."

"The leader whispered something in your ear before he pushed you. What did he say?"

She looked at her feet and muttered something in Chinese.

"What does that mean—in English?" Nick asked.

"It means, *back off, bitch, or next time we'll kill you.*"

"Obviously they're talking about Kizilsu. Major Li must have sent these guys," he said through gritted teeth.

"These are not men of my government, Nick Foley. They are not military. These men were thunks."

"Thugs," Nick said, correcting her absently with a nod. "Yes, but who sent them?"

Dash shook her head.

"Someone besides Major Li who does not want me knowing who killed the Uyghurs in Kizilsu."

"And someone who does not want you asking questions about the weapon used to kill them."

"Yes, precisely."

She raised her hand to signal a taxi, and within seconds a taxi had pulled along the curb. Nick opened the door for her and then handed the driver a wad of money from his pocket.

"Are you going to be all right?" he asked her, ducking his head to look at her in the backseat through the open rear door.

She smiled at him—a beautiful and genuine smile.

"Yes, Nick," she said, dropping the formal "Nick Foley," he noticed. She touched his hand on the door-frame. "Thank you."

"Will I see you again?" he asked, surprised to hear the words spilling from his lips.

She looked down. "Yes, maybe," she said, and she looked up to meet his gaze. "I may still need your help."

He closed her door and watched the cab pull away until it disappeared into traffic.

He stood at the curb, suddenly exhausted, his hip and left elbow throbbing. Right now, his number one priority was sleep.

Tomorrow, he would think about his next move.

Tonight's events had settled the only decision that really mattered—come hell or high water, he was not leaving China.

SEVENTEEN

THE SHAKING STARTED in her legs, despite the fact that she was sitting.

What is happening to me? Dazhong thought as she trembled uncontrollably in the backseat of the taxi.

The doctor in her head answered, calm and clinical: *Physiological response to an adrenaline surge triggered by a traumatic, life-threatening event. Epinephrine release causes elevated heart rate, increased respiration, muscle contraction, and the rapid metabolism of glycogen and lipids. Shaking is completely normal. Take slow, deep breaths and try to relax.*

She inhaled and blew a long, stuttering exhalation through pursed lips. She felt the taxi driver's eyes on her and glanced up at the rearview mirror to confirm her suspicion. She quickly looked away from his judgmental gaze and exhaled another shaky breath. Her mobile phone rang inside her handbag, startling her despite the familiar ringtone. With clumsy fingers, she fumbled with the bag's zipper and managed to retrieve the phone before the call went to voicemail.

"Hello?" she said, trying to sound normal.

"You said you were going to text me when you got home," Jamie Lin said accusingly on the line. "I sent you three text messages. Is everything all right?"

"Yes."

"Are you sure? Your voice sounds funny."

Dazhong felt tears coming and tried to steel herself. "I'll be fine."

"You'll *be* fine?" Jamie Lin said. "Now I'm worried. I'm coming over."

"No. You can't... I'm not at home."

"Where are you?"

"In a taxi."

"Dazhong, tell me what the hell is going on. You're scaring me."

"After I left the club, some men pulled me into an alley," she stammered. "I thought they were going to... I thought they were going to hurt me, but they didn't."

"Oh my God. Did you call the police?"

"No."

"You shouldn't be alone right now. Tell the taxi driver to drive you to my apartment. I'll be waiting outside at the curb."

"Are you sure, Jamie Lin?"

"I insist."

"All right, see you soon."

Dazhong ended the call and informed the taxi driver of the change of address. Fifteen minutes later, she was inside Jamie Lin's apartment, sitting on the sofa, her best friend cradling her in a hug. When the tears came, they came in heavy, violent sobs—weeks of pent-up emotion, frustration, and uncertainty spilling out in a much-needed emotional release. She had been strong—assertive in her dealings with Director Wong and Commander Zhang, brave in confronting Major Li and her unpredictable husband, and confident in front of Nick Foley. But the attack in the alley had unwound all that in a single instant. She felt like someone had kicked her feet out from underneath her, landing her flat on her back and gasping for air in a state of emotional hyperventilation.

When Jamie Lin asked her what happened, *everything* came spilling out in one long, incoherent, blubbery diatribe. She vented about her professional frustrations working for the CDC and what an asshole Major Li was. She talked about the gruesome deaths she had witnessed in Kizilsu and her concerns about a scandalous cover-up sanctioned at the highest levels of government. She explained how an American named Nick Foley had single-handedly fought off three thugs in the alley and saved her life. Throughout her long and detailed purge of the events, a voice whispered quietly for her to stop, to shut up, that she was sharing government secrets she had sworn to protect. But she ignored the voice. She was tired of being alone. She was tired of being strong. She made no effort to filter details or her emotions, and eventually the little voice gave up and disappeared entirely.

Then she cried about Qing and her tragedy of a marriage. She confessed how she longed to have children, but not with a man she didn't love and never could. Through it all, Jamie Lin listened, stroked her hair, and said how proud she was to know such an amazing and accomplished woman.

When she was done crying and confessing, a comfortable silence lingered between them. Jamie Lin eventually stood and fetched two glasses of water from the kitchen. When she returned, she invited Dazhong to spend what remained of the night with her in the apartment. With a grateful smile, Dazhong declined and said she was ready to go home.

"At least let me escort you," Jamie Lin insisted. "Just to be safe."

"Are you sure?" she asked, secretly grateful for the offer.

"Of course I'm sure," Jamie Lin said.

A surge of paranoia suddenly washed over Dazhong as the gravity of what she'd shared with Jamie Lin began to register.

"Now what's that look for?" Jamie Lin asked, putting on a concerned face.

Dazhong forced an anemic smile. "I should not have told you all those things. Some of that information was confidential. I could get in very big trouble if anyone found out."

"It's okay," Jamie Lin said, placing a hand on Dazhong's shoulder. "You have nothing to worry about. Your secrets are safe with me. Besides, all that CDC microbiology stuff you do is way over my head. Half of what you said, I don't understand."

"Promise me you won't tell anyone?"

"I promise," Jamie Lin said. "Besides, who on earth would I tell?"

"Big Mac at Vic's?" Dazhong said.

Jamie Lin burst out laughing. "Now *that* really would be a disaster," she said, finally managing to catch her breath. "But seriously, Chen, it's okay to vent from time to time. It's healthy, in fact. Everybody needs somebody to talk to. Someone who can help unload emotional baggage without judgment. I know Qing is not willing to be that person for you, but I am."

"Do you really mean that?"

"I do," Jamie Lin said, pulling Dazhong in for a hug. "That's what best friends are for."

EIGHTEEN

ViaTech Corporate Offices, eighth floor
Xinjuan South Road, Chaoyang District

CHET LANKFORD RESTED his elbows on his desk, pushed his reading glasses up on top of his head, and rubbed his tired eyes until white stars began exploding like fireworks on the inside of his eyelids. When his eyes began to ache, he leaned back in his cheap swivel chair with a tired sigh, looked up at the cheap ceiling tiles, and wondered how many new listening devices were up there now. The newest edict out of Beijing, veiled under a guise of counterterrorism, had stepped up close surveillance measures on all foreign corporations. The most crippling facet of the new rules was the banning of all virtual private networks, which might allow the tech savvy to defeat or at least complicate surveillance by Uncle Mao. Without a VPN, secure, private communication over the Internet inside China was almost impossible.

Lankford leaned forward again on his elbows and tried to compose an e-mail message on his no-longer-even-remotely-secure mail client. His e-mail would be intercepted and read; this was indisputable. The trick now was to compose a message that would convey the necessary information to his bosses in Virginia without raising any flags for the Chinese cybersurveillance team. Losing security could be financially crippling for corporations that needed that security to keep an edge in the uber-competitive marketplace. In his world, security was a matter of life and death. For a moment, he thought about deleting the e-mail and moving to a secure location to use his encrypted comms gear. But that would require ditching the surveillance team that was watching him right now, and he was way too tired for that. Besides, why risk his cover for a routine status report?

Hell, I don't even know anything.

For as long as he'd worked for the CIA, Beijing was his least favorite assignment. It was a chief-of-station-level job, though they didn't call it that, since it was run out of the East Asia station and was considered a covert operational assignment. That was how the world was changing. Twenty years ago or more, *all* the chief-of-station assignments were covert with an OC, or official cover—now that was a special gig. The problem here was that he needed to function daily as a full-time regional operations manager of an international tech company that actually did the business it was supposed to. He actually had a P&L, for Christ's sake. Then he was supposed to find another twenty hours a day to actually run his assets, manage his organic operators, and process and convey the data they collected. The end result was predictable—trying to excel at both jobs simultaneously translated to subpar performance in both.

Lankford tapped the delete button and erased his last sentence, deciding his reference to the flu would raise too many flags. How was he supposed to send a routine e-mail to "Corporate" at ViaTech that would tell his bosses at Langley about a possible biological event in the boondocks of western China?

This job is really starting to suck. I'd rather be running assets in Kabul than this shit.

He sighed. Before he sent the message, he should probably work out the more important question—did *he* really believe that something important to world security had struck a handful of impoverished Muslims in the middle of the desert in western China? This was China, so it wasn't like you could just turn on Fox News or CNN for late-breaking news and investigative commentary. These people kept their own citizenry in the dark as much as they did the rest of the world. Hopefully, Jamie Lin could tease some intel out of the Chinese CDC doctor she was running. When the lead medical scientist of the CDC's Ebola task force is dispatched to a domestic location on a moment's notice, it raises some eyebrows. Not the way it would in the West, but still, it was something, so he needed to report *something*.

His mobile phone vibrated on his desk. He leered at the thing with the same disgust one would a cockroach scurrying across a kitchen counter. Whoever it was, he was not in the mood. He picked it up and glanced at the caller ID: Jamie Lin's number flashed on the screen. He raised an eyebrow. He had not expected to talk to his agent again until morning. Maybe she had some *actual* information on what the hell was going on in Kashi.

"Lankford," he said into the phone.

"Hey, handsome," said a tipsy voice—faux tipsy, he hoped. "Wanna get a drink?"

"I don't know," he said, reciting lines from their mutual script. "It's awfully late."

"It'll be worth it," his agent said in a sexy voice—their code for urgency. Now both eyebrows went up. Either something really bad or something really significant must have happened or Jamie Lin would not be contacting him at this hour. She was only twenty-seven years old, and this was her first assignment running agents, but she had as much raw talent as any field operative he'd ever managed.

"Okay," he said with forced reluctance in his voice. "I'll meet you at the usual watering hole."

"Twenty minutes," she said with a giggle. "Don't be late."

One hour—I might have been followed.

"Don't start without me," he said.

Be careful.

The line went dead and Lankford set the phone on his desk.

He reached into the bottom desk drawer and pulled out the messenger bag that held his Glock 17. He rarely carried in China, but something told him the stakes had just gone up. He stood, slipped the leather strap over his shoulder, secured the office, and left. He stood a little taller, walked a little faster, felt a little younger. His senses felt sharper; his lethargic wits felt keener. It was good to be back in the spy game—the real spy game, not the mind-numbing bullshit reporting on Chinese cyberincursions and omnipresent surveillance of Western businessmen and diplomats. He was starting to like this job...well, better than he did five minutes ago, anyway. He glanced at his watch—he would devote a full hour to his surveillance detection route to scrub any ticks off. Tonight, he had reason to be careful.

It took only forty-five minutes to be certain he was

clean. Apparently, the Chinese surveillance teams had other priorities than to follow a nobody middle manager at ViaTech. The Noodle Bar was just what it sounded like: a small venue for late-night noodles and beer. It was located at the edge of the diplomatic and business district of Chaoyang—nearly in Xicheng. It was so off the beaten path that making the trek told a story. The story was one of impropriety: a disgruntled boss having an affair with one of his attractive young staffers. Theirs was a business of stories, each narrative designed to mimic the intricacies and intimacies of real life. Details mattered.

While the other eateries and bars in Chaoyang would be getting crowded at this hour, the Noodle Bar had only a few younger customers sitting inside. Lankford ordered two large bowls of Zha Jiang Mian—fried noodles and sauce. After a long night of partying at the clubs, his agent could probably use some protein and carbs. He ordered a Xiang Dao beer for himself and a bottle of water for Jamie Lin. He shifted in his uncomfortable chair. He hated this place; eating hot, fried noodles at this hour would have him up with heartburn the rest of the night. He would eat them anyway. His discipline had gone as soft as his belly.

He was starting to get anxious. His agent better have something important to report.

The steaming bowl of spicy noodles in a thick, meaty sauce arrived at the table just as Jamie Lin waltzed through the door. He kept his grin to himself as she strutted like a supermodel in her tank top, impossibly short leather skirt, and black leggings. The makeup, the piercings, and the purple streak in her frosted hair made her look even younger and buffer than usual. This creature bore zero resemblance to the girl he had met in Langley before their pairing almost a year ago. He'd heard she was a rising star, but her performance thus far had surpassed all his expectations. She had become her OC. All hints of the Duke-educated, Division I women's lacrosse star were scrubbed from her persona.

"Hi, sexy," she said, kissing his cheek and collapsing into the chair beside him. He scanned over her shoulder toward the entrance while she scanned the room for a reaction to her arrival. There was none.

"I'm famished," she said, then leaned in and whispered, "Clear."

He nodded and whispered back. "You too."

"Thanks for this," she said, shoving a huge bite of noodles into her mouth with chopsticks. "I'm starving."

He smiled at the girl and tipped his beer up. "What do you have for me?"

She slapped his arm and laughed—another ruse for whoever may be watching that they had missed—and then leaned close, digging into the noodles again. She kept her voice low.

"It's something," she said. "My girl is working with the Snow Leopards as well as the army. Joint task force operation."

It took great effort for Lankford to keep his face neutral. He had expected a surprise, but sure as hell not this.

"The Snow Leopards are counterterror. What the hell are we talking about?"

"Not sure," she said, shoving another heaping noodle bite into her mouth and then wiping her chin with a napkin. "My girl was really upset. They sent her out west for a few days, but then a heavy hitter from the army shut her out. Everything's been cleaned and compartmentalized."

"What about the Snow Leopards? Is there a terror component?"

"My girl thinks yes, but the Snow Leopards were sent home, too. PLA is running the show now."

"Did she give you any names?"

"The Snow Leopard Commander is called Zhang. The PLA lead is Major Li."

"What else?"

The young agent shrugged, but her face looked serious.

"It was not Ebola, but whatever it was has scared the hell out of her."

"What's scarier than Ebola to an epidemiologist?"

"Smallpox," Jamie Lin mumbled, her mouth full of noodles. "But it's not that either."

"What else?" Lankford pressed. He was getting irritated now. "Gimme the gold."

"She's scared and angry. She suspects a cover-up, but like I said, they've black-balled her."

"You've gotta push her. Encourage her to keep digging. She's our only fucking asset in orbit near this thing."

"You think I don't know that?" Jamie Lin fired back with an adoring smile on her face.

Lankford resisted the urge to rub his eyes.

Shit.

Shit, shit, shit...

He looked down at his bowl of untouched noodles. His mouth began to salivate like a Pavlov dog. The heartburn would be murder.

He picked up his own pair of chopsticks and took a bite.

Fucking delicious.

He needed to get a handle on this shit, like, right now. Snow Leopards + PLA + CDC = big red flag.

"This is big," he said, and then lowered his voice. "It screams bioterrorism."

"I thought the same thing, but the target is nonsensical."

She's right, he thought. *Then again, Kashgar is becoming a problem for Beijing.*

"Good work," he said, taking a swig of beer. "See what else you can find."

"There is one more thing," she said, flashing him a coy smile.

Lankford raised an eyebrow.

"There's an American involved."

"What?" He coughed and then chastised himself for raising his voice. "Who?"

This was his turf. He knew every American operating in China.

"His name is Nick Foley," she said. "My girl met with him tonight. She says he's an NGO guy working on some water project outside of Kashi. He was at the scene, I think, and he was admitted to the hospital for possible exposure."

"She met with him tonight?"

"Yes."

"Why would she meet him at night in a club, unless they had something 'off book' to talk about?"

"My thoughts exactly."

"All right," he said. "I'll reach back for information on any other GAs or task forces operating in China.

Foley better not be one of those Joint Interagency Coun-terrorism jackasses playing in our sandbox without a heads up. I've had enough of those dipshit cowboys."

His agent nodded and then yawned.

"Sorry, I'm hitting the wall now," she said sheep-ishly. "What do you want me to do? I can rally, boss."

Lankford smiled. What a go-getter. She was going to do great things in the Company.

"Nothing else tonight," he said. "Get some sleep. Come in late to the office and we'll catch up over lunch." He put a fatherly hand on her wrist. "This is great work, Jamie. Just keep doing what you're doing."

She smiled at the compliment. "Thanks, boss," she whispered softly. Then she stood up abruptly and pushed from the table. "It's your loss, Romeo," she said, her voice slurred. "I was really, really in the mood."

"I don't like it when you're this drunk," he said harshly.

"Then take me out somewhere nice," she demanded and faked a few tears.

"You know we can't do that," he said.

She flipped him the middle finger and then stumbled for the door, knocking over a chair on her way. Lankford tried to look pissed as she left, but it was hard. She had gathered a month's worth of intel in one night.

Now it was his turn to get to work. He committed three names to memory: Zhang, Li, and Nick Foley.

His stomach growled and he looked down at his bowl.

"Fuck it," he said under his breath and began shov-eling noodles and sauce into his mouth.

There would be no sleeping tonight anyway.

NINETEEN

POLAKOV WAS SEETHING.

When he was a younger man, he had killed a French intelligence officer while in the throes of such a rage. As it happened, that event had been his last foolish and glorious act as a KGB operative before the collapse of the Russia he loved—the Russia he had spent the rest of his career helping Putin reanimate.

He was not so impetuous now.

He had evolved.

The world was a different place: more complex, but less forgiving. Greater access to information, but fewer places to hide. For Polakov, the last two decades had been a constant exercise in adaptation and self-control.

But tonight, he would take a step back into the past. The old methods had their place. The old methods could still be effective.

He touched the Polish Radom P-64 9×18 caliber semiautomatic pistol tucked in his waistband. The small gun, a variant of the more classic Makarov pistol from the glory days of the KGB, was thin and light—far less aggravating to his growing love handles than the MP-443 Grach preferred by his contemporaries. He probably should have left the weapon in his room. With his temper flaring, it would have been better not to have the option of a trigger to pull. He reminded himself that manipulation and psychological engineering were far more important tools of tradecraft than the pistol.

He spotted the arrogant bastard sipping a drink at a corner table of the highly Westernized coffee shop. Polakov scanned the café. Nothing suspicious. He strode to the table and sat boldly down beside Prizrak.

"Your recklessness and stupidity are going to unmask us both," he said softly. "Do you know what they do to spies and traitors in this country?"

Prizrak set his chai on the table and smiled in a way that made it difficult for Polakov to resist the urge to choke the man to death.

"Then I suppose Moscow had better hurry and bring us both home."

"Your demands are absurd and arrogant," Polakov said, fingering the butt of the pistol in his waistband.

"But they have agreed nonetheless?" the Chinese scientist asked, unable to suppress a large, smug smile.

Polakov leaned forward on his elbows and grumbled. "Yes."

Prizrak's face glowed. "That is wonderful news, comrade."

They both knew Polakov's chastisements and posturing were nothing but a game. Moscow would never risk Prizrak's invention going to some terrorist organization or one of Russia's enemies. Still, Prizrak was naïve if he thought he was immune to retribution. Even in this post–Cold War world, Moscow was quick to issue kill orders when "problems" began to get out of hand. Losing the weapon was not an option. If it could not belong to Russia, then it would not belong to anyone. Either way, Prizrak's latest stunt had sealed his fate. Once the weapon technology was safely in Russian hands, accounts would be balanced. Oh, how he would enjoy killing this scorpion of a man.

Now it was Polakov's turn to smile. "I am afraid that we cannot leave just yet, *comrade*," he said, his tone slow and mocking. "But Moscow has concerns that need to be addressed before entrusting you with a director-level position in VECTOR." Polakov nearly choked on the title—the absurdity that this arrogant psychopath would believe he would hold such a powerful position in the Russian military-science complex after betraying his own country. He shook the thought off and relished the confusion on his asset's face.

"Concerns about what?" Prizrak demanded.

"Why, your wife of course," Polakov said, and he watched Prizrak's face flush.

"She will come with me, of course," Prizrak said, but he was clearly caught off balance by this shift. "She is loyal to me," the Chinese scientist growled. "That is all you need know."

Polakov was enjoying himself now and crossed his legs at the knee and smiled. "Moscow doesn't share your opinion, especially since your wife has been observed interacting with the American CIA."

"Absurd," Prizrak said, a vein standing up on his forehead. "I can assure you, my wife would never betray me. Nor would she betray China. You are either mistaken or lying. You're trying to manipulate me."

"Take care with your voice," Polakov said, relishing every syllable of the conversation. "We don't care how much your wife parties or who she fucks in her spare time—"

"How dare you insult me," Prizrak interrupted, his voice nearly hysterical.

Polakov grabbed the man's wrist near the base of his thumb and applied pressure. "Silence," he commanded, and for the first time in a few years, the Chinese scientist did exactly as he was told.

"Nothing is impossible. Your arrogance will get us all killed," Polakov said, releasing the man's wrist and leaning back in his chair. "The only question is whether your wife has been turned or not. All that *matters* now is what your wife knows about the technology, our plans, and how much she's told her CIA handler."

"She knows nothing," the Chinese traitor stammered. "She thinks I'm developing implantable diagnostic microarrays."

"Perhaps," Polakov said. He had his asset right where he wanted him. "But we must assume there is a chance she may have pieced something together. We must be safe and assume that the CIA is close to figuring this out, if they have not already. And we must assume that your own government is not far behind."

"They are all fools," Prizrak scoffed, but his voice lacked true conviction. "By the time they put the pieces together, we'll be long gone."

Polakov stood. "My sentiments exactly, which is why the time has come, Prizrak," he said, his hand on the man's trembling shoulder. "We must leave now. You will transfer the technology immediately and then I will get you safely out of China."

"We are leaving for Russia now?" Prizrak asked with incredulity.

"Yes," Polakov lied. "Once I have the weapon technology transferred, I will accompany you to Koltsovo so you can start your new life."

The asset looked up at him with eyes that were clouded with something other than fear. A wife's betrayal stings deep, Polakov knew. "How much time do you need?"

"Twelve hours," Prizrak said.

"Nothing can be left behind," Polakov instructed. "No data, no inventory, no feed stock, nothing—do you understand?"

"I understand."

"Do you need me to review how to operate the incendiary devices?"

Prizrak shook his head.

"Very well," Polakov said. "A word of caution, Prizrak. Stay away from your wife. Do not go home. Do not confront her. Do not do *anything* that could jeopardize our departure. When you are ready to leave, text message me the word 'Raven' and I will give you the location of our meeting place."

"I understand," Prizrak said, but Polakov did not like the ice in the man's voice. "Twelve hours."

"Be careful," Polakov warned as the man rose. "Time is running out for us, and I would hate for anything *unexpected* to happen to you."

The scientist scurried out of the coffee shop, shoulders drooping. Bravado gone.

Polakov looked at his watch.

In less than twelve hours, the creator of the most powerful weapon in the world would be dead, and Polakov would be on his way home...a hero of New Russia.

TWENTY

AS A TEEN growing up in Chanute, Kansas, Chet Lankford spent every spare minute reading spy novels. His favorites he read multiple times, searching for nuances, the secrets of tradecraft, and dark truths about the human condition. Unlike most boys his age, his first true love had not been football or the girl next door, but the complete set of Ian Fleming's Bond novels. He was shy, despite his raging hormones, and found himself living vicariously through Bond, who never seemed to run out of opportunities for exotic adventure and gratuitous sex. As he matured, so did his reading list, with John Le Carre, Ken Follett, and Robert Ludlum relegating 007 to the bottom shelf.

When it was time to apply for college, his father pressed him to pursue engineering at a state university. A surprise acceptance letter from Dartmouth College, coupled with a generous financial aid package, changed all that and set him on fate's path. During his final semester, the spymasters found him when the CIA's Ivy League recruiter did what he did best—spotted raw talent. The recruiter sensed what young Chet Lankford thirsted for and tempted him with allusions to a cloak-

and-dagger world just behind the curtain. It only took a couple of years working under the growing federal oversight demanded by the Clinton administration before the CIA of his imagination faded away and was replaced with the stark reality of bureaucratic espionage. James Bond was allegory…nothing more.

During the early years, Lankford kept his head down, his nose clean, and worked his ass off. Advancement became his primary focus. But just when he thought he'd found his groove, some Islamic terrorists slammed a couple of planes into the twin towers and the world went insane. The cold war intelligence community of his youth was gone forever. He adapted. He matured. And he did what the Company asked him to—running assets in Afghanistan, Africa, and Iraq.

Now he was in China, and the Agency asked that he adapt yet again. The rise of China as a superpower was changing the global militarypolitical landscape. Had a new cold war begun? Was China tomorrow's Soviet Union? No, probably not. The veins and arteries connecting the economies of America and China did not exist between America and Russia last century. Sever too many blood vessels and the economic heart keeping the world alive would go into defibrillation. Nonetheless, it was obvious to Lankford that not everyone got the memo, because the global level of clandestine activity had reached epic levels.

"Moscow rules" were back, only this time in Beijing.

He folded his paper in his lap and adjusted his trousers, trying to get comfortable in the God-awful modernistic chair in the Four Seasons lobby. He'd adjusted his seat to the perfect angle to cover the main entrance, the elevators, and the front desk. He feigned checking his e-mail on his phone and thumb-typing a message as he scanned the room with his peripheral vision. He held back a boyish grin. *This* was the kind of spook shit that he had signed on for all those years ago. He would be having the time of his life if he only understood what the hell was going on.

And if my surveillance target wasn't an American ex–Navy SEAL.

His research—well, the research conducted by a team of analysts thousands of miles away and transmitted in real time to his mobile phone via encrypted satellite feed at the speed of light—would have given Ian Fleming a hardon. Lankford, however, did not have a hardon. The kids at Langley had not found jack shit on Foley. No one could even guess whom Foley was working for. There were a myriad of small joint task forces in play nowadays that could have employed him, but no one would raise a hand to claim their lost pit bull.

He knew Foley was working for someone, and that someone was not the CIA.

In Lankford's mind, Foley fit the perfect profile for a covert operator: former Navy SEAL, in the prime of youth, well trained, and well educated. The man had three combat tours in total and had earned a Silver Star with a combat V in addition to numerous other awards, including two Purple Hearts. Navy SEALs were the most highly skilled, intelligent, and committed killers in the world. The Agency's own Special Activities Division was busting at the seams with former frogmen for this very reason. There was no way in hell that Nick Foley had quit the world's most elite special operations force to dedicate his life to bringing clean water to the poverty-stricken religious minority in remote western China.

No way. It would be too tragic of a waste of talent.

Foley's record, and what must most certainly be his NOC—his nonofficial cover—was exactly what he would expect from a clandestine service operator. But whatever outfit was working this guy, they were some spooky sons of bitches. The current crop of analysts in Langley were the best he'd ever seen; if they couldn't find anything on Foley, then the architects of Foley's NOC were cybergods. If Foley truly had squandered the training and expertise the US Navy had bought and paid for by joining a nonprofit to dig ditches in the desert... Lankford shuddered in abhorrence at the thought.

The elevator dinged.

Lankford raised his paper, flipping the page and using his peripheral vision to scan the three people emerging through the ornate doors. Towering a foot above two Chinese businessmen was his target, dressed in a form-fitting Under Armour T-shirt and gray running shorts.

Very subtle, Foley. Jeez, why don't you just wear a SEAL team ball cap?

That was the problem with former operators—they always *looked* like former operators.

Foley walked past him without a glance, popping in some ear buds and looking at his phone. Lankford waited, just so, and then followed Foley out of the lobby onto the sidewalk. He followed for two blocks before deciding to close the gap. As Foley turned left, Lankford reached out a hand for his shoulder and then thought better of it. An undercover ex-SEAL on a mission might just accidentally break an arm for that.

Lankford called out instead.

"Mr. Foley—excuse me," he said, loud enough to be heard over whatever the SEAL was listening to on his ear buds, "MR. FOLEY?"

Foley turned, surprised but not startled or defensive. The SEAL looked Lankford up and down and then popped his ear buds out.

"Can I help you?" There was a hint of suspicion in his voice, and Lankford noted how Foley made a quick scan of the area around them.

Checking for enemies, assets, and escape routes. There's my little spook.

"Do I know you?" Foley asked, draping his ear buds over his shoulder.

"No," Lankford said. "I'm from the US embassy here in Beijing. Can we talk for a moment?"

Foley pursed his lips. "Sure," he said with a shrug. "Is this about what happened in Kizilsu? Did you speak with Commander Zhang? That asshole *still* has my passport, you know."

Lankford reeled at the mention of Kizilsu. He didn't expect to be caught off guard and tried to cover his surprise with a smile.

"Perhaps we could sit and talk for a moment? Somewhere quiet?"

Foley shrugged again and looked at his watch.

"Sure," he said. His eyes held Lankford's a moment, sizing him up. "What did you say this was about?"

"I didn't," Lankford said, smiling again. "Please, Mr. Foley. It will only take a moment."

"Okay."

Lankford put a guiding hand on the small of Foley's

back. Finding no weapon, he gestured to the right along Liangmaqiao Road.

In response, Foley widened his gait, separating himself a half pace while glancing over his shoulder. "Embassy Row is the other way, isn't it?"

"Yeah," Lankford answered, giving his best bureaucrat smile. "I thought we would just sit and chat away from the office, if that's okay? I know a little bakery just a half block down—they have the best bings. Have you had Chinese pastry during your time here? I'm positively addicted," Lankford said, relaxing into the role. He laughed and patted his waist.

Foley slowed until their shoulders were even but opened an arm's length gap between them.

"You said you're with the embassy, right? Forgive me, but do you have some identification?"

Lankford stopped and laughed with a good-natured eye roll.

"Of course. Gosh, I'm so sorry, Nick. Mind if I call you Nick?"

He pulled out a black case with a photo ID that identified him as part of the embassy staff and showed it to Foley. The SEAL studied the ID intently for a moment, glanced at Lankford's eyes for a long second, then handed it back.

"This *is* about the accident outside of Kashi, right? You guys gonna get my passport back for me?"

"Sure—of course," Lankford said. "We didn't know you lost it, actually."

"I didn't lose it," Foley snapped. "I told you it was taken by the head of the Chinese counterterrorism unit when I was in Kizilsu."

"Right," Lankford said. What the hell was Foley up

to? Why was he letting out so much information? Hiding in plain sight, maybe? "Commander Zhang, you said?"

Foley nodded. "From the Snow Leopards."

"The Snow Leopards? My God," Lankford said, trying to sound amazed. "Seems strange they would get called in to investigate an industrial accident."

"My thoughts exactly," Foley said, shaking his head.

"Why do you think Zhang is interested in you?"

"As I'm sure you know, I work with an NGO on a clean water project out west. But given my background, I'm not surprised I popped on Zhang's list. He thinks I'm involved."

Lankford stopped and turned to the SEAL, his face hardening. He looked into Foley's eyes the way he would a hostile interrogation subject.

"Were you?" he asked. He let the question hang a moment and then continued just before Foley could answer. "Were you or the organization you work for involved in a bioterror attack on a Uyghur mosque in Kizilsu, Nick?"

"Of course not," Foley said, his voice calm and even. "Were you or the organization you work for?"

Lankford held the SEAL's gaze, loving the dance, loving the bravado this kid had.

"As a general rule, the US Department of State tries not to get involved in such matters."

"True, but as a general rule, the Central Intelligence Agency does—Mr. Lankford, did you say it was?"

Okay, now that we've established we're on the same team, let's talk turkey, Lankford thought. *Like what the fuck is Foley doing operating in China without the courtesy of notifying him. China was his playground...*

"Here we are," Lankford said with a smirk, gesturing behind him at the Honglu Mill Bakery, set back from the road and just short of the Guang Ming Hotel.

"Your treat," Nick said.

"Of course," Lankford said. They had sniffed each other out and settled motives. Now they could get to the business of haggling for information—spook to spook.

Lankford bought a sticky, sweet bing for each of them and two cups of dark roast coffee. Then he joined Foley at a small, round table in the corner.

"So," Lankford began, sipping at his coffee. The Chinese made a helluva pastry, but they didn't know shit about coffee. "Now that we've made our introductions, how about we start with you telling me exactly what you guys are doing here in China?" Lankford knew he would get the information much more quickly if he pretended to know who "you guys" were.

"Or," Foley said, not touching his pastry. "We could start with why the CIA is trying to get information from a private American citizen doing charity work instead of directing the *actual* embassy staff to help me get my passport back."

"Oh, please," Lankford snorted. "Give me a break, Foley. You have the gift, to be sure, but come on. Whoever built you your NOC didn't do you any favors setting you up as charity worker digging ditches for the Uyghurs. Good Lord, man."

Lankford watched the SEAL closely and saw his eyes go somewhere else for moment before drilling into his forehead like two blue lasers.

"I don't know what you're talking about," Foley said, his face a blank slate.

"Look, Foley," Lankford said and leaned in. "We're

on the same team, bro. We have the same goals. I'm not one of those 'protect my rice bowl' guys. I want what you want. I want to keep Americans safe and American interests protected. I have no interest in getting in your way. If I can help—let me."

Foley said nothing and looked down at his untouched pastry.

Lankford went in for the kill.

"All right, look," he said. "I get it. You don't know me. You need to vet me through your task force before you'll talk. But even then you don't really know me, because we haven't logged time together. How can you trust a guy unless you've logged time in the field with him? But I've worked with team guys a lot—hell, we may even have met downrange somewhere. The point I'm trying to make is that I want to help you, Nick. I have resources at my disposal. I have information that could help keep your op moving forward."

Foley looked up, his eyes a little less hostile.

There it was.

"What kind of information?"

Lankford smiled and sipped his coffee.

"I have an agent working an asset—a high-level official in the Chinese CDC who was directly involved in the 'incident.' She has some information about the attack that you may be interested in—things that could help you."

"I didn't say it was an attack. Do you know something I don't know?"

Gotcha.

"I sure hope so. We're on the same team, right? We really should pool our resources here."

"How is your agent connected to your asset?" Foley asked.

Lankford hesitated. *What the hell was this all about?*

"What difference does that make?"

"It might make a big difference in vetting your information," Foley said coolly. "You're saying you have a spy in the CDC?" Then he folded his hands on the table and waited.

"I didn't say we had a mole or a spy. It's social," Lankford said. He needed to protect Jamie Lin above all. She was *his* team. "That's all I can tell you."

"Okay," Foley said. "I get it. What can you tell me about Kizilsu? You think it was a bioterror attack?"

Shit, Lankford thought. *He doesn't know anything.*

He looked at his watch. He needed to get Foley and his guys into the fold.

"How does your schedule look?" Lankford asked, stalling. "We should meet again."

"Why?"

"Because my agent is still digging. Still vetting. I'll have more details by tonight."

Foley looked unconvinced. He stood to leave.

"You need to talk to your people, Nick," Lankford said, pressing his back hard into his chair. "We need to work together here—pool our resources. If there is some bioweapon out there in play, then we don't have time to worry about territorial bullshit. I have a big machine that can help us figure this out."

"Yeah," Foley said. "I've worked with you guys before in Afghanistan. I know what you can do."

Lankford watched the SEAL's expression become clouded. A bad sign. Sometimes the goals of the military operators and the spooks came into conflict. When that happened, the end result was usually raw feelings and perpetual distrust. But Foley was a spy now. He was read into the big-picture briar patch called "strategic policy" and all the complications that generated. "Aim, point, shoot" was a myth. Foley got that, right?

"We can discuss next steps when we meet tonight," Lankford said, pressing.

Foley seemed to chuckle to himself. "One step at a time. Let me talk to my people first. How can I reach you?" he asked.

"I'll find you," Lankford said.

"Right," Foley said.

Then the SEAL was gone without a backward glance.

Lankford chewed the inside of his cheek. Something felt weird about this guy. He checked his phone—no messages or missed calls from Jamie Lin. He'd let her sleep a little while longer and then call her in. Maybe he should have her back off for a couple days. Just to be safe. Just until things came together with Foley and whoever the hell he was working for.

Lankford popped the last bite of pastry into his mouth and then his eyes wandered to Foley's untouched bing across the table. With an outstretched index finger, he dragged the little ceramic plate toward him.

"My treat," he mumbled, lifting the sticky bun to his lips. "Yeah, right."

TWENTY-ONE

DAZHONG WAS EXHAUSTED—physically, emotionally, and intellectually wiped.

When she got home from Jamie Lin's last night, it took her a while to calm down enough to fall asleep, and now it seemed like only seconds later that her alarm was buzzing in her ear. With less than two hours sleep, she dragged herself into work, where she promptly and thoroughly caffeinated herself. Thirty minutes before lunch, she got a call on her personal mobile phone. When she checked the caller ID and saw "NF," it took her several seconds to register who was calling. She had been so absorbed in the hyperfocused rhythm of work at the CDC that the events of last night had faded, like a childhood nightmare years removed. Her secret meeting with Nick Foley, the brutal attack in the alley, the sobbing confessions at Jamie Lin's apartment—those things had happened to some other girl, a foolish crusader trying to tackle a government conspiracy in thousand-dollar high heels and a mask of makeup. In the light of day, even superheroes feel the fool. And she was not a superhero. She was Dr. Dazhong Chen, Project Director for Research, Screening, and Testing of Emerging Diseases at the CDC, and she did not have time for petty interruptions. But Foley's voice was ripe with distress and urgency, so against her better judgment, she left work and took a taxi to Wangfujing Snack Street.

She scanned the crowd. A two-meter-tall American should be easy enough to spot, she thought, but when she felt a hand gently touch the small of her back, she startled.

"Thanks for coming, Dr. Chen," a familiar voice said to her left.

She whirled to face Nick Foley beside her. A switch flipped inside, and suddenly, she was back in the cloak-and-dagger world.

"I am taking a big risk meeting you here," she said. "If anyone sees us together—"

"I know," he said, nodding, "but I wouldn't have called you if it wasn't urgent. Walk with me."

They walked shoulder to shoulder until they came to the elaborate, multicolored archway at the entrance to Wangfujing Snack Street. The famous bustling outdoor food market was crowded with tourists and the local lunchtime rush. If there was one place to get lost in the crowd in Beijing, this was it. She could not remember the last time she'd been to this place—five years if she had to guess. She grinned as she watched Nick's eyes go wide as he surveyed the exotic fare being peddled by sidewalk food vendors. On "Snack Street" almost every creature imaginable was showcased for human consumption. The smell of deep-fat fryers, roasted meat, and boiled offal hung in the air. To their left, fried scorpions were showcased on wooden skewers next to rust-colored centipedes the size of her hand. On the right, giant water beetles, with shells as black as midnight, were displayed alongside jumbo-sized grasshoppers and deep-fried seahorses. She saw him smirk as he passed one peddler aggressively advertising a tray of sheep penis and ox testicles.

"Hungry, Nick?" she said, nudging him with her elbow. "My treat."

"No thanks," he said, patting his stomach. "I've already had lunch."

"At this place, I am only—how do you say it in America? A window shopper?" she said, grinning.

"Ah, c'mon. I thought for sure you were one of those girls who loves to eat giant scorpions."

"Is that why you called me here, Nick? To watch me eat fried bugs?"

His expression darkened. "No, I called you here so we could talk in private, face to face, about a conversation I had this morning that concerns you."

She cocked an eyebrow at him.

"A man I've never met—an American—approached me this morning at my hotel. He started asking questions about what I was doing in China. He accused me of working covertly for the American government and immediately started probing for details about what happened in Kizilsu. Then he started talking about you."

"Me?" she said, butterflies suddenly fluttering in her stomach. "Why me?"

"He didn't give me those details. The conversation was a bit one-sided, if you know what I mean."

"Who was this man? Who does he work for?"

"His name is Chet Lankford, and I'm ninety-nine percent sure he works for the CIA."

Dazhong felt the blood drain from her cheeks. "How does he know me?"

"He's been keeping tabs on you."

"He's been spying on me?"

"Not Lankford, one of his agents. Someone who—I suspect—has probably been running you for some time now. This agent made a report last night that got Lankford all spun up and twisted out of shape."

"Last night?"

"That's right. Did you meet with anyone else last night besides me? A woman perhaps, who you might have mentioned my name to?"

A wave of nausea washed over Dazhong, followed immediately by a red-hot surge of anger. "Jamie Lin!" she seethed.

"Who is Jamie Lin? A work colleague?"

"No, she's a friend," she said, choking on the words.

"Did you tell Jamie Lin about me, Dash?"

She heard the question, but Nick's voice was already fading into the background din of Wangfujing Snack Street as she set off through the crowd.

"Where are you going?" he asked, jogging to catch up.

"To see Jamie Lin, of course."

"No, no, no," he said. "That's not a good idea, Dash. Not a good idea at all."

"Why not?"

"Because that's not how you play the game. If you go in hot and confront her now, one of two things is going to happen: (a) she'll deny everything and try to placate you so she can keep you in play, or (b) she'll admit the truth and then use scare tactics to convince you that you're a traitor in the eyes of the Chinese government, so the only way you can protect yourself is to agree to become a double agent and work for the CIA. Either way, you've lost any element of control you had in the relationship and she owns you."

"Sounds like you know a lot about this," she said, glowering at him. "Maybe you're a spy for the CIA, Nick Foley."

"You and Commander Zhang vetted my background in that interrogation session, remember? I'm an ex–Navy SEAL, not a spook."

"I thought I knew Jamie Lin, but according to you, she's been lying to me from the beginning," she said, stopping and crossing her arms on her chest. "I don't know who to trust anymore."

"I understand how you must feel but—"

"Do you, Nick?" she interrupted. "Do you know how it feels to be betrayed by someone you trust? Do you know how it feels to be lied to by the CIA?"

"Yes," he said, looking her straight in the eyes. "I know *exactly* how that feels, and being lied to by the CIA is the reason I'm no longer a Navy SEAL."

She held his gaze, and deep in his pale-blue eyes, she saw that he was telling the truth.

Her mobile phone buzzed in her purse. She broke eye contact and fished it out. A text message from Jamie Lin flashed on the screen.

"What's it say?" Nick asked, staring down at the Chinese characters.

"It says, 'Need help. Can't breathe. Think I'm dying,'" she said, translating the message. "More lies—she probably knows I'm meeting with you."

"No, I don't think so," he said, grabbing her by the arm and tugging her in the direction of the towering Wangfujing Snack Street archway. "Not this time."

"Where are we going?" she said, jogging to keep up with him.

"To Jamie Lin's apartment, before it's too late."

TWENTY-TWO

"MAYBE SHE'S NOT HERE?" Dazhong said, turning to look at Nick.

He pressed his ear against the outside of the apartment door and listened. "Maybe," he said. "But I think she is."

"Then why won't she answer the door?"

"Maybe she can't answer the door," he said, worry lines suddenly tracing his forehead.

"What do we do?"

"You wouldn't happen to have a key for her place, would you?"

"Actually, I do," she said, fetching a silver key from her purse.

"Too bad," he said with a chuckle. "I used to be a professional door kicker."

She shot him a curious glance.

"It's a Navy SEAL thing, never mind," he said, extending his palm to her.

She handed him the key and stepped aside. She watched in silence as he took great care to unlock the door without making a sound.

"Stay behind me," he whispered as he turned the knob and took a cautious step across the threshold.

She nodded and followed him inside. The air in Jamie Lin's apartment felt stale and empty, as if all the qi had been drained out of it. Even the plants on the window ledge seemed to droop. The sunlight streaming through the windows was pale and clinical. The stillness was so detached and cold, she felt goose bumps stand up on her forearms and the nape of her neck. Dazhong had spent many hours in Jamie Lin's apartment, and never had it felt like this before.

"Something is wrong," she whispered.

"I feel it too," he said. "Call to her."

"Jamie Lin? It's Dazhong," she called. "Are you home?"

After a beat, she heard a groan, faint and barely audible.

"Did you hear that?" she asked Nick.

He nodded and led her in the direction of the noise. "Call out again," he said.

"Jamie Lin, it's Dazhong… Are you okay?"

Another groan—this time a terrible, terrible sound that reminded her of a dying animal.

"She's in the bathroom," Dazhong said, shouldering her way past Nick. The bathroom door was cracked open and the light was on inside. She glanced back over her shoulder at Nick for confirmation.

He nodded.

Tenuously, she pushed the door open.

Dazhong found Jamie Lin in the bathroom, writhing on the floor beside the toilet. Jamie Lin's back was to them, her mobile phone clutched in her right hand. Dazhong knelt and cautiously reached out her hand to touch Jamie Lin's shoulder. Before she made contact, Nick stopped her with a hand on her shoulder.

"Don't," he said, his voice stern and authoritative.

Upon hearing his voice, Jamie Lin whipped around to face them.

Dazhong lurched backward at the horror of Jamie Lin's face. "Oh no," she gasped. "Not again."

Suddenly, she was grateful to have Nick with her.

"This is the same disease presentation I saw in Kizilsu, with my friend Batur," he said.

All the anger and venom Dazhong had been harboring on account of Jamie Lin's betrayal immediately began to drain away, like dirty bathwater spiraling down the drain. Rushing in to fill the void were a strange mix of emotions—compassion, dread, and most of all, fear. There was no recovery from this scourge; the mortality rate for the victims at the Artux People's Hospital had been 100 percent. Judging from Jamie Lin's symptoms, the disease had advanced even more quickly. Her friend did not have much time left.

"Dazhong?" Jamie Lin wheezed.

"Yes, Jamie Lin. It's me, Dazhong. I'm here."

"Can't...see."

"I know, sweetie. That's because your eyes are swollen shut."

Jamie Lin coughed and sputtered and then let out a long, agonizing groan. "Am I dying?"

Dazhong looked at Nick. He gave her a solemn nod.

"Yes," she finally managed, the word catching in her throat.

Jamie Lin shuddered and Dazhong looked on in horror, powerless to do anything.

"I have...something...to tell...you," Jamie Lin whispered, each syllable a labor now.

"I know you work for the CIA," Dazhong said. "It's okay."

Jamie Lin began to sob, but the effect was more like a convulsion. "Our…friendship…was…real…forgive me."

Dazhong wanted to stroke her dying friend's hair, but she couldn't. Just being in the same room with Jamie Lin, breathing the same air without a respirator, put her and Nick at terrible risk.

"Who did this to you, Jamie Lin?" Nick interjected suddenly.

Dazhong jerked her head to look at him. Nick's forensic assumption hit her like a brick. *Of course*, she thought. *This infection is not random. This is murder. Jamie Lin was murdered because of me!*

"Didn't…see…his face," Jamie Lin labored, her voice barely audible now. "He…" She stopped and began to gurgle. Grayish-purple blood laden with mucous bubbled from her lips. As she wheezed for air, a death panic took hold of her and she began to thrash about on the floor, clawing at her neck.

Dazhong reached out and clutched Nick's arm. He looked at her and she at him, begging with her eyes. He shook his head.

Tears welled up in Dazhong's eyes, and it took every fiber of strength in her being not to try to help clear Jamie Lin's airway. As she stared at her friend through tear-filled eyes, she watched dark blood begin to drip, and then pour, from Jamie Lin's eyes and nose, followed by her ears. Her friend wretched, and a waterfall of dark, foul-smelling blood exploded from between her swollen lips. Then, a dark stain began to grow around Jamie Lin's waist, as she lost control of her bladder and bowels. Dazhong recoiled, gagging.

Jamie Lin stiffened, arched her back violently, and then went limp.

"We need to get her to a hospital, Nick," Dazhong said, shaking him until he looked at her.

"You know we can't do that," he said, grabbing her by both shoulders. "This was murder—you realize that, right?"

"But there's still time…"

"There's nothing we can do for her. Nothing anyone can do for her."

Dazhong shook herself free from his grasp and ran out of the bathroom. She needed to think. She needed air.

"Stop," he called, just as she reached the apartment door. "We need to do an autopsy."

"What?" she said, whirling to face him, tears welling in her eyes. "Are you insane?"

"I know it sounds crazy, but this might be our only opportunity to discover the truth about what the hell this thing is. You told me that Major Li confiscated all the patient data from Kizilsu, right? Well, now's your chance to perform a postmortem analysis of your own. Do you have access to laboratory and analysis equipment at the CDC?"

"Yes, of course."

"Okay, then we need to collect samples and run tests before they find out what happened here and confiscate the body."

He was right—of course, he was—but just the thought of performing an autopsy on Jamie Lin made her stomach turn.

"I don't know if I can."

"You don't know if you can do what? Perform the autopsy or analyze the samples?"

"Both."

An awkward pause hung in the air between them. Nick broke first and said, "What if I did it?"

"Did what?"

"The autopsy. If I do the autopsy, will you analyze samples?"

She wiped her eyes. Would he really do that?

"Well?" he said.

"We'd need to get her to an autopsy suite. I have some connections at local hospitals I could—"

"No," Nick said, cutting her off. "Too risky. It has to be here."

"You really are insane."

"Think about it, Dash. There is no way we'll get a body that looks like that into a hospital without drawing someone's attention. Our only play is to do this right here, right now. We collect tissue and blood samples and then get the hell outta here before the police show up and arrest us."

He's right, she thought. They only had one chance, and their window of opportunity was closing rapidly.

"We'll need PPE, surgical supplies, sample vials, and a cooler," she said, thinking aloud.

"Yeah," he said, nodding. "I'll stay here with the body while you make the supply run."

"Okay," she said, feeling a surge of adrenaline kicking in.

"One more thing," he said, stopping her at the door. "Keep your phone close. If things go bad here, or the police show up before you get back, I'll text nine-one-one to your mobile and that will be your signal not to come back. Got it?"

"Got it," she said. "But what about you, Nick Foley?"

"I guess you'll just have to find a way to get one very pissed-off ex–Navy SEAL out of Chinese prison," he said with a smirk.

TWENTY-THREE

Jamie Lin's apartment
1425 hours local

THE HOUR AND a half Nick waited in the apartment—
alone and trapped with the reek of death—was more
than ample time to question the stupidity of his offer. In
what universe was he qualified to perform an autopsy,
for God's sake? He'd performed some dissection during his Eighteen Delta training and clinicals, and he'd
assisted on two autopsies with the medical examiner,
but that was the extent of his training. The thought of
autopsying Jamie Lin made him sick.

But what other choice did he have?

Despite his initial misgivings, he now believed he
could trust Dash. During the past twelve hours, she
had assumed as much—if not more—risk than he had
in this quest for answers by putting her personal safety
and her career on the line. And she certainly couldn't
autopsy her best friend alone. Clearly, she needed his
help as much as he needed hers. He had already risked
his life for her once in the past twenty-four hours; why
stop now?

Because you hardly know this woman. Because if
you get caught helping her, it's your dumb ass that is
going to end up in a Chinese prison, not hers. Because
you do not work for the CIA, have not seen her case

*file, and the only information you know is what she's
told you. And because she's married.*

He hated arguing with himself.

He tried to clear his head and concentrate on the
task. What they were about to do was unthinkable.
He couldn't even imagine the horror Dash must be
feeling—watching her best friend die in front of her
and then preparing to conduct the postmortem autopsy.
Not to mention the feelings of betrayal and anger she
was undoubtedly trying to work through after learning
Jamie Lin was a CIA agent. When she walked through
that door, he fully expected her to be an emotional train
wreck, which meant that he would—

His phone vibrated in his back pocket.

He pulled it out and read the text from Dash:

Coming up

Nick tapped in his reply:

Ready here

The woman who walked through the door was *not*
a train wreck. Her jaw was set and determined, her
eyes bright with a fire. Dash was in the zone. All business. Not a hint of the emotionally haggard girl with
tear-streaked cheeks who'd left ninety minutes earlier.
He hustled to the door to unburden her of the stack of
plastic-wrapped supplies that reached all the way up
to her chin. Then he helped her unsling the oversized,
duffle-style gym bag whose strap was biting into the
base of her neck. To his surprise, she hugged him. It
was a real hug—full of gratitude, trust, and earnest in-

tent. The feel of her body against his was the solidarity he needed to push away the creeping thoughts that she might betray him.

She let go first.

"Thank you, Nick," she said. "I would be lost without you today."

"You're welcome." Unsure what else to say, he focused his gaze on the last item hanging on her shoulder: a large, lunch-box-sized cooler bag.

Dash opened the gym bag and pulled out two sets of coveralls and handed one to Nick. She walked across the room, hesitated at the doorway, and glanced back over her shoulder, her face flushed.

"I'll turn my back and promise not to peek," he said.

She lowered her eyes. "Thank you, Nick. You are a gentleman."

If she only knew how many times he'd undressed her in his head, she'd take that comment back.

He turned his back as promised but caught her reflection in a starburst mirror on the wall beside the TV just in time to see her bent over and stepping out of her pants. The black thong she wore framed her nearly perfect...

He squeezed his eyes shut and waited.

"Thank you, Nick. I am finished," she said a moment later.

He turned as she was slipping on foot booties.

"Your turn," she said with a little smile, and she turned her back.

Obediently, he stripped to his underwear and pulled on his own suit. At least the suit was bigger than the child-size coveralls they had given him at the Artux hospital a few days earlier. The booties, however, were another story, and they required him to curl his toes just to pull them on.

"Okay," he said, turning to her. "Gloves?"

She handed him a pair of long, yellow rubber gloves, along with a purple respirator, mask, and goggles. He pulled up his hood, cinched it tight under his chin, and then donned the mask, goggles, and gloves. She did the same, and when they had finished dressing out, they stared at each other like two bug-eyed aliens in space suits.

He smiled behind his mask and gave her a thumbs-up.

"I will walk you through what to do and what tissues I need," she said, her voice muted and breathy through the respirator. "I will try to help you, but if I cannot, you can describe for me what you see, and I may add some additional tissue requests. Are you sure you are okay to do this?"

Nick nodded and shifted uncomfortably, already roasting inside the suit. He felt a trickle of sweat rolling down the small of his back, and another behind his left knee snaking down into his left bootie. On the plus side, the pungent stink of rubber from his mask completely replaced the reek of dead tissue, blood, and excrement he had fought to stomach over the last hour.

"Yes, I'm okay," he said. "I only hope I can do it right."

Of course, I would rather be on an assault team kicking doors right now with an M4 carbine in my hands.

"You will do fine," she said. "We do not need very much precision. We just need some chunks of tissue from a few places and that will be all. I will tell you everything to do."

She handed Nick a surprisingly heavy, rectangular package wrapped in plastic. He felt the metal box inside and understood—it was a surgical instrument tray. He carried it ahead of himself like some sort of burnt offering to Hades and headed down the short hall. At the bathroom door, Dash touched his shoulder. He turned and saw her wide eyes though her fogged goggles.

"May I wait here a moment while you set up?"

"Of course," he said. "If you can tell me what to do from the hall, you won't have to come in at all."

She smiled at him with her eyes.

Nick took a deep breath and then stepped around the corner of the door and into the bathroom.

It was tight quarters. He leaned back against the wall beside the pedestal sink in a low squat. Then, he removed the plastic wrapper encasing the surgical instrument box and unfolded the blue paper draping. He spread out the paper and then set the tray down, unlocked the simple latches, and took off the top. He made a conscious effort to focus on the instruments and not yet look at the swollen corpse lying on the tile floor only a foot away.

"Are you ready?" Dash called from the hallway.

Nick swallowed hard to keep his stomach contents down where they belonged.

"Almost," he called back.

The box held rows of large clamps, small and large scissors, a giant silver pair of what looked to be garden shears—God only knew what the hell he would do with those—and then a handheld circular saw with a blade perhaps the size of a drink coaster. There were two green-handled scalpels with opaque plastic covers over the blades. Nick gritted his teeth and forced his gaze on Jamie Lin.

The dead girl looked almost nothing like the gray, bloated thing he had watched die ninety minutes ago. The thing before him barely resembled a person—which could make it easier...or not. There was a puddle of thick, congealed, black blood in a huge oval around the body, and the crotch of her sweat pants were stained black and brown up to her waist. Reflexively, he immediately began tactical breathing to calm his nerves and steady the tremor in his hands. Unfortunately, the exercise did precious little for his rising nausea. He took one more long, rasping breath and called out to Dash: "Okay. What first?"

"There is a small and large scalpel in the kit," she said, and Nick marveled at how her voice sounded so strong and clinical now. "Take the ten-blade—the larger-bladed scalpel—and you will need to make an incision in her abdomen."

Awesome, he thought, rolling his eyes. *Let's just dive right in.*

"Okay. First I need to roll her."

"Do you need my help?" she called, her tone less convincing than her words.

"No," he grunted, shuffling toward the body in a squat. "I got this."

He grabbed the dead girl's shoulders and his fingers sunk into the flesh like Jell-O. The tissue was way softer and squishier under his rubber-gloved hands than he expected. This felt like the opposite of rigor mortis, but his limited interaction with cadavers gave him little frame of reference for expectations. The bloated body was heavier than he expected, and he grunted as he rolled the swollen corpse to the left. It rolled onto its back, and a puffy, gray hand thunked against the toilet bowl. The face now looked directly up at him—or would have, if the eyelids had not swollen to the size of tennis balls. Nick touched the chin and pushed until the dead face looked away, at the wall beneath the sink. He took one of the blue towels from the surgical kit and draped it over the head and face, which helped settle his nerves. He shuffled down toward the feet and set his metal tray down beside him. Then he fished out the larger of the two scalpels and pulled the plastic guard off the blade with a shaking hand.

"Okay," he said. "I have the knife."

He pulled Jamie Lin's shirt up to expose a bloated abdomen.

"Make a deep cut from just beneath the breastbone all the way down past the navel—you know, the belly button."

"Yes," he said. "I know, the belly button." He grinned tightly. He felt for the breastbone, blinked hard once, and then plunged the knife in deep. The puncture hissed, releasing trapped gas, and he choked back a reflux of vomit.

"Disgusting," he muttered, and he dragged the blade down toward the dead girl's waist.

The motion was easier than he expected, and in one long pull, the abdomen gaped open. He lost his balance at the end of the cut, and his right hand plunged into the warm goo. He jerked his hand out and several loops of gray intestines came from the cavity of dark liquid. The guts squirmed over his arm and spilled onto the floor with a wet splat.

He gagged hard.

"Did you do it?"

"Yes," he called back. "Just a minute, please."

While I throw up inside my suit.

He scooted back a few inches, but the guts followed him like a wriggling snake and then rested against the bootie on his right foot. He closed his eyes and commenced another round of four-count breathing.

It's not a person, he told himself. *It's a thing... It's not a person.*

"Are you okay in there, Nick?" Dash called.

"I'm fine. Almost ready."

Just go clinical, dude. Like Dash did. Hardcore clinical.

He exhaled, opened his eyes, and peered into the belly cavity.

What he saw was not right. The human abdominal cavity was tightly packed, with a tidy arrangement of clearly discernable organs. But Jamie Lin's insides looked like someone had dumped a bunch of organs into a barrel of motor oil. Everything seemed to just slosh around inside the dark liquid that spilled out and dripped down onto the tile floor.

"I don't know, Dash. This doesn't look right."

"What do you mean?" she called.

"The blood, for starters—looks like motor oil," he said. "And the organs are just sorta floating around in it."

"I don't understand. Are you okay to continue, Nick?"

"Yes. Never mind. What tissues do you need?"

"I need a piece of liver, intestines, kidneys, and the larger blood vessel in back—the aorta. Wait a moment, please. I need to see."

Dash came in from the hall and knelt beside him,

leaning in for a good look. He looked at her eyes behind the fogged goggles and saw fascination instead
of fear or disgust.

"This is most interesting," she said, and she reached
over, taking the scalpel from him without asking. She
extended the lower part of the incision another inch or
two. "It is most strange indeed. Things are not what
they should be."

She plunged her hand in and felt around, no disgust
at all in her eyes or voice, while Nick struggled to keep
his stomach contents where they belonged. It seemed
they both had skills they brought to the table, and this
arena was clearly hers.

"We need some liver first," she announced, but he
didn't think she was talking to him anymore.

Nick hesitated. In the top right side of the gaping
hole, he saw what he thought was liver, bobbing free
and unattached in the oily goo. He watched as Dash
grasped the friable gray tissue. It crumbled under her
forceps and then floated loose in the motor oil. He swallowed hard.

"Oh my God," she breathed.

Nick looked up at her. "Have you ever seen anything
like this before?"

The rubber mask with its dual purple discs shook
comically back and forth.

"Never," Dash said in a calm, clinical voice he had
not heard before. She was all doctor now.

She reached her hand into the dark pool and then,
with a sucking sound that made Nick's stomach turn,
pulled out a kidney. The organ lay flaccid in her hand.

"The kidney was not connected," she said. "It should
be connected." With her fingers, she pulled a chunk,

like wet, raw hamburger, from the kidney. "It is as if all the connective tissue in the body is gone," she mumbled, rolling the flesh around in her fingertips.

He reached around behind her and used his left hand to grab a small, plastic Tupperware container. He lifted it, the top already off, and she dropped the soggy tissue into the shallow container. He grabbed two more containers and slid them into the bathroom.

She took a large sample of liver and placed it in a separate container.

"We will take a piece of pancreas as well and then take some of the liquid, I think." Her voice was calm and steady, as if they were simply lab partners in a freshman biology class. The trauma of her friend's death had been buried under the fascination for whatever biological anomaly had dissolved Jamie Lin from the inside out.

Moments later, they had pancreas and abdominal fluid added to the neat row of shallow Tupperware containers. Nick realized he was more of an observer than a participant now, as Dash reached into the metal box and fished out the small, handheld saw by its gleaming handle. It appeared to be battery operated, because she pushed a button and the silver disk of the blade spun with a loud, high-pitched squeal.

"What's that for?" Nick asked.

"Brain tissue," she said.

The sudden ring of a mobile phone nearly caused Nick to lose control of his bowels.

"Is that you?" he asked.

"No," Dash said, turning to pull the blue cover off of the corpse's head.

"I'll check it," Nick said, and feeling the coward, he

scurried from the room. The sound of the saw and then, a second later, the sound of it biting into wet flesh and changing pitch as it hit the hard skull brought his stomach into the back of his throat.

On the fourth ring, he found Jamie Lin's phone on the floor in the kitchen. It rang once more and then stopped, and the green "missed call" icon appeared with the initials "CL" beside it.

CL... Chet Lankford. Has to be. He's her boss.

The screen lit up again, and he read the text that appeared.

Everything okay? Lots to discuss. You coming in or want me to swing by your place? I could be there in ten. Text me back—CL

"Shit," he breathed and hollered over his shoulder. "Dash, we gotta go."

He sped down the hall to help her clean up.

"What's wrong?" Dash asked, looking up from her ghoulish task.

"We gotta go, Dash. I think we're about to have company."

"Who?" she asked, dropping a glob of gray tissue into the final Tupperware container.

"The CIA," Nick said, snapping lids on containers furiously.

"What?" Dash sprang up from beside the now horribly mutilated corpse. They both washed their gloved hands in the bathroom sink and then moved into the hall to pack the containers.

He grabbed a permanent marker to label them.

"What are you doing?" she asked.

"Labeling them," he said.

"No labels," she scolded. "I have to be very careful, Nick."

"Okay, sorry."

She sprayed each container with aerosol disinfectant, stacked them inside the lunch box among cold packs, and then zippered the top closed.

"Hurry, Dash," he urged, reaching to remove his goggles.

"Wait, we have to decontaminate," she said, her voice frantic.

"How?"

"With this," she said and blasted him head to toe with a fog of hospital disinfectant. She tossed him the spray bottle. "Now me."

Nick returned the favor, making sure to cover every square inch of her body.

"We gotta go, Dash," he said, ripping off his mask and goggles. "Right now."

"Okay, okay," she said, stripping down to her underwear right in front of him. Nick did the same, both of them too stressed to waste time gawking. Moments later, they were dressed, out of breath, and headed for the door.

Dash stopped and looked back.

"What about the gear and the PPE?" she asked.

"No time," he said and grabbed her by the hand.

"But they can be analyzed. They will find our DNA," she argued.

"Maybe, but right now, we have to go. We'll deal with the consequences later."

She looked over her shoulder and then into his eyes.

"You are right, Nick," she said simply. "We'll work it out later."

He tugged her by the hand out of the apartment. They sprinted down the stairs and used the fire escape door to exit at the back of the building. Five minutes later, they were walking south on Shanglong Xili East Street. As they walked, he felt eyes on his back—watching, judging, following. He tried to resist the urge to look back over his shoulder but failed. No Chet Lankford. No Snow Leopard commandos, no Beijing police.

"Are we being followed?" Dash asked, keeping her gaze straight ahead.

"No."

They each exhaled a long, slow breath in unison, which made them both smile.

He slowed their pace, and after two more blocks, he stopped at the corner to hail her a taxi.

"How much time do you need for the analysis?"

"To do a thorough investigation will take days," she said. "Maybe weeks."

"We don't have that kind of time," he said. "How long to just get an idea what the hell we're dealing with? Enough to prove that things are not as your government and the CIA want us to believe?"

She shrugged.

"Four hours perhaps."

Nick looked at his watch.

"Okay. Meet me at nine thirty," he said. "You choose the location."

"There is a small shop known as Emily's Coffee," she said. "It is on Jinghua Street, not far from here. Can you find it?"

"Yes."

"Okay, at nine thirty then."

She slid into the cab with her large lunch box.

"Please text if you're running late," he told her.

"I will," she said, patting him on the hand through the open window. "I promise."

He watched her through the back window as the taxi sped away. Just before disappearing from view, he saw her turn and look back at him.

She waved.

He waved.

And for the second time that day, he wondered if he would ever see her again.

TWENTY-FOUR

Chinese Centers for Disease Control and Prevention
1543 hours local

DAZHONG'S LEFT EYELID twitched furiously as she approached the employee security checkpoint. She resisted the urge to jam a knuckle into her eye socket and instead smiled furtively at the security attendant on duty. She did not recognize this guard. That, coupled with his young face, meant he was probably new. By her observation, new guards tried to conceal their inexperience behind a maniacal adherence to protocol. She watched his gaze lock onto the lunch cooler she carried in her left hand. A bead of cold sweat trickled down her right armpit. The cooler contained six plastic containers—Tupperware, Nick Foley had reminded her—with snap-tight plastic lids. Two of the six containers held actual food, the other four contained pieces of Jamie Lin.

"Good afternoon," she said to the guard, swiping her ID badge through the card reader.

The guard checked the computer monitor and then made brief eye contact with her. "Good afternoon, Dr. Chen." Then, pointing at the lunch bag, he said, "What do you have there?"

"Just my lunch," she replied.

He checked his wristwatch. "A little late for lunch."

"I know," she laughed. "I worked through lunch, and now I'm starving."

"Can you open it for me please?"

"Of course."

She set the little cooler on the counter in front of him, unzipped the top flap, and tilted it toward him. "See, just lunch," she said and, after a beat, began to zip it closed.

"Stop," he said. "Please remove all the contents, one at a time."

She squinted her disapproval at this instruction and said, "Are you serious?"

"Yes, Dr. Chen, I'm quite serious."

Clenching her jaw, she removed the first container and handed it to him.

"Noodles and sprouts," she said.

He tilted the container to look through the glass side. Satisfied, he set it down.

"Next."

She handed him the second container.

"Roasted chicken."

"Okay, next."

She hesitated an instant, before selecting the container with fifty grams of Jamie Lin's liver. "Beef liver," she said.

With a grunt, he repeated the same process of tilt and inspect.

"Next."

"Kidney."

"You like organ meat?"

"Oh yes," she said. "Very strong healing properties."

"My mother says the same thing, but I don't care. I don't like it."

"Jellyfish," she said and handed him the next container with twenty grams of Jamie Lin's pancreas and abdominal fluid.

This time, he took his time surveying the container. "You eat this?" he asked, crinkling his nose at her.

"Oh yes," she said. "Jellyfish is considered a delicacy. What? You don't like seafood?"

He shook his head. "No, I hate it. Especially shellfish. Oysters make me sick."

"That's too bad," she said, her mind racing to think of her final menu item. With her new insight into the guard's culinary preferences, she handed him the final container and said, "Sea cucumber."

He took the container and held it up to the light. While scrutinizing Jamie Lin's brain tissue, he said, "This doesn't look like a sea cucumber to me."

"Well, that's what's inside," she said, her cheeks flushing.

"You must be really hungry," he said, smirking at her. He set the container on the counter and repositioned his thumbs to open the lid. "I've got to see this."

"No," she blurted, stopping him.

"Excuse me?"

"I wouldn't do that if I were you," she said.

"Why not?"

"The smell is very strong. Just like oysters."

"Oh," he said, thrusting the offensive container back at her. "In that case, take it."

Her eyelid twitch went into overdrive as she repacked the cooler.

"Are you okay, Dr. Chen?" he asked, gesturing to her left eye. "I have never seen someone's eye twitch like that."

"Too much caffeine and too little sleep," she chuckled. "It will stop after I eat something. I should not have skipped lunch."

"Hmm," he grunted with a shrug. "Have a nice day, Dr. Chen."

"Thank you."

She managed to keep her composure all the way to her office, but the moment she shut the door, a wave of light-headedness forced her to the floor. Sitting with her head between her knees, Dazhong squeezed her eyes shut and fought hyperventilation as images of Jamie Lin—flayed open in autopsy on the bathroom floor—flooded her mind. The grisly truth of what she had done hit her like a semitruck.

Be brave and be strong and everything will be okay.

When she finally felt her self-control returning, she opened her eyes. Slowly, she got to her feet and took a deep, cleansing breath. Both the light-headedness and the twitch were gone, and she felt ready to push on. Her first priority was to reserve microscope time. To reduce the risk of interference by a curious colleague, she would wait to view the samples until after the general staff had gone home for the day. That would just barely give her time to prepare the slides anyway. She logged onto the network to check microscope availability. Everything was booked until eighteen hundred hours. She reserved two hours on the CDC's recently acquired microsphere nanoscope—a novel optical microscope that permitted wet sample viewing at a magnification down to fifty nanometers.

While not possessing the extreme magnification of a scanning electron microscope, or SEM, the microsphere nanoscope possessed one critical advantage—

its user could view wet slides at ambient temperature and pressure. Whereas SEM required chemical fixation or cryo-vacuum preservation of the subject tissue, the nanoscope could be used to observe living tissue. Equally important, the nanoscope could view viruses, bacteria, and cellular structures previously not visible at the two-hundred-nanometer threshold of traditional light microscopes. In Dazhong's mind, being able to see below the two-hundred-nanometer threshold would be critical to determining the nature of the pathogen that killed Jamie Lin. If she was really lucky, she might even catch the pathogen interacting with a host cell. The trick now was simply finding a way to do her work without getting caught.

Protocol dictated that any work involving the manipulation and handling of an organism as dangerous as this should be carried out in a biosafety level-four laboratory. However, the Chinese CDC headquarters did not have a BSL-4 laboratory. The only civilian BSL-4 laboratory in China was located a thousand kilometers away at the Wuhan Institute of Virology in Hubei province. The CDC did have several BSL-3 laboratories, so that would have to suffice. Besides, she and Nick had just performed an autopsy on Jamie Lin on a bathroom floor using safety controls barely up to BSL-1 standards, so having access to a BSL-3 cabinet with a containment hood suddenly felt indulgent.

Maybe it was a fool's hope, but her experience in Kizilsu made her think this pathogen did not actually qualify as a BSL-4 agent. Yes, it was lethal, and yes, there was no cure or vaccine for it, but she suspected that the transmission mode for this particular organism was neither airborne nor direct contact. In Kizilsu, she'd found no evidence that the infected patients functioned as vectors. Granted, Major Li had confiscated all the lab data and patient records shortly after his arrival, but to her knowledge, there had not been a single case of the disease being transmitted person to person. Nick Foley was living proof of this. He had been in prolonged direct contact with a terminal victim and managed to avoid infection. Her present transmission hypothesis was based on Nick's insightful comment during interrogation—the scourge of Kizilsu behaved more like a chemical toxin than a pathogen.

She smirked.

She wouldn't be surprised if Major Li had gotten his bogus cover story idea of an "industrial accident" from her interrogation notes. She looked down and noticed her clenched fists. Just thinking about Major Li sent her blood pressure soaring.

None of that matters now, she told herself. *Major Li is a thousand kilometers away, and I have the tissue samples and equipment necessary to finally learn the truth. All I need now is to be left alone to work.*

But being left alone proved more difficult than she imagined. Everywhere she went in the building, someone wanted to talk to her. Apparently, CDC division directors can't fly below the radar at headquarters, no matter how hard they try. Covertly transferring sample material from her lunch box containers to actual sample vials was an absolute nightmare, taking her two hours and three aborted attempts. By the time she was actually able to prep and view the first slide, it was after 7:30 pm.

The nanoscope was physically located behind a glass partition under a BSL-3 containment hood. Unlike a

traditional tabletop light microscope with an eyepiece
and manual focus adjustment knobs, this microscope
was equipped with state-of-the-art automation and controls, including a slide caddy and mobile microscope
head. The actual lens image was digitally encoded and
displayed on a 4K HD monitor with joystick-style pan
and zoom controls, making it simple to change view-
finder position and magnification. She had never used
this microscope before, but once she figured out how
to load the sample, using the controls was as intuitive
as using an iPad for the first time.

Dazhong played for a moment with the joystick until
she got the feel for the gentle motions required. She cen-
tered on the grayish-brown, hazy blob and then raised
an eyebrow as the system autofocused for her. Very impressive. Once the most superficial layer was in focus,
she was able to control the depth of focus with the con-
troller and scan across the specimen like a spaceship
skimming across the surface of a strange planet.

It was strange indeed, since the specimen looked
nothing like the normal histology slides of human liver.
Dazhong looked away and checked again that she had
loaded the correct sample.

She had sectioned the sample thinly, but a gross
specimen—unpreserved and unstained—should still
retain the normal architecture of liver tissue. However, this specimen held no organization whatsoever.
It looked like a disorganized lump of tissue—nothing
like the elegant architecture of the liver. A normal liver
sample would present layers of parenchyma, neatly organized and divided into blocklike regions, surrounded
and separated by monotonous lines of septae and bands
of connective tissue to support the blood vessels and

the biliary structure meant to collect and transport the products of liver metabolism. There was no such structure here.

The sheets of connective tissue should have organized the liver tissue into thousands and thousands of lobules—hexagonal structural units of the liver with portal triads at the vertices and then a central vein. This tissue had no resemblance at all to the familiar and predictable pattern of a healthy liver.

"Damn," she sighed, but she decided to keep looking at the sample anyway.

Fully adjusted now to the new machine, she tapped the zoom button twice. She watched the magnification flash twice and then the autofocus began to sharpen the new, greatly magnified image. When the image became clear, she raised both her eyebrows and then wrinkled them in confusion.

In the center image, she saw the very distinctive, polygon-shaped image of a mature, adult hepatocyte—a liver cell. Around it were scores of other, also easily recognizable hepatocytes, but they were clumped in piles of totally disorganized cells. It was as if a city had been destroyed, but the buildings were left intact, lying in a jumbled heap on top of one another. The liver cells were there—as were the blood vessels and the bile ductules—but they were no longer held together.

"Ah…" she said softly. "I was right."

Her earlier supposition had been correct. It was as if all the connective tissue—the sheets and bands of fibrous tissue that provide structure throughout the body, forming everything from tendons, to the basement membrane beneath tissues, to the tissue holding liver cells together—had somehow been dissolved away.

She increased the magnification again with the simple click of a button and let the machine scan slowly over the clumps of jumbled cells. She watched intently, her finger poised to stop the image once an organism—whatever the hell organism could have resulted in such chaos—came into view.

But there was nothing—just piles of useless, disorganized cells. She saw not one bacterium or even any macrophages. Either would be easily seen at this magnification, as they were in the same range as the hepatocytes—of roughly twenty to thirty micrometers. There was some much smaller, scattered, black debris—perhaps in the five micrometer range or less—but she assumed that was just debris from their incredibly crude tissue collection.

Using the microscope's menu controls, she selected the next sample for viewing. Barely audible in the background, electric motors hummed and precision gears whirred as the automated slide caddy indexed to the second tissue sample. A few seconds later, a chime sounded, indicating the slide was in position. She took the joystick controls in hand. With a twist of her right wrist, the screen image blurred as she dove deep into the hidden universe of the microscope—life and death at fifty- nanometer resolution.

The brain tissue came into focus and then shifted out of focus as something zoomed across the image from left to right, disturbing the computer's depth perception a moment. Dazhong blinked and rubbed her eyes. Probably a floater, she thought, or some contaminated debris floating in the tissue prep. She had seen that thousands of times. The computer scanned in and out a moment and then the picture became crisp and clear. In the center of the screen, she saw the triangular-shaped gray-matter neuronal cells, and to the right was a clump of unidentifiable tissue. Again, she saw a flash of movement just to the right of her field of view. She tapped the joystick and scanned a fraction to the right.

In the center of the clump of cellular debris was something out of a science-fiction movie—a black orb with spiderlike appendages coated in something that appeared more biologic. The two smaller legs were feeding tissue into the center of the orb, where bits of debris spread outward from the microscopic machine. Whatever the machine was, it was destroying everything in its path. Wait. No, not everything. The neuronal cells were intact, untouched and scattered among chunks of what looked like blood vessel wall. What she was witnessing was the targeted destruction of human connective tissue.

Dazhong sat back on her stool and shook her head in disbelief. If she had not seen it with her own eyes, she would not have thought it possible—a fully automated, cell-sized nanobot operating inside the human body capable of seeking specific tissue types for destruction. Someone had invented a synthetic macrophage! *Absolutely incredible*. The clinician in her thought immediately of the therapeutic applications. The possibilities were limitless: precision treatment of cancer, removal of arterial plaque, dissolving of blood clots, destruction of resilient parasitic organisms such as malarial Plasmodium and Naegleria fowleri amoeba, or even the hunting down and destruction of cells infected with viruses before the commandeered cell could churn out more viral copies. But in Jamie Lin's case, the nanobot macrophage had not been programmed to do any

of those things. It had been programmed to seek and
destroy healthy connective tissue cells, analogous to
how native viruses and bacteria attack the body. Just
like with the victims in Kizilsu, Jamie Lin's nanobot
infection had spread quickly—very quickly—which
indicated that the nanobot macrophages were self-replicating. For micromachines operating at the scale of
fifty micrometers to consume hundreds of millions of
connective tissue cells in less than eight hours, an ex-
ponential replication rate had to be at work.

How many of these things were inside Jamie Lin?
Millions? Billions?

An epiphany hit her like a slap to the face. She
jumped off her roller stool, tripped over one of the castors, and stumbled backward, arms windmilling wildly.
She knocked a clipboard and a stack of folders off the
lab bench behind her, sending paper flying everywhere,
before catching her balance against the edge of the table.

"Oh, shit. I need to tell Nick," she mumbled in English, surprising herself. "He won't believe this."

Her mind started racing in a hundred directions all
at once. This technology was not a therapeutic breakthrough gone awry; it was a biological weapon. No, not
a biological weapon—it was an entirely new class of
weapon, unlike anything conceived before. A precision
weapon that the human body had no biological defense
against. This explained why the preliminary bloodwork
from all the victims in Kizilsu presented like it did. How
can the immune system identify and categorize a threat
as a threat if the pathogen is not made of proteins and
lipids? During a nanobot infection, the body's entire
immune response would be limited to an innate activity by macrophages and fibroblasts—which would fail,

of course, because *biological* macrophages cannot digest nanobots via phagocytosis. No phagocytosis, then no antigen presentation. No antigen presentation, then no T-cell activation. No T-cell activation, then no directed B-cell activation. No B-cell activation, then no antibody production.

The adaptive immune response never gets triggered, she realized, bracing her palms against the lab table. *That's why I couldn't find any trace of infection in the blood samples I took in Kizilsu, before Major Li intervened.*

The sudden and disturbing sensation of millions of tiny insect feet crawling over her skin sent a shiver through her entire body.

This must be a Regiment 54423 project. That's why Major Li took control of the task force and confiscated all the records. That's why he seized the cadavers. He knew what this was. He knew what I would be looking for, and he knew that when I didn't find anything, I would raise questions.

Her heart rate skyrocketed. She whirled around, checking to see if anyone was watching her. She stared out the narrow glass pane in the microscope lab door and into the hallway outside. No face in the window. No shuffle of footsteps.

She glanced at the mess on the floor.

I have to clean this up.

Her gaze shifted to the nanoscope behind the glass partition.

I have to destroy the samples.

The room was getting hot; the air was turning thick and heavy. She felt herself starting to hyperventilate.

I have to get out of here.

Her mobile phone buzzed in her pocket.

That was all it took to send her flying—out the door and down the corridor. She knew she shouldn't be running. Running made her look guilty, or crazy, or both, but she wasn't in control anymore. Fear was driving this train. She rounded the corner to the next hallway and gasped. Three men abreast, armed and dressed in uniform, were heading straight toward her. She locked eyes with the soldier in the middle and her legs went to jelly.

Major Li had come for her.

TWENTY-FIVE

1830 hours local

POLAKOV LINGERED IN the stairwell linking the parking garage to the finely appointed marble lobby of Prizrak's apartment building. He surveyed the lobby through the small square window in the steel fire door. The charade was over. He no longer needed to protect the identity of his asset. The Chinese entrepreneur had been working for him for years, feeding intelligence to the Russians. At first it had been for money, but over the years, it had become something more. Perhaps he should have controlled his asset differently, but if he had, then perhaps they would never have had the opportunity to obtain this amazing weapon. Very soon the weapon would be in his control and the pompous, erratic Prizrak would be dead, a thought that made Polakov smile.

The building did not have a doorman or lobby attendant as was typical in New York or London. The Chinese elite liked to keep their privilege a bit more concealed, Polakov surmised. Still, before he stepped out, he wanted to make sure the lobby was deserted. He had disabled the security cameras and inserted a blind loop into the DVR that recorded the feeds and then broadcast them over the web to the security company for remote monitoring. If someone was actually paying attention and recognized the loop, by the time a security patrol arrived, he would be long gone. Of course, it was possible that the apartment had separate government surveillance in place, but that footage would only be useful for "event reconstruction," which would take place days, or even weeks, after Prizrak's disappearance was confirmed. In that scenario, the Ministry of State Security would eventually identify him, but that was of no concern. After tonight, he would never set foot in China again. In any case, he planned to leave with his agent, not hurt him here. He would kill Prizrak once the technology had been transferred. He smiled, imagining the look of anguished astonishment on Prizrak's face as he inserted a blade into the side of the man's neck while chatting over a glass of wine.

His mobile phone vibrated in his pocket once, twice, and then stopped. The all-clear signal from his spotter. Polakov had kept Prizrak under surveillance since their meeting at the coffee house, tracking all the scientist's movements during the day. The plan was to surprise the man at home and tell him the timetable had been accelerated and that they were leaving immediately for a private airport outside Beijing. He wanted to catch Prizrak early, alone, and supersede any opportunity for last minute "cold feet."

Everything was in place.

The GRU agent opened the door and moved quickly across the lobby, past the ornate elevator to the stairs. He took the stairs two at a time at first but tired quickly—his fifty-eight-year-old heart and worn-out knees reminding him he was not the young KGB agent he liked to picture himself as. By the time he reached the landing at the thirteenth floor, he was panting and sweating profusely. Perhaps he should have maintained better fitness these last ten years. He took a moment to collect himself before walking to the apartment door.

The apartment door was cracked open, and the security keypad above the doorknob was blinking red. Not a good sign. He pulled his semiautomatic Radom P-64 pistol from the holster concealed beneath his jacket.

I know he's here. If he had left the building, the spotter would have seen him…but that doesn't mean someone else could not have arrived before us.

Leading with his pistol, Polakov slipped inside the darkened apartment. He cleared the small foyer for threats before easing the front door shut. Then he paused, letting his eyes adjust to the dark while he listened for movement. The apartment was as quiet as a vault. He debated his next move: sweep the apartment or call out to his agent? Both actions were risky.

If he was lucky, Prizrak had absent-mindedly left the door open and had fallen asleep in the bedroom, waiting for his call. Polakov would love the look on the arrogant scientist's face when he woke to find his handler standing at the foot of his bed, pistol in hand. He missed such old-school encounters. He remembered shooting a Russian scientist, a traitor and defector from the former Soviet Union, in the forehead as he sat up beside his wife in a bedroom in West Berlin. That man had gifted him with such a look—that shocked, "this can't possibly be happening" look. Polakov considered himself a *collector* of such moments—moments of vanquish and vulnerability at his hand.

He decided to err on the side of covert progression—a rule that had served him well over the years—and sweep the apartment. The GRU agent stepped lightly on soft, rubber-soled shoes from the foyer into the dimly lit kitchen. He stood a moment, scanning the room, and then eased into the dining room. He felt his pulse quicken. Something was wrong. He inhaled through his nose, checking for olfactory evidence of foul play, but the only two odors he could identify were benign— air freshener and roasted duck. The kitchen had been clean and orderly, the same with the dining room. No apparent signs of a struggle. He crouched, both hands gripping the Radom, and moved into the living room.

Only one room left to search—the bedroom.

A soft whisper, like socks shuffling on a hardwood floor, sent his pulse soaring. He was not alone. Adrenaline and endorphins poured into his bloodstream. Hunter and hunted. Who was who? Just like in the old days. This is what he loved. This is what he lived for. He held his position, trying to pinpoint the sound. To his left? Yes. He started to rotate, but just then, he heard a click to his right. He whirled right, his barrel trained on the swaying curtains as the air handler turned on. The old Russian killer smiled and chided himself: *Perishable skills. I have become both fat and stupid.*

The apartment lights switched on, blinding him.

Something hard and heavy hit him on the back of the head. The blow sent him to his knees, dazed and disoriented. He raised his left arm above his head in anticipation of a second blow, but a second blow did not come. As his pupils constricted, adjusting to the light, a blurry figure came into sharper focus and his chest tightened in horror. The thing standing in front of him looked like an alien creature from a science-fiction movie—a faceless, bug-eyed humanoid dressed in a space suit.

He raised his right hand to shoot it, but the pistol was no longer in his grip.

He shook his head and felt his wits returning to him. "Prizrak?" he asked, squinting at his assailant, who he now recognized was a man wearing a full hazmat suit, complete with a military-grade respirator and goggles.

The man in the suit laughed, the timbre modulated by the respirator, creating an effect both demonic and robotic. Despite the distortion, this was a laugh he recognized, and it sent a shiver down his spine.

"What the hell are you doing?"

"I like seeing you this way," Prizrak said. "On your knees. You Russians are so proud. So arrogant. And yet such fools."

"What the hell are you doing?" Polakov said. "It's time. I came to get you. The plane is fueled and waiting for us."

"I want you to beg," Prizrak replied.

"Excuse me?"

"Beg for your life, old friend. Or are you too proud, even now?"

Polakov's mind was racing. His asset had finally snapped under the pressure, and he, Polakov, had become the target of the Chinese scientist's violent mania. His only chance was to redirect his rage, to shift the focus onto a different, more dangerous threat. "They know about us," he said. "Your government knows about the weapon, and they are coming for it. If they catch us, they will confiscate your work, arrest us, and execute us as traitors. We don't have much time. My car is waiting, Qing. It's time to go." As he spoke, Polakov glanced at the floor, searching for his P-64. He spotted it lying on the carpet, two feet from his left knee. He looked back at Prizrak and saw that the scientist was hiding something in his right hand behind his back.

A knife? A pistol? The thing the bastard had clubbed him across the head with? Polakov's instincts told him that Chen Qing was beyond reason. To survive, he had only one play, and that was to go for his gun and empty every round in the clip into to the mad scientist's chest.

"I trusted you," Qing growled. "I put my life's work in your hands, and this is how you repay me? With lies and betrayal?"

"I did not betray you," Polakov said. "I'm here to save you."

"Silence!" Qing shouted, his voice manic and full of rage.

"Listen to me, Prizrak—"

"Do not call me that," Qing screamed, cutting him off.

Polakov went for his gun…but he was too slow.

Qing's right rubber boot connected with Polakov's chin before his fingers could find purchase. The blow sent his lower jaw crashing into his upper, and he felt multiple teeth crack in his mouth. Stars danced in his eyes, and when they cleared, he watched Prizrak's second kick send his gun skidding across the carpet and under the living room sofa.

"Have you gone mad?" Polakov said, spitting tooth fragments onto the carpet. *I will not die on my knees*, he said to himself, and with a grunt, he struggled to his feet. When he leveled his gaze at Qing, he was nose to nozzle with a stainless steel pressure canister aimed at his face.

"Robert Oppenheimer once said, 'I am Death, the destroyer of worlds,'" Qing said in stilted English. "Was Oppenheimer mad, Polakov? No, he was a genius misunderstood. As am I."

"What are you going to do?" Polakov asked, truly afraid for the first time in his life.

"I am going to walk in the blood of all who stand against me. I am going to turn Beijing red."

The canister hissed and a wet mist bloomed around him. Polakov gasped in horror, choking inside the acrid cloud of microscopic certain death. He exhaled forcefully, pulled his shirt over his head, and ran. He ran holding his breath, barely able to see because of the shirt over his face. He clipped a doorframe with his hip on the way into the foyer, stumbled, but kept on going. His lungs were screaming at him to take a breath, but terror ordered that he not. He fumbled for the doorknob, found it, and flung himself into the hallway. He turned left toward the service stairwell, threw open the fire door, and sprinted across the landing. His tried to descend the steps two at a time, but on his third stride, his left foot missed its mark and sent him sailing. As he tumbled down the concrete stairs, he felt a rib crack and then his left wrist snap. When he crashed to a painful stop on the twelfth-floor landing, he immediately began stripping off his clothing—shirt, pants, shoes, even underwear and socks.

He felt himself begin to swoon from the rising carbon dioxide levels in "his" bloodstream as his brain screamed for oxygen. He scrambled down the next flight of stairs, not daring to take a breath until he was clear of the contaminated clothing. At the next landing, he collapsed naked onto the cold floor. The only sound in the stairwell was the rasping echo of his lungs in hyperventilation. Exhausted and in excruciating pain, he collapsed onto his back. With each new breath, he began to regain mental focus, and as he did, the gravity of his situation became deathly apparent.

He had inhaled Qing's death gas. Certainly he was now infected. Certainly? How many hours until he was dead? At this very moment, tiny robots were coursing through his blood like an armada of Special Forces cellular assassins in microscopic fast boats. The Chinese scientist had suffered a psychotic break—and now it appeared he intended to use the weapon to kill thousands, if not millions, of innocent people.

Polakov rose on unsteady feet. He would take the stairs to the lobby. Then he would cross bare-ass naked to the garage stairwell and use the magnetic key under the fender to unlock his car. In the trunk, he had his go bag—complete with extra clothes, extra passport, and backup weapon. He would regroup. He would contact Moscow. Then, he would hunt down Prizrak and kill him.

Halfway down the stairs, Polakov's eyes felt funny. The world around him began to turn pink and hazy, then crimson, and he realized his eyeballs were filling with blood. After a moment, he was completely blind. His head exploded with pain—the worst migraine imaginable. He pawed at his eyes and tried to express his confusion and anger in words, but the words were suddenly lost to him. His ears began to ring. He felt hot, wet trickles begin to run from both ears, down his neck. The ringing got louder, and louder, and louder, until finally it stopped and the world enveloped him like a womb—silent, dark, and thick. He felt dizzy and lost his balance. He fell head forward and tumbled down yet another half flight of concrete stairs. More bones broke, but he had trouble comprehending this.

His tongue went numb and he lost control of his bladder. And then the pain began to fade, which made him happy. His thoughts turned to death and revenge and killing...killing someone he hated.

But he could not remember who he wanted to kill.

He could not remember anything.

He was confused.

He was tired.

He was...

TWENTY-SIX

Chinese Centers for Disease Control and Prevention
2008 hours local

"STOP THAT WOMAN!"

Major Li's voice boomed like a shotgun blast down the corridor.

Dazhong tasted fear. It was the taste of self-doubt and dread. Of desperation and subjugation. They would catch her; it was inevitable.

Then someone screamed the word "No," and it took her a second to realize that the voice she'd heard was her own—an unfamiliar voice, ripe with strength, outrage, and defiance. She would not take the blame for *this*. She refused to be the scapegoat for their demented bioweapon field test.

She spun around and, without a backward glance, sprinted off in the direction from which she'd come. She darted past the microscopy labs and cryo-preservation facilities. She navigated a dogleg in the hallway and leapt over a cooler-size lockbox someone had left on the floor, all without breaking stride. Her legs felt powerful; her senses were clear and crisp. If she could just reach the west stairwell, then she might make it down to the ground floor and out the building before they secured the exits.

She drove her shoulder into the stairwell door at full

speed. The impact sent an electric stab of pain down her arm all the way into her fingertips, but the heavy steel door crashed open, swinging all the way into the concrete wall. She crossed the landing in a single stride and bounded down the steps two at a time, using the inner railing to steady herself. There were six switchbacks between her and the ground floor. When she had reached the fourth one, she heard a door slam open above.

"There's nowhere to run, Dr. Chen," echoed Li's voice overhead.

Footsteps thundered in the stairwell as Li and his men converged on her. After the fifth flight, she leapt over the railing, bypassing the final switchback in favor of a six-foot vertical drop. She landed square on both feet and glanced up, expecting to see gun barrels trained on her. But there were no guns, just three black leather gloves sliding impossibly fast toward her along the metal railing.

She whirled one hundred eighty degrees to face salvation. Bold, white kanji stenciled across the red emergency door warned against foul play: "Warning. Alarm will sound. Use only in Emergency."

I've always wanted to do this, she thought with a smirk and drove both her palms into the door's rocker bar. To her dismay, even with the rocker bar depressed, the door wouldn't budge. She cycled the rocker bar and tried again, but the door held shut.

"No!" she screamed, pounding her fists against the cold, unyielding steel. "Emergency exits are not supposed to be lockable!"

The footsteps stopped behind her and the stairwell fell silent.

"Dr. Chen," a voice said. "Will you please end this foolishness and come with me?"

"Am I under arrest?" she panted, her back still to him.

"Dr. Chen, please don't make this any more difficult than it has to be," said Li, sounding as clinical and superior as she remembered.

She turned around, again expecting gun barrels and again surprised to find none. She met Major Li's hard, cold eyes and knew it was over. He'd won.

Again.

"All right," she said, simply. "I'll go."

He nodded at her, with more exasperation than triumph, and gestured for her to walk beside him. She crossed her arms on her chest and fell in step with the army man. Then, to her surprise, instead of escorting her out the stairwell to an idling police cruiser for handcuffing, he led her back up the stairs to the second level. They walked shoulder to shoulder down the main transverse corridor until they reached the CDC's executive conference room. Through the glass sidelights flanking the double mahogany doors, she caught a glimpse of two men talking. The one facing her she knew instantly—Dr. Wong, the CDC director. The other man had his back to her, but there was something familiar about his stance.

Li stopped in front of the mahogany double doors and signaled the two escorting soldiers to open them. As she stepped into the room, the man talking to Dr. Wong turned to face her.

"Zhang?" she breathed, unsure whether she should be relieved or terrified. For the Snow Leopard Commander to come here, with Major Li no less, could only mean one thing:

They must think I'm working with bioweapon terrorists.

Zhang met her gaze, and for an instant, she thought she saw a hint of a smile before his expression darkened.

"I apologize for keeping you waiting," Major Li said, shooting her a stern sideways glance. "It took me longer than I thought to *chase down* Dr. Chen."

"No need to apologize," said Director Wong. "It gave me a chance to talk with Commander Zhang. Now please, everyone, take a seat."

Li glanced back over his shoulder and the two army guards immediately shut the conference room doors and posted themselves outside. Li headed for a seat on the left side of the conference table next to Zhang, so Dazhong went right and sat down beside Wong.

"Dr. Chen," Major Li said, not wasting a second, "we have some important matters to discuss with you, matters concerning highly sensitive and compartmentalized information. But before we do, we have some questions for you."

She nodded and glanced at each of them in turn.

"Dr. Chen," Li continued, "tell us everything you know about biomedical microelectromechanical systems, a.k.a. Bio-MEMS technology."

Her left eyelid twitched.

"I… I would not claim to be an expert in that field, not by any stretch of the imagination, but I have a rudimentary understanding of certain Bio-MEMS products and applications."

She paused.

"Very well. By all means, enlighten us with your rudimentary knowledge," Li said, crossing his arms on his chest.

"Well, most of my experience with Bio-MEMS has to do with diagnostic applications. Here at the CDC we've begun using proteomic microarrays for genome analysis. Despite their miniature architecture, microarrays have high throughput, making gene analysis and sequencing faster, easier, and cheaper. I've also used microarrays for PCR amplification, peptide and protein analysis, and oligonucleotide mapping of genetic mutations."

"Excuse my ignorance, but what exactly is a microarray?" Zhang asked.

"A microarray is essentially a laboratory on a microchip. Most people call them LOCs—labs on a chip. LOCs take advantage of microfluidic conditions to perform complex analyses while only using picoliters of sample material."

"So you put one of these chips inside a person and it analyzes his blood for you?" Zhang asked.

"No, not presently. The chips are installed in instrumentation. But implantable LOCs, in my opinion, are where the future of diagnostic medicine is heading."

"What else do you know about Bio-MEMS?" Li interjected.

She shifted her gaze from Zhang to Li.

He knows, she thought. *He's like an attorney using leading questions to drive me into a confession of guilt.*

"That's about it," she said, resisting the urge to jam a knuckle into her twitching eye. "Like I said, my knowledge of Bio-MEMS only encompasses those devices that intersect with conducting epidemiological research, which is my field of expertise."

"Curious," Li sniffed. "I would have thought you'd be intimately versed with Bio-MEMS technology given who your husband is and the fact that his company is a successful Bio-MEMS start-up in China."

The weight of their collective gaze made her shrink in her chair, and she suddenly felt nine years old again.

"You think Qing had something to do with this?" she said at last.

Li sat up in his chair and leaned forward, like a panther ready to pounce. "Something to do with what, Dr. Chen?"

"With what happened in Kizilsu. With the outbreak that claimed dozens of human lives that you called an industrial accident."

Li glanced at Zhang.

"Who said anything about Kizilsu?" Zhang said, his tone almost too casual. "We were talking about Bio-MEMS."

Her left eyelid was fluttering so bad she couldn't stand it anymore; she bowed her head and jammed the pad of left thumb between her upper lid and eye socket. She could feel the tiny little muscle fluttering beneath her touch.

I could never be a professional poker player, she thought and began to chuckle.

"What's so funny, Dr. Chen?" Director Wong asked, speaking up for the first time.

"It just occurred to me, sir, that we're all sitting around this conference table pretending to have a meeting, but *this* is not a meeting."

"If this is not a meeting, then what is it?"

"It's a poker game," she said releasing her thumb, setting the twitch free. "And we're all terrible bluffers."

Zhang laughed out loud, a big, genuine grin spreading across his face. The laugh was so infectious, she began to laugh, and then so did Director Wong. Even Major Li cracked a smile. When she finally stopped laughing, the twitch was gone.

"Because I am a terrible poker player, I am going to take a chance and lay down all my cards and see what happens," she said, looking at them each in turn. "There's been another attack."

"What?" Li said. "Where?"

"Here in Beijing," she said. "I know the woman who was targeted. She is—was—my friend."

"When?" asked Zhang.

"This morning. She called me as she was dying. I went to her apartment, but there was nothing I could do. It was just like Kizilsu. After she died, I performed an autopsy and snuck tissue samples into the lab. I was conducting an analysis with the microsphere nanoscope when Major Li showed up."

"What were you thinking?" Director Wong shouted, jumping to his feet.

"There is something terrible going on, and some-how I seem to have landed in the middle of it. People are dying, Director Wong, and I needed to understand why. This was the only way."

"You should have talked to me, Dazhong," Wong growled. "There are strict protocols for the handling and transport of these sorts of pathogens. After your time in Liberia, you, more than anyone, should know this. We could have taken precautions. Major Li could have helped you."

"Like he helped me in Kizilsu?" she fired back. "When he took unilateral control of the task force, confiscated all the data, cremated the victims' bodies, and made me write my signature on a falsified report? No thank you," she said, shaking her head. "You and Major Li are the reason I *had* to do what I did."

Wong's cheeks flashed crimson. "By bringing it here, you've jeopardized the lives of everyone in the CDC, including the four of us sitting around this table."

"No," she said, firmly. "The macrophage nanobots are not contagious. They don't vector like viruses and bacteria do."

"Wait," Li interjected. "What are you talking about? What do you mean when you say 'macrophage nanobots'?"

From the look in his eyes, she suddenly realized she knew more about the bioweapon than he did. "Have you not actually seen them?"

"No."

"Then how did you know we're dealing with nanotech?"

"It's been my working hypothesis since Kizilsu. When we didn't find antibodies in the victims' blood, I was forced to rule out viral or bacterial infection. I had tissue samples taken from every victim and ordered detailed autopsies on ten cadavers: five men, five women. What we found was like nothing we'd ever seen before—all the connective tissue was simply gone. The victims' organs were liquefied—as were their tendons, as you might imagine. I pushed my technicians to find the root cause. I sent tissue samples out for SEM evaluation, and all the reports came back the same. Nonbiological debris was found in every sample. That was the germination of my Bio-MEMS weapon hypothesis."

She nodded. "Impressive detective work."

"Not as impressive as yours, it seems," Li said. "Tell

me, Dr. Chen. What have *you* discovered? What do you think we're dealing with?"

She talked for twenty minutes without interruption, explaining everything she'd observed in Jamie Lin's tissue samples. Then she fielded their questions—answering those she could and formulating hypotheses for those she couldn't. When the talking finished, she slumped in her chair, mentally and emotionally drained.

Zhang turned to Li and with an ironic smile said, "I suppose we can consider Dr. Chen officially 'read in' to this operation now."

"Not quite," Li said, rubbing his temples. "There's still the matter of the other Dr. Chen to discuss."

"I don't understand," she said, her eyes darting back and forth between her two inquisitors.

Li sighed and fixed his now bloodshot gaze on her. "I knew your husband in postgraduate school, many years ago. Even then, he was obsessed with nanotechnology. He was fascinated by the concept of von Neumann machines. He loved quoting Eric Drexler and talking about gray goo. He was especially enamored of Stanislaw Lem and loved to brag about how he bought an English-translation copy of *The Invincible* at a science fiction conference in San Diego. Four years ago, when I learned that a Bio-MEMS startup called Invincible Nanotech Industries—INI—had received one hundred million dollars in venture funding from ALP Capital, I knew instantly the founder was Qing. How much do you know about your husband's work? Does he discuss INI's research and development with you? Does he share bioengineering details or ask for your scientific opinion on technical problems?"

She suppressed the urge to chuckle. "What you need

to understand about my husband, Major Li, is that he loves to grandstand. With Qing it's always, 'INI is going to revolutionize health care,' or 'Ten years from now, when I'm on the cover of *Time* magazine, they'll call me the man who changed the field of medicine.' Qing only talks to me about his grandiose plans, never about minutiae of INI projects and operations. He never asks for my counsel or opinion on anything of substance… not anymore, that is."

Li fixed her with a stern gaze and said, "What I'm about to tell you is highly classified. Possessing this information puts your career and personal liberty at risk. Divulging this information to any unauthorized person is a treasonous offense punishable by death. Do you understand, Dr. Chen?"

"Yes, I understand."

Li took a deep breath and exhaled from his nose. "ALP Capital, the venture firm that invested in Qing's company, is not your typical venture capital firm. It is a state-funded defense technology incubator. ALP Capital seeks out promising nascent technologies in the private sector that could have military applications. If the technology passes all the necessary hurdles, the intellectual property is sold off to a state-owned defense contractor for late-stage testing and production. If the technology does not pass muster, then ALP will seek a buyer in the commercial market to recoup the initial capital investment, usually at a considerable profit. So far, this covert incubator model has proven to be extremely successful. When ALP Capital invested in INI, it put the company and Qing on the fast track."

"How do you know all this?" she asked.

"Because I regularly serve as a technical consultant

to the ALP board, evaluating technologies that might apply to the weaponization of, or defense against, nuclear, biological, and chemical agents."

"Did ALP Capital ask you to consult on early stage funding for INI?"

"No. The board is very careful to spread the work around. Compartmentalization is very important to them. To use an American expression, they don't like to 'put all their eggs in one basket.' They're careful to prevent any one person from knowing too much. As such, I'm only invited to consult on three or four technologies a year. I know of others in Regiment 54423 who also consult for ALP, but we don't discuss it. Sharing information between consultants is strictly forbidden."

"I understand."

"No, I'm not sure that you do," he snapped. "A one-hundred-million-dollar investment by ALP Capital in INI can only be interpreted one way. Despite your husband's grandiose claims, despite the marketing materials INI disseminates to the press, the company's *real* charter is to develop Bio-MEMS technology for military applications."

"Is that why you cut me out of the loop in Kizilsu? Because of my husband?"

Li nodded. "As soon as I suspected the outbreak might have been caused by the uncontrolled release of nanotechnology, I started making calls up the chain of command. Little did I realize I'd just kicked the hornet's nest. Within four hours of my first call, the Central National Security Commission held an emergency meeting. The result of that meeting was to give me unilateral authority over the joint task force and charter me with finding out the truth about what really happened in Kizilsu."

"All right, but what about Commander Zhang? Why did you kick him out of your inner circle too?"

"In hindsight, that was a mistake. I'm a subject-matter expert on terrible weapons, not on the terrible people who mean to use them. That's Commander Zhang's specialty. When I realized my error, I contacted him directly, apologized, and read him in."

She turned to Zhang. "When did this happen?"

"The day before yesterday," Zhang said.

"What did you say?"

"I accepted and then told Major Li that I thought we should read you in immediately. But he convinced me to wait until after we finished our investigation of INI."

"I'm confused. You're talking to me now, so does that mean your investigation of Qing is complete?"

"We haven't found anything linking Qing to Kizilsu yet," Zhang said, "but we're still looking. I've had an undercover audit team at INI doing record reviews for the past two days."

Her stomach felt heavy, almost nauseous. "The investigators showed up at INI the day before yesterday?"

"Yes."

"The day we flew back from Kashi?"

"Precisely," Zhang said. "Why? What's on your mind?"

"It's probably nothing, but Qing was acting very strange the night I got back from Kashi."

"Strange in what way?" Zhang asked.

"Like a guilty child suddenly on his best behavior. I assumed he must have done something bad while I was gone."

"Bad like what?"

"Like sleeping with another woman," she said, managing to keep her tone unaffected. "It would not be the first time."

The three men stared at her in awkward silence.

After a beat, Zhang said, "But now you think it might be related to the surprise audit?"

"Yes."

"Why is that?"

"Because Qing seemed particularly interested in what happened in Kashgar. He asked me more questions about my time in Kizilsu than he did when I returned from months in Africa. We actually had a *conversation* during dinner; I can't remember the last time that happened. Now that I think about it, Qing specifically mentioned knowing you, Major Li."

"You told him about me?" Li asked, narrowing his eyes at her.

She shrugged. "Your behavior really upset me, so I vented."

"What else did he say?" Li said, pressing.

"He was particularly keen to learn what the official cause of the outbreak was. He didn't seem to care whether it was an Ebola outbreak or a chemical release—just that the cause was found and would be reported to media."

"What do your instincts tell you, Dr. Chen?" Zhang asked, stepping in. "Do you think your husband is a man capable of murder?"

She thought of Jamie Lin, writhing on the bathroom floor as the macrophage nanobots liquefied her organs. Was Qing responsible for her death? Had he discovered Jamie Lin's link to the CIA and murdered her because of it? Had her husband sent the three thugs to rough her up in the alley outside the club?

"Dr. Chen?" Li said, growing impatient.

She blinked twice and said, "My husband wears many masks, has many secrets, and has always kept his true thoughts and feelings to himself. Maybe I should be ashamed to admit it, but I do not know my husband. I do not know the real Chen Qing. Five years ago, if you had asked me if he was capable of murder, I would have said no. Today, I'm not so sure. If he was pushed to the limit, I don't know what kind of malice Qing is capable of unleashing."

The confession took her by surprise, but it was also profoundly liberating. She did not consider it a betrayal. She did not love her husband. She hadn't for a very long time.

"Is there anything else you'd like to tell us, Dr. Chen?" Li asked. "Any details or thoughts you might have left out that could be relevant to this investigation?"

Like the fact that my best friend was a CIA agent? Or maybe the secret parallel investigation I have going with an American Navy SEAL?

Dazhong glanced at the row of clocks on the wall above Director Wong's head. It was after eleven pm—she was more than two hours late for her meeting with Nick. She had promised to text him if she was going to be delayed, and she suspected he must be worried sick. She needed to call him as soon as possible and apologize. Certainly he would understand.

But she needed to close this loop first.

"Nothing I can think of," she said at last while resisting the urge to fold her arms across her chest.

With a sharp rap of his knuckles on the table, Zhang stood. "Then what are we waiting for? I think it's time to go have a chat with the *other* Dr. Chen."

"Are you sure direct confrontation is the best strategy, Commander?" Li said, not moving in his seat.

"Oh, I don't plan to confront Dr. Chen," Zhang said. "I plan to take him."

"I would feel more comfortable with a joint operation," Li said. "This is not the sort of thing that should be rushed."

"Unfortunately, Major, I must disagree. Rushing is a necessity for all counterterrorism operations. Time is our single biggest adversary."

"Yes, that may be true, but I am the ranking official here."

"The moment Dr. Chen became classified as a terrorist threat to China, operational control for his apprehension shifted from your unit to mine."

Li eyed Zhang for a moment and then said, "Keep me posted as events unfold, but let me be clear. Dr. Chen is not to be harmed during his apprehension."

"Dr. Chen's personal safety is a priority, but let *me* be clear—his safety does not and will not supersede that of my men and the general public."

Major Li sniffed but had no retort.

Zhang turned to Dazhong. "Do you know where your husband is at present?"

"He is most likely home at our apartment, but we have not spoken this evening," she said, her mind still reeling with thoughts of nanobots and all the innocent people her husband might have murdered.

"Has he tried to contact you in the last twelve hours?" Zhang asked.

"I don't think so," she said, checking her mobile phone. "No text messages. No voicemails."

"All right. We start with your apartment and branch out from there," Zhang said. "If he suspects you are working with us, we may be too late. He could already be on the run."

She touched Zhang's sleeve as they all exited the conference room. "Why would Qing do this?"

"I don't know," Zhang said. "Most likely, he is working with a foreign government. Perhaps the Americans or the Iranians. Possibly the Russians."

"So not only is my husband a psychotic mass murderer," she said through clenched teeth, "but he is also a traitor to China."

"I'm sorry, Dazhong," Zhang said, turning to her, his face an unreadable mask. "For what it's worth, I've never suspected you had any involvement in this."

"Thanks," she said, wondering how much longer she could bear the crushing weight of the world she was carrying on her shoulders.

"Are you sure you want to come with me?" he asked with genuine concern. "You don't have to, you know. We've got this under control."

Do you? she wondered, thinking about the sequence of events over the past five days. *It seems to me he's been operating one step ahead of all of us since the beginning.*

"I'm coming with you," she said, staunchly. "I wouldn't have it any other way."

Zhang nodded. "And if things get ugly, are you ready for that?"

"If the accusations about Qing are true," she said, balling her hands up into fists, "you might have to stop me from pulling the trigger myself."

TWENTY-SEVEN

One block south of the Chen residence
Chaoyang District
0045 hours local

NICK HAD THE eerie sense that everyone was watching him. No, not watching—*surveilling*. Was he being overly paranoid? Yes. Was someone actually watching his every move? Most likely. Somewhere in the thin crowds and the dark cars with their dark windows were agents of the CIA, the Snow Leopard counterterrorism unit, the Chinese Ministry of State Security, the People's Liberation Army, and of course whoever was actually behind the insane attacks in Kizilsu.

God only knew what other governments had agents following him now as well.

Nick was out of his lane in this world. His dismal performance with Lankford today had proven that. He'd played his best cards on his opening hand, ceding his advantage immediately to the Company man. Now, here he was, playing spy games without training. He had tried some of the rudimentary countersurveillance techniques he had used in the teams, but those were not techniques designed to thwart true professionals in this environment. If he had, by some miracle, shaken some surveillance teams on his way here, he was just picking up new ones with his arrival. But what other choice did he have? His repeated calls and texts to Dash had gone unanswered, and she was more than three hours overdue for their meeting. She had promised to text message if she was tied up so he would know not to make the meet, but she had not done so. He had sat for nearly two hours at the coffee shop on Jinghua Street, supplementing adrenaline with caffeine as the time ticked by. Nick realized—with a modicum of shame—that he was far more concerned about Dash than he was about the next bioterrorism event.

He tapped his thumb on his thigh, dissipating some nervous energy.

Where the hell is she?

Coming to her apartment was a big risk. If the watchers hadn't observed them together yet, this would change that going forward. He glanced at the map on his phone where the little blue dot (him) was closing in on the little red dot (her apartment). He prayed he had properly understood the address she had given him, but Chinese words gave him fits. Given the late hour, if she was home, then certainly her husband would be home with her. She had not spoken to him about her husband, other than notifying him of her marital status. Now he realized that he should have asked about her husband's profession. For some reason, he imagined the man was some variety of doctor, too, but he could not recall why he thought this.

He looked up and down the quiet street. There were a couple of cars parked along the curb, but none with their engines running. In movies, the bad guys always sat in running cars, but that was the extent of his expertise on the matter outside of a war zone. Nick grinned tightly and snorted as he realized that, for the first time in years, he very much wished he had a weapon. A SOP-MOD M4 rifle with EOTECH Holosight and a PEQ-2 laser designator was his preference, though the circumstances called for something a little less overt—a semiautomatic pistol with hollow points would do. Hell, he'd be grateful just having a pocketknife in his sock.

He checked his phone again. The blue dot and the red dot were right on top of each other.

"I'm here," he said and tried to resist looking up at the apartment building to his right. He turned the corner and walked with feigned confidence and certainty toward the entrance. The apartment building was new but had an ornate, classical façade—like a university or embassy building. Block out the rest of the skyline and the building could have been an Upper East Side luxury co-op in Manhattan. As he strode up the short flight of steps to the lobby, he wondered what excuse in God's name he would give for asking to speak with Dash if the husband answered the door.

At the top of the steps, he glanced casually around, saw nothing of note, and then reached for the heavy door and pulled. The door did not budge. No rattle meant it was secured with an electromagnetic lock. Nick noted an intercom panel to the right of the door, which he assumed was a call box for the residents of the building. All the writing was in Chinese hanzi. He had no idea which button to select.

So much for getting buzzed in.

He looked left and right, searching for a decent hide where he could wait to follow a resident covertly into the building. But there was nothing—no alcove, no basement egress, no short alleynowhere he could conceal himself.

"Shit," he sighed.

Now what?

He decided to circle the block. A solution would come to him in time.

The roar of an engine snapped him out of his head. Reflexively, he moved toward cover behind a stone column as a black Mercedes SUV tore up the apartment complex driveway. The SUV screeched to a halt, the left tire popping up onto the curb a few yards away from where Nick had been standing. The driver's-side door flung open and black boots dropped into view below the sill of the door.

"Stay where you are, Nick Foley," a voice boomed from behind the dark-tinted window. "Raise your hands above your head."

Nick's mouth dropped open as Commander Zhang—head of the Snow Leopard Commando Unit—stepped into view, a pistol pointed at Nick's head. Zhang was in uniform, but thankfully not kitted up in combat gear. Nick immediately noticed the large, triangular-shaped canvas bag clipped to the Snow Leopard Commander's belt. MOPP gear—*Not a good sign.* His instinct had been right—he was being surveilled. The passenger door opened and a smaller man in a military uniform sprang out and then took a knee beside the vehicle, taking aim at Nick with a combat rifle, just as a second SUV screeched to a stop behind the first. This second man barked something at him in Chinese.

"My colleague," Zhang said as he lowered his own pistol and walked toward Nick with a smirk on his face, "would like for you to kneel on the ground with your hands on top of your head." The Snow Leopard Commander barked something at the smaller soldier, who nodded, but his face suggested he was unsure about his Commander's order, whatever it had been. "I told him that will not be necessary, but I really must insist you keep your hands in view so that my teammate does not shoot you dead here in front of Dr. Chen's home."

Three other Snow Leopards now fanned out in a loose half circle from the second SUV, their rifles at the ready but at least not pointing at his head.

"What do you want?" Nick said, the calm in his voice incongruous with the dread blossoming inside. He was not afraid of combat. He was not afraid of death. But to be thrown into a deep, dark hole for a very long time was a fate he could not stomach. For an instant, he considered making a run for it—he could find Lankford, agree to help the CIA. If the spooks couldn't get his ass out of China, then he'd go to the embassy and let the diplomats fight over him. But the little red dot on his chest implied that running would be a very bad idea.

"I think the question, Navy SEAL Nick Foley, is what do *you* want? And more importantly, why are you here at the residence of the most-wanted terrorist traitor in China?"

What the hell was Zhang talking about? Dash was no traitor. The Snow Leopard Commander must surely know that. This was insane. Unless…they had pieced together a damning triangular of connections: Dash and Jamie Lin, Dash and Nick, Nick and Lankford. In this unfortunate geometry, all lines pointed to the CIA.

Oh shit. We'll both be prosecuted as traitors and framed for the massacre in Kizilsu.

"Stop—please," called a woman's voice in English.

Nick looked over Zhang's shoulder in disbelief as Dash stepped out of the back seat of the Mercedes SUV.

She walked to them and placed a hand on Zhang's shoulder. Nick's confusion replaced his fear, to be trumped seconds later by rage. Had everything that transpired been a setup? Was Dash a confederate, put in play by Zhang to manipulate him and ferret out Jamie Lin's OC? Or had she simply used him to collect enough evidence to build a case against him so Zhang could frame an American SEAL in an effort to keep China's image clean? The anger made it hard to think clearly. Something didn't feel right. None of this felt right.

"This is not what you think," she said.

"And what do I think, Dr. Chen?" Zhang said, his eyes never leaving Nick. "That Nick Foley is an ex-Navy SEAL employed by the CIA, bent on helping a bioweapons terrorist escape China, so that America can obtain the technology for itself? Does that spell things out clearly enough for you?"

"No, you have drawn the wrong conclusions," she said, her voice low and deliberate. "Nick Foley is with me."

"What?" Nick and Zhang spoke the question in unison, and this time Zhang did turn to her. "What are you saying? That this American spy was here to meet with you?"

Nick opened his mouth to speak, but she silenced him with a look.

"Yes, he was here to meet me," Dash said, speaking in English, no doubt for his benefit. "But he is no spy, I assure you."

"I'm sorry, Dr. Chen, but you have been deceived by this man. We have surveillance footage of him meeting with a ranking CIA field officer only hours ago. Did you know that?"

"Yes," Dash said, "but that does not make him a spy. He was trying to help me."

The young Snow Leopard, the one with the rifle pointed center mass at Nick's heart, barked again in Chinese. Zhang scowled but nodded.

"Yes," he said. "My junior officer is right. Explain why you have been in communication with this American and how he has been helping you."

Dash stepped in front of Nick, shielding him from the barrel of the Snow Leopard's rifle. "This *American* saved my life last night. He also risked his safety and reputation to help me obtain tissue samples so I could investigate this bioweapon. I will explain all this in detail later, but for right now, can we please get off the street? Qing may have people watching the apartment—warning him as we speak. We need to go inside and search for him immediately. Nick is coming with us."

Nick watched Zhang's mouth twist into something resembling a smile. The girl had brains and balls: two traits that apparently went a long way with the Snow Leopard Commander, because he barked something at his team.

The junior man grudgingly secured his rifle and walked directly toward Nick, his face a mask of professionalism. He said something to Dash, and she stepped aside. The soldier frisked Nick roughly and thoroughly for weapons. Finding none, he then gestured for the group to move out.

Nick looked at Dash and forced a smile. "Mind telling me what the hell is going on?"

"It appears likely that Qing—my husband—is the inventor of a terrible weapon and the person behind the terror attacks in Kizilsu."

"What?" Nick said, shaking his head with incredulity as they jogged after Zhang. "That's unbelievable... and terrible. I don't know what else to say."

"Yes, there are no words," she said. "This day is like a nightmare, only I am already awake."

"And your husband is upstairs right now?"

"I don't know," she said. "But I am most glad you are here, Nick. I would not want to confront Qing alone."

Her words resonated inside. She was not alone. Zhang and his team were here, but that was the point, wasn't it? She viewed him as her protector now.

When they reached the entrance, Dash entered a code and buzzed them in. Feeling naked and awkward, Nick trailed Zhang and three operators, as the Snow Leopards advanced in a two-man clearing pattern. They covered each other's corners fluidly as they moved quickly and expertly through the empty lobby. Nick felt like a bystander and again wished he had a weapon so he could be more than just baggage. The presence of the other two Snow Leopards behind him—where they could keep an eye on him as well as cover the flank—was not lost on the former Navy SEAL.

Zhang gestured to the stairwell. An assaulter pulled the door open, and Zhang entered in a tactical crouch. A beat later, Zhang gave an all-clear signal, and the group began the ascent in pairs. Nick took the rear position behind Dash, who was behind the assault team, figuring he could at least be a barrier between her and any surprise attack from behind should the other two soldiers be too focused on him to identify a threat from their rear. After ten flights, Zhang called for them to halt, and then Nick heard a loud, short conversation in clipped Chinese. Zhang called down the stairs from the landing above.

"Dr. Chen, please come up slowly."

She looked at Nick, her expression grave.

Nick nodded encouragement: *Whatever it is, I'm right beside you.*

The strain in Zhang's voice had been unmistakable. Whatever the Snow Leopard Commander had found, it was bad. Nick peered up the stairs to the next landing, where Zhang stood against the wall, MOPP mask now pulled over his face, his huge alien eyes staring down at them. Zhang raised a hand, stopping them. It was then that Nick noticed a thin stream of dark blood dribbling down the steps above. Zhang tossed down two small, green bags, which Nick caught in midair.

"Each of you put on a mask. There are latex gloves inside as well. Put those on too, but don't touch anything," Zhang directed. He then issued a curt command in Chinese, and the two soldiers on the landing took up defensive positions, looking back down the stars, rifles at the ready. "Also, please watch where you step. Dr. Chen believes that the weapon should not be contagious, but until that is confirmed, we must take great care."

Nick handed a bag to Dash and then unpacked his own.

"I have a theory that the nanobots self-destruct once the target tissues have been completely destroyed, but I am not certain of the mechanism or the timing," she explained before putting her mask on.

Nick donned his gloves, then pulled on his own mask. After checking that the seal was satisfactory, he looked at her and said, "I have no idea what you're talking about."

"I know," she said, slipping on her latex gloves. "I have very much to tell you, Nick. Soon."

Soon...great.

He followed her up the stairs and took a position beside her on the landing. Three feet away, a dead man lay naked in a pool of blood. Nick stared at the scene, perplexed. *Why is this man naked? Why is the blood always dark purple instead of the red he had seen in combat? And why is there so much blood?*

"This one looks different," Dash said, under her breath.

Nick nodded. Where Batur and Jamie Lin had been swollen to the point of bursting, the man at their feet was gaunt, the cheeks sunken and gray. The eyes were gone, except for some gelatinous goo that pooled in the corner of the otherwise empty sockets. It was as if his eyes had been gouged out and then the sockets used as a spigot to drain the body of blood. Dark blood dribbled down the corpse's neck from the ears and ran from the nose over the mouth and chin, but this was nothing compared to the river of blood pouring from of the gaping holes that had once been eyes.

"What the hell happened to him?" he asked, his voice strange and unfamiliar through the rubber mask.

Dash looked over at him with fogged bug-eyes. "Murderedby the same weapon that killed the others."

"But the presentation is nothing like the others."

"Yes, that is the power and beauty of my former husband's weapon," she said, her voice strained with emotion. The sudden use of the word "former" was not lost on him.

"What are you talking about? This body looks absolutely nothing like the others," he said, careful not to mention Jamie Lin's name. Since he still didn't know what information she had shared with Zhang, he thought it better to err on the side of compartmentalization.

Dash nodded, patiently.

"The weapon can select different tissues. I am guessing he delivered the nanobots on a vector specific for a central nervous tissue antigen. I will explain soon, I promise."

Nick nodded understanding, but inside, his frustration and anxiety were mounting.

"There will be time to examine the corpse later," Zhang snapped. "We need to go." Again he barked a command to the soldiers below.

The unlikely fellowship moved up the stairs to the thirteenth floor; the battle rattle from the two soldiers behind Nick was familiar and reassuring. Zhang and his three operators cleared the hallway, and then they advanced to the Chen apartment. The apartment door was shut and locked. With gloved fingers, Dash entered her security code into the keypad. The lock beeped and then clicked. She stepped clear of the door.

"Wait here," Zhang whispered over his shoulder, and then he entered the apartment with his team.

Nick took Dash by the hand and repositioned her clear of the door. While they waited silently in the hallway, Dash bounced nervously on her toes and mumbled in Chinese. He could hear the men barking short, coordinating bits of information at each other, and except for being in Chinese, it was exactly how they would have cleared rooms in a two-by-two formation in his SEAL team. The lack of gunfire and shouting suggested they were not finding anyone. Less than a minute later, Zhang was back.

"Qing is gone," he said in English. "But he was here, not long ago."

Obviously, Nick thought, picturing the sunken corpse with the blood lakes for eyes on the landing.

"Your house safe has been emptied," Zhang said. "Looks like he took almost everything."

Dash said nothing.

Nick followed Dash through the luxurious apartment. In the living room, a hinged bookshelf hung open, revealing a hidden walk-in safe nested in the wall behind. Black metal shelves built in a *U* shape lined the inside walls. All the shelves were empty.

"My god," Dash mumbled.

"Is something missing?" Nick asked.

Dash shook her head, the weird green rubber mask making the movement a caricature.

"I cannot say," she said, looking up at him. "I had no idea that this room was here."

Nick's stomach went to knots. Not for himself, but for her. He could not imagine the horror and betrayal she must be feeling. Her husband—the man she had shared her life and her bed with—was a monster.

"Listen, Dr. Chen," Zhang said, stepping between them. "It is important that you think carefully. Is there anything missing or left behind that might offer a clue as to where Qing went?"

Dash pulled her mask off and let it drop to the floor.

She looked shell shocked to Nick, almost fugue-like. "No," she muttered. "I do not know this man. I can't help anyone."

Zhang pulled off his own mask. He placed his hand on her shoulder and spoke to her in Chinese. His tone was compassionate, his cadence slow and deliberate.

She did not make eye contact with him, but she nodded as he spoke. Then he said something that made her smile, and at that moment, Nick realized that Zhang was not the enemy. Despite his bravado and bluster, the Snow Leopard Commander was a good man. A sudden strange sense of camaraderie washed over Nick. Maybe SEALs and Snow Leopards were closer to brethren than he'd considered before. If he squinted just right, maybe he even saw a hint of his old Senior Chief in Zhang.

She waited until Zhang had finished before answering, this time in English. "It is my own fault for being so easily deceived, but as you say, the past is in the past. I need to move forward. I need to help you find Qing. Give me a little time to think, and maybe I will remember some clues."

"That's all I ask," Zhang said. He nodded to Nick, who was unsure what the nod implied but preferred it to the barrel of a gun pointed at him.

Zhang stepped away to conference with his junior officer in Chinese. When they finished, Zhang turned back to Nick. "We must go. There is much to do and many people to talk to. Beijing is at risk. The joint task force has a new mandate—hunt down Chen Qing and secure his bioweapon."

"We will go with you," Dash said, picking up her mask off the floor.

"No," Zhang said. "I am sorry, Dr. Chen, but for the next few hours, you would serve only to slow our progress. We have much to do." He handed her a small phone. "This phone is secure and will dial me directly by pushing pound-one. I am sorry to ask you to remain behind. I know that must be very difficult for you, but I must insist that you stay here and look for clues as to what Qing's next move might be. As ironic as it sounds, this is probably the safest place you can be right now, because it is the last place Qing will want to be. I've ordered two of my men to remain behind as your protection detail. When you're finished here, pack a bag and my team will drive you to secure, temporary lodging."

Dash nodded.

"Nick Foley, I will permit you to remain here with Dr. Chen and assist her," Zhang said.

Nick raised his eyebrows in surprise.

"Suddenly you trust me?"

Zhang laughed. "Warrior to warrior, you've earned it. Don't do anything to make me regret it."

Nick nodded and flashed Zhang a sarcastic grin. "Yeah, well, you still have my passport, so I don't really have a choice, now do I?"

The joke fell flat and Zhang stared at him.

"That was a joke."

Zhang responded with a polite smile and then turned to Dash. "If you find any clues to where Qing may be hiding or heading, call me immediately." Then he said something in Chinese that made her smile. To Nick's surprise, she stepped in and gave Zhang a hug, which the Snow Leopard Commander received with awkward stoicism.

"Good luck, Commander," Nick said when Zhang turned to leave.

"Thank you, Nick Foley. I expect that the next time we meet, it will be under more favorable circumstances."

"As do I."

Nick watched Zhang conference briefly with his team and then depart via the back stairs, the same way they had come in. The two Snow Leopard "babysitters" that stayed behind split up—one taking a position near the rear exit and the other at the front door. Nick turned to look at Dash and realized she was not at his side. He scanned the living room, but she was gone.

"Dash?" he called, wandering out of the living room. "Dash?"

"I'm in here," she answered, her voice coming from the next room over.

He walked out of the living room, down a short hall, and into her bedroom. He found her sitting in the middle of the floor cross-legged, cradling what looked to be a broken toy in her hands. Around her, the bedroom was in shambles—broken furniture, shattered lamps, and shredded women's clothing were strewn around the room. The room looked as hell-worn as if a grenade had gone off.

He took a knee in front of her. "What is that?" he asked, looking at the jumble of brightly painted wooden shards in her palms.

She looked up at him, a single tear snaking down her left cheek. "It was a gift from my father," she said. "And the last little piece of my soul."

TWENTY-EIGHT

Building 16, fifteenth floor
West Area, Jianwai SOHO
Central business district, Chaoyang District
0215 hours local

QING PEERED OUT from behind the darkened window of the empty office. As with so many properties built under the rejuvenation project in Beijing, Building 16 was only partially occupied. For a modest sum, he had secured an office with an eastern exposure that looked out over Henghui Road. More important, this office gave him a clear vantage of INI's main office and laboratories across the street, half a block away. Invincible Nanotech Industries was his biotech company. His brainchild.

They think they can take it from me?
They think I would let them?

"Fools," he whispered.

In moments, it would all be gone. Disappeared, as if it never existed. And afterward, he would disappear as well, like a ghost. Polakov had dubbed him Prizrak for a reason. Polakov understood him. Polakov appreciated his intellect and his talents. But Polakov made the same mistake as everyone else and tried to control him. Chen Qing was no man's puppet.

He checked the timer counting down on his mobile

phone. Less than a minute and everything would be gone. Well, not everything. His most important creation was archived digitally on multiple encrypted hard drives and stored physically inside twelve pressurized canisters locked in a metal cage beneath the city—in a darker, forgotten Beijing.

Commotion at the end of the block caught his eye, and he strained to see north to the corner of Henghui Road and Jingheng Street without moving closer to the window where he might be noticed. He pursed his lips as two black Mercedes SUVs pulled into the intersection and blocked traffic, blue-and-green lights flashing in their windows. Two other SUVs screamed south on Henghui to block the other corner while a fifth led two large, black military-style trucks onto the oval-shaped access road in front of the INI building. The first truck stopped, and a dozen armed men clad in body armor and helmets poured out the back like angry hornets. The other truck sped around the corner—out of view— presumably to assault the rear in a similar fashion.

He glanced again at his phone: *0:09, 0:08, 0:07...*

He frowned.

He didn't have time to reprogram the timer. Pity—if he could have added just two minutes, the blast would have evaporated the entire assault force and left many fewer enemies to worry about.

It doesn't matter, he told himself. *They will never find me.*

With two seconds left on the countdown, he shielded his eyes. Despite the hand in front of his face, the flash was blinding. The shockwave and the roar hit an instant later, rattling the window in front of him as the explosion incinerated the INI offices across the street. Soldiers who had mobilized on the sidewalk fell in unison to the ground, arms protecting their heads as glass and debris washed over them like crystal rain. The soldiers did not fare well in the maelstrom. He counted one, two, three impalements, one severed arm, one crushed skull, maybe more…it was hard to tell at this distance.

"This is your fault," he yelled through the window at them. "You did this. Not me—not me!" he screamed, spittle spattering the window in front of him.

He sniffed and straightened his shirt.

"Not me."

He slipped his phone into his pocket, turned, and walked out of the empty office. Upon exiting, he calmly locked the door behind him. He walked to the end of the hall, pushed the call button for the elevator, and waited. Moments later, the elevator chimed, the doors opened to greet him, and he rode the glass-and-chrome carriage down, inspecting his fingernails all the way to the lobby.

The next several hours would be difficult and dangerous for him. For the first time in his life, he felt completely alone. For years, he had relied heavily on Polakov and the Russian Intelligence agency he worked for. It was that apparatus that had planned, procured, and installed the demolition charges he had just detonated to cover his tracks. It was that apparatus that had the means to safely and secretly extricate him from China. But now it was gone, and his escape was no longer guaranteed. What he desperately needed now was a new team with equivalent capabilities—state-level brawn to protect him and his big ideas. Perhaps his new ally, with its underground global terror network, would be able to fill this deficit.

The elevator doors opened and he strode confidently across the marble floor toward the lobby exit on the west side of the building—away from the chaos he had just created. He adjusted the leather messenger bag on his shoulder and nodded at the security guard running toward him.

"Did you hear that?" the guard asked, slowing his pace.

Qing shrugged and shook his head.

"There was a massive explosion across the street," the guard said, his breath labored and his face sweating. "I think someone just blew up the INI building."

Qing wondered if the man might be having a heart attack.

"That's terrible," he said, the words incongruous with the serenity he was feeling. "Who would do such a thing?"

It was a shame he had not created more of his biological agent. It would have been an interesting experiment to have combined the MEMS with the explosives. If only he had thought of that before. He made a mental note of this—each new deployment of the weapon was an opportunity to experiment. He had every reason to believe that the nanobots, and the immune vectors they relied on, would survive such an explosion. In fact, if the charge was designed properly, the explosion might even enhance the infection rate, propelling and dispersing the bots in a wider area than his aerosolizing canisters were designed to do. He felt a twinge of excitement at the prospect of testing the idea. Unlike the Russians, who were focused on covert applications of the technology, his new ally might find the idea of an explosive delivery very appealing indeed.

A conversation for another time, he mused.

He continued out the west doors and then moved southwest at a quick clip along the empty sidewalk between Building 16 and Building 15 to the south. Then he continued west two more blocks, turned south on Yong'anli East Street, and a minute later was heading east on the Tonghuihe North side road that paralleled the Tonghu River. As he walked past Henghui, he glanced left. Fires burned, sirens wailed, and chaos reigned supreme in the place that had once been INI. He smiled. That would keep his enemies occupied for a while. It would take less than twenty minutes to walk to the vacant shop with secret access to the Underground City.

No one would think to look for him there.

No one except Dazhong…

He glanced at his watch, surprised at how much time had gone by. He picked up his pace. This was not a meeting he wanted to be late for.

TWENTY-NINE

Chen residence
0225 hours local

DAZHONG STARED AT the splintered remains of the puzzle box cradled in her hands. Considering everything else that had happened to her in the past forty-eight hours, a broken puzzle box should be the least of her anxieties. A broken puzzle box should not trigger such angst and loss in a grown woman. But here she was, holding this broken thing, and the emotions were real. Maybe there is a reason emotions are difficult to articulate. Emotions are the bridge between the concrete and the abstract. They are the bridge between that which is external, the world, and internal, the mind. The mind ascribes worth and hierarchy to objects, people, and events in the world; each value judgment is unique from mind to mind. To 99.999 percent of the people in the world, her broken puzzle box would hold no more value than a novelty toy—its worth as inconsequential as a taxi fare. In Dazhong's world, it was an intimate treasure that transcended a monetary analog. The puzzle box was a metaphor—it was the yin and yang of Chen Dazhong: plain in form yet beautiful when painted; impenetrable to the uninitiated, yet accessible with intimacy; secure in the right hands, yet vulnerable in others…

"I'm sorry," Nick said, interrupting her thoughts,

his voice soft and cautious. "It must have been very beautiful."

"It was. I think you would have…" She stopped and let the words trail off.

"You think I would have what?"

"I think you would have appreciated it—for what it really was. Qing never understood it, and so he resented it. And he resented me," she said. "He did this to hurt me."

Nick stood and turned to leave.

"Where are you going?" she said, confused.

"To the kitchen," he said. "Be right back."

She heard the clamor of cabinet doors and drawers being exercised sequentially and then he returned carrying a plastic bag. He held the mouth of the bag open and presented it to her.

"Put the pieces in here," he said. "I will fix it for you."

"No, Nick. It is destroyed."

"Nah," he said with a cocky little grin. "That's just plain-old broken. In my world, the word *destroyed* has a different definition."

"Well, it looks destroyed to me," she said, placing her cupped hands over the open bag and letting the pieces fall inside.

"Trust me. Destroying things used to be my profession. It's not destroyed."

"If you say so," she said, unable to suppress a smile at his foolish optimism. "But I still don't see the point of this."

"Maybe when things calm down a bit, I'll see if I can put Humpty back together again."

She raised an eyebrow at him. "I thought you were a professional destroyer of things."

"Yeah, well, that was my old job. Now I'm a professional fixer of things."

She laughed and felt a little flutter of hope that maybe he could make good on the promise. After all, he'd made good on all the others. Side by side, on hands and knees, they scoured the floor for every last shard of the puzzle box. When they had finished gathering them, he helped her to her feet.

They looked at each other expectantly.

"Zhang's men should be ready to move us out of here any minute," Nick said, hooking his thumbs in his cargo pant belt loops, "so if there's anything else you want to grab—some clothes, toothbrush, clean underwear—you might want to do that now."

"As you can see," she said, gesturing to the wardrobe carnage all around them. "My choices are limited."

"Good point," he said. "In that case, we could look around for clues. Something Qing might have accidentally left behind or overlooked—anything that might give us an idea as to his next move or possible whereabouts."

"What is *whereabouts*?" she asked. "I don't know this word."

"It means location," he said.

"And what is *Humpty*?"

"What?" he said.

"Before, you said the word *Humpty*, when you were talking about my puzzle box."

"Ah yes, I suppose I did," he said, chuckling. "Humpty is an egg."

"An egg?"

"Yeah, but not a real egg," he said. "It's an English nursery rhyme: 'Humpty Dumpty sat on a wall. Humpty

Dumpty had a great fall. All the king's horses, and all the king's men, couldn't put Humpty together again.'"

"This does not make sense, Nick. Why would the king try to use horses to fix a broken egg?"

"I know," he laughed. "It's absurd, but like all children's rhymes, there is another meaning."

"What does it mean, this story of Humpty Dumpty?"

"Supposedly, Humpty Dumpty was the name of a cannon used to defend a walled city in England back in the 1600s. It's said the cannon was loved and revered by the city's soldiers and residents because it had such an excellent service record fending off invaders. Then one day, the city fell under siege. During the attack, a parliamentary cannon shot the wall out beneath Humpty Dumpty. Humpty fell to the ground and broke into pieces. The soldiers tried to repair it, but they were not able to put Humpty back together. They left the cannon abandoned in place."

She nodded, thoughtfully. "So the point of the story is that if you want to destroy a cannon, the best way is to use another cannon?"

"I suppose that's one way of looking at it," he said. "Now that I think about it, the story reminds me of US military policy in Iraq last time I was there. The bean counters in Washington somehow decided it was more economical to disable multimillion-dollar equipment and leave it abandoned in place than to ship the stuff back stateside. Which is completely ridiculous, if you ask me. I can't believe—"

"That's it!" she said, interrupting him. "The interstitial debris. I didn't understand it before, but now I think I do. It's Humpty Dumpty."

"Okay, now I'm the one who's confused," he said. "What are you talking about?"

She thought a moment about how best to explain the concept to Nick, but then one of the two Snow Leopards came through the door.

"Time to go, Dr. Chen," he said politely in Chinese, but there was no doubt in her mind this was not a request.

"Just a moment, please," she said. Her mind was reeling and she needed to get back on balance before the germ of her idea evaporated.

"I'm sorry, Dr. Chen, but we must leave now. Come with me, please."

"What is it?" Nick asked, his hand on her arm. The Snow Leopard now had her by the other arm, leading her out toward the front door. She felt herself very much pulled in two directions by the two hands on her.

"Time to go, it seems."

"You've thought of something, though," Nick said, excitement in his voice.

"Yes," she breathed. "I think so… I will tell you on the way."

As they approached the foyer, the second Snow Leopard unlocked and opened the front door.

Then, everything went to hell.

There was a blinding flash, a deafening pop, and an acrid smell that filled her nostrils. A hand tightened on her arm and pulled her to the floor as gunfire erupted all around her. Someone screamed and something heavy fell on top of her. She realized her eyes were closed, and she forced them open. The next scream was hers as she found herself staring into the dead eyes of the younger of the two Snow Leopards—the right side of his forehead obliterated, brain matter dribbling out and down his cheek. She cocked her head away from the grizzly visage and came cheek to cheek with Nick, who she just now registered was shielding her with his body.

"Stay on the ground," he whispered, "no matter what happens."

There was a calm certainty in his voice, and in that moment, she trusted him unconditionally.

As the smoke engulfing them cleared, she saw two men in suits standing an arm's length away in the foyer. They looked like businessmen except for the submachine guns slung from their shoulders. They were both pointing their weapons at Nick, who was making a big show of holding his hands above his head and getting slowly to his feet.

"Thank God you're here," he said in English. "Do you speak English? I'm Dr. Foley and this is Dr. Dazhong Chen. The men you shot were holding us hostage— they are Snow Leopards. Thank you for rescuing us."

Nick was on his feet now and moving slowly toward the closer gunman, who was surveying the carnage around them. The man shifted his gaze to Nick and leaned right to say something to his friend in a language she didn't understand—Russian, she thought.

The Russian gripped his machine gun at the ready, but she noticed the barrel had dropped lower now. "You are American?" the Russian said.

"Is it that obvious?" Nick laughed jovially, while his feet continued to shuffle, inching him closer. "Damn accent always gives it away. I grew up in Texas, but—"

Midsentence, Nick's body transformed into a blur of motion. One instant he was a hapless academic, and the next he was holding the first gunman's rifle in his hands, the strap pulled tight around the Russian man's throat. The second gunman reacted reflexively, swinging his own weapon around, but he was too slow. There was a horrible burp as tongues of fire leapt from Nick's machine gun and the Russian's face exploded in a shower of blood and bone. Nick twisted the rifle in a half circle and jerked hard, snapping the first gunman's neck. In what seemed like slow motion, she watched in horror as both of the vanquished gunmen crumpled to the floor with the sickening crunch of collapsing bone. Nick looked down at her, and she saw hellfire in his eyes. A heartbeat later, the look disappeared, replaced by the familiar calm, compassionate eyes she had come to know and trust.

"Are you okay?" he asked and extended a hand to her. At first, the thought of taking the hand of the man who had robotically taken two lives was repulsive. Then the gravity of what had just happened registered with her. Nick had saved her life again.

She reached for him and he pulled her to her feet.

"What was that?" she stammered.

"We need to go. Right now," Nick said, grabbing her forearm and tugging her toward the door. "I'll explain it to you on the way."

"Who were these men?" she asked, her feet still frozen to the floor.

Nick looked at the dead men at his feet.

"Russians," he said. "No friends of ours, that's for sure."

He retrieved a pistol from the thigh holster of one of the dead Snow Leopard commandos and shoved it into the waistband of his pants. He tugged gently on her arm again. "We have to go, Dash. There may be others."

She recoiled at the words and then followed him out the door.

She followed Nick into the stairwell beside the elevator bank. He moved like a soldier now—scanning over the barrel of the submachine gun as they descended.

"Where are we going?" she asked.

"Away from here," he said, his voice even and cool.

At the bottom of the stairwell, Nick ditched the machine gun and untucked his shirt to hide the pistol butt protruding at the small of his back.

"Walk slowly and calmly," he whispered, taking her hand. "We exit through the lobby just like nothing happened. Can you do that?"

"Yes," she said, steeling herself.

Moments later, they were on the sidewalk outside the building, walking hand in hand. As they walked, Nick coached. "We are just a couple out for a stroll…smile and nod… I just told you a joke…laugh if you can." To accent the point, he tilted his head back and chuckled. She tried to laugh, but the sound seemed to catch in her throat. They walked three blocks and turned left. A half block later, he abruptly pulled her into the shadows of a short alley between two apartment buildings. He made her crouch behind him while he watched the street for what felt like an eternity.

Finally, he turned to her and smiled. "Are you okay? Are you injured?"

She nodded and was angry when she felt tears rim her eyes. She squeezed them away. "I'm okay," she said, glad to hear certitude in her voice.

"Good," he said with a sigh. "Jesus, Dash. That was a close one."

"I need to go back to the CDC," she said, not wasting

anytime. With the threat of imminent death now gone, her body was electric with energy from the new insight she had back in the apartment. "I need to go back to the microscopy lab. I need to test a new theory."

"Are you crazy? Russian gunmen just killed two of Zhang's men. Do you still have the phone he gave you? We need to call him immediately," Nick said.

"I lost the phone, Nick," she said, meeting his gaze.

"Shit," Nick seethed through clenched teeth.

She reached out and took his hands in hers. "You have to trust me, Nick. This is important. We can call Zhang from the CDC, but right now we are wasting precious time."

"You just figured something out, didn't you?" he said.

"Yes."

"Something big?"

"I think so."

"As in, how to stop your husband and save the world big?"

She met his gaze and nodded once.

"In that case," he said, trotting off ahead of her, "what the hell are you waiting for?"

THIRTY

Grandma's Kitchen restaurant
One block east of Henghui East First Road
Chaoyang District
0300 hours local

QING WAS BREATHING hard as he crossed the parking lot outside of Grandma's Kitchen. Despite the cool nighttime air, his skin was dappled with sweat. He was desperately out of shape, and the hurried walk over from Building 16 had proven it. No matter—physical exercise had never been of interest to him. There were too few productive wakeful hours during the day as it was. Why would he squander any portion of that time on exercise? He possessed the most powerful bioweapon on the planet—what did it matter if he couldn't run five kilometers?

He reached into his pocket and retrieved a small key ring. The key seemed to shiver, but this was a product of the adrenaline coursing through his veins. Finally, he managed to slip the quivering key into the lock and spin the deadbolt with a click. He removed the key, stepped quickly inside the building, and closed the door behind him. He was standing in the pantry, just off the kitchen. The shelves to his right were full of the foodstuffs needed to prepare the tasteless Western food that the restaurant specialized in. Grandma's Kitchen catered to Western businessmen and tourists, giving them a convenient outlet to continue stuffing themselves with the familiar garbage they loved instead of the many fine Chinese delicacies Beijing had to offer. It was a travesty, in his opinion. But he hadn't come for the food. He'd come to access the restaurant's hidden treasure—a concealed entrance to the Underground City. The entrance existed long before the restaurant occupied the location. He had paid the restaurant manager a hefty bribe for a key to the back door and unfettered, unreported access. At the corner of the long shelf, he grabbed the frame and pulled, and the entire rack slid easily on silent castors away from the wall. Qing slipped behind it and then spun the combination into the old-style padlock on the aged metal door that blended into the wall. Again, his excitement caused his hands to shake, and he made a soft click with his tongue when he had to enter the combination a second time. This time the lock dropped open. He removed it and placed it on the top shelf. Then he carefully pulled the rack back into place as he stepped backward across the threshold of the hidden entry. Once inside the passage, he eased the rusted steel door shut.

He paused, giving his eyes a chance to adjust to the dark. He reached out with his right hand, felt the cinderblock wall, and swept his palm in an arc until he felt the familiar metal box. He flicked the switch and a series of battery-powered, red LED lights illuminated the concrete stairs that stretched out and down before him. He had installed these lights himself after missing a step in the dark, taking a nasty tumble, and nearly breaking his neck. Had he actually broken his neck, he imagined it would have been months before anyone discovered his body. As far as he knew, he was the only person who habitually accessed the Underground City from this entrance.

He descended slowly, listening for movement in the tunnel below. The air was cool underground, eighteen degrees Celsius year round, but stagnant. It had a faint but pervasive odor that he had come to identify as an amalgam of damp concrete, rodent, and mold. He was not bothered by the smell; in fact, the familiarity soothed his nerves. Down here, he was invisible—immune to Beijing's CCTV security cameras, surveillance spotters, patrol cars, and do-gooders with camera phones who could identify him. Down here, he was safe from the state police, the Snow Leopards, and the army. Down here, he was a man in control of his own destiny. He was safe. He was comfortable.

He was a ghost.

The Underground City was exactly as the name implied—a sprawling subterranean complex spanning eighty-five square kilometers built under the heart of Beijing. The excavation project began in 1969 under Chairman Mao's direction and was originally designed to accommodate half of Beijing's then population of six million in the event of a nuclear attack. More than three hundred thousand laborers toiled for a decade, excavating and building a complex web of tunnels, stairwells, ventilation shafts, drinking-water wells, sewage lines, food production and storage nodes, and mixed-use chambers. But the massive project ended during the cold war, incomplete, unutilized, and unknown by the rest of the world. Plans had been entertained by the government in the years leading up to the 2008 Summer Olympics to convert the Underground City into a tourist attraction with shops, restaurants, and bars, but the plans fizzled after the money ran out, leaving the Underground City once again forgotten.

Forgotten by most, but not all.

Eighty-five square kilometers of climate-controlled real estate infrastructure in a city as crowded and expensive as Beijing does not go unnoticed. Economics is omnipotent, and arbitrages will always be exploited. The Underground City was no exception. A vibrant black market economy of illicit commerce and real estate brokering flourished beneath the streets of Beijing. Down below, anything could be had for a price—drugs, sex, weapons, black market tech, and shelter. It was an *Underground City* in the truest sense, with its own law and leadership. Patrolling gangs who worked for Gang Jin—the Underground City's "mayor"—kept order, enforced the rules, and collected "taxes." The money that flowed through the Underground City now was millions more than city planners had dreamed of for legitimate enterprise. This black-market economy was Qing's ticket to salvation, yet danger still lurked. An unfortunate encounter with a drug addict—or worse, Gang Jin's enforcers—could delay or even derail him from reaching the critical meeting with a new buyer, and this was one meeting he could not afford to miss. His life depended on it.

He moved cautiously, but quickly, down the red-lit tunnel at the bottom of the stairs. Soon the lights he installed would end, but by then, his eyes would be much better adapted, and if need be, he could always use his flashlight. As he walked, he remembered the time Dazhong had followed him here—years ago when she was still content with being his wife and not distracted from her marital obligations by professional and other less worthy intrusions. Their sex had been satisfying for him, but far from adventurous. He whispered his fantasies in her ear during their lovemaking to test her appetites, but she had balked. He had soon become a regular at Club Pink—an establishment specifically designed to discretely cater to the desires of wealthy clients, no matter how kinky or bizarre. There was no sexual appetite that could not be curbed in the Underground City—for a price. His own interests were usually more pedestrian and less expensive, but no less devastating to his young wife, who followed him and found him indulging his appetites.

It had been a disaster. She had run off and nearly been attacked in the process. It had taken years to mend the damage to their marriage. Perhaps it never really had been mended.

What he would give to drag Dazhong back down here with him now. He imagined her naked, bound, and helpless. He stiffened as he visualized himself dominating and then breaking her. After her punishment was meted, he imagined her loving him as an obedient wife should.

Qing stopped and pressed his thumbs into his temples.

Enough thoughts of Dazhong and her treachery. If given the opportunity, he would avenge her infidelity and punish her properly. If not, then she would simply perish with the rest of the corrupt in Beijing.

Darkness forced him to retrieve the LED flashlight from his bag. He clicked on the beam and a rat squealed, scurrying across the floor in front of him so close he almost stepped on it. He jumped back a step, his heart pounding in his chest. A drop of water fell from the ceiling and splattered on the bridge of his nose, startling him again.

He collected himself and forced his mind to the task at hand. As he made his way down the tunnel, he saw a dim light several hundred meters in the distance. Yes, good, the turn was close. He walked ten meters forward and felt a subtle shift in the air currents. He arced the flashlight beam right and found the next passage. He turned into the new tunnel and resisted the urge to jog. He was close. He checked his mobile phone for the time and smiled. Perfect. He would arrive on time. These were not the type of people who liked to be kept waiting.

A few minutes later, he reached the stairwell and climbed back up toward the surface. He had selected the meeting location—an unoccupied warehouse—because it afforded several strategic advantages. First, it was unoccupied. He knew this because he had purchased the warehouse fourteen months ago via a shell company. Second, it had an entrance to the Underground City, which meant he could enter and exit without being seen or followed. His original plan had been to sell the building to INI for a hefty profit, evade capital gain taxes, and set up nanobot incubators. He would maintain an office at the facility and have handy access to the Underground City. Never had he imagined that the building might someday save his life.

He came to the recess in the wall and shined his light inside, revealing a metal gate and the stairs beyond. He opened the gate and then clicked off the light and stowed it in his bag. He quietly opened the door at the top of the stairs, slipped into a small utility closet he'd had made to camouflage the entrance, and closed the secret panel door back into place. Then he waited a moment behind the ordinary closet door that opened out into a hallway at the rear of the warehouse. He pressed his ear against the door. Hearing nothing, he slowly opened the door, grimacing when it creaked slightly. He stepped out into the hall and shut the door behind him.

He glanced left and right and found the hallway empty as expected. He walked softly down the hall to the access door to the warehouse and pulled it open. Beside the door, a man holding a submachine gun startled and whirled to face Qing. The sentry raised his weapon and then glanced quickly over his shoulder at his boss, who was standing in the middle of a tight group of men in the center of the room. The leader nodded, and the guard stood down.

"Where the hell did you come from?" the guard grunted softly.

Qing said nothing and flashed the muscle a condescending smile. He walked across the tile floor and extended his hand in greeting to the leader, a man known in the underworld as Mok the Broker.

Mok looked at Qing's hand and frowned. "You left me in a rather awkward situation, Doctor," he said, pursing his lips and refusing to shake hands. Then he turned his back and walked a few paces, leaving Qing alone in a cone of light cast by an industrial yellow halogen light above their heads. "You made promises, and so I made promises. You provided me with milestones and timelines, and so I provided milestones and timelines. Do you see where I'm going with this?"

"I'm sorry but—"

"My clients do not care about sorry," Mok said, cutting him off. "These are very serious, very violent people. Surely you've seen what they do to their captives? They chop their heads off with machetes." Mok finally turned back to look at Qing, the trained killers on his flanks staring impassively—attack dogs on a leash.

Qing was not intimidated by this charade. In fact, he expected this. Mok had always been his contingency plan, but the broker of the underworld didn't know that. Pride needed to be swallowed; face needed saving.

"Of course, you're right. I've put you in terrible situation for which I apologize most sincerely," he said, bowing his head slightly and crossing his arms behind him. "I assure you that this delay was not of my own making."

Mok the Broker lifted an eyebrow. "Go on."

"I fear my operation might be under investigation, and I did not want to risk your safety or anonymity. Extra precautions were necessary, and such things always take longer than anticipated."

The man's mouth dropped open. Then his face flushed with anger.

"You are under surveillance and you still came here to meet me? Are you insane?"

Qing put on his most disarming smile. "Quite the opposite. It is with an abundance of caution that I came here today. Everything is in order, and I am ready to proceed."

Mok shook his head. "I am not certain we can still proceed," he said. "There is more risk than you had led me to believe."

"The greater the risk, the greater the reward," Qing assured. "You have explained to your client what the agent can do?"

The broker laughed.

"My reward is money, which I must be both alive and free to enjoy. I do not share your passion for this weapon of mass destruction, nor do I share our client's zeal for punishing nonbelievers. I am a businessman, and the cost-benefit ratio of our relationship has just shifted."

Qing nodded. "Of course, which is why I suggest raising your fee from twenty percent to thirty percent— a very substantial sum of money. I will also add a five-million-euro bonus after you complete one additional task I require."

"I am listening," Mok said.

"It is imperative that I leave immediately."

"You want us to arrange passage out of Beijing?" the man asked.

"Out of China," Qing clarified. "I require a private, secluded residence where I can wait safely and comfortably until my new lab and residence are established in Manama."

"How soon?"

"We must leave Beijing this afternoon."

Mok snorted. "You ask a lot."

"And I give as much," Qing said. "I offer not just money but information to protect you and your organization—and your loved ones, if you have them—from things that are coming."

Now he appeared to have the man's full attention. Mok glanced down, thinking perhaps, but more likely stalling for affect.

"I can get you out, *if* we move forward," Mok said.

"If?"

"Yes, if," the arms broker said with a smirk. He nodded to one of the brutes beside him, who moved off toward a black SUV Qing could see parked inside the warehouse near the loading door. "The client needs a demonstration first."

"Of course," Qing said, not surprised. The event in Kizilsu was compelling but had not been witnessed firsthand. He slipped the messenger bag from his shoulder and from it pulled out a black case, about the size of a large textbook. As he did, the armed guard returned with a barefoot man, his torn clothing matted with blood and his bare feet swollen and purple. He could not see the man's face, because the man's head was covered with a black hood. The guard dragged the man with one hand and a folding metal chair with the other. The pair stopped three feet in front of Qing, and Mok's goons went to work. One bodyguard forced the hooded man to sit on the chair, while the others used plastic ties to bind his arms and legs to the structure.

"This is the subject?" Qing asked, opening the black case. Inside was a small metal canister he had been using and three syringes full of a pink liquid, each a bit darker than the last and lined up perfectly in the foam cutouts inside the box.

Mok shook his head in apparent amusement and snorted again. "Subject? Yes, Doctor, this is your *subject*."

Qing smiled, hiding his irritation at Mok's insolence. "Of course," he said and tapped the darkest of the three syringes—the highest concentration—to check that no air was present. Silly, wasn't it? A few ccs of intravenous gas would be the least of this man's concerns in a moment.

"What did this man do?" Qing asked as he located a bulging antecubital vein in the crease of the hooded man's elbow.

"Perhaps he did not bow low enough to Mecca; perhaps he drew a cartoon picture of Mohamed," said Mok the Broker. "I don't know, and I don't care."

Qing took position at the man's side and then, careful to not stick himself, plunged the needle into the man's vein. The man jerked his arm, but Mok's bodyguard clamped down on the poor soul like a vise. Qing pulled back on the plunger and saw the swirling cloud of blood in the syringe that let him know he was in the vein, and then injected the pink liquid. He then dropped the syringe into a small clear case built into the side of his black box.

As Qing packed his case, he noticed that Mok and his goons were staring expectantly at the hooded man. One of Mok's men was recording video of the event with his mobile phone camera.

"It's not working," Mok said with irritation after a minute had transpired.

"Patience," Qing said. "If the buyers wanted to watch a bullet spill this man's brains, then they would have bought a gun. The death that you are witnessing is happening on the cellular level. This is a precise and sophisticated biological weapon that can kill anyone— covertly, quietly, and without a trace."

"He is not contagious?" Mok asked, taking a step back.

"No," Qing assured, neglecting to mention that it was best not to be exposed to the target tissues until enough time had lapsed for the nanobots to scavenge completely.

"How long?" the man asked.

"The weapon was given intravenously, so tissue decimation will progress quickly."

He had selected central nervous tissue as his target—
like he had with Polakov. He had also injected a highly
concentrated dose, so effects would manifest quickly.
No time for games today; he had a tight schedule to
meet. He took a bottle of sparkling water from his messenger bag and drank from it.

"Please send me a text message when you have the
client's decision," Qing said, screwing the cap back on
the bottle. "Remember, we need to be out of Beijing by
three o'clock this afternoon."

Mok waved a hand at him but kept his eyes riveted
on the subject.

Qing strolled away, sparkling water in his hand.

The broker would be calling him very quickly. Until
then, he had other important business to attend to in
the Underground City.

THIRTY-ONE

Chinese Centers for Disease Control and Prevention
0320 hours local

"I'M SORRY, NICK, but you have to wait in the car," Dazhong said, chewing her lower lip.

"Impending bioterrorism attack in Beijing, Snow Leopards on high alert, unsanctioned American Navy SEAL seeking entry into CDC after hours," he said with sarcastic lilt. "Don't worry, I get it."

"Please stay in the car," she said.

He narrowed his eyes at her. "Hey, I'm not the one who has trouble following orders, remember?"

"Keep your phone turned on so I can call you if I need you."

"Of course, but I'm not the one who has trouble answering and returning phone calls either."

She shot him a playful scowl, opened the driver's-side door, and stepped out. "And whatever you do, don't leave."

"Cross my heart," he said, and traced an *X* over his chest.

"I should only be an hour…maybe two."

"Just go, Dash," he said, scooting up and over the center console to take her place behind the wheel.

"Okay, I'm going. Bye, Nick."

Ten minutes later, she was badged in, cleared through

security, and pulling open the door to the nanoscope laboratory. She exhaled with relief to find the room exactly as she had left it hours ago. She powered on the nanoscope and began her search for nanobots. If her theory was correct, she would not find any in the prepared samples—only nonbiological, interstitial debris. She searched all the slides in the caddy but couldn't find a single nanobot. Given the amount of tissue material she needed to search and the search magnification, she was certain to have missed one, or two, or maybe even half a dozen active nanobots in each sample. But finding the needle in the haystack was not the point. Twelve hours ago, there had been *millions* of nanobots in Jamie Lin's tissues. The question she needed to answer was this: "Where did all the nanobots go?"

To her knowledge, she was the only person who had actually seen an intact nanobot—excluding Qing, that is. Major Li and his team of researchers had encountered the "smoking gun" problem during postmortem analysis of tissues harvested from the Kizilsu victims: pervasive tissue damage, no identifiable pathogens, but abundant, interspersed nonbiological debris. Unlike Li's team, she had harvested her tissue samples only moments after Jamie Lin's death, and she had put the samples on ice, thereby slowing cellular motility. The combination of these factors—time and temperature—probably explained why she had seen the nanobots in action, but Li's team had not.

Her initial hypothesis for the mechanism behind the nanobot disappearance had been that the nanobots self-destructed after a predetermined time period—like a bomb detonating after the timer counts down to zero. The problem with this theory was that the empirical evidence did not support it or, at least, did not support it completely. The nonbiological debris that both she and Major Li had observed was uniform and unspecific. Every chunk looked like every other chunk. There were no identifiable pieces that screamed, "Nanobot Death Machine." The task was analogous to being shown a pile of demolition rubble and then being asked to identify the architecture of the building that had been demolished. The fact that Major Li had possessed the insight to make the leap from indiscernible trash to a Bio-MEMS weapon was impressive. Had their roles been reversed, she doubted she would have made the same cognitive leap. Li, however, had not offered any theories as to what happened to the nanobots postmortem. If she could solve that mystery, then she could move on to the next step—figuring out how to stop them.

Her revised theory was simple: The nanobots did not self-destruct.

They were shredded—shredded by other nanobots.

The idea had germinated when Nick told her about Humpty Dumpty—not the egg, but the origin story. In the seventeenth century, the best way to blow up a cannon was simply to use another cannon. In the case of Qing's nanobots, the same was true. The human immune system was incapable of destroying them; that was the genius of the weapon. The hardware advantage of a synthetic macrophage over a biological one was insurmountable. But as is so often the case, a great advantage does not often come without a great disadvantage. Yin and yang. In his quest to build the perfect bioweapon, Qing recognized that stealth was a prerequisite. Killing people is easy. Killing without leaving fingerprints is hard. Leaving millions of self-replicating nanobots in the tissues of a victim was one hell of a fingerprint. To safeguard his technology—from discovery, duplication, and defensive countermeasures—Qing turned to biology for the answer.

Apoptotic phagocytosis.

Apoptosis, or preprogrammed cellular death, is a highly regulated, essential biological process in the life-cycle of multicellular organisms. In contrast to cellular division, which provides the body a mechanism to generate new, healthy cells, apoptosis is a mechanism to rid the body of aged, defective ones. In healthy adult humans, cellular division and apoptosis are in equilibrium—averaging fifty to seventy million events per day. After a cell dies, phagocytic cells, such as macrophages, engulf and digest the remains. Dazhong was very familiar with apoptosis because of the essential role that preprogrammed cell death plays in a healthy, functioning immune system—providing an elegant, efficient means to rid the body of infected and cancerous cells. Now it appeared Qing had taken a page from nature's playbook and programmed his nanobots to phagocytize each other once all the target tissue was destroyed.

The man is brilliant, she mused. *Diabolical, but brilliant.*

She backed her stool away from the monitor, arched her back, and groaned. She was exhausted. She couldn't remember the last time she slept. She closed her eyes for just an instant. Her head bobbed with microsleep, and she snapped back awake.

Got to keep going. Got to keep pushing.

She stood and smacked her cheeks with her palms. Then she jumped up and down to get her blood pumping. It helped a little.

Time to make more slides.

Her theory was sound, but she needed proof—visual confirmation of nanobot phagocytosis. The samples loaded in the nanoscope were too old. She needed fresh tissue, but that wasn't an option. Her only hope was that the refrigeration had slowed the motility of the nano-bots in the remaining samples of Jamie Lin's liver to the point that nanobot apoptosis was incomplete.

It took her thirty minutes to prepare two additional samples for the nanoscope, ten minutes to load them, and twenty minutes to find her holy grail, and when she did, her heart skipped a beat. There, in the center of a pile of black debris, a nanobot was busy tearing another nanobot to pieces, its legs beating furiously as it pulled its brother machine into a macerating maw in the center of the orb. She bellowed a victory howl so primal and loud it made her blush despite the fact that she was alone. Then a stab of panic washed over her. Had she remembered to press the record button for the nanoscope video feed? She glanced at the controls and breathed a sigh of relief—recording in high definition.

The fatigue she had been battling earlier was gone, replaced by endorphin-driven euphoria. She grabbed her mobile phone and dialed Nick. He picked up on the second ring.

"Hello," Nick answered. He sounded tired.

"It's me," she said, "Dash." As she spoke, it regis-tered that this was the first time she had referred to herself by that name, which made her feel strange and good all at the same time.

"Yes, I know," he said.

She could feel him smiling.

"Were you sleeping?" she asked.

"No," he grumbled. "Were you?"

"Of course not."

"It's been nearly two hours," he said with a hint of irritation in his voice. "I was beginning to get worried."

"I'm fine," she said. "I'm calling to tell you some news. Do you remember what I told you during the drive here from my apartment—my theory about nano-bot apoptotic phagocytosis?"

"You mean the part when you said you think the nanobots eat each other after they've killed their target?"

"Yes, that part."

"I remember."

"Well, I was right, Nick. I have video proof."

"That's incredible, Dash," he said, suddenly sounding very much awake. "And super creepy."

"Yes," she said. "It is very creepy. And I have you to thank for the idea. If you had not told me the story of Humpty Dumpty, I would not have thought of this."

"Somehow I doubt that, but you're welcome," said Nick, chuckling on the line. "Now what? Should we call Zhang and tell him where we are? I imagine he's pretty angry with the two of us right about now."

"You can call him and tell him where we are, but I am not finished here. I have much more work to do. This was just the first step."

"I don't understand," he said. "You figured it out. You solved the mystery of the weapon. What else is there?"

"Oh, Nick," she said, frowning at the phone. "Understanding the function of this bioweapon is only half my job."

"What's the other half?"

"Developing a way to stop it."

"I watched what these things did to Batur. We both saw what they did to Jamie Lin. How do you stop something that is unstoppable? There are no antibiotics for nanobots, and the human immune system doesn't have the capability to fight these things by itself."

"You are right, Nick. The human immune system cannot fight nanobots," she said solemnly.

There was a long pause on the line before he finally said, "Then how do you propose to stop them?"

"The only way to stop nanobots," she said, clenching her fist, "is with nanobots."

THIRTY-TWO

Club Pink
Underground City
0545 hours local

QING RECLINED IN the oversized leather chair, a black leash clasped tightly in his right hand. His eyes were closed as he concentrated on the pleasure. When the woman on her knees between his legs began to tire and slowed her rhythm, he jerked the leash, pitching her forward until her chin smacked painfully, and erotically, against his pubic bone. The tears streaming down her cheeks pleased him, so he lightened the tension on the leash to allow her more freedom to work. He closed his eyes.

The sound of his phone startled him and he sat up. He picked the phone up from the armrest of the chair, saw the text message, and smiled. A picture of the test subject—dead and bleeding in the warehouse—appeared on the screen. The image gave him great pleasure and drove him to immediate climax. He yanked the leash, delighting in the sound of his sex slave's gagging sobs. Then he pushed her backward with his foot, sending her toppling onto her back. He stood, cleaned himself, and then pulled on his pants. He stepped over the girl and walked into the small, private sitting room connected to the "pleasure room" he had rented. He had not honestly been in the mood for his favorite Underground City diversion, but he needed a place to hide out where he would be safe from wandering eyes. What better place than a very expensive, members-only club with private security and underground cellular service?

He dialed Mok the Broker.

"Your 'experiment' is complete and my client—our client—is pleased," Mok said.

"I told you they would not be disappointed," Qing said. "How long did it take?"

"Nearly thirty minutes to die, but he was incapacitated and then comatose within minutes, just as you said."

"So we have a deal?"

"We have a preliminary deal," the middleman said. "The buyer would like to see an event-level demonstration, but afterward they will agree to all your terms."

"Very good," Qing said as he tightened his belt and smoothed his expensive shirt. "Do you and I have a deal as well? I must be out of Beijing by three pm today. The *demonstration* will follow shortly thereafter."

"It will happen here, in Beijing?" the man asked, and Qing smiled at the uneasy fear he heard in the voice.

"Yes," Qing answered. "You may want to have your people out of town with us at three pm. But don't worry, it will be safe to return as early as tomorrow."

There was a long pause as his new "partner" digested that information.

"Do we have a deal?" Qing asked.

"Yes," the man replied. "We have a deal. My people are working on travel arrangements as we speak. Would you like to meet now?"

"No. I have work to do," Qing said as he slung his

messenger bag over his shoulder. "I will meet you at two pm."

"Very well, two pm," the man replied. "At our last meeting place. Do not be late."

Qing suddenly realized that Mok the Broker possessed one more thing that he needed. He had lost much when he had severed his ties with his Russian handlers. He had no team now, and he would need one desperately in the coming hours. "Actually, I could use some assistance."

"What kind of assistance?"

"A small security detail," Qing said, "to watch my back while I work."

"A security detail?"

"Yes," Qing said. "Just a few men to make certain no one interferers with my efforts while I make preparations for the demonstration."

"You will pay extra?"

Qing laughed. Small-minded men like Mok the Broker were so predictable. "No," he said, not for lack of funds, but for the sake of dominance. "The money you will make from this transaction—your brokerage fee plus your bonus for getting me safely out of China—will make you a very wealthy man. Who knows, Mok? I would not be surprised if you chose to retire when this deal is done."

There was a short pause.

"Very well," his new, official business partner relented. "I will assign you three men. Where shall they meet you?"

Qing told him.

"Ah," the man said with what Qing heard as admiration and respect. "Now I understand how you have been avoiding surveillance. Very clever."

"I need them armed and ready to move in thirty minutes."

"Thirty minutes," Mok said, and the line went dead.

Qing slipped his phone into his pants pocket and then pushed through the frosted-glass door back into his pleasure room. The woman bowed her shaved head and stared at the floor. With two fingers, he raised her head by the chin and smiled down at the frightened eyes, rimmed with tears.

"I'm afraid I must go, my dear," he said and kissed her on the top of her head, the stubble tickling his lips. As he closed the door behind him, he purged the session from his mind and shifted his thoughts to the future.

By this time tomorrow, Beijing would be engulfed in death and chaos.

And he would be watching it all unfold on television, while enjoying a bottle of very expensive wine.

THIRTY-THREE

Jamie Lin's apartment
0550 hours local

IT WAS MORE than a sixth sense. Experience and training were in control now. Any lingering question about whether something untoward had happened to his agent had long vanished. Lankford did not expect to find her here, at her apartment, but he hoped he might find some clue as to where Jamie Lin was or what had happened to her.

He was hardly surprised when she had called to say she was not feeling well. Her schedule the last few months had been physically and emotionally arduous—working at ViaTech, working her assets in the field, mining data and preparing intelligence reports, and of course keeping up appearances as the late-night party girl her cover demanded. The girl had run herself ragged. He had told her to take the morning off and call him in the afternoon. When he hadn't heard from her by dinner, he thought nothing of it. But when all his calls and text messages went unanswered well into the night, he became concerned.

Lankford entered her access code and the lobby door clicked loose from its magnetic lock. He resisted the urge to look up at the lobby camera as he crossed to the elevator. He pressed the call button and the doors opened immediately. As he rode the lift to the fifth floor, he contemplated his feelings for Jamie Lin. Becoming too emotionally invested was a real risk of his position, and sexist or not, the tendency was far worse managing a female agent—especially a young agent like Jamie Lin. Since the beginning, he had felt like a big brother to Jamie Lin, fiercely loyal and overprotective. This played well for their cover relationship—a perpetual not-so-secret "secret" office tryst. But lately, if he was honest with himself and factored in their twenty-three-year age difference, his devotion had evolved. Now he viewed Jamie Lin more like the daughter he never had than a sister.

He balled up his fists.

If someone hurt her...

The elevator chimed and the doors opened. He moved swiftly down the hall, acutely aware that he was being recorded. At her apartment door, he pulled out his key and resisted the suddenly overwhelming urge to pull his pistol. He tried the deadbolt first and found it unlocked. As he shifted the key into the doorknob, his instincts were screaming. Jamie Lin always locked the deadbolt, whether she was home or not. Lankford positioned his right hand near the pistol in his waistband and pushed the door open.

"Jamie Lin? Sweetheart, it's me—I'm sorry about the other night..."

The smell hit him like a slap in the face.

He moved swiftly left, kicked the door closed behind him, and pulled his pistol. He'd spent enough time in Iraq and Afghanistan, hunting evil in torture chambers everywhere from the Hussein palaces to basements in Kandahar, to recognize this smell. It was the miasma of death. The reek of decay. His pulse spiked. His movements became reflex.

He scanned the room over his subcompact Sig Sauer 320 and regretted not bringing a weapon with more rounds. The apartment was silent, the air perfectly still. He heard nothing, except for the thumping pulse in his eardrums. He moved right, away from the window, and slid along the wall of the eat-in kitchen. His eyes darted back and forth, clearing the kitchen behind the small pass-through bar. Next, he scanned the short hallway that led to the bathroom and Jamie Lin's bedroom.

He advanced, leading with his Sig.

The light reflected off something on the hallway floor. He inched forward and saw that it was a puddle of dark, congealing blood, beside it a bloody footprint. He paused, his hearing now hyperacute, and held his breath. Nothing—no breathing, no rustling of cloth on skin, no shifting weight on floor boards.

He moved swiftly into the hall. Blood was everywhere. He nearly stepped in one of the pools but stutter-stepped and caught himself against the wall. He looked into the bathroom as he continued down the hall, his brain registering the horror of the body—what looked like a bloated, short man—naked and lying in a pool of black blood. A few loops of intestines lay drying on the floor beside the swollen mass of tissue. He left the nightmare in the bathroom and moved on to the bedroom.

The bedroom door was slightly ajar. He crossed the threshold and fluidly cleared both corners. He rapidly moved on to clear a small closet and then dropped to a knee to clear under the bed. With his peripheral vision, he kept watch on the hallway, his gun hand instinctively drifting that way. He stood and his gaze fell on Jamie Lin's bed, the sheets stained in dark-gray circles that still looked damp. The pillow was spotted with blood, and on the floor by the nightstand he noted a puddle of blood and vomit. Despite himself, he couldn't help but notice the undigested remains of her last meal—the meal she had shared with him at the Noodle Bar.

Jesus Christ...what the hell happened here?

He swiveled back toward the hall, his gun still up but his mind already piecing together the gut-wrenching truth. Dread bloomed in his chest, and it felt as though a thorny rambler was entangling his heart. He moved slowly, reluctantly, out of the bedroom and into the hall. He was keenly aware of each step, a part of him not wanting to step in any bits of Jamie Lin spattered about the floor. Using the tip of his gun, he pushed the bathroom door inward until it bumped against the gray, naked legs of the corpse. He tasted bile in his throat and felt tears spilling onto his cheeks.

The bloated corpse was Jamie Lin—his agent, his friend, his adopted daughter. Her face was a grotesque and deformed caricature of a woman, the lips and eyelids split and gray with blood. He recognized her hair—streaked in electric blue—and he recognized the bracelet that was barely visible on the swollen wrist, biting into the edematous tissues that had swollen to at least three times their normal size.

The corpse had been opened from breastbone to pelvis—the cut ending just above a patch of neatly trimmed pubic hair. Looking into the abdomen was like looking into a vat of motor oil. A flap of scalp was flipped down over her left eye, just beneath where a hole had been carved through her skull. He gagged and looked away, but it was too late. He vomited, adding his own wretch to the horror on the floor. With the purge, his brain suddenly rebooted, and the CIA operator inside him started asking questions.

Was this a murder? Why was the body mutilated? Was someone sending a strong, sick message, or was this something else entirely? It was almost like...an autopsy.

His mind went to the bioterrorism attack in Kizilsu. He remembered Jamie Lin's asset was the CDC director for emergencies like Ebola.

Oh shit.

Lankford pulled his shirt up over his mouth and nose and backed quickly out of the bathroom. He sprinted down the hall through the living room to the front door, where he kicked off his shoes. He felt an upwelling of panic and fear driving him to that place where fight or flight takes control. Every fiber of his being wanted to strip off all his clothes and run screaming from the apartment. But the training saved him from himself. Thank God for the training. He returned his subcompact Sig Sauer to his holster. Then he stepped out of the apartment, closed the door, and locked the dead bolt. Aware of the cameras, he walked as calmly as he could manage toward the elevators.

He rode down, every brain cell still screaming to strip naked and find a scalding hot shower. But he doubted a shower would do any good. If this was a bioweapon, he had been either infected or not. His life was in fate's hands now.

He moved across the lobby at a quick walk and banged out the door. When his shoeless feet hit the sidewalk, he lost the battle. He took off at a sprint down the block, running like he had not run in years. When he reached his car, he glanced in both directions and then tore off his shirt, pants, and socks. He put his gun, wallet, and keys on the driver's seat and then shoved the contaminated clothes down a nearby storm drain. Wearing only his underwear, he strode to the back of his car, popped the trunk, and pulled gray sweat pants, a T-shirt, and a pair of Nikes from a gym bag.

Lankford quickly dressed, scooped up his wallet and gun, and collapsed into the driver's seat. He took three deep, cleansing breaths and then slipped the key into the ignition. He reached to put the transmission into drive, but the weight of the last few minutes buried him like an avalanche. He gripped the steering wheel in both hands and pressed his forehead against his clenched fist. Tears came and he gulped for air.

I'm so sorry, Jamie Lin... I'm so, so sorry.

He let himself suffer, condensing and compacting months' worth of grief into thirty seconds. He would give himself that luxury—thirty seconds to mourn. Then he turned it off like a toggle switch, and his angst was replaced instantaneously by cold, calculated anger.

Whoever did this—this horrible, disgusting thing— to his agent would pay.

He put the transmission in drive and pulled away from the curb.

An image of Nick Foley, the SEAL turned spook, popped into his head. He remembered Foley's smug expression and holier-than-thou attitude as they had chatted in the cafe. Why? Why did Foley take that tack with him? Because Foley was one step ahead. Whatever outfit Foley was working for was way ahead of the CIA

on this Kizilsu thing. To find out who carved up Jamie
Lin, he needed to find Foley.

I'm coming for you, Foley, you Navy SEAL sonuv-
abitch. I'm coming for you right now.

THIRTY-FOUR

Chinese Centers for Disease Control and Prevention

THE HUMAN LIVERS arrived at the CDC by helicopter exactly one hour after Dazhong telephoned Major Li with news of her discovery. Of that hour, ten minutes had been committed to her explaining her plan. Five minutes had been devoted to Major Li yelling at her and arguing why her plan would not work. Two minutes had been consumed by Major Li waffling and then changing his mind. The remaining forty-three minutes had been composed of pulling cadaver livers previously dissected from Kizilsu victims out of cold storage, loading them in biohazard transport containers, and flying them at God's speed to the Chinese CDC from Regiment 54423's undocumented, unacknowledged, top-secret research facility, located on the northern outskirts of Beijing. In the world of high-stakes government bureaucracy, this achievement was nothing short of a miracle.

With the livers in her possession, she worked feverishly to execute her plan. Unlike most plans to save the world, hers was simple—so simple it would either work perfectly or fail completely: *Use Qing's own creation to defeat him and then destroy the technology forever.* The logic was sound; the trouble lay in the execution.

She used a centrifuge to separate as many intact nanobots as possible from five kilos of cadaver liver tissue and then divided the collected population into cryogenic canisters for preservation. According to her agreement with Major Li, 10 percent of the collection was to be earmarked for reverse engineering by the army's greatest technical minds. With the resources and full support of the Chinese government, the army would eventually crack all Qing's secrets, including how the nanobots were fabricated, programmed, and deployed with optimal lethal efficiency. And maybe, if Dazhong was lucky, someone might devote some thought and effort to developing nanotechnology safeguards.

The remaining 90 percent of the collection was for creating nanobot "vaccines." Inoculations would be reserved for Commander Zhang's Snow Leopard commandos, who were presently canvassing the city for Chen Qing, and for emergency first responders, who would be conducting lifesaving operations at "Ground Zero" in the event Qing launched a bioterror attack in Beijing. When Major Li asked her how many doses she thought could be harvested, she'd said she estimated around two hundred.

Her plan had offered Li a solution for both his short-term and long-term agendas—giving him the opportunity to be the savior of Beijing but also control over a powerful new weapon on which to build his career. She'd sold the lie so effectively that she almost convinced herself of the plan's merits.

Almost.

In reality, she used all the harvested nanobots to make two vaccine doses—a primary and a backup. Even with the higher concentration, she did not know if the population of *good* nanobots was sufficient to counteract an infection. Hell, she wasn't even sure her idea would work at all. Hers was not a "vaccine" in the conventional sense of the word. Her vaccine was simply a collection of nanobots that had already made the transition from infection mode to apoptotic phagocytosis mode. Simply put, the nanobots she planned to inject were those carrying out their final program mode of finding and killing other nanobots. Her plan was to wage a nanobot war, and the battlefield was the human body. The invading army would be met head-on by an identical defending army. The soldiers in both armies were the same mass, moved at the same speed, and would be equipped with the same armor. Unfortunately, her army of defending nanobots possessed one major disadvantage compared to the invading nanobots: the infecting nanobots replicate, while the defending nanobots consume indiscriminately...including themselves.

Victory was a numbers game.

For her vaccine to work, the inoculating dose would need to be orders of magnitude larger than the exposure dose. To further complicate matters, the injection would need to be administered immediately *prior* to exposure—early enough to circulate the bots through the body but not so early that they would have time to consume each other to extinction before the infection occurred. Ordinarily, she would test her hypothesis by performing dozens, if not hundreds, of computational simulations. If the simulations demonstrated proof of concept, next she would conduct bench-scale testing in media. After that, she would conduct rodent trials...and so on and so on. But these were not ordinary circumstances, and instead of months to prepare, she had only hours. This was simply the best she could do.

Am I just as crazy as Qing? she wondered.

Hopefully, none of this would be necessary. Qing would be captured and arrested before getting the chance to do the unthinkable. The city would be safe, and she could go back to her old life...no, not her old life. Her old life was over.

There is no going back. There is only tomorrow.

To get to tomorrow, she had to make it through today. To make it through today, she had to stop Qing. As much as she wanted to place that burden entirely on the very capable shoulders of Commander Zhang and his elite squad of Snow Leopards, her gut told her that to do so would be a mistake. They would not find Qing unless he let them. If he let them find him, then it would be a trap, and a lot of very brave men would die agonizing, gruesome deaths. No, she knew what she had to do. One final deception to set things right.

Only hours ago, she had confessed to Li and Zhang that she didn't know her husband—that the real Chen Qing had deceived her for years. But that was only a half truth. The whole truth was that she had deceived herself. All the signs had been present, but she had chosen to ignore them. She had chosen to minimize, rationalize, or excuse every disturbing behavior and belief that Qing exhibited. Somewhere along the way, she had subconsciously decided that being married to a lie was better than being married to a monster. Divorce had never been an option with Qing. He was a sociopath— a charming, brilliant, cruel, obsessive megalomaniac. For him, life was a game of seduction and domination, obedience and punishment. With time, she'd learned the tools to coexist as his wife: appeasement, flattery, and submission. Stroke Qing's ego and stay out of his business affairs, and he was happy to leave her to her own pursuits. Over the past few years, Qing's workload and responsibilities as CEO at INI had skyrocketed, just as her own workload and responsibilities had at the CDC. Seventy-hour workweeks were not uncommon for both of them. Add travel on top of that and, well, they practically never saw each other anymore. That separation had given her a false sense of security. Qing was still Qing, and the power and wealth he had accumulated were only fueling his pathological tendencies. Yet, despite everything he had done over the years to dominate and manipulate her, she would never have thought him capable of murder. He was a sociopath, yes, but a psychopath? Four days ago, she would have said no, but now the evidence was damning.

She checked the time. Li would be arriving to collect the vaccines within the next twenty minutes, which meant it was time to leave now. She packed the inoculation canisters in a cryogenic container and then sent a text message to Nick:

Wake up. Time to go.

His response came in seconds:

Ready here. What's the plan?

She exhaled with relief. That was the response she had been hoping for. With Nick Foley at her side, she could do this. Hopefully, when she told him her plan, he would understand.

She typed her answer:

The plan is simple. Stop Qing and save Beijing.

THIRTY-FIVE

Guangao Railway Station parking lot
Two miles east of the Chinese Centers for Disease
Control and Prevention
0930 hours local

RAGE YIELDED TO tedium and tedium to exhaustion. Lankford had been swimming against the current over the last twenty-four hours, and now the undertow was beginning to drag him down. His head bobbed with microsleep. He slapped at his cheeks, but it only helped for a minute before the fog of sleep settled back in.

He had never been a stakeout kind of agent. He had spent most of his time with the CIA hunting Muslim terrorist wack jobs across the desert with the US Special Forces, not in the cloak-and-dagger world that had lured him to the Agency in the first place. Ironic that only now, when he was too old to care, would he finally get a taste of the cold war surveillance game. Doubly ironic, he mused, that his surveillance target was a product of the very US Special Forces he had come to respect and depend on during the breadth of his career.

He yawned and glanced at his watch and then over at the screen on his tablet computer, where the blue dot of Nick Foley's phone still pulsed on a map in the Chinese CDC complex two miles away. He looked out the window at the nearby train station terminal building and wondered if there was a coffee kiosk inside. A jolt of espresso might revitalize him, but to get it, he would have to leave the tablet behind. The tablet was his only lifeline to Foley, so he reminded himself not to break the cardinal rule of modern espionage.

Thou shalt not be separated from one's tech.

He was just so damn tired.

Screw coffee, he decided. *I'm gonna start smoking again.*

He checked the glove box for cigarettes, but then he remembered how Jamie Lin had rummaged through all his possessions and thrown every pack away. She'd even found all his supersecret hidden stashes.

He couldn't help but smile at the memory.

He tried moving his legs to get the blood circulating. He pinched the skin on the side of his thighs and squeezed the pressure point between his thumb and index finger, but it didn't help. Finally, he did what he told himself he would not do—he let his thoughts drift back to Jamie Lin's naked, eviscerated corpse abandoned on the bathroom floor. The poor kid's parents would not even be given the closure of a proper burial. When Jamie Lin's body was discovered by the Chinese authorities, it would be cremated.

He clenched his jaw and sat up tall in his seat.

Anger always trumps drowsiness.

He stared at the blue dot: *blink, blink, blink, blink...*

That was the only possible explanation for the ex–Navy SEAL being here—at the Chinese CDC—mere hours after Jamie Lin's gruesome murder and autopsy. Nick Foley was a traitor. Lankford had asked the boys at Langley to make poignant inquiries around the independent contractors to see if anyone wanted to claim a prodigal son, and still the answer that came back was a big fat goose egg. In Lankford's mind, this confirmed the SEAL's traitor status. Foley had gone off the reservation and was now working with evil forces inside China on something terrifying. Now he, Chet Lankford, was the only one who could stop him. While the thought of blowing his nonofficial cover on an American operator gone rogue was not something he would normally risk, the stakes in this case were too high. Time was running out, and he was the only one close enough to the situation to do anything about it. Was there a chance that he was wrong about Foley? Yes. Was there a chance that Foley was so black within the community that even the director of the CIA did not have knowledge of his task force or his mission? Yes. There was always a chance, but it was a candle burning in a hurricane chance. And now it was too late. If someone important wanted to keep their guy safe and in play, then that someone should have spoken up.

No one did.

Lankford had his marching orders from Virginia: confront Foley and decide whether to assist or eliminate. The split-second, life-or-death decision was Lankford's to make. God pray his instincts were right. But nothing could happen while Foley was inside the Chinese fucking CDC. Lankford assumed Foley was with the female Chinese doctor. No new information had returned on her either—no surprise there, since Jamie Lin had been the one running her.

Nothing about this entire situation made any damn sense.

His tablet computer beeped.

He glanced at the screen and watched as the blue dot

flashed three times and then became brighter. Lankford's pulse jumped, and he relished the adrenaline surge that followed. Better than caffeine, better than nicotine, better than rage—he was amped up and ready to go. Foley was on the move. Lankford started the engine.

The tracking parameters were set at a tight five-meter radius; that way he could track Foley easily whether he was in a vehicle or on foot. Based on the speed of movement, Lankford knew Foley was in a car. He watched the dot for several seconds to verify the heading. If the blue dot headed east on the government extension of Fuxue Road or south on Longshui Road, he would wait and then fall in behind. If it headed west to pick up the Province Road 216 south back into downtown or north to God only knows where, he would have to haul ass to catch up. He waited a moment and the blue dot paused, then it headed toward the CDC exit north of the complex and then…headed west.

Shit!

Lankford moved the gearshift into low and accelerated out of the train station parking lot. He was going to fall behind and would need to catch up. He wanted to ID the vehicle while Foley was still outside downtown, ideally on the highway. He needed to get close enough to make a visual and verify that the blue dot was really Foley. That was the problem with tracking phones instead of targets: decoys and diversions could mean game over at any second. Unfortunately, in this case, Lankford had no choice. It was follow Foley's phone or go home.

If Foley was still carrying the phone he had made contact on, the guy was either arrogant or sloppy. Or maybe, just maybe, he wanted Lankford to find him. The thought made the CIA agent purse his lips. Was it possible that Foley was under duress? Perhaps he was a prisoner and was *counting on* Lankford to track him. In his tired and emotional state, he had not even considered that possibility. Different scenarios began playing out in his mind. What if in his haste to mete out retribution for Jamie Lin's murder, he killed an innocent man? Or what if in stopping Foley, he prevented a deeply embedded black operative from stopping another bioterrorism event? He better be damn sure he got this right, because the truth was he had no idea who all the players were, nor what objectives they were working to accomplish. An error in judgment could cost thousands—hell, maybe even millions—of lives.

No pressure, he thought, shaking his head. *Just another day at the office.*

Gripping the steering wheel with his left hand, he adjusted the tablet on the seat beside him. The blue dot was merging onto the expressway and turning south, back toward downtown Beijing. He had closed the gap a little, but he needed to make up more ground. Lankford merged onto the highway and accelerated cautiously. He glanced frequently at the tablet as he sped south, the distance between his red icon and the blue dot getting shorter and shorter. As they passed the exit for Shahe, the highway changed names from Province Road 216 to Badaling Highway. The tablet chirped and a note box appeared, informing him he was now five hundred meters from the target.

Minutes later, he had closed within thirty meters.

Lankford scanned the vehicles ahead. The traffic was heavy, but he managed to narrow the field of possibles down to five vehicles. He slowed and matched speed with the group: two trucks, two sedans, and one black SUV. If he were Foley, he'd have picked the boxy, silver sedan that was in the lead. Low profile and ubiquitous. The silver sedan was moving faster, pulling away from the other four vehicles in the cluster, but a glance at his tablet showed the blue dot holding steady at about forty meters, so he could nix that car. He also nixed the two semitrucks, as they were unlikely candidates.

That left the green sedan and the black Mercedes SUV.

He moved into the far left lane and accelerated slowly past the two trucks. The sedan—a faded-green four door that in the States would be a very 1970s color—occupied the far right lane, and the SUV was just ahead of it and in the center lane.

The rising sun in the east put a wicked glare on the rear window of the sedan, making it impossible for him to make out anyone in the car. He inched forward until the flash disappeared, and he made out two adults riding in the front seats. He pursed his lips. He had expected Foley to be alone, but maybe the CDC doctor had decided to tag along. He shifted his attention to the SUV. The windows were tinted—too dark to see inside.

He needed a clear look inside the green sedan, but he was already too close for comfort.

He eased up on the gas, drifted back, and moved into the center lane. Over the next few minutes, he strained to catch a glimpse of the sedan driver in the side view mirror, but it was no use. In a few more minutes, they would be coming into downtown, and already the traffic density was picking up. A fast-moving BMW, weav-

ing through traffic, passed him and then moved into the
right lane behind the green sedan, blocking his view.

"Shit," he mumbled under his breath.

As they approached North Wuhuan Road, the expressway gained an exit lane and the sedan moved
right into the new fourth lane. Lankford worried the
car would take the exit. The BMW accelerated, moving even with the green sedan, blocking his view of
the turn signal.

His pulse jumped as he debated what to do. Braking
and changing two lanes would call attention to himself.
With a single glance, Foley would recognize him. Just
being the tall white guy in a car on Badaling Highway
was enough to get a double take from most of the other
drivers. Most Western tourists and businessmen did not
drive themselves around in Beijing. He took his foot
off the accelerator and changed lanes, moving into the
right lane behind the BMW. He glanced right and saw
that the green sedan was now behind him. The exit was
less than two hundred meters away. He still had time to
take the exit by swerving in front of the sedan.

He glanced in his rearview mirror, looking through
the windshield of the green sedan.

Driver male. Passenger female.

That's gotta be Foley and the doctor.

He jerked the steering wheel right, swerving into
the exit lane.

He glanced at the tablet just to be sure.

The blue dot was ahead of him—thirty meters according to the message box.

Shit! It's the SUV.

He jerked the wheel back to left, barely missing the

exit guardrail. His palms were sweating. He smirked and shook his head.

Jesus, that was close.

Foley, or at least his phone, was heading into downtown Beijing.

With the target identified, Lankford opened his range and followed at a safer distance. At Madian Park, Badaling Highway ended and became Deshengmenwai Avenue—the main artery into the city. Traffic slowed to a crawl. Following Foley's SUV while maintaining adequate separation was easy now; he would only need the tablet in the unlikely event he lost visual contact. They inched through the city and then headed southeast toward the business district.

I've got you now, you son of a bitch.

He tapped the nine-millimeter in his belt and smiled.

Twenty minutes later, they were back in the familiar Chaoyang district. To Lankford's surprise, Foley appeared to be heading to Grandma's Restaurant—a popular hang-out for Western expats in Beijing, especially Americans and Brits. Over the past year, Lankford had become a regular—stopping in whenever he had a craving for bacon and eggs, cheeseburgers, or fried shrimp. He paused at the south corner of the parking lot that served the restaurant and several other businesses on the block and watched the SUV. It would be torture sitting in his car and smelling breakfast wafting out of Grandma's.

What the hell was Foley doing?

Instead of pulling into the one of the many empty spots in front or on the south side of the restaurant, the SUV swung west to the rear of the building. They parked twenty meters away and the taillights clicked off, but no one exited the vehicle. Were they meeting someone? Was Foley watching someone else?

After a long pause, the driver's-side door opened and Foley stepped out. He walked around to the front of the SUV and met his passenger, a woman who Lankford immediately recognized as Dazhong Chen. She said something to Foley and then gestured to a door at the back of the restaurant. Foley looked around and then nodded. Together, he and the doctor approached the door. They paused and listened before disappearing inside.

It was time.

Lankford sped across the parking lot and jerked the car to a stop four spaces south of the SUV. He scanned the area and, seeing no threats, exited his sedan and hustled across the parking lot. Like Foley, Lankford paused to listen outside the door. He could hear the hushed sound of Foley and the doctor, but he could not make out what they were saying.

He took a deep breath and steeled himself.

In the next thirty seconds, either he would hear an explanation worthy of fireworks from the American former Navy SEAL, or he would shoot the bastard dead.

And maybe the doctor, too.

Drawing his pistol, Lankford reached for the door.

THIRTY-SIX

Nick followed Dash into the storeroom, wondering if Dash had lost her mind. She had been under so much pressure, experienced so much emotional trauma, and had so little sleep the past two days, he would not be surprised if she had gone loopy on him. He'd seen it before with guys in the military after traumatic events. Sometimes the mind checks out from reality as a defense mechanism. Watching her rummage through a shelf full of canned goods and foodstuffs, he told himself to be patient and stay calm. The woman had proven her brilliance, so he owed it to her to let this play out. If the restaurant manager walked in on them, he would simply play dumb. He was good at that.

"He's been here," Dash said, sliding an oversized can of lard out of the way. "Or someone has."

"How can you tell?"

Dash grabbed a padlock from the back of the shelf and held it up for him to see.

"Okaaay," Nick said, staring at the lock.

"You still don't believe me?" she said, firing him a look.

"I'm not sure what the lock has to do with——"

"Look here," she snapped, cutting him off. She gestured for him to look *past* the shelves.

He obliged and ducked his head. Behind the shelves,

he spied a door, almost perfectly concealed in the wall. "Well, I'll be damned."

"I was worried Qing might have entered another way," she said, setting the lock down. "Because I have no idea what the combination is for this lock."

Nick chuckled at the comment. As if after everything else they'd been through, a padlock would have been the insurmountable obstacle that ended their mission. "We would have gotten the lock off, Dash."

She blushed and smiled back at him. "Help me move this shelf."

Nick stepped back as she gripped the corner of the long shelf. He reached over to help her, but the entire shelf was already gliding easily away from the wall, rolling on a nice set of castors. He traced his finger along the nearly invisible seam in the wall and then reached for the handle.

"Ready?" he asked.

"Ready."

Just as he started to pull, the room got bright and he heard the back door open.

"Step away from the wall and turn around, Foley," a voice— an American voice—boomed. "Keep your hands where I can see them or I'll shoot you."

There was terror in Dash's face as they both turned to face their aggressor. Nick gave her a tight smile and then grabbed her hand in his and raised their hands together overhead.

"Just be cool, Lankford," Nick said, facing the CIA agent. "This is not what you think."

Lankford shifted a pace to the left so he could have a line on both of them and then pulled the door closed behind him. "And what do I think? That a rogue American SEAL has betrayed his country and is working with a high-ranking Chinese national on a weapon of mass destruction? Could that be it?" Lankford's voice was controlled and professional, but there was a rage in Lankford's eyes, a rage that meant he had found his agent—Jamie Lin—or what was left of her.

"I understand how this looks on paper, Lankford," said Nick, staring into the barrel of the CIA man's nine-millimeter pistol. "But you don't have all the facts."

"Oh really? Then why don't you enlighten me with *the facts*, Foley?"

"We're on the same team. We're working toward the same end game, okay? Something horrible is about to happen, and I'm trying to stop it."

Lankford took a half step toward them, but not nearly enough to allow the SEAL to be in arm's reach of his weapon. "If we're on the same team, Foley, then why hasn't a single task force in the entire intelligence community claimed you or acknowledged your operation in China?"

Foley grimaced. He had led Lankford to believe he was with a covert team on purpose, in the hope of shaking loose some information. Now that mistake was biting him in the ass.

"Look, I lied to you," he said. "I admit that. I needed information and I let you believe I was with a covert team. The bottom line is I'm not working for anyone. I really am just an NGO volunteer who was working on a clean water project outside Kashi." Lankford snorted, but Nick continued. "Something terrible happened in Kizilsu, and a lot of innocent people died. One of those people was a friend of mine on the project. I didn't ask to get involved in this, Lankford. The *suck* found me.

It's the story of my fucking life, if you haven't figured that out by now."

"Even if I did believe your peacenik volunteer *in the wrong place at the wrong time* story—which I don't for a second—but even if I did, it still doesn't explain why are you standing here in the pantry of Grandma's Kitchen with a high-ranking Chinese biological weapons expert."

The clock was ticking, and Nick's hackles were up. He had no interest in explaining. Instead, he simply said, "Dr. Chen is here because she is the only one who knows where the madman with the weapon of mass destruction is hiding."

Lankford raised an eyebrow and lowered his gun slightly.

"So there is a bioweapon in play," he said softly.

"Yes and no," Dash said from beside Nick, letting go of his hand. "The weapon is not an infectious agent like a virus or bacteria but a vector-specific nanotechnology. Once the target is infected, the agent destroys the target's tissues at an astounding rate. There is no countermeasure for this weapon, and it has a one hundred percent mortality rate."

Nick saw that Dash's explanation had a sobering effect on Lankford. She had his complete attention.

"Who is the target?" Lankford asked.

"Civilians," she said. "It could be anyone, or everyone. Do you understand the risk now?"

Lankford looked at Nick.

"She's right, Lankford. We have to stop this asshole before he gets out of Beijing. We had sixty-seven deaths in Kizilsu, and we think that was just a single canister released in a mosque. Can you imagine what would happen if he sold this technology to al-Qaeda, or ISIS, or Iran? The stakes are big. Not just for China, but for the rest of the world."

Lankford pursed his lips, and he lowered his weapon a little. "I will have to verify this."

"There is no time," Dash said, her voice trembling with urgency. "We must stop him or I fear he will kill thousands."

"Yeah, you said that already," Lankford said, his face not hiding the internal battle he was fighting. "Assuming I believe you, you still haven't explained what you're doing here in this food closet."

"This is a hidden entrance to the Underground City," Dash said. "We believe we can find him there."

"The Underground City?" Lankford said, confused.

"Look," Nick said, growing impatient. "We don't have time for this shit, Lankford. We need to go. Now."

Nick watched Lankford's face flash red with anger, but after a beat, the coolness of a professional operator returned. The CIA agent was beginning to understand the stakes and was weighing his options. Nick hoped Lankford could find a way to put his personal feelings aside and focus on doing what was right.

"You better make time, Foley. Because you're each one trigger pull away from going nowhere ever again. Now tell me, what happened to my agent? What happened to Jamie Lin?"

"Jamie Lin was murdered," Dash said softly. Then she raised her eyes and defiantly held Lankford's gaze. "But we had nothing to do with that. She was my friend. Even after I found out she had lied to me and was using me for the CIA, I still cared about her."

"How was she murdered? Who was responsible, and how is it tied to this plot?" the agent asked.

"My former husband killed her with the biotech weapon," Dash said evenly. "He must have somehow learned about her—perhaps even about her role in the CIA—and when he did, he targeted her. But because of her death, we were able to discover what this weapon was, and maybe even how to stop it."

"Wait a minute. Are you saying you're the one who cut her up?" Lankford's voice was tight.

"Yes," Dash said. "We autopsied her, and that is how we discovered the weapon and eventually that my husband was involved."

Lankford shook his head. "Your husband is the one behind all this?"

She nodded.

"I can't let you go," Lankford said, shaking his head. "This is all too crazy."

Nick clenched his jaw and lowered his hands.

"You have a choice, Lankford. Either come with us and help us stop the next attack," Nick said, turning his back on the CIA agent, "or shoot me in the back. Either way, you need to decide right now. Because we're leaving."

Nick grabbed the handle and opened the hidden door in the wall.

"I will answer all your questions on the way, Mr. Lankford," Dash said.

"You win." Lankford sighed and lowered his gun. "You're lucky I have a gut feeling about you, Foley."

Nick winced. "And?"

Lankford chuckled and then, after a pause, holstered his weapon under his shirt.

"You're not a traitor, Nick," the CIA agent said with a smirk as he joined them by the hidden door. "Only an idiot would make up a story like that if it wasn't the truth."

Nick's shoulders sagged with relief.

"What exactly is the play here?" Lankford asked.

It was Nick's turn to chuckle.

"It's a little loose," he said. "We're improvising as we go."

"Great," Lankford said.

Nick peered down the stairwell with its eerie red lights. He turned back to Lankford. "Creepy. Maybe we should kit up a bit? I have a weapon, but only one magazine of ammunition."

Lankford rolled his eyes.

"Jesus, Foley," he said, and he shook his head as Nick stared at him hopefully. "Pushing your luck a bit, aren't you?"

"If you have a backup, we'll double our firepower."

Lankford lifted his right pant leg and pulled a small pistol from an ankle holster. He pulled two short magazines from his pocket.

"This is all I have," Lankford said.

"Way more than I had a minute ago," Nick said. He pulled the slide back to check a round in the chamber on the subcompact pistol. "Sig three-two-oh?"

"Yeah," Lankford said, handing him an extra magazine. "Twelve rounds staggered in the magazine and then one in the pipe. Not a lot of ammo."

"Thirty-seven is better than the ten I had before," Nick said. He slipped the pistol into the waistband of his pants. "You ready?"

"Hooyah," Lankford said, mimicking the SEAL battle cry.

Nick smirked. "Hooyah."

Nick led, with Dash behind him and Lankford taking up the rear. After a few paces, he felt Dash's hand find his shoulder. He led them down a steep set of concrete steps, lit softly in red with lights placed at ankle level along the wall. At the bottom, they entered a tunnel—a massive rectangle of concrete with red lights stretching into the distance.

"What the hell is this place?" Lankford asked.

"This is an entrance to the Underground City," Dash said.

"How far does this tunnel go?"

"Many kilometers. The Underground City is very, very big. It is said the Underground City was designed to provide shelter for six million citizens of Beijing in the event of a nuclear attack on the city during the cold war. The long tunnels like this one are escape routes from the heart of the city to what were the outlying districts at the time of construction."

"What is it used for now?"

"Officially, nothing," she said. "Unofficially, it has become a black-market economy for unregulated, underground housing, the drug trade, and prostitution."

They walked in silence for several minutes until Lankford said, "Do you have a plan to find your husband, Dr. Chen?"

Nick looked back at Dash, not sure what he expected to see in her face. Her eyes were wide in the darkness, but her jaw was set firmly.

"I have some ideas where to look."

"If we find him, what then?"

"We must kill him," she said simply.

Nick raised his eyebrows, surprised at her stoic conviction. It seemed like a thousand years ago that those beautiful eyes had scrutinized him with quiet curiosity from above a surgical mask. The events of the past two days had changed her. She was like a blade after finishing—first quenched to be hard and now tempered for toughness.

"*If* we find him," Lankford grumbled.

"Oh, we'll find him," Nick said.

"How do you know?" Lankford asked.

"Because we have to," Dash answered for him.

The three of them continued down the dark tunnel, toward a dim yellow glow in the distance. As they walked, the light gradually intensified along with Nick's anxiety. Dash's search-and-destroy plan for Qing sounded good in principle, but Nick knew the devil lurked in the details. In his experience, evil rarely menaced alone, and he would be shocked if Qing did not have "associates" in the mix. As far as Nick was concerned, Qing's weapon was officially in play, and that meant their objective could be infinitely more complicated depending on how much of a head start Qing had. Nick realized that having Lankford with them could be a blessing or a curse.

On the one hand, Lankford had decades of experience successfully tracking and stopping men like Chen Qing. But could he trust Lankford with their lives? With the lives of thousands, possibly millions, of Beijing citizens? As crazy as it seemed, at that moment, Nick thought he might actually trade Commander Zhang for Lankford. Zhang understood the political and philosophical differences between the United States and

China. Zhang knew the inner workings of the Chinese system and had intimate knowledge of Beijing. Lastly, Zhang was part of the brotherhood. They were both blooded Special Forces warriors who—regardless of the insignia, patches, and flags stitched on the uniform—were committed to stopping terrorism and the murder of innocents above all else. Maybe Lankford was cut from the same stuff, maybe not. Nick did not know the man well enough to say.

Eventually, they reached a section of tunnel brightly lit overhead by regularly spaced yellow halogen lights. They had yet to encounter another living soul, but Nick was certain that could change at any moment.

"Where are we going?" he whispered to Dash, wondering why he was whispering.

"A placed called Club Pink. I believe Qing is a regular customer there," she said with acid in her voice. "It will be a good starting point."

Fifty meters ahead, Nick saw that the tunnel intersected a larger space—a hub with other tunnels and hallways leading off of it. As they approached, he noted two dark side passages off their tunnel: one on the left, one on right. In his peripheral vision, he caught movement in the shadows from both. He reached instinctively for the pistol in his waistband and pulled Dash behind him, but it was too late. Two men, each bearing submachine guns, greeted them at gunpoint. Nick raised his hands to shoulder level, stepping completely in front of Dash.

"Good morning, gentlemen," Nick said.

The men were dressed identically in black cargo pants and black short-sleeve shirts with a symbol embroidered over the left breast pocket. They wore radios clipped to their belts with wireless headsets and a wired microphone transceiver clipped to the right shoulder epaulet. In another setting, he would have assumed they were police or security officers. The taller of the two, still a half foot shorter than Nick, barked something at them in Chinese.

"He wants to know who we are and where we are going," Dash whispered from behind him. She answered the man in Chinese and then said to Nick, "I told him we are going to Club Pink to find my husband, Chen Qing."

The man stepped to the side and spoke into a radio at his shoulder, much like a cop.

"You do not belong here," he said in broken English, his accent thick. "Nah welcome. Needs permissions to coming here."

He gestured with his rifle back down the tunnel.

"Now what?" Nick asked over his shoulder at both Dash and Lankford.

Dash stepped out from behind him.

"We wish to speak with Gang Jin," she said boldly. "I am Dazhong, wife of Chen Qing."

The two men looked at each other in surprise, but then the taller man barked something else and they both cackled. The apparent leader gestured again with his rifle at the tunnel behind them.

"You go."

Then he raised a hand to the earpiece in his left ear, listening. He spoke softly into the radio at his shoulder again. Then he whispered something to his partner, who raised both eyebrows, then lowered his rifle to point it at the ground. He looked nervous.

"One minutes," the taller man said and glanced nervously over his shoulder.

"What's going on?" Lankford whispered.

Dash and Nick shrugged their shoulders in unison.

A moment later, two more men, dressed the same as the first two, approached from the far tunnel. These men were also armed, but their rifles were slung casually across their chests. They joined the first two sentries and then parted to allow the grand entrance of a fifth man.

This man was all smiles and wore a tailored suit rather than tactical clothing. From appearances alone, he might have been a Wall Street banker or high-priced London barrister, except for the expensive gray leather cowboy boots—ostrich, Nick guessed, having seen many such boots back home in Texas.

"Welcome," the man said with a broad smile. He extended his hand to Nick, who shook it. "I am Gang Jin, the mayor of Underground Beijing. It is my pleasure to meet you." He reached back and shook Lankford's hand as well and then opened his arms and his smile broadened. "Ah, the lovely Dazhong. You are even more stunning than I remember from our last meeting." He took her hand in both of his, bent at the waist, and gently kissed her wrist. "I must admit I am surprised to see you here. Of all the places in the world, this is the last place I imagined running into you. Is there something I can help you with…again?"

Nick realized his mouth was hanging open and snapped it shut.

"Who did you say you were again?" Lankford said.

"You may call me Jin. I run the city beneath the city."

"You called yourself the mayor?"

"Yes," Gang Jin answered. He glanced at the armed men behind him and whispered a command. The sentries lowered their rifles but fanned out in a semicircle behind him. The "mayor" was not completely trusting, it would appear. "Mine is not an elected position like your New York City mayor Bloomberg, but then again, China is not a democracy. Nonetheless, my underground approval rating his quite high…or so I'm told," he said with a chuckle.

Nick smiled and decided it best not to inform Gang Jin that Mayor Bloomberg's tenure in New York had ended. Instead, he said, "I appreciate a man who knows the value of a fair reputation."

Jin's eyes brightened at the comment. "What is your name? How is it you find yourself in my city?"

"Nick," he said. "Nick Foley, from Texas."

"Ah, a real American cowboy. You like my boots? Imported from Texas—Tony Lama."

"I've been admiring them since you arrived. Ostrich leather?"

"Very good, Nick Foley. I think I like you," Jin said, still sizing him up. Nick suspected Jin would happily kill all of them in a heartbeat if the man felt threatened. In many ways, Gang Jin reminded Nick of the Afghani tribal leaders he had met in the Hindu Kush—gracious hosts with secret loyalties and hidden agendas, men who would slit your throat if circumstances did not bend to their needs.

Jin turned to Lankford. "Who are you?"

"Lankford. Chet Lankford," Lankford said and gestured to the sentries. "Who are these guys? Your police?"

Jin's smile tightened. "Yes, exactly. The Underground City would be a very dangerous place without the order of law. I'm sure you can appreciate the value of personal safety, Mr. Lankford."

Dash subtly stepped in between Gang Jin and Lankford and smiled. "Sorry to interrupt, but you said if I ever needed your help again, well…"

"I remember," Jin said, shifting his attention to her. "Very unpleasant business that night, if I recall."

"I am forever in your debt for what you did for me, but right now, we need your help," Dash said. Her voice betrayed the urgency of their situation, and Jin's face became serious.

"Of course," he said. "How can I help?"

"I need to find Chen Qing," Dash said. "He has done something terrible, and the lives of thousands, maybe tens of thousands, are in danger."

"What has your husband done?" he asked, undoubtedly probing whether switching allegiances in the future would benefit him and his enterprise.

"He's created a terrible weapon and plans to betray China by selling it to terrorists," Dash said, her voice hard and even. "We fear he intends to use the weapon against the people of Beijing."

Jin's face was now a mask, his jovial persona gone. He clenched and unclenched his jaw and his eyes narrowed.

"And you believe he is here, in the Underground City?"

"Yes."

Jin looked the three of them over closely for a moment.

"Then we must find him," Jin said finally. "Come with me. I have systems in place that may help us locate him, if he is here in my city," he said, looking at

Dash now. "On the way, you can explain why there are two Americans helping you and not officials from our own government."

"Of course," Dash said. "I will tell you everything, but we must hurry."

"We're the advance party, but rest assured we have back-up. The Snow Leopards are standing by to assist us once we find Qing," Nick said to Jin.

"The Snow Leopards? That is impressive. This should be quite a story—one I look forward to hearing." Jin paused and looked back and forth between Nick and Lankford, "I will not insult you by having my men frisk you like common criminals, but I must insist you give me your weapons."

Nick raised a hand to object, but Jin shushed him.

"You will get them back, I assure you. You will be quite safe while you are with me, but we do not allow weapons in the city center except for members of our security force."

Dash put her hand on Nick's arm. "It's okay," she said.

Nick nodded and then pulled the pistols from his waistband and handed them to Jin, who passed the weapons to one of his men.

"Jesus," Lankford hissed, but he forfeited his pistol as well.

"Thank you, gentlemen," Jin said. "Now, please follow me."

The three of them followed the mayor, his cowboy boots clicking on the concrete floor. The security detail fanned out and flanked them, and Nick likened the formation to being under the protection of the secret service.

"Was this part of your plan, Foley?"

"Not exactly," Nick snorted. "But adapt and over-
come, right?"

"Awesome," Lankford huffed.

Nick glanced at Gang Jin and wondered if the man
could be trusted. The mayor of Underground Beijing, in
his Armani suit and ostrich-leather boots, was a show-
man. A flamboyant mafioso. Yet, one does not acquire
a position of such power with smiles and kisses. Gang
Jin was a criminal and a killer, and Nick would not let
himself be fooled into thinking otherwise. The man
clearly had a moral compass, but like so many underworld bosses, that compass needle usually skewed in
the presence of large sums of money. Nick prayed Chen
Qing had not gotten to Gang Jin first, because if he had,
they were walking directly into a trap.

THIRTY-SEVEN

Underground City tunnel beneath the China World
Trade Center
1115 hours local

QING BRUSHED THE dust from his slacks and smoothed his shirt. He had forgotten how filthy the Underground City was. He looked up the ladder and sighed. Deploying the canisters around Beijing had been more time consuming and tiring than he had expected, but so far, everything had proceeded smoothly and without interference from the authorities. He was glad for the manpower and weapons that working with Mok afforded him. With a cadre of hired guns under his command, he could move quickly and confidently through the Underground City. He checked his watch. He had four hours and forty-five minutes to place the remaining three canisters and escape before the countdown ended and the weapon was automatically discharged at a dozen locations around Beijing. Each canister was equipped with a programmable activator device with an integrated cellular modem. If things went wrong and he needed more time, he could delay the release. If events progressed ahead of the timetable, he could activate all the canisters at the push of a button on his phone. He smiled. Death by mobile app.

He glanced at the burly thugs fanned out around

him, rifles gripped and at the ready. He knelt and extracted one canister from his duffle bag, leaving two canisters remaining inside. With each sortie above, he left the bag behind with his borrowed muscle. Three of the five killers had been present in the warehouse to witness his earlier demonstration of the weapon's capabilities. Despite their caveman intellects, they knew better than to mess with the metal canisters inside the bag. Still, compulsion got the better of him, and he repeated the same instructions before each departure.

"I'll be back in fifteen minutes. Whatever you do, don't touch the bag," he said, and then he began his ascent.

As he climbed, he adjusted the strap of the large messenger bag on his shoulder. The bolt cutters and metal canister inside were beginning to grow heavy as the day wore on. The trip back would be easier without the canister, but bolt cutters were a necessity. Officially, the Underground City was closed. Every "known" entrance was chained and locked shut by the police to prevent unauthorized access. So far today, he had cut nine locks off of chains. He suspected this gate, which was located between a laundromat and novelty store, would be locked as well. At the top of the ladder, he exited into a short horizontal passage that led to a metal door. This door was locked from the inside. He cut the lock off and unthreaded the chain. He took a long breath and then pushed through the door and stepped out into a recess between the door and an accordion-style metal gate. The gate was locked too. With another quick snip, he was out. He walked briskly to a nearby public restroom, where he retrieved his folded suit jacket from his messenger bag and shrugged it on.

He lingered for two minutes, exited, and walked a half block to the China Unicom headquarters building. He strolled into the lobby, walked past reception and the elevator banks, and then entered the men's restroom. He walked into a stall and shut the door. Qing opened the messenger bag and retrieved the canister and one of the two remaining paper shopping bags he had obtained from an upscale women's lingerie boutique. He slipped the canister in the bag and checked the control unit settings. Countdown timer running: check. Cellular modem connectivity: check. He cinched the top of the lingerie bag shut using double-sided adhesive tape. Then he exited the stall, washed the grime from his hands in one of the ornate marble sinks, and looked at himself in the mirror and smiled.

He wondered which picture they would use when they talked about his deeds on the international news. Not even China could keep an event of this magnitude secret from the world. He wondered how much of the truth they would be able to conceal. It would be difficult for the Chinese government to admit that one of their leading military scientists had turned on China. To admit this would be too shameful. They would manufacture a scapegoat to take the blame—the Uyghur dissidents perhaps. That would make an effective cover, especially after Kizilsu.

Major Li and Commander Zhang will know it was me. The Standing Committee and President Xi will never forget my name.

With his weapon, China could have ruled the world. But did they laud him for his vision? No. Did they give him the respect and accolades he deserved? No. Their investment in INI was a charade. Their plan had always been to let him do all the hard work and then steal his creation when it was operational. Did they really think he was such a fool? He knew what ALP Capital really was—China's version of DARPA. He knew where his "venture" seed money really came from. If they thought for a second that he would forfeit the greatest scientific breakthrough of the twenty-first century to Major Li and his brigade of uniformed baboons, then they deserved to suffer.

He left the washroom and crossed the expansive lobby, nodding politely at the two security guards who paid him little mind. In addition to the uniformed security presence, he was keenly aware of the CCTV cameras recording his every move. No matter, even if Zhang's men were searching the feeds in real time, he would be back underground and untraceable before they arrived.

He scanned the lobby and noted the vacant small white leather sofa beside a trio of potted plants. Qing walked to this sofa and sat, placing both his bags on the floor by his feet. He glanced around the lobby, and when he was certain the security guards were not watching, he used his right heel to slide the lingerie bag underneath the accent table between the sofa and the plants. The bag would be hard to see beneath the table and would be partially occluded by the three planters. Next he retrieved his mobile phone, sat with his legs crossed, and made a show of checking his voicemail messages and e-mail. When four minutes had elapsed, he stood, slung the messenger bag over his shoulder, and pretended to make a call on his phone as he exited the lobby.

He walked briskly back to the little unmarked door

tucked between the novelty store and the laundromat. A minute later, he was back on the ladder heading down into the Underground City.

He stepped off the bottom ladder rung onto the concrete floor. He glanced at the ground and was pleased to see that the duffle bag lay undisturbed, exactly as he had left it. He picked it up, stuffed the messenger bag inside, and slung it over his shoulders. Without a word or a glance, his bodyguards followed him over to the 112cc motocross bikes that Mok the Broker had provided to expedite their underground travel.

He climbed onto one of the bikes, started the engine, and checked the countdown timer.

Still on schedule.

Ten down...two to go.

THIRTY-EIGHT

City Hall, the Underground City
1145 hours local

NICK BREATHED A sigh of relief.

This was not a trap. Not a setup. Gang Jin had not duped them, nor was he handing them over to Chen Qing so that he could infect them with nanobots that would dissolve their flesh from the inside out. No, this was something else entirely—something Nick could not have imagined in his wildest dreams.

This was déjà vu.

As he surveyed Gang Jin's "city center," he noticed the room was not unlike an overseas military TOC—a tactical operations center. Instead of plywood desks fashioned by Seabees, Jin's workstations were industrial metal tables with Formica tops. Instead of real-time drone and satellite imagery of the sprawling desert, here he saw CCTV feeds of underground passages and cavernous rooms. Half a dozen workstations—each with its own computer, flat-screen monitor, and phone—formed a half oval. The half oval faced a large flat-screen TV monitor mounted on the far wall, the screen divided into eight squares—four to a row—displaying different feeds.

"Welcome to our security operations center," Jin said, gesturing broadly at the busy room. The room was modestly equipped if judged by Pentagon standards but compared comfortably to the downrange TOCs Nick was accustomed to with the teams. The six black-clad "security professionals" kept focus on their tasks despite the new arrivals. Two other technicians, a man and a woman, stood in the far left corner, drinking coffee. The whole thing was surreal—almost more like a police or military operation than a criminal enterprise.

"I'm impressed," Lankford said from beside Nick as he scanned around the room. "The Beijing authorities don't bother you down here?"

Jin laughed.

"Why would they?" he asked. "We pay our taxes and fees to local government officials like any other business enterprise."

Nick smiled and nodded with an epiphany: Bribery was the lifeblood of Beijing. Nothing moved in the city without compensation. With the Underground City, the case for a man like Gang Jin was even more compelling than just the sum total of the tribute he paid. Like it or not, the Underground City existed. No matter how many entrances were closed, no matter how many gates were sealed, the city beneath the city was never going away. Better to have someone to manage it, prevent chaos, and keep any unpleasantness from spilling up. A big revenue stream from a little problem was a much more appealing proposition than a little revenue stream from a big problem. Why not let someone like Jin profit from managing Hades?

"Let's get to work," Jin said. A deadly serious look had replaced his grandiose smile since learning what Qing was up to.

"Where do we start our search?" Lankford asked.

Nick looked at Dash. She was not just holding it together; she now seemed to be keeping *them* all together. His delusion that he would be somehow protecting the demure doctor he had met in Artux had evaporated.

"My theory is that Qing is using the tunnels to move about undetected as he sets his trap. But knowing my husband, he may have trouble avoiding a stop at Club Pink."

Jin nodded. "Yes, that is his favorite place here in the Underground City. He makes visits there often—at least once a week and sometimes more."

Dash's face clouded and she seemed to bite the inside of her cheek.

Jin continued: "He also has met occasionally with other businessmen to secure various types of tech. We arrange, but also monitor, all such transactions here in our city."

"What kind of tech?"

Jin shrugged. "We closely monitor dangerous substances that may exchange hands, but other than that, we do not censor activities. We simply monitor the interactions. In any case, it has been some time since any such dealings have occurred in the Underground."

"What do you mean?" Lankford asked.

"Simply that it is not unusual for principles whom we introduce to continue their business dealings up above. We make no efforts to prevent or manage such interactions. I know that he has relationships with both tech dealers and others, but I have no control of information about any dealings above ground. We collect a fee for making introductions, and we arrange—also for a modest fee—for safe and secure meetings in our many meeting areas here, but these relationships often grow and continue outside my jurisdiction."

"How do we find him?" Nick asked. The backstory was interesting, and it might be useful in building a legal case against Qing, but this was not the priority. All that mattered was finding Qing before he could set his plan in motion. As far as Nick was concerned, the only trial Qing would get was Underground justice. Either they would kill Qing, or he would kill them, and if it turned out to be the latter, then tens of thousands of innocents would perish with them.

Jin motioned for them to the right side of the room.

"We monitor and record activities at dozens of locations within the Underground City," Jin said and gestured to an empty workstation near the wall. He snapped his fingers and gestured to one of the men by the wall, who set down his coffee and hustled over. "Mostly these are in areas where more remote tunnel systems converge on our retail spaces, so unfortunately, if he is staying in the periphery of the underground, our cameras will not see him. We also can do targeted searches with facial recognition—inexpensive but reliable software similar to that used by your intelligence agencies. However, unlike the CIA, we have a much smaller database to search. Anyone who is admitted with regularity to the Underground City is recorded in our database, and we build profiles on them."

Nick looked at Dash, who raised her eyebrows. What Jin described was analogous to how big government intelligence collection programs functioned. Beside her, Lankford looked equally as impressed. Nick thought perhaps Dash was wondering if she was in Jin's database.

The shorter man from the kiosk joined them and spoke to Jin in clipped Chinese. The man nodded, sat at the workstation, and began keying in data. A moment later, Qing's face popped up on the screen. A few more taps and a picture resembling a government ID photo filled a monitor on the center wall. Nick wondered how deep Jin's cybernetwork penetrated the government networks above ground. Jin turned and addressed the room in Chinese while a series of red dots and lines began to flash across the picture on the screen, the computer mapping out key elements of Qing's facial structure to form a template for the facial recognition.

The man seated beside him said something softly to Jin, who nodded.

"Our records indicate that Qing was at Club Pink in the last few hours and left not long ago. We show no official entry into the city."

"Official entry?" Lankford said, and Nick noted he was unable to keep both the sarcasm and the admiration from his voice.

"Yes," Jin said. "We have checkpoints restricting access to the Underground City."

"Like customs and immigration?" Nick blurted out.

"Yes," Jin said patiently. "Much like customs and immigration. However, many of our regular citizens have other entry points into the city. We discourage this, but we also understand their need for privacy and discretion and make little effort to prevent it for those who are properly vetted and well known. In any case, they will be keeping their entry secret from other citizens—not from us."

"How do they get in and out?"

"The portion of the Underground City I control is

only a small portion of the original project. An extensive tunnel system exists outside of the areas we monitor. Very few people know of the many entrances scattered about the city, primarily in older businesses. You entered from such an entry point, yes?"

"I suppose we did," Nick said.

Jin nodded. "We detected you as you approached the city center—and we happen to know about the entry Qing likes to use from the restaurant—but we don't monitor it. There are many such entries, and in any case, monitoring them is pointless. We see everyone who gets to our business district before they arrive and—like you three—if guests are unknown or blacklisted, we greet them."

"So you will have a recording of my husb..." Dash stopped herself and then continued, "...of Qing entering the city?"

"Yes," Jin said. "He entered a few hours ago—not from your tunnel, but from one to the east."

Dash looked at Nick.

"We know he entered through the restaurant as we did," he said to Jin. "We don't know when."

"Then he went somewhere in the time between," Jin said.

All eight screens began to flash with various views of small groups of people throughout the Underground City, pausing as the red lines and dots flashed across the faces on the screens before moving to the next images. Jin spoke to the man at the console beside him, who nodded.

"We will reconstruct his activity and route as best we can, but I must warn you, it will be difficult to pinpoint his current location if he left the surveillance zone."

"You mean the areas covered by cameras?" Lankford asked.

"Yes, but that is only part of it. Technology has strengths but also weaknesses, which is why I employ considerable manpower. I have roving security patrols throughout the area, and we just sent them a screenshot of Qing. We will do our best, but it will take time. We will also review the DVR data to see if we can reconstruct his movements."

"How long?" Dash asked urgently.

Jin smiled and placed a sympathetic, almost fatherly, hand on her shoulder.

"Not long, my dear," he said softly. "We will find him."

"And then?" Lankford asked.

"He is a traitor to China," Jin said. "We will help you track him down and then you may do with him what you will—kill him, I assume. It would be best if you do this and not my people—I would not want our involvement to be misconstrued by our clients."

A technician suddenly shouted in Chinese from a workstation across the room, and Jin rushed to his side. "This is Qing only twenty-four minutes ago," Jin said, excitement in his voice.

"Where is that?" Lankford asked.

"The tunnel comes from the north," Jin said. "From there it would have numerous points of entry within the central business district and the China World Trade Center."

"Where did he go next?" Dash asked.

The lower far-left screen froze and flashed red for a moment. A man was starting up a ladder, flanked by a team of men armed with assault rifles.

"There," Jin said. "This was fifteen minutes later. That ladder leads to a complex of four office buildings three-quarters of a kilometer south of the World Trade Center."

"That footage was taken only ten minutes ago?"

"Yes," Jin said and snapped his fingers. Another, taller man hustled toward them.

"How long to get us there?"

"Fifteen minutes in vehicles," Jin said. "We will get you close and then you will proceed on your own. But don't worry; if you fail to stop him, he will not be permitted admittance into my city."

"You should stay as far back as possible," Dash said, looking at Nick. "If he is armed with weaponized aerosol canisters, a single release would be rapidly redistributed by the closed ventilation system and could kill every soul in the Underground City."

"In that case, I advise you to shoot him quickly," Jin said, grim faced. "I will provide you with rifles so you can engage Qing's security detail at a distance."

A man handed a silver case to Jin and then nodded and moved away. Jin clicked it open and pulled our four small boxes, each with a wire leading to an earpiece and boom mic. "This will give you access to our communication network. We will guide you and monitor for any other threats."

"That is very generous," Nick said. "Thank you."

"I do this for China," Jin said, and then he smiled at Dash. "And for the lovely Chen Dazhong," he added.

"We need to go," Lankford said. The CIA agent seemed all in now, any lingering doubts about the plan apparently long gone.

"Agreed," Jin said. "Follow me. I will provide you

with Kevlar vests and rifles from the armory before
you go to the vehicles."

"Just a moment," Dash said, removing a silver pendant of a rat from her neck. She extended her arms,
fastened the chain around Gang Jin's neck, and kissed
him on the cheek. "From one rat to another," she said
with a coy smile.

"You honor me, Chen Dazhong," Jin said with a gracious smile. "But now we must hurry. I fear your opportunity to catch him may be slipping away."

THIRTY-NINE

Northwest-bound tunnel, Underground City

NICK FELT LIKE a SEAL for the first time in years, and he was surprised at how much he liked it. The sway of the Sig Sauer 516 rifle slung across his shoulders, the snugness of the Kevlar vest around his chest, and the crackle of radio static in his ear from his integrated earpiece and boom mic—these were the poignant, familiar sensations of being all kitted up that he missed, and it struck a nerve. He was a warrior; that part of him would never die. But this morning, he was leading the least qualified assault team he had ever been associated with—a jumpy CIA case officer and a female epidemiologist who had never held a weapon before.

Face it—you're a team of one.

Nick and Lankford knelt in the back of the Argo six-by-six all-terrain vehicle while Dash rode in the front passenger seat next to Gang Jin's appointed driver as they tore at breakneck speed through the tunnel. A second ATV cruised along beside them, this one a four-by-four trail-riding model.

"You are two minutes out. We still hold five armed men at the stairwell, but Qing has not returned," said Jin's voice in Nick's earpiece, and it was strange to have the heavily Chinese-accented voice acting as his guide.

"Roger. We need stealth on the approach," Nick said

into his voice-activated mic. "We should stop soon and walk in. If we spook Qing, we may not get another chance."

"I agree," Lankford said.

"Yes," Jin answered. Then Jin said something in Chinese over the same comms channel that must have been meant for the driver, because the man behind the wheel backed off the accelerator and pulled over along the side of the tunnel.

"We'll go in from here," Nick said, jumping out of the Argo. It was not lost on him that once they had kitted up, Lankford was quick to pass on operational control to Nick. The CIA man was an experienced covert operator, but Nick was, after all, a SEAL.

And this is what SEALs do.

Dash and Lankford disembarked from the vehicle and huddled together.

"Here's the plan. Lankford and I will advance on and secure the target. Dash, you stay here with Jin's men. They'll protect you and provide emergency egress if things go wrong."

"Agreed," said Lankford.

"I concur," Jin said over the radio.

"Absolutely not." It was the first thing Dash had said since he had given her a forty-second in-service on her weapon before they boarded the ATV. "I have to come. Qing is unpredictable. You will need me with you if something goes wrong." Dash looked at him pleadingly but then also tapped her right vest pocket and raised her eyebrows.

Nick hesitated. He knew she was right. Dash was the most qualified to assess Qing's state of mind and the biotactical situation. Besides, she possessed the only protection from Qing's WMD. *Well, possible protection.* Her vaccine was untested and unproven. Despite what she witnessed in the microscope lab, Nick put the odds of the harvested nanobots actually saving their lives at about 10 percent.

"Okay, Dash is coming with us," he announced. "She is the only one qualified to assess the threat from Qing's tech."

Lankford pushed his boom mic aside and covered it with his hand. "Assess the threat from the tech? What the hell is that supposed to mean?"

Nick clicked the radio on his vest to mute it.

"She's coming with us," Nick said softly. "It's not up for debate."

"Is there something you're not telling me?"

Nick looked at the CIA officer. He was starting to trust the guy, but they didn't have time to get into the backstory of the possible cure that Dash had developed.

"You've gotta trust me on this," Nick said and clapped a hand on Lankford's shoulder while looking him in the eye.

Lankford pursed his lips but nodded and clicked his own radio off of mute. Nick did the same and then announced, "I'm point, Dash and Lankford two by two in a spread behind me. How's the video feed, Jin?"

"You are in between cameras at your current location," came Jin's reply over the wireless. "But I still hold the armed men at the bottom of the stairwell. They are perhaps five hundred meters farther down the tunnel. The stairwell camera is the last one on the perimeter we monitor. I have no way to tell you who or what lies beyond."

"Check," Nick answered. "Just watch our backs."

"There is nothing to your rear but my men and the two vehicles. One other thing you should know, Nick: beyond this point there are many branches and other exits. If Qing and his men flee to the north, I will not be able to guide or assist you."

"Roger that," Nick said, and he looked at Dash and Lankford. "From here on in, no talking. Complete silence. Understood?" They both nodded. He could see the uncertainty in Dash's face, but he was surprised by her lack of fear. Even team guys had fear—you simply learned to harness its energy. Dash looked determined and anxious, but not afraid. Her awkward holding of the small rifle and her oversized Kevlar vest made her look like a little girl dressed up for Halloween. He smiled at her and she tried to smile back. "Let's go," he said. "On me."

He turned and began to lead his team down the tunnel. Nick had his rifle up and moved in a tactical crouch, advancing as he had done countless times in his former life. Muscle memory drove his movements. He covered the distance quickly and quietly. The same could not be said for his companions. Every squeak and shoe scuff from Lankford or Dash made him cringe.

But this was his team, and there was nothing he could do about it now.

Fifty meters past the last of Gang Jin's tunnel lights, the tunnel began to grow dim. He slowed their pace to give everyone's eyes time to adjust as they headed into darkness. What he wouldn't give for a pair of night vision goggles and a PEQ-2 IR target designator. *With just those two items, we would make quick work of Qing's three bodyguards.* He glanced over his shoulder and was pleased to see Lankford in a reasonable combat crouch to his left. To his right, Dash was making a rather child-like, but still impressive, impersonation of the same.

A sound made him stop, and he raised a closed fist with his left hand.

A loud shoe squeak from Dash made his pulse jump.

He took a knee and peered over his iron sights into the darkness.

"I think they heard you," Jin's voice said in his ear. "The guards are talking and one of them is shining a flashlight in your direction. How far out are you?"

Nick didn't answer but scanned ahead. Jin's report was spot on, as he saw the dancing flicker of white LED light ahead.

"One of them is on the move, heading your way," Jin added, his voice reflecting anxiety for the first time.

Nick gestured for his team to press their backs against the walls. He intentionally positioned himself in the lead, between Dash and the approaching gunman.

"I lost him now. He is out of our camera range," Jin said. "Nick, can you hear me?"

Nick clicked his microphone in acknowledgement and raised a hand slowly, a gesture of silence he hoped the others understood. The flashlight beam suddenly went dark. Nick wasn't sure if that meant the advancing gunman had given up and turned around or if he was astute enough to continue his reconnaissance in the dark. Nick strained his eyes, willing the darkness away as he searched for movement in the shadows.

There!

The gunman was creeping down the center of the tunnel—an amateur mistake. Quietly, Nick moved his right hand off his rifle grip and into his cargo pocket. His fingers found his folding knife, which he opened quietly in the dark with his thumb. The blade was only three inches long, but used correctly, it would be enough. The gunman was only five meters away now, and still he had not seen or heard them.

Four meters...

Nick raised the blade to the ready position.

Three meters...

He could hear Dash's nervous breathing and prayed quietly that the approaching gunman could not. Nick stepped away from the wall, advancing silently into position to intercept the gunman just as he passed abreast of their position. Nick planned the killing sequence in his head: he would clasp his left forearm around the man's throat, constrict the airway to silence any attempt to shout, and plunge his knife into the base of the man's skull, severing the spinal cord at the brainstem and silencing him forever.

Nick moved a pace to the left.

Gang Jin's voice crackled in his ear and sent Nick's pulse racing: "I see shoes climbing down the ladder... It may be Qing returning... Confirmed. I have a visual on Qing."

One meter...

A voice barked something in Chinese from the tunnel ahead. The advancing gunman looked over his shoulder and hollered back. Nick hesitated. This was the moment to make the kill, but to do it now would alert Qing to their presence. He needed Qing in the tunnel. If the bastard scurried back up the stairs, they would lose him. Nick stayed frozen in place. Dash's raspy breathing sounded like a freight train to him, but the gunman still did not seem to hear it. The man shouted again in Chinese, spun around, and hurried back down the tunnel.

"Qing is carrying something," said Jin over the comms circuit. "Looks like a leather messenger bag. He's transferring something from a duffle bag into the messenger bag. It looks like a coffee thermos."

Nick held his left hand up with a closed fist and prayed no one would make a sound. They were predators now, and any noise would send the gazelles scattering. Their best chance was catching them in a tight group.

"Qing is talking with his bodyguards... Now they are walking to their motorcycles. If you're going to engage, you need to do it now, before they leave," Jin reported on the radio.

The decision to engage wasn't that simple. If Qing and his men planned to go south, then they would be easy targets as they passed. Whack, whack, whack, game over, Qing loses. But if Qing's orders were to drive north, then the window of opportunity was lost. The odds of catching Qing outside Gang Jin's camera perimeter were virtually nil. Nick knew he needed to move now, before they egressed. He slipped the knife back into his cargo pocket and slinked back to the wall. He gave the "advance" command with his left hand, brought his rifle up to the ready, and rested his right index finger on the trigger guard. He advanced the team quickly, too quickly apparently, because the rattle from Dash's loose-fitting kit was like thunder echoing in the tunnel.

"They've heard you," squawked Jin over the wireless. "Three gunmen are heading your way. The other two stayed behind with Qing."

Nick could make out three distant figures in the soft light streaming down from the ladder well. The gunmen were fanning out. Just five more seconds and he would take them all out.

"Help," a female voice called out. "Help me, Qing!"

Nick did a double take at Dash, not believing what had just happened.

Lankford dropped an F-bomb.

Then the bullets began to fly.

Qing's gunmen dropped to their knees and began to fire blindly down the tunnel. Had Nick not kept his team along the wall, they would all be dead as tracers screamed down the center of the tunnel.

Nick advanced in his crouch and fired, his first shot hitting the gunman on the far right in the neck. The man screamed and dropped his rifle. He reached for his neck but then collapsed. Nick's second shot caught the middle gunman dead center in the middle of the chest. The man grasped his chest and then pitched forward face first onto the floor of the tunnel. Nick aimed farther down the tunnel for Qing next and squeezed the trigger, but the bastard was prescient and ducked just as cement fragments exploded from the tunnel wall where Qing's head had been a half second earlier. Qing's two bodyguards were hustling him deeper into the tunnel. They fired back over their shoulders blindly. Nick knew from combat that stray rounds kill just as quickly as targeted ones, so he stayed low, angling himself between the fleeing gunman and Dash to his right.

Lankford's rifle barked fire and Nick watched the third gunman in the tunnel take a round in the hip, spinning him around. Nick finished the wounded man with a shot to the head as he fell.

Qing grabbed one of his protectors and spun the man around as a human shield. As they backpedaled, the bodyguard screamed something in Chinese and unleashed a prolonged burst of automatic fire, spraying the tunnel from wall to wall. Nick leapt backward and yanked Dash to the ground, shielding her with his body.

"Qing!" Dash screamed from beneath him. Then, she shouted something else in Chinese, and Qing straightened up behind the gunman. Nick raised his rifle and aimed for Qing's forehead, but the shot went wide to the left, tearing through the top of the head of the man Qing held between himself and his enemy. The man crumpled to the ground and Qing spun around and ran.

"Shoot him, Lankford," Nick shouted as he tried to get a better angle without crushing Dash.

Qing yelled at the lone remaining gunman as he fled to the motorbikes. The gunman unleashed a punishing volley. And then another.

Nick pushed up onto his right elbow, ready to fire, but before he could, he heard Lankford yell, "I'm hit!"

Nick glanced right and saw Lankford was down.

A motorbike engine growled to life and screamed with a high-RPM whine followed a half second later by another one.

Nick took aim and squeezed off a burst down the tunnel, but it was too late. They were gone. He rolled off Dash and felt a sudden surge of fury toward her.

"What the hell were you thinking?" he growled.

She glared at him, her jaw set defiantly. "I was trying to make him hesitate so you could shoot him before he got away."

"Damn it."

He scurried over to Lankford and found the CIA

man with both hands clutching his right hip. "Let me take a look."

Lankford grimaced. "It's not bad. Clipped my hip and went out my ass cheek, I think."

Nick was in full combat-medic mode now. He knew there was no way Lankford would know if the bullet had torn through his guts or not. Bullet trajectories through bodies were unpredictable. He'd seen some unbelievable injuries over the years. He took Lankford's pulse at the wrist—strong and fast. Good.

"Go," Lankford said. "We can't lose him. I'll be right behind you."

"Stay down," Nick said. The CIA operator would be more of a liability now. He checked the wound and Lankford's initial assessment appeared to be right. The bullet clipped him in the meat just outside the hip and exited straight. Nick pulled a bandana from his pocket, rolled it in a tight ball, and pressed it onto the wound. His hands did not come back soaked in blood, which was usually a good sign—unless, of course, all the bleeding was inside. "Keep pressure here," he said. Then he keyed his microphone and said, "Jin, we have a man down. We capped four bad guys, but Qing and one gunman escaped. Send the vehicles."

"Roger," Jin said, then issued orders in Chinese to his men with the ATVs.

Nick squeezed Lankford's wrist. "You okay?"

"Go kill that son of a bitch," he answered.

Nick nodded and got to his feet. With Dash standing at his side, he watched and waited as the two ATVs roared up the tunnel to their position. "Go with Lankford in the Argo," he said to her, making a beeline for the four-by-four.

"Like hell," she said, running beside him. "I'm going with you."

"Like hell you are," he shouted at her. "Not after that stunt you just pulled."

"We started this together. We're going to finish it together. Do you understand me, Nick Foley? This is the way it must be."

He whirled to face her and clutched her by her shoulders. His intention was tell her no and shove her away, but then he met her gaze. She was right. This was the way it was supposed to be.

They would kill Chen Qing together.

FORTY

DASH LEAPT ONTO the ATV's tandem seat behind Nick and wrapped her arms around his waist.

"Go!" she shouted into his ear, and go he did.

The acceleration nearly sent her flying off the back of the vehicle, but her nails found purchase in the Velcro straps of his bulletproof vest. She clamped her knees against the frame and held him tight as they flew through the Underground City. The roar of the ATV's engine was deafening—amplified and reverberating off the concrete tunnel around them. If Nick was cursing her for what she'd just done, she could not hear it. She would not blame him. She had not shared *that* part of her plan with him.

Turbulent wind whipped her hair about, stinging her cheeks and the nape of her neck. She peered over Nick's shoulder down the darkened tunnel ahead. Two red taillights—the dirt bikes they were pursuing—glowed faintly in the distance. Ventilation ducts and metal pipes materialized from the darkness, snaking overhead and along the walls, and then disappeared in a blur. The effect was hypnotic and disorienting, so she tried to ignore her peripheral vision and focus on the ground ahead.

The ATV's anemic headlights illuminated only twenty meters of the upcoming passage, if that. Nick was driving at a lunatic pace, yet he couldn't see what was coming at them. She yelled at him to slow down, but at the same instant, the ATV hit a puddle, hydroplaned, and started to slide toward the concrete wall. She felt Nick ease off the throttle and watched him try to steer into the slide, but the wall just kept coming. Her stomach went queasy and she screamed. With collision imminent, the tires regained traction and the ATV lurched onto a new vector. Her right knee kissed the wall and the concrete chewed through the fabric of her jeans. Nick got them off the wall a heartbeat later, and she felt the burn on the side of her knee where the skin had been sanded off.

She resisted the urge to look at her knee to check the damage and instead focused on the scene ahead. The two red taillights were growing dimmer.

"They're getting away," she yelled over his shoulder.

"I know," he hollered back.

The motor whined and she felt the wind pick up as Nick accelerated to pursuit speed. She repositioned her grip, digging her fingertips deeper into his straps. If the tunnel were illuminated, maybe the ride would be exhilarating, but *this*—this was terrifying.

She squinted in the wind, trying to back Nick up by watching for hazards ahead. Suddenly, the taillights ahead disappeared. She leaned left to look over Nick's other shoulder, hoping for a different angle, but the lights were definitely gone.

"We lost them," she yelled.

"Not likely," he yelled back. "I think they turned."

She nodded.

"Hang on," Nick yelled, his voice ripe with panic. "Stairs!"

He braked hard, but it was too late. They took the

stairs head on. She screamed as the ATV pitched forward and headed down the steep incline. The angle felt all wrong, much too steep, and she was certain the vehicle was going to topple end over end…but somehow, it didn't. Instinctively, she leaned back, reclining almost fully until her shoulder blades were bouncing against the tubular steel cargo deck behind her. Nick shifted his hips forward and leaned back also, while keeping his hands on the controls. The ATV shuddered and bounced down the stairs, bucking like a wild bull trying to jettison its tandem riders, but they did not fall off. Just when she was beginning to get in synch with the bone-jarring rhythm, the ATV hit the bottom with a gut-shaking thud, which sent her pitching forward. Her forehead smashed into the middle of Nick's back, and she heard him grunt.

The tunnel ahead was pitch dark—no sign of the red taillights.

After a beat, she heard Nick's voice over her headset: "Jin, this is Nick. I think we've lost them. I could use a little help."

"I don't have any cameras in that sector," came Jin's voice over the wireless. "But I can try to plot you on the map if you give me landmark details."

"We just drove down a big-ass flight of stairs."

"Okay, I know where you are. In one kilometer, the tunnel will split. One passage goes southeast and one passage goes southwest."

"Please tell me you have a camera there," Nick said.

"No, I'm afraid not," Jin replied. "If you can't see which path they took, you will have to guess."

"I don't guess," Nick said, twisting the throttle. The ATV's tires squealed and they were off again. This time,

Nick brought the vehicle up to its maximum speed. Dash shut her eyes and pressed her forehead against his back. She didn't want to look. She couldn't. If they crashed at this speed, they would die, and she'd rather not see it coming.

She listened to the *whoosh, whoosh, whoosh* as they passed ventilation duct after ventilation duct. Just as she began to wonder if Nick had somehow missed the junction where the tunnel split, the high-pitched whine of the ATV's engine began to fade into a throaty growl. She felt the ATV slow as Nick backed off the throttle. She looked up and over his shoulder and saw the fork in the passage ahead. He turned off the ATV's headlights and killed the engine.

All went dark and quiet.

"Did you see which way they went?" she whispered.

"No." He climbed off the ATV, machine gun raised. "Get behind the ATV," he instructed. "This could be a trap."

She did as she was told.

Squatting behind the rear fender, she watched him duck into a crouch and move toward the tunnel on the right. After a few meters, he disappeared completely into the darkness. She waited anxiously, certain that the next thing she would hear would be a barrage of automatic weapon fire.

It never came.

"They went right," a voice out of nowhere said, making her jump.

"How do you know?" she asked.

"The echo is louder that way," he said. "Let's go."

They climbed on the ATV and took off down the right tunnel. Gripping him tight, she settled in for the ride. She noticed that now, instead of driving down the center of the tunnel, Nick was hugging the left wall, staying on the inside radius of a gradual bend to the left. She didn't understand why until two minutes later, when a volley of bullets and tracers ripped down the center of the passage, barely missing them. Nick killed the headlights on the ATV and immediately returned fire. The staccato *pop, pop, pop* of gunfire in the dark shredded her nerves. She made herself small behind him and wondered why he hadn't stopped moving. Then she realized that Nick had gained the advantage of timing over their unseen adversary. Somehow, he seemed to time his volleys a split second before the other gunman, dominating and controlling the tunnel.

"Give me your rifle and get off," he yelled at her between bursts. "Stay against the wall until I call you."

She handed him the machine gun slung across her back and slid off the left side of the ATV. Then, to her surprise, Nick twisted the accelerator, the ATV engine roared, and he was gone—a torrent of bullets and malice. She pressed her back against the wall and waited. The gunfire intensified and she pressed her hands over her ears. The racket was so loud it hurt. Then there was a blinding light and a boom. She heard someone scream in agony and then another volley of gunfire before silence fell once again.

She waited for Nick's call, but it did not come.

She waited in the dark, frozen and silent...

Footsteps.

Someone was running in her direction, and deep in her gut she knew it was not Nick. She reached for the subcompact pistol in the small-of-the-back holster Gang Jin had given her. Despite the darkness, her fingers found the grip and the trigger. She had never shot a gun before, but Nick had assured her that all she had to do was point the barrel at the target and squeeze the trigger—the bullet would do the rest. She extended the weapon in the darkness, aiming at the footsteps, which were getting louder and closer. And louder and closer.

Her arms began to tremble.

She wanted to call out Nick's name, just to be sure. What if she shot him? What if she shot and killed Nick just when he was coming back to her? But the person running toward her was not Nick, she was certain of it.

She heard him breathing now, the runner, and the footsteps were almost on top of her.

With her index finger, she put tension on the trigger, ready to shoot, and...

The footsteps ran past her.

She followed the sound with the barrel of her gun, confused and uncertain what to do.

"Qing!" she yelled, taking herself by surprise.

The footsteps stopped for a beat but then resumed anew at a harder, faster pace. She chased after him into the darkness. A volley of gunfire erupted in the tunnel behind her, but it sounded farther away than before. She didn't look back; she just kept running after the footsteps, holding the pistol in her right hand.

A flashlight flicked on ahead of her, and she saw the shadow of a man running. It was Qing; she knew his shape, his gait, his form.

The light flicked off.

They kept running.

"Qing, wait!" she yelled.

The light flicked on again, but Qing did not stop.

This time she noticed a darkened cutout in the tunnel wall ahead and a sign overhead.

The light flicked off.

After a few more seconds, the sound of Qing's footsteps changed direction and took on a new quality.

He turned.

She had not had time to read the writing on the sign, but she knew what it said: EXIT. She veered left and extended her left arm until her outstretched fingertips brushed against the concrete tunnel wall. After five meters, the wall disappeared. She stopped, breathless now, and turned left into the darkened exit tunnel. She could hear Qing's footfalls directly ahead as he climbed the concrete steps. She followed, slowly at first, feeling for the first step. When the toe of her left shoe hit the bottom step, she almost tripped, but she managed to catch herself and not discharge the pistol. She felt for a railing, found one, and began the long ascent. Pretty soon, her lungs were burning, and she realized what terrible shape she must be in. Her only solace was the fact that she knew Qing's fitness was no better.

Light flooded the stairwell from above, and she looked up to see Qing, a silhouette in an open doorway. He was looking down at her, but she could not see the expression on his darkened face.

"Qing, wait!" she called, between gasps.

The door slammed shut, and she was once again in the dark. She stowed the pistol in her holster and took the steps two at a time. When she reached the top, she felt her body slowing with fatigue. She pushed against the exit door and it didn't move.

"No!" she screamed and drove her shoulder into the

metal door. This time, the door pushed open a couple of centimeters.

The bastard blocked the door with something.

She hit it again, and again, and again—shifting the heavy mass on the other side—until at last she could squeeze through the gap. On the other side, the light was blinding. She squinted, surveying her surroundings, and realized this entrance to the Underground City was in an alley protected by a metal cage with an iron gate. She stepped around the metal trash receptacle Qing had used to block the door. A chain and a cut padlock lay on ground beside the open gate. She ran through the open gate and sprinted down the alley. When she reached the intersection, she scanned the crowd, frantically looking for Qing. The hair on the nape of her neck stood up when she saw him, standing directly across the one-way street, staring at her.

She heard a crash in the alley behind her. She whirled around and saw Nick emerging from the Underground City, rifle in hand. He looked at her, then past her at Qing, then back at her. He shook his head: *Don't do it.*

She mouthed the words *I'm sorry* and then pulled one of the nanobot vaccine canisters from her vest pocket. She raised it to her mouth, depressed the lever, and inhaled the fog. She dropped the canister, smiled wanly at Nick, and turned to face Qing.

"Don't leave me," she called out to Qing and took a step into the street toward him. Then, placing both her hands on her abdomen, she met Qing's gaze. "Take me with you. I'm pregnant."

She watched Qing's face contort through a series of emotions: confusion, joy, and then doubt. A black SUV rounded the corner and screeched to a halt at the

curb in front of Qing, blocking her view of him. She
checked traffic, which was stopped a half block away,
waiting for the light to change. She began walking toward the SUV.

"Please," she begged. "Take me with you."

For a moment, nothing happened. In her peripheral
vision, she could see the cars to her left beginning to
move. Just when she thought he would leave her, the
rear passenger door opened. Qing extended his hand
and beckoned her. She smiled at him and dashed across
the street just ahead of an oncoming wave of vehicles.

"No!" she heard Nick yell as she climbed into the
SUV and slammed the door behind her. Qing tapped
the driver on the shoulder, and the engine roared to life.
Dash looked over her shoulder out the rear window as
Nick chased after them, his machine gun trained on the
SUV. She watched him until he disappeared from view.

She turned to face Qing.

"You're pregnant?" Qing asked expectantly. Cautiously.

"Yes."

"How long have you known?"

She hesitated. "Two weeks."

His cheeks flashed crimson. "Two weeks and you
didn't tell me? Two weeks and you went to Kashi, risk-
ing the life of my unborn child?"

This was precisely the reaction she'd wanted from
him. Hot, passionate, and genuine. She needed him to
believe. "Please don't be angry with me," she said, looking down at her lap. "It was too early to tell you."

"Too early to tell me? I don't understand."

Keeping her eyes averted, she said, "This is not the
first time."

He did not respond for several long moments. "You've been pregnant before?"

She nodded. "I lost it, during the first eight weeks."

"Look at me," he seethed, and when she did, he reached out and clamped a hand under her chin, squeezing her cheeks terribly. "You lied to me, Dazhong, about a great many things, it seems. How could you lie to me about something like this?"

"You're hurting me," she managed with a whimper.

He narrowed his eyes at her. A chill settled over him and it spread to her. His eyes went cold and she shuddered.

"I found your birth control pills," he said. "Tell me, Dazhong, how does a woman become pregnant while taking birth control pills?"

She was prepared for this question. "After miscarriage, there is a waiting period. The doctor advises two months on birth control before trying again. The body needs time to heal and for the cycle to normalize."

He studied her, searching for any trace of insincerity or doubt. Finally, he released his grip.

"With the first miscarriage, I didn't know what was happening. I didn't even realize I was pregnant. I was so ashamed. I thought you would be angry with me. I thought you would blame me for losing the baby because I did not know I was pregnant," she said, her voice raw with staged emotion. "This time, when the pregnancy test came back positive, I became afraid. Afraid that it would happen again, so I decided to wait until after the first ultrasound to tell you."

"I understand why you were afraid and confused," he said and placed his hand on her knee. "But honesty is the foundation of a marriage. If we are to be together, we must be honest with each other about everything. We must trust each other. Without trust and honesty, there can be no love."

"I'm glad you feel that way," she said, "because honesty and trust must work in both directions."

He stiffened. "What is that supposed to mean?"

She steeled herself. It was time to rattle the hornet's nest.

"The American CIA approached me. They told me you created a biological weapon and that if I didn't help them stop you, you were going to sell the weapon to terrorists."

Qing smiled at her, and the smile gave her goose bumps.

"They are deceivers," he said. "They deceived you about my work, just as you tried to deceive me about your secret life. I know about the CIA and your friend Jamie Lin. I've known for some time now."

"I did my best, Qing," she said, choking back a sob. "I tried to insulate you by playing the game, but I'm a scientist, not a spy. I'm sorry I failed you, but I want you to know that I have never broken my marriage vows. Despite what worries you may have, I have always been faithful to you."

He held her gaze for an uncomfortably long time before finally responding. "I believe you. But it's over now. We're safe and we're together." Then, placing a hand on her belly, he added, "You, me, and my baby."

She exhaled her relief and snuggled up next to him. He put his arm around her shoulders and cradled her. She laid her head against his shoulder.

As they rode in silence, she stared at the duffle bag on the floor between Qing's feet.

Her heart was pounding. She felt flush and cold at the same time. Her stomach was queasy and the cabin of the SUV suddenly felt small. Too small. She felt claustrophobic and afraid and…

"There's something I want to show you," Qing said suddenly. "Something I am very proud of that I'm ashamed to say I have kept secret from you."

She lifted her head and looked at him with endearing, grateful eyes. "What is it?"

He reached between his legs and lifted the bag onto his lap. He unzipped the main flap. She sat up straight for a better view. Light glinted off the curvature of a metal cylinder inside.

Her nerves were on fire. She tasted the bile of anticipation and dread in her mouth, and it was a struggle to keep her breathing steady and slow.

He reached into the bag and pulled out the stainless steel cylinder. Mounted on the top of the cylinder was some electronic device attached to the nozzle. A thumb-sized metal lever stuck out the opposite side, which she recognized to be the manual vent release.

Her left eyelid twitched.

She smiled and squinted hard to conceal the twitch.

"This is what the Americans are so afraid of," he said, holding the canister as if it were some sacred offering. "This is my creation."

"What is it?" she asked tentatively.

"The future of medicine," he said, beaming. "A universal cure for cancer, for malaria, for parasitic infection, for clearing arterial plaque to stop heart attacks and strokes…the opportunities are infinite."

"What is this?" she asked, pointing to the device on

the nozzle. Her instincts told her it was a remote actua-
tor, but she needed to be sure.

"That's nothing you need to concern yourself with,"
he snapped. Then, looking at her left eye, he said, "Your
eye is twitching."

She smiled and rubbed her eyelid with a knuckle. "I
know. I'm exhausted, Qing."

He narrowed his eyes at her. "Is there something *else*
you're not telling me?"

She sensed the suspicion, the distrust, the malice
welling up in him. She noticed the tendons on the back
of his right hand grow taught as he gripped canister
tighter. It was now or never. She leaned in slowly, as if
to kiss him. With her right hand, she found the top of
the canister and said, "Good-bye, Qing" as she pressed
the manual pressure-release lever. The canister hissed
and a thick, hazy fog filled the passenger compartment
of the SUV.

Qing jerked the canister away from her and then
turned to her, eyes wide. "What have you done?"

She scooted away from him, pushing her back up
against the far rear passenger door.

Qing went frenetic, shouting at her and then the
driver and then talking to himself. He fondled the canister and then threw it at her head. She ducked and it
smashed against the window behind her, cracking it.
He lunged at her, but she raised her knees and kicked
him with both heels, driving him back. His eyes were
insane with rage. He yelled at the driver to pull over
and pulled the lever to open his door before the SUV
had even stopped.

Eyeing him, she reached into her vest pocket and
retrieved the second vaccine dose. She held the final

minicanister to her mouth, pressed the release, and inhaled deeply. She repeated the process a second time
until the gas was expended and prayed the concentration of scavenging nanobots inside her would be enough
to save her life.

Qing whirled to face her. "What is that?"

She smiled at him.

"What is that?" he screamed.

"The cure," she whispered, and tossed the spent minicanister on the floor.

He lunged for it and pressed it to his lips, squeezing
the release lever to no avail. She watched him, wondering how long until it happened. Wondering if she would
die too. There was only one last thing to do.

"How do I stop the other canisters from going off?"
she asked.

"What?" he said, incredulous and confused.

She picked up Qing's canister with the remote trigger
device off the seat beside her and held it up for him to
see. "How do I stop the other canisters from going off?"

He flashed her a malevolent grin. "You can't. In fact,
I'm going to make sure that no one can." He reached
into his front left pant pocket and retrieved his mobile
phone.

"Qing, don't do this."

He shook his head. "Thousands will die for your betrayal. Their blood will be on your conscience. You did
this, Dazhong. You killed them."

She watched him enter his security passcode, then
she swung the metal canister, bringing it down on his
forearm hard. Qing's phone flew out of his hand and
landed in the footwell behind the driver. Qing leaned

forward to grab it, and she swung the canister again, connecting with the back of his head.

He howled with rage and turned on her, ready to lunge, but he didn't. Instead, he waived his hand in front of his eyes.

"I can't see," he mumbled. Then, more frantic, "I can't see!"

"What tissue did you have it programmed to attack?" she asked him.

"Central nervous system," he said, the words beginning to slur.

The SUV was stopped now, and she noticed that the driver was missing. She looked out the window and saw the man stumbling down the side of the highway, gripping his head. She turned back to Qing. He was drooling now and beginning to sag. The nanobots were consuming his brain and central nervous system tissue before her eyes. Soon, he would be like Jamie Lin—unwhole, unhuman.

Undone.

She assessed herself. She felt alert—no pain, no confusion, no sensory degradation. Was the vaccine working? Had she been right? Or was this delusion, false hope? A blissful, ignorant reprieve before her nanobot defenses were overwhelmed?

While I still have my wits, I have to use them.

She reached down and picked up Qing's mobile phone. The screen showed a map of Beijing superimposed with the Underground City tunnel system. A dozen red dots flashed at various coordinates throughout the city. These were the canister locations. A countdown timer was displayed at the top of the screen. It read: 01 hrs 52 min 43 sec. She exhaled with relief.

There is still time.

She felt a sharp pain in her left forearm. She gasped and saw that Qing was biting her and pawing for the mobile phone in her hand. Reflex took over. She snatched the phone out of her left hand with her right and stuffed it in her vest pocket. Then she picked up the canister and wacked him repeatedly until he relaxed his jaws. He looked up at her—a horrid creature, with blood spilling from every orifice. She kicked him away from her, and he tumbled out the open passenger door and onto the ground beside the SUV.

She got out of the vehicle, stepping over him as he screamed slurred, unintelligible curses at her. She watched him roll around in blind agony until she couldn't take it anymore.

"This is no way to die," she muttered, drawing the pistol from her holster. She pointed the barrel at his head. "For Jamie Lin."

She squeezed the trigger and Chen Qing was still.

She leaned her back against the side of the SUV, suddenly exhausted.

One more thing to do, she said to herself. *Then I can rest.*

She pulled her mobile phone from her pocket and dialed Nick. He answered on the first ring.

"Dash? Tell me you're okay," he said, breathless.

"I'm okay," she said. "At least, I think I am."

"And Qing? What happened? Did he let you go?"

"I did it, Nick. I beat him. It's over."

"Oh my God, Dash. When you climbed in that SUV, I thought I was never going to see you again," he said, his voice steeped in relief, "If something had happened to you—"

"I know, Nick, I'm sorry," she said. "But I had to do it. It was the only way."

"Where are you?"

"I don't know," she said, looking around. "On the side of the highway outside Beijing. Call Commander Zhang. Tell him to track my phone and send someone immediately. I have Qing's phone. It shows the locations of all the canisters he set. We have just under two hours to collect them before they activate."

"Okay, I'll call him right now."

"And Nick?"

"Yes?"

"In case something happens to me, the passcode for Qing's phone is five three four two."

"Five, three, four, two. Got it."

"And Nick?"

"Yeah."

"If something happens to me," she stuttered. "I want you to know that I... I—"

"Yeah, I know. Me too."

FORTY-ONE

Snow Leopard Commando Unit headquarters building
2030 hours local

IT WAS THE Artux People's Hospital interrogation all over again: same spartan room, same irritating fluorescent lights, same players. It was Nick's personal Groundhog Day, with one important exception.

This time Dash was sitting at his side.

Commander Zhang tapped his thumb on the top of the white Formica table. His face was contorted with irritation—irritation he made no effort to conceal. At last he spoke: "What part of 'Go nowhere' did you not understand? My instructions were only two words long, and I spoke to you in English, so that there could be no miscommunication. Tell me, Mr. Foley, how could I have been more clear?"

Nick resisted the urge to grin. "You could not have been more clear, Commander."

"Then you admit to violating my direct orders."

"Yes."

Zhang cocked his head, seemingly surprised to have won Nick's confession so quickly and effortlessly. No browbeating required, no threats of incarceration necessary, no torture required.

Dash opened her mouth to speak, but Nick silenced her with a subtle touch of the hand.

"Why did you not notify us before going into the tunnels? Did you not think my team of counterterrorism operatives could lend you assistance?"

Nick decided to err on the side of humility and hope that *results* were his best defense, just like when he was back in the teams. "In retrospect, we should have coordinated with you. You and your men have the superior skills and training to handle such situations. But at the time, we were afraid a large presence would alert Chen Qing to the pursuit and he would react by deploying the weapon immediately. Our plan was to identify his position and then call in your team to take him down."

Dash reassuringly caressed his finger with hers, then pulled away when Zhang's eyes flicked to their hands.

"But that is not what happened," Zhang said, his gaze rising from their sophomoric touch and back to Nick's eyes. In that moment, Nick wondered if Zhang might not have a little crush on Dash. "Instead, you obtained illegal weapons from an underground mafia leader and pursued Chen Qing on your own, while enlisting the help of the CIA, correct?"

"Correct, except the part about the CIA. The man who assisted us was an American expat named Chet Lankford who works for a technology company here in Beijing," Nick said, unable to suppress the grin any longer.

"Please," Zhang snorted, waving his hands. "We know about ViaTech and the CIA's activities in China. And we know all about Mr. Lankford—his real name is Terence Broadwell if you are curious. It may interest you to know you both served in Afghanistan during the same period, leaving me to wonder if you do not know each other much better than you claim. You are also CIA, yes? A common career change for those with your background, I believe."

"I work with an NGO. My background has been thoroughly vetted by your government, as you are well aware."

"Yes, yes," Zhang said, his voice more angry than irritated now. Nick felt the Commander's eyes on his right hand, a few inches from Dash's, and he pulled his hand away and dropped it into his lap. "So you keep saying. You wish only to bring clean water to our underprivileged religious minority in the west. You were in the wrong place at the wrong time. Amazing how you somehow managed to kill three Chinese citizens, with the help of your CIA friend, with your illegal weapons. Do not insult me, Nick Foley."

"And you saved thousands."

Nick and Zhang stopped their sparring to look at Dash, who had been silent until now.

"What?" Zhang asked, his face now resigned and confused.

"He saved thousands, perhaps tens of thousands, of Chinese citizens and our Western guests. He stopped a madman whose plans would have threatened the lives of millions of people around the world, including many with our security interests."

"Well, yes, but—"

"There are 'official' ways we must do things, I know," she said. Beneath the table, her foot brushed gently along the side of Nick's leg. "But Nick is not Chinese. Nick does not work for our government. His actions were selfless. Did China benefit from his courage? Yes. Did he risk his life for our people and for me?

Yes." She turned to him and smiled. "I think Nick is a hero of China."

Nick met her gaze and felt a rush of emotion. Had he really saved her, or was it the other way around? She was the one who had climbed into the SUV with Qing. She was the one who had injected herself with an untested nanobot vaccine to save the world. Now here she was, saving him again. Dazhong Chen was the real hero of China.

Zhang sighed.

"Well my government agrees." He looked up and shook his head. Then came a hint of a smile. "I suppose if our roles had been reversed…" his voice trailed off.

Nick grinned and decided he was beginning to like Zhang a little more every time he saw him. "If our roles were reversed, I can't say I would be as diplomatic and understanding as you have been. Next time, I promise I will follow your instructions to the letter."

Zhang narrowed his eyes at him. "Next time? There better not be a 'next time,' Mr. Foley."

"Of course, you're right. What was I thinking?"

Zhang opened the file on his desk, glanced inside, and then closed it and shook his head. "I understand you are seeking a visa to remain in China?"

"Yes," Nick said, forcing himself not to look at Dash. "I've been offered a job with my NGO—as director of global operations. I accepted the position, pending the approval of my visa."

Zhang leaned back in his chair. Now it was his turn to enjoy himself. "We will see what happens with your visa. If you are permitted to stay in China, I will be keeping a very close eye on your activities."

"I would expect nothing less, Commander," Nick said.

Then Zhang's expression went cold. "Know this. If it is determined that you have not been truthful and that you are employed as an agent of a foreign government, you will be held accountable. The punishment for espionage in this country is quite severe, Mr. Foley, and I will not be able to protect you."

"Understood," Nick said with a grave and respectful nod.

Zhang stood. "Thank you, Nick Foley—for your selfless service to China. The prime minister considered presenting you with a civilian service award, but I counseled that such an award might cause you problems with your government. Instead, I will give you this." Zhang extended his right hand and handed Nick an intricately embroidered patch depicting a roaring, white snow leopard, set against a field of blue, above a golden laurel and crossed arms. It was a patch he had seen before, sewed to the uniformed shoulder of every Snow Leopard commando.

Nick accepted the patch, studied the detail, and then shook Zhang's hand. "Thank you, Commander. It's been an honor."

Zhang released his hand and acknowledged Dash with a long glance and a courteous nod. "Dr. Chen, thank you for your courage. If you ever need me, you have my private number."

"Thank you, Commander Zhang…for everything," she said.

Zhang turned back to Nick. "I will send someone to escort you out of the building."

Then he turned and left, closing the door behind him. Nick resisted the urge to sweep Dash into his arms. He had no idea how she might react, but now was not the time or the place. It didn't matter—her eyes reflected his feelings without the embrace.

"What now?" she asked, expectantly.

"Dinner, perhaps?" he said.

"Maybe we should start with coffee," she said with a coy smile.

"Then coffee it is."

EPILOGUE

ViaTech Corporate Offices, eighth floor
Xinjuan South Road, Chaoyang District

NICK COVERED HIS yawn and then smiled at Lankford across the spook's cluttered desk.

"Sorry," he said. "I still haven't caught up on my sleep."

"Yeah, well, sometimes you gotta get away from things to decompress."

Nick laughed. He wasn't sure how much farther away he could get. The last few days were a blur, but he felt at peace. He had never been one to need time to decompress. It was over. Things were what they were. He was happy with his decisions, no matter how impulsive.

"Getting settled in?" Lankford asked.

"Yeah," Nick said. "I've got some shopping to do yet. The apartment is mighty barren, but I kind of like it that way."

Lankford smiled and shook his head. Then he slid a blue passport across the desk.

"I got you your visa," Lankford said.

Nick picked up his passport and flipped it open. The stamps were so fresh, they almost looked wet. "That was quick," he said, snapping the passport shut. He slipped it into the breast pocket of his Columbia quick-dry shirt. "Bai told me it would take months. I was worried I might have to leave the country and come back."

Lankford laughed out loud. "Yeah, well, I know a guy."

Nick laughed too. "I'm sure you do."

"Sure you don't want the paycheck? It's a lot of money, and you earned it," Lankford said. "There's more where that came from too, you know."

"Thanks, but no thanks," Nick said, remembering Zhang's warning. "I've got a job."

"Right, delivering clean water to poor people around the world. You'll be working in Beijing, right?"

"Right," Nick said. "Director of operations for the NGO."

"Director of operations. Excellent," Lankford said, nodding. He retrieved a glass bottle of amber liquid from the bottom desk drawer.

Nick recognized the distinctive, faceted shape and the pewter horse and rider atop the stopper. "Blanton's?"

Lankford's lips curled into a knowing grin. "The man knows his bourbon."

Nick shrugged. "There was a time…"

Lankford set two glasses on his desk.

"No thanks," Nick said.

Lankford snorted. "Jesus, Foley. What the hell kind of frogman are you, anyway? Have a drink. Toast our success. We saved a lot of lives together. Hell, we might have even saved the world."

"Ex-frogman, and it's Dr. Chen who we should be toasting," Foley corrected.

Lankford smirked and poured two glasses. He slid one to Nick and raised his own. "To the brave and beautiful Dr. Chen."

"Don't forget brilliant," Nick added.

They clinked rock glasses and Nick took a gulp—savoring the burn and the smooth finish that followed.

"Speaking of Dr. Chen," Lankford said, cradling the rock glass in both hands. "Your new office is close to the CDC, isn't it?"

Nick nodded and looked at his hands.

"Coincidence?"

Nick shrugged. "We'll see."

"You know, we could really use you, Nick," Lankford said and took a long pull on his own drink. "I don't want to sound trite, but your country could use you too."

"I'm not your guy," Nick said softly but firmly. "I appreciate the offer, though."

"Oh, you're our guy all right," Lankford said. "But I knew you would say that. So here is my counteroffer: How about we give you a small retainer, just while you're here in China. We can have lunch occasionally, maybe grab a beer from time to time, and if something pops up, I can call you. You would be like a...like a consultant."

Nick had to admit the idea was intriguing. He missed being "in the know." When he quit the teams, they had cut the intelligence umbilical cord, and it hit him hard. He didn't like being disconnected from the shadow world; it left him feeling naïve, vulnerable, and anxious. *Keep your friends close and your enemies closer*—that was the old saying, and over the years he had come to appreciate the meaning. But Lankford's proposal was the devil's bargain. There was no such thing as being a part-time spy. Dip your toe in the drink and you're all wet. Zhang's warning had been unequivocal. The Chinese would be watching.

And there was Dash...

"A retainer sounds a lot like an obligation," Nick said at last.

"No obligation," Lankford assured. "I'll even put it in writing. You keep your finger on the pulse of things and only do more if you're interested. You can walk away anytime."

"Anytime, huh?"

Lankford nodded, his face hopeful.

"Is that a yes?"

Nick finished his drink, stood, and shook Lankford's hand. "That's an 'I'll think about it.'"

"What do you say we grab a beer on Friday?"

"I have plans Friday."

"In that case, tell Dash I said hello," Lankford said with a coy smile.

"I will if I see her," Nick said, couching his reply as he headed for the door.

"You'll change your mind," Lankford called after him. "You had a taste and you liked it. You're like me, Nick. You hate not being in the know."

"Thanks for expediting my visa. See ya around," Nick said, closing the door behind him.

He pulled on a ball cap and kept his head down as he left ViaTech. He knew *they* were watching, but he saw no point in making it easy on them. He arrived home an hour later, after picking up some much-needed groceries for his empty fridge and bare cabinets. His new apartment was a studio, which was all he could afford in the high-priced Beijing real estate market. He surveyed the dirty floor and bare walls and dreaded the thought of cleaning, organizing, and decorating. The apartment could probably use a fresh coat of paint too. He sighed and sat down on his cheap, new sofa in front of his cheap, new coffee table. On the table sat a Ziploc bag full of broken wooden pieces.

He opened the bag and turned it upside down, spilling the contents. Dazhong's broken puzzle box clattered onto the table, a daunting jumble of wooden levers, slides, and interlocking blocks. Staring at the pieces, he reminded himself that he knew nothing about Chinese puzzle boxes. In fact, this was the first one he'd ever seen, and it was smashed to bits. To rebuild something with this level of complexity would require careful study and patience. He would probably need to consult a craftsman with subject-matter expertise to learn how puzzle boxes operated. He would not be surprised if handmade beauties like this were unique—each one an artist's snowflake. How does one locate a puzzle-box master craftsman anyway?

He began sorting pieces, grouping them by paint color. Next, he subdivided the broken pieces and shards into clusters that he perceived had once been whole. Satisfied with his piles, he went to the kitchen and fetched a bottle of beer from the fridge and a bottle of wood glue from a box of hardware supplies he had bought. He returned to the sofa, opened both bottles, and began the slow, tedious process of making the broken components whole. As his fingers worked, his mind wandered. Thoughts of Batur, Jamie Lin, Commander Zhang, Lankford, and of course Dash circled around and around in intersecting orbits in his mind. Two hours passed, and instead of growing weary, he found his focus renewed. He was a fixer—a mender of broken things. He had come to China to find purpose, but the irony was that he had never lost it.

He had simply forgotten it.

His life's mission was simple and clear: go where

he was needed most and fix the broken things that others could not.

But he didn't have to complete his mission alone.

He had found a partner.

And so he would stay in China...

Until the day came she ordered him to go.

* * * * *